I0599693

GOLD MINE

GOLDEN OMEGAVERSE
BOOK TWO

R. L. RANDOLPH

Cover image: *Flowers in a Vase* by **Philip van Kouwenbergh** (1700)

Image sourced from the National Gallery of Art

Editing by: DerpyWickedFox Editorial

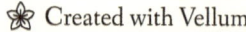 Created with Vellum

For the people pleasers who need to hear this:
Choose your own happiness

PLAYLIST

i. *Howl* by Florence + The Machine

ii. *Jaws* by Sleep Token

iii. *shivering gold* by Tove Lo

iv. *The Gold* by Manchester Orchestra, Phoebe Bridgers

v. *June* by Florence + The Machine

vi. *You're Gonna Go Far* by Noah Kahan

vii. *I Love You, I'm Sorry* by Gracie Abrams

viii. *Dinner & Diatribes* by Hozier

ix. *the warmth* by Paris Paloma

x. *The Manuscript* by Taylor Swift

A NOTE

This book contains sensitive content.

This book takes place in a version of our current world where every person has a secondary designation: *alpha, beta,* or *omega.* If you're unfamiliar with the omegaverse, there is a guide specific to this world in the back matter. The guide contains no spoilers, and is meant to provide further context.

You can also view the content warnings and spice list for a better understanding of the content included in this novel. These are all in the back matter.

THE HEAT

CHAPTER ONE

JUNE

ALPHA.

He's not here. *He left me.*

I can't think. I can't *breathe*. Between sobs, I fist the blankets around me in the nest and pull them closer, trying to inhale the lungfuls of fresh rain wafting off of them. The smell is so warm, so good — and it's mixed with other, fainter scents. There's decadent chocolate fudge, fresh oranges, and bright, sharp mint. All of them familiar, all of them comforting in their own right, and all of them belonging to my alphas and my beta.

But it's my other alpha that abandoned me.

My chest smarts — my skin feels too tight for my body, aching and *hot*. God, everything is so hot — my neck, my head — there's sweat dripping off my brow —

Where did he go? Why didn't he want me?

My wet hair drips down my bare back as I turn my head, burying my nose in blue fabric. Even if he walked away, I still have this. I can just... stay here.

A faint buzzing makes me look up, but it fades, going

quiet after a moment. I sniffle, rubbing my eyes as I look at the door to the nest — he could just be outside. What did he say again?

"*I need to go.*"

That wasn't a "*I won't come back.*"

Theo will be back. He has to. He wouldn't leave me.

I sit in the center of the nest, blankets wrapped around me, oscillating between shivering and sweating, just staring at the door. The buzzing sound happens a couple more times, but my focus is on the space where he'll appear any minute now.

He'll be back. He's coming right back.

A cramp seizes my abdomen, all my muscles tensing at once, nausea rushing in as bile fills my mouth. Fighting to keep it down, I curl into myself, gasping and whining at the sensations. There's so much *pain* — I don't feel right, something is wrong —

The door opens as another violent shiver wracks my body, and with it is a wash of perfume, but it's not the clean, rain-soaked smell of the space around me.

"Can I come in, baby?"

Fudge — sugar and cocoa powder, so thick and delicious slides into my veins.

I nod rapidly, sucking in a ragged breath as I look up at my beta, my *Seth*. His long brown hair is pulled back in a loose ponytail, tanned olive skin highlighted by the dim light from the hallway. He kicks off a pair of loafers, climbing into the enclosed area with me and the mattress in a pair of trousers and a button up shirt. His arms move, snaking under the blankets, wrapping around me tightly, seeking out my naked body, his hands splaying across my back.

"I don't feel right."

"I know, come here. It's okay." One of his hands strokes my damp hair and I lean into him, fighting to get my hands free so I can touch him as much as I *need* to.

I press my palms against his shirt, then wiggle between the buttons, forcing it open so I can touch his warm chest, burrowing closer and climbing into his lap, sticking my head against his neck so I can breathe him in. I want to be *in* him, I want to claw my way into his chest and just curl up against his heart and live there, it's the only thing that's going to stop this bone-deep feeling of discontent.

"I need you." I push at his shirt, kissing his jaw and throat. "I need you right now, please, Seth, *please*."

"Okay." His voice softens as his hands slide over my spine. "June, your first heat started."

His lips aren't on mine, and that is *stupid*.

I lean up and kiss him, muffling whatever else he was planning on telling me — maybe that grass is green, or that the sky is blue. As I slide my fingers into his long hair, I snap the band free so it can cascade down his back. Pressing myself against his body as he groans, half undressed underneath me, I focus on my task. Trousers first — shirt can stay on for all I fucking care — all I need is —

"God, you're *distracting*." He pulls back, sucking in a breath.

I flash him a smile, running my palm down his exposed chest. "I want you, I want my beta."

He hums and lets me push his shirt off his shoulders. I drop my head, kissing his exposed body while running my tongue over one of his pecs, unable to resist. His hands cover mine as they dip lower, reaching for his belt. The smells on his skin are muddled, like the outside, sterile cleaners — but I can fix it. I can make him smell like me, my sweet perfume of tea and honey — and maybe we can add oranges.

My mouth waters as his hands curl around my wrists.

"June."

I blink, looking up at him with a frown. "*What?*"

He has the *audacity* to grin at me. "Are you lucid? Are you here with me?" Seth dips his head, his hazel eyes searching mine. "Or do I need to get you off and *make* you lucid for half a second?"

I don't know if it's a rhetorical question, but I'm choosing that option. Wiggling my hands free, I unlatch his belt and go for the button on his slacks — I'm on a fucking mission, and getting off sounds *great* right now.

"God help me."

Seth grabs me again and suddenly I'm on my back, pinned to the mattress. I grunt as he hovers over me before he shakes his head and kisses me heatedly. With my hands pinned by one of his, I stretch out under him, spreading my legs with a whimper, begging with my body while my mouth is otherwise occupied.

I moan, loud and shameless as his thumb brushes my clit.

Seth's breath puffs against my jaw. "So fucking wet — I need to focus." He kisses my skin again, soothing it with each press. I roll my hips up, gasping as two of his fingers slide into me with ease. It's *nothing* compared to Theo's thickness, but they'll do —

"*Oh fuck!*" I shriek, my toes curling as Seth's fingers crook. Bowing forward, I struggle against his hand, gasping and writhing under him as he laughs, kissing my throat.

His thumb swipes over my clit as he thrusts his fingers in and out. "That's it, baby. I've got you. You're already so wet.

It's not going to take much, is it? I can just *hook* right there — *yeah*. Come on, come for me."

I gasp, pressing up against him, my legs shaking as I thrust up against his hand. The orgasm races like lighter fluid in a line up my spine, fire igniting in a rush. His name comes out of my mouth like a plea, and then I'm *coming* — slick gushing around his fingers as he kisses me, his hand letting mine go as he hums against my parted lips, breathing me in as I spiral somewhere in the stratosphere before returning to my senses.

"Hi." I blink up at him, my mind suddenly ten times clearer, the haze parting as I take in the man above me. Seth's long brown hair is tousled, his lips slightly swollen already, and a darker tint highlights his cheeks. He's so fucking *pretty* it makes my heart clench.

He pushes my hair away from my face, then kisses my forehead. "Hi, baby." Seth sits up partially, pulling me with him as he gives me a gentle smile. "Bennett and I were on our way back when Theo called. Your heat is here."

I nod, feeling a dull cramp that confirms what I already know. It's like I'm not in sync with my own body. I feel empty and needy, but also fractured, like there's a limb missing as I flinch and grimace.

He kisses my jaw, adjusting the blankets around my bare shoulders. "You told Arin you wanted him, Bennett, and I to be with you during this. Is that still okay?"

"Theo —" I jerk, rushing to get his name out as I stare at Seth with wide eyes, my throat closing as my heart smarts with a dull, throbbing pain that's different to the hollow feeling in my bones. "He *left* —"

"He didn't leave." Seth shushes me, grasping my cheeks. The feeling of his palms on my skin soothes the startling panic. "He went downstairs and called Arin because he didn't know what to do. It's okay. You are okay, and he is okay."

"He didn't *want* me."

Seth looks around the nest, then his eyes fall on me. "I don't think that's true, June. Have you seen this place? Have you seen *yourself*?"

I lift my head. There's clothes on the floor, and bottles of water in the corner — memories of Theo's body on mine, pressing me against the mattress, *fucking* me until I saw stars, bombard me. He only left once to get water and I was on him again in seconds when he got back — *oh*. I shift, glancing down at my bare chest. Bright red marks cover my breasts from his teeth, his lips. My stomach didn't escape either, and in the dim light I see bruising on my thighs too.

"Are you mad?" I glance up at Seth, biting my tongue.

He arches an eyebrow. "That you and Theo finally worked it out? No" — Seth taps the tip of my nose — "*but* I need you to focus and tell me if there's anything off limits while you're in this heat."

I blink at him, my brain muddled. *Limits?* I should have made a list — Arin asked for one days ago. I reach out for Seth unconsciously, touching his arms, my fingertips pressing down against his skin as I whisper, "I don't... I can't think — I —"

Seth leans up and I move to follow him. He pauses, his hands sliding over mine and carefully pushing me back to kneel on the mattress. I huff, but my eyes immediately go to his trousers as he finishes unbuckling his belt and pushes them off.

"Okay." He drops back down, crawling to box me in before he kisses my jaw, whispering, "*Jesus*, Theo did everything but bite you. Fucking unhinged alphas." He shakes his head, one hand splaying across a thigh before he lowers me to the mattress, kissing me softly, pressing himself against every inch of my body as his hand wraps around a leg, pulling me open, baring me to him.

"We're going to take this heat nice and slow, baby. How does that sound?" Seth's voice is silk as he whispers in my ear, his fingers sliding to my inner thigh, knuckles brushing through the curls between my legs. "I'm going to get you nice and ready for Bennett and his knot, and when Arin gets home, I'm *sure* he'll make you feel good. And not a single one of us will do *anything* with you unless we've already done it before."

I stare down at his hand, transfixed as he plays with me, parting my lower lips and gliding a finger over my clit. "Mhm." I swallow, breathing out as I arch against him. "But —" I jerk, opening my eyes quickly to find his. "No spanking."

Seth pauses, his smile devastating. "Got it. Just for the heat or..." He licks his lips. "In general?"

"For the heat," I clarify, wiggling lower so I can reach for his hips, kissing him gently as my nose wrinkles. "My skin is hot and tight, it's kind of sensitive right now." After a moment, I nip at his jaw and murmur, "But I like it rough any other time."

He barks out a laugh against my lips, then kisses me back, his fingers resuming their exploration. I moan as he whispers, "Look at this messy fucking pussy." Seth nips at my lower lip. "I'm going to make it even filthier so Bennett has something good to come home to."

I gasp as he pulls his hands away, replacing them with his tip. Seth rubs against my clit first, then he kisses me harder. Everything feels so *good*, like sparks shooting through my skin as he thrusts in. I drag myself forward so I can chase the kiss as he hikes my hip up, thrusting deeper and groaning.

A whine escapes from my throat as his lips move down, sucking and biting on my chest, irritating the marks already there. His hands guide my hips into his as he breathes out. "You were made for me, June."

Meeting him thrust for thrust, I keen out when he sinks all the way to the hilt, my toes curling from the pleasure. It doesn't matter that he doesn't have a knot — the feeling of his fingers threading through mine, holding onto me, his lips grazing my heated skin — it all makes me unravel. I gasp, breathing hard as the orgasm leaves me clenching and fluttering around him, arching into his chest as the blankets tangle under us.

Seth grunts, his hips kicking forward. "Oh *fuck*," he gasps, grabbing onto my hip as he slams into me two more times, then his cock jerks. Our foreheads press together, and I relish the feeling of him coming inside me as his labored groan skates across my skin.

Sliding my fingers into his hair, I inhale the scent of him, humming as I kiss across his face, touching every inch I can. "So good." With a languid mumble, I nuzzle his nose with mine. "I like you so much. I wanna keep you forever."

He stills. "Yeah?" Seth's fingers map my sides and his head drops to my shoulder, smiling against my skin. "You're going to keep me, huh?"

"Yeah." I lean into him, feeling drunk off the euphoria. The smell of oranges hits me and I roll my hips up, clenching around him again. *Need* — hot and insistent crawls through my veins. "I want our alpha."

"You're in luck." Seth raises his head, touching my chin and turning it so my gaze falls on the doorway.

Bennett leans against the frame, his tall body coiled. My heart rises in my throat at the sight of him, a smile lifting the edges of his lips. From my place under Seth, I can see the tightness in his shoulders as he holds himself from entering the space meant for only me.

"Can I come in, darling?"

I shiver, nodding as Seth kisses down my chest again. His lips wrap around a nipple and I mewl as he sucks and pulls out of me at the same time. I'm not empty for long, because his hand creeps between my thighs, playing with the mess the two of us made, sliding through it, and then pushing it back into me.

The nest dips and I look up, breathless as Bennett lowers to the space next to our bodies. His shirt is partially unbuttoned, his pants open at the fly, like he couldn't undress for wanting to get to us.

I lean up, bracing on an elbow as I stare at him. "Welcome home, alpha."

"Hello, sweet omega." He crawls forward, dipping his head down and kissing me slowly. I hum against his lips, one of his dark-skinned hands coming to cup my face sweetly. He's all orange zest, bright on my tongue, a citrus tang chaser to the layers of sugar from Seth and I.

I wiggle down, gasping as Seth's fingers toy with me again, shallowly thrusting. With a little whine, I pull back and look down as the beta smirks up at us both, pulling his hand away and licking his fingers as he stares at Bennett. "She's more than ready for you."

Bennett curses under his breath, kissing me one more time before he drops lower, his lips ghosting over my body.

He settles next to Seth, sliding his own hand between my thighs and I spread them wider, watching the two men as they kiss each other, lingering in the familiar embrace for a breath that makes my heart tug with affection. Bennett turns his head, kissing my inner thigh as Seth shifts out of the way. The beta moves up, laying next to me, one hand moving over my chest as he pulls me into another kiss, distracting me.

When we part, Bennett's naked body fills up my field of view as he settles overtop me. Seth grabs my hand and presses my palm against Bennett's lower stomach. I feel the heated skin, soothed by it instead of recoiling. *This* is what my body needed.

My fingers sink lower as Bennett's lips replace Seth's. As my hand brushes his hard length, I whisper, "Knot me?"

He nods into the kiss, settling between my legs as one hand guides himself and my hand lower, rubbing through the mess between my legs. "You and Seth did such a good job." He murmurs the praise, his voice wrapping me up as the orange scent of his perfume washes over me. "So fucking wet and messy for me, you're going to take me so well. You'll stretch perfectly for my knot, won't you? You're going to let me fill you up?"

I moan, pressing up against him, panting out. "Both of you."

Bennett pauses, the tip of him just barely breaching me. My throat feels dry and I turn my head to look at Seth. "Please?"

"Well, since you asked so fucking politely," Seth groans, leaning in to kiss me.

Bennett pulls back and the loss of him stings, but it's only for a moment as I sit up, my hands in Bennett's. He pulls me into his lap, Seth's lips leaving mine and dropping to my shoulder as I straddle Bennett, turning my focus to the alpha in front of me as I grind down with tiny circles of my hips.

He breathes out heavily, his eyes only on me as I feel Seth's lips brush down the back of my shoulder, his fingers spreading me as he lines Bennett up. I lift — and then sink down, taking Bennett with a little hiccuped gasp, pressing my forehead against his.

"*God*," Bennett groans, kissing my jaw, my neck, my ear, his voice breathless. "You are a fucking *wonder*."

I smile as I run my fingers over his short hair, the soft curl pattern tickling my palms as Seth's fingers toy with my clit, winding me up almost casually as Bennett lazily thrusts into me.

From behind, Seth murmurs, "I need to get you ready, June. Are you sure?"

"Mhm." I smile back at him, glancing over my shoulder as I lean further onto Bennett's chest, watching as Seth's eyes dart from my face down to my ass, his pupils blowing out with lust.

"We have a captive audience, alpha." I turn my head, kissing Bennett slowly as he bounces me in his lap.

He groans, grabbing onto my hips, his fingers digging into my skin. "Better put on a good show, darling."

Seth curses from behind me and I gasp as Bennett's hips begin to thrust up a little faster. I feel Seth's finger ease over me, spreading the slick and our combined release. His breath fans over the back of my neck as his finger circles, thrusting into me as Bennett moves. My attention is split and I whine both of their names, muscles clenching and fluttering around Bennett as Seth stretches me.

"You're such a good omega, you're going to let Seth take you while I knot you?"

I nod, breathing Bennett in as I bounce faster, his knot kissing my cunt with each thrust. "Now, now please." I reach behind me for Seth, feeling him press against my back. "I can't wait, I need you." Even half-full, I feel unbearably empty, like nothing will soothe the scorching heat in my body except for the two of them together. One alpha, one beta, one omega — how it should be, how it should *always* be.

The tip of Seth's cock presses against me from behind and I bear down as Bennett's lips fall to my right shoulder, sucking on my skin and giving me a focus point. Seth's head presses against mine, his lips right next to my ear. "*Fuck,* you're so tight. You're going to strangle me, aren't you? I won't even last long enough to get my fill."

I moan as I push back against him, feeling stretched and full, but *right* as he thrusts in. Crying out, Seth settles in me as I tug Bennett's head to mine, kissing him roughly and nipping at his lips. *Fuck* going slow, my skin is going to combust if they both don't *move* —

An inhuman noise leaves my mouth as Bennett slams his hips up, kissing me back with just as much force, all while muttering, "I can *feel* Seth." His hand moves behind me, grasping onto his bonded's shoulder for stability. "I can't knot you like this, June. What if I hurt you?"

Thousands of arguments rise — the fact that my newfound designation has *made* my body able to take this being the top one — but I give up on them all and slam myself down, rocking harder until I feel the thick knot of muscle around the base of Bennett's cock press slowly against my entrance. I want it. I *need* it.

"*Please*," I whine, throwing my head back to Seth's shoulder. "Please, someone make me *come*."

Seth slams into me, all the way to the hilt, his voice ragged. "Bennett, *fuck* her for god's sake."

Bennett's hand tightens on Seth's shoulder as his other digs into my hip, and then pounds up into me, the knot breaching me and settling against my inner walls as I gasp. The pressure makes my body *sing* with pleasure, every inch of me meant to be taken up by the feeling of him.

I explode, screaming their names as I come hard enough that the beta roars behind me, pushing me forward with a thrust. Rocking against Bennett, the tug of his knot locked in me pushes me into another, shallower orgasm. As Seth comes, it sets Bennett off, his nails digging into my thigh to hold me in place.

Boneless, I droop into Bennett's chest when Seth pulls out. The room feels fuzzy and warm as I hum and slump against the alpha. His chest rises and lowers in quick succession, breathing out his orange scent all over me. A warm blanket slides over my back, covering us up as Bennett sinks down to lie on the mattress.

I sprawl on top of him, clenching down on his cock still buried inside me, locked in place with his knot. He grunts, once, then exhales a little laugh, kissing the top of my head as Seth stretches out beside us, kissing Bennett's chest right next to my head. Bennett's hand rubs my back, soothing touches lingering.

This is what safety feels like.

The knot will go down. I already feel the flush of desire at the thought of making him press into me over and over again — until both of us are delirious. Nuzzling his chest, I relax overtop of him, drifting off with my mind finally quiet in my alpha's arms, our beta beside us.

CHAPTER TWO

SETH

She's so fucking pretty.

Even flushed head to toe, her pink lips swollen, I can't stop kissing her and neither can Bennett. June's auburn hair looks like strands of fire in the dim light. It's a tangled nest at the back of her head, her lush, curvy pale body marred with marks from our lips, hands, and grazes of teeth.

We got the call from Theo on the way back from Heathrow. I wish we hadn't even *left* — but shareholders wanted a meeting and happened to be in Dublin. I tried everything to get out of it, but they won't ever just see me, it always has to be Bennett and I.

I'd nearly thrown open the door to the car and ran back to the townhouse. The only thing stopping me being the fact it was faster to just stay seated.

I *knew* her heat would come early. The idiots at the designation center swore that she had two weeks, but they weren't *looking* at her when I charged in there. She'd been exhausted, tired, and out of it — leaving her in their incapable hands wasn't an option.

I make a lot of rash decisions, but she's my best one.

My muscles feel like jelly as I pick up another orange slice, guiding it to her lips as I kiss the side of her head. Her body leans back against my chest, curled up in my lap as I murmur, "One more bite."

She sighs, parting her lips and letting me feed her. The lucid moments are touch and go, sometimes I swear the only thing she wants to feel is pleasure, over and *over* again — but a few times she's just cuddled against mine or Bennett's chest, seeking out our general presence. I have no idea how anything to do with omega heats work, but I'm fine with figuring it out on the fly as long as she's taken care of.

"I'm tired." Her voice is hoarse and I turn, wondering where Bennett is with the water bottles. It's barely been twenty-four hours since we've gotten home and I don't doubt that she's exhausted. The stupid pamphlets the center gave Bennett said a heat could last anywhere from five to seven days. Endless days of sex, insatiable need, a burning hot fever, full body shakes, and cramping — I can't even fathom it. The most terrifying part is that if she doesn't get the care she needs, it can irreparably damage her body.

I rub her side, pulling her closer. "Want to nap on me for a bit?"

June nods, finishing chewing the orange. The slices are perfect segments, with every strand of white pith picked off. Theo left them by the door an hour ago without a word.

She turns in my arms, her body soft and languid as she nestles herself against my chest. I look down at her, sliding my fingers over her hair, just watching her for a moment as her face slackens, sleep pulling her under for a few stolen moments of rest.

Her breathing evens out as I rest my head back against the nest wall for a moment, closing my eyes too. I already sent Bennett away twenty minutes ago, reminding him that Arin will be back as soon as the contracts are signed in Paris. He's selling some huge property in the countryside and I already pulled him away from it once when I made the last-minute decision that the woman in my arms was coming home with Bennett and I.

Never did I expect we'd all find ourselves in this situation, but I don't take her trust in us lightly.

June's begged for Bennett's knot more times than I can count, and I'm slightly worried he'll be totally out of energy if he comes back into the nest without a nap. I don't know why it didn't click just *how* insatiable she'd be, since that's the entire point of the heat — to make her beg and beg for *days* until the ultimate biological goal is achieved — getting her pregnant.

I take some comfort in the fact she has a birth control implant. She was on it when she was still a beta, and the designation center doctor assured her it's also used with omegas too. I don't envy her, waking up one day with a totally different designation sounds horrifying. I always knew I was just... normal and it's worked for me. Meeting Bennett and feeling attraction to him wasn't life-changing until he sunk his teeth in me, giving me a silver bond mark at the junction of my neck and shoulder and a connection to him forever.

The bond in my chest hums, low and tired, but he's clearly taking *care* of himself, and that's all I want for him. I push love back at him, receiving an immediate swell of affection in return, smiling to myself as I whisper to the darkness of the nest. "I love you too."

Glancing down, I take June in while she rests, lifting a hand to smooth out the line between her brows.

I love her too.

It's not a hard thing to do.

The world insists betas are benign, that there are no biological instincts one way or another, no true bonds forged between a beta and omega — because omegas are really *meant* for alphas one way or another. Alphas are the ones with a knot, or a lock. They're the ones predisposed to care for another person to the level an omega needs.

But the second I saw the woman in my arms in that elevator, I knew she was missing from mine *and* Bennett's lives.

She stirs, breathing out against my neck as she wiggles in my lap. One of her hands moves, and then she's touching me, wrapping fingers around me and pulling slowly, coaxing my cock back to life as I groan.

"Already?"

Her lips twitch, her eyes still closed as she turns and kisses my chest, jerking her hand. "Please?"

She's so fucking *polite* when she's out of her mind with lust, if it wasn't an insane scenario, I'd find the humor in it. Also, it makes it hard to think about how amusing it is when her fingers keep trying to push me into the tight, wet sheath of her.

I kiss her head, sliding my hands down to grasp the curve of her ass. I grab two handfuls of her body as she moans, sliding a leg over mine. The smell of her slick floods my senses — it's so goddamn sweet, like licking dripping honey off a spoon, tinged with a herbal, tea leaf aftertaste.

Grinding against her, I whisper, "How do you want me this time, baby?"

I'm selfish, I kind of want her ass again, or to just eat her out until my jaw locks — but my body is hers to use right now.

June leans up, her eyes hooded as she cups my face and kisses me slowly, like she's savoring me. She slides away and I arch an eyebrow as she rests her forearms on the edge of the nest wall, cushioned for this *exact* reason. I watch as she bends her body over, sighing softly as she arches, not saying a word.

I can take a fucking hint.

Sliding a hand over the dip of her back, I move behind her, bending down to kiss her shoulder as I rub the head of my cock through her folds. She writhes, her breathing growing more and more labored as she grasps the plush wall. I thrust into her, punching my hips forward, as deep as I can go, rewarded by the sound of her soft keen, slurring out, "*so good.*"

Grinning, I rest a hand on the small of her back. I push her down for me before pulling out and slamming in again, watching her ass jiggle as I do. *Jesus.* My own head spins for a moment as I move at a steady pace, tired but doing my best to block it from mine and Bennett's bond. I can last another round — or two, most likely, because it's taking more and more to satisfy her. I should have bought more toys. The two little bullet vibrators that Bennett and I used last night have already died. They didn't even make it to the early hours of this morning.

Some help would be *great*, but the only other alpha in the house is lurking downstairs like a fucking specter.

As if I conjured him, I look up, pausing mid-stroke to see Theo in the doorway, his eyes zeroing in on June.

The alpha fills the space, his broad shoulders hunched

slightly, clad in a tight t-shirt and a pair of sweats that do nothing to hide the clear arousal straining in them. I continue thrusting as I bite my tongue, my eyes sweeping over him, from his bare feet, up to his pale arms covered in black tattoos, to his slightly long blond hair, pushed back. It's not long enough to pull into a bun — yet, but I think June would dig it if it was. I would.

"You're doing so well for me, June," I groan as I reach between us, toying with her clit as my eyes focus on Theo. "Does that feel good, baby?"

She arches into me, turning her body into a literal work of art as she cries out. I increase the pace, slightly breathless as Theo's eyes flicker over her, then land on me, his nostrils flaring.

I smirk back at him, my voice even. "Don't you want her, Theo?"

June whines, her head lifting slightly, and I *know* she's looking at him, as much as she can when she's blissed out with my cock buried inside her.

"Don't you see how good she can take it?"

Theo's hands clench into fists at his sides. He'll break soon, there's no way he's going to survive this little starvation hissy fit to the end of her heat.

I strum June's clit faster, making her release another gush of slick around me, the smell of her arousal permeating the air. I move faster, a little harder, and I'm rewarded by her cunt spasming around me. "Do something for me, baby," I grunt, leaning down to whisper in her ear just to watch goosebumps rise on her skin. "Say Theo's name when you come around my cock."

The words do the trick. She gasps, her body trembling as she scrambles for purchase on the side of the nest. I feel it before she comes, a rush of heat through her body, burning me as I sink into her steadily. She gives into the orgasm, her voice a soft whine. "*Theo.*"

I never knew I'd be so into making her say other men's names, but *fuck* if it isn't the hottest thing in the entire world. I pull out, grabbing myself and stroking quickly, leaning up so I'm positioned over her back before I come, breathing hard as I cover her skin in my release. It's not much, and I'm exhausted, my balls ache, my body shaking as I look up at Theo.

"Look at that." I smear it on her back, leaning down to kiss her shoulder lovingly as she sinks down into the blankets. I adjust them around her, making sure she's comfortable as I stumble to my feet, fully naked. "Her perfume is so thick, I know it's dripping down your throat, Theo. Are you still going to stand there and deny her?"

His breathing turns ragged as I climb out of the nest, moving to the doorway. Theo's nostrils flare when I get close enough. He's no Bennett — but Theo and I have done our fair share of dancing around each other, and he *does* like to occasionally join Bennett in wrecking me. This is fair game. I do wonder sometimes if Theo wouldn't enjoy being put in *his* place, but I don't know what he and Arin get up in their spare time.

Theo licks his lips, backing up and colliding with the side of the wall in the hallway outside the nest. "I can't." I step closer, following him as he glances at the nest doorway, his expression breaking. "*Fuck,* I started all this, didn't I? I'm the reason she's so miserable."

I reach out, touching his chest, my voice softening. "Yeah, you did. And she's wanted you since I got in there with her. She wants *all* of us."

There's something dark in Theo's eyes as his palm presses against the front of his sweats.

I watch as his hand tries to alleviate the length straining in his pants, raising an eyebrow. "Problem?"

"Yeah." He rasps the word and then pushes the waistband down, exposing himself as he barks at me. "*Fix it.* Be a good beta and *suck me off*, because you got this started and need to finish it."

I grin at him, running my tongue over my teeth before I drop to my knees and wrap my hand around his cock, the same one coated in June's slick. I take him into my mouth without preamble, sucking him down as he groans above me. It won't take long, he's already twitching in my mouth as his hand fists my hair, tugging on it as his hips jolt forward, pushing him to the back of my throat.

I wrap one hand around his knot, swollen and hot under my palm, and use the other to toy with his balls as I pull back and gasp, "Did you knot her while we were gone? Bennett said it feels like heaven. I could feel him nearly black out from the pleasure in the bond."

With that image planted in Theo's mind, I deep throat him. He rewards me with a roar, bending over as he comes down my throat. I lean back, laughing as I look up at his confused expression.

"I was just supposed to bring water."

I glance at the two bottles near the door, then grab them, slapping Theo on the shoulder as I crack one open and down half of it.

"You know you could go in there."

Theo gives me a haunted look as he pulls his sweats back up, his throat bobbing. "No." His eyes dart away. "I can't. Not until Arin says it's alright."

I nod, crushing the bottle in my palm as a beat of anger flashes through me.

It passes in a heartbeat. I don't know the full story about his background, but I've made a few educated guesses through the years. We all have our differences, but it's what makes this pack work.

"It'll be okay. She'll be lucid again. You didn't... hurt her."

Hesitating with the bottles in my hands, I raise my chin at the taller alpha. His eyes are purple underneath, the pale skin bruised from lack of sleep. Theo hasn't been in the nest, but he looks just as wrecked as June does — and that doesn't sit well with me.

"I don't know what happened between you two, but she *was* upset — only because you left her."

Theo makes a strangled sound, and when he looks up at me, there are tears in his eyes. Bennett once gave me a look that lost — completely beholden to his own biology and designation, like he couldn't escape the shackles of his own innate desire.

I sigh. "Get out of your own head, for your sake and hers."

Pushing the nest door open, I let it shut behind me as I climb back into the bed with June, adjusting the waters so they're within reach as I wrap myself around her, waiting for her to wake up again so I can feed her more fruit and get her to drink something.

Fucking alphas.

CHAPTER THREE

ARIN

I'VE NEVER HEARD Theo so panicked before.

"*Arin, I don't know what I did — she's — it happened — the heat started and I don't know what to do about it. I don't want to hurt her. I can't end up like my fathers.*"

Trapped in Paris, with my entire pack frantic, as my new omega goes into her first heat? Yeah, that's just what I wanted for this week.

I barely remember to thank the driver before I sprint from the car and up the walkway to the front door, ignoring everything around the townhouse in favor of just getting *inside it.* Unlocking the door, I step inside, inhaling sharply on instinct. It doesn't smell like anything but cheese and garlic, wafting from the kitchen. Dropping my bag in the foyer, I pivot toward the smell, stopping when I see Theo stirring a pot of risotto on the stovetop.

He looks up, then lets out a breath, stepping away from the stove and heading toward me. I feel the pull in my chest, wrapping my arms around the other man, tugging him to me. Now *Theo* smells like more than just his fresh rain scent —

26

mixtures of Seth and Juniper lingering on his skin. I'll get the details later, but for now, I touch the back of his head gently, my voice low.

"How is she?"

With the question, his rainwater scent sours, going muddy as his face twists. Theo pulls away, going back to the pan and stirring it quickly — I don't know enough about Bennett's specific risotto recipe to know if he's *supposed* to be doing it or not, but it doesn't deter me from staring him down.

"Fine." Theo mumbles the word under his breath. "Bennett and Seth have been upstairs the entire time. They're probably tired though. Bennett told me how to make this" — he motions to the pot — "and said she wanted it."

Within the span of a breath, Theo's voice takes on a gentle, almost loving tone. His eyes focus on the rice as he mumbles, "I need to get her to eat something, she's only had two clementines and some water."

I push my sleeves up, nodding as I move around the kitchen. Crackers, pre-sliced fruit, and anything with high enough nutrients in small bites goes into a basket I got for this *very* reason. I shouldn't have let myself get distracted when she was in my bed days ago. It was the perfect time to get her to give me a list of the things she likes to snack on.

But this will have to do.

Pointing at one of the oversized mugs I bought, I mutter, "Spoon her food into that so it's easier to hold."

I anticipate she's probably too tired to feed herself, but that's why I'm here.

Theo portions out the risotto, then slides the mug across the marble counter to me.

I look up as I wrap my hand around the mug. "I'm

sending Bennett and Seth down. Make sure they shower, eat, and sleep."

Theo dips his head at me. "I'll help where I can down here."

His shoulders sag, his head dipping lower as his eyes stay on the stove.

"Theo, you are *not* your fathers." I should know, I've had the misfortune of being around the two bastards for a majority of my life. "You're not going to cross a line with her. You won't *hurt* her during this."

He looks away, his jaw flexing. "I might."

I growl, unable to help myself as I abandon June's food on the counter. It'll be fine for a moment. Rounding the corner of the island, I step into Theo's personal space, making the other alpha look up sharply. His eyes widen as I grab him by the back of his throat, my lips pulling back in a snarl.

"Theo, you are *not* them." I give him a stern look, making sure he hears me. "I would not have *formed a pack with you* if you were even remotely similar. I don't know *what* happened when I was out of this house, but I wouldn't have *left* you with her if I was worried about your behavior. Are we clear?"

Something vulnerable shatters behind his eyes. "She's just so *small*."

I squeeze the back of his neck, feeling the snarl leave my face as quickly as it came. "And I *trust* you. More importantly, she was okay with being alone with you. I *asked* her before we left."

Theo closes his eyes, dropping his head as he nods. I let him go. I don't have *time* to work through every tiny issue he has with his alpha designation, but I do hope that he eventually gets it through his thick skull that I didn't make the choice I did lightly. I would have never left them in the position I did if I didn't trust him. And I *do* trust him — implicitly.

Snatching the food, I turn on a heel and jog up the stairs, reaching the topmost floor of the townhouse and sucking in a breath. I wish I could have gotten her back home to Rochester — because the nest there is more comfortable and set closer to the kitchen — but this is what we could make do with. After this is over, she can come *home.*

I reach for the door, opening it slowly and glancing in to see Bennett on his side, running his hand up and down June's spine as she lies on her stomach. Her pale back is flushed, a sheen over her skin as she sighs softly. Seth is on her other side, stroking her hair. Bennett and Seth both look up at me, and I see the dark circles and bags under their eyes — a little pile of water bottles and food scraps in a corner.

I'm proud of how well they've done, but I'm here now.

Clearing my throat, I focus on the naked omega in the nest. "Juniper, can I come in?"

She lifts her head, her eyes widening as she scrambles to sit up. "*Arin.*" Her voice is so raw and soft, worn out from use.

I smile gently, lifting her mug. "I brought food."

The smile she gives me makes my heart ache. In the light from the hall, I can see the shadows caressing the curves of her body, thick hips, bare breasts, utterly unconcerned with the state of herself. I feel a little out of it as her focus flickers over me, like she's seeing into my mind.

Her voice is husky when she whispers, "Come into my nest, alpha."

I step in, moving over to her as I drop the basket of

snacks within reach of the mattress. My eyes dart to Bennett and Seth, tone brooking no argument. "Go. Go eat, shower, and rest."

Bennett hesitates before he nods. He bends down and kisses June's head before he passes her, naked, to leave. Seth wraps an arm around our omega, kissing her jaw and lingering to whisper something in her ear. She laughs, a light, giggling sound as she turns into the beta. I watch as her arms wrap around him, squeezing tightly, clinging to him.

I hear them shut the door, but don't see it as I step down onto the mattress with bare feet. Suddenly surrounded by the mixture of their perfumes, my brain clouds, instinct and desire warring. Her full attention turns to me, hazel eyes blown out as she crawls across the mattress. When she reaches me, she sinks back to sit, ass to heels, perched in front of me. The picture of a perfect submissive, hands in her lap, eager to please.

Fuck.

I suck in a breath as I lower myself down to sit, leaning against one of the walls, opening my arms. "Come here."

She leaps forward and I grunt as she launches herself at my chest. Grabbing her, I help her crawl into my lap and hum as she wraps her arms around my neck. June bends her head down, barely giving me a glimpse of her sweet face up close before she kisses me, sliding her hands through my hair. I hold onto her as she moans, wiggling her hips.

I can't think. She smells *so good*, damn near edible.

Her whine is breathy in my ear. "Missed you, need you." Her lips slide across my jaw, rubbing over my beard. "Alpha, *please.*"

I jolt my hips up, unable to help myself when she's bare

on top of me. Sliding my hand over her hip, I work to swallow. "You should eat."

"After, please," she mumbles against my lips, kissing me again as she pushes at my button-up.

I pull back, watching her pout as she rests her hands on my chest.

"Don't make me *beg*, Arin."

My lips twitch — she's more lucid than I expected — but she also smells like sex, and my mouth fills with saliva at the thought. I'm not predisposed to watching as much as Bennett is — but *god* — I have two handfuls of a stunning woman on top of me and picturing her overcome with pleasure from all of us makes my blood heat.

I kiss her jaw, muttering against her skin. "You beg so prettily though."

She wraps herself around me, kissing me heatedly as her hands fumble with my trousers. I help her push them down, just enough to pull myself out, then I flip her onto her back and settle between her thighs. Running my thumb over the skin between her thigh and pussy, I stare down at her, my brow furrowing. "You've got bruises all over you."

Her smile scrunches her nose as she grabs my hand and pulls my chest flush to hers. "Theo got a little carried away. I like them."

I dip my head down, relenting and kissing her slowly as I slide myself against her slick entrance. Humming, I press my tip into her. "Should I add mine to the collection, Juniper? Would you like my teeth marks next to his? Or my bruises beside Bennett's?"

She nods, her hands sliding over my shirt. I feel like a deviant, dressed on top of her as I thrust into her deeply, kissing her entrance with the knot at the base of my cock.

She moans, a gentle sound, her neck arching as she sighs. "It's so different with you."

My heart stops as I stare at her, pliant and willing under me. Fumbling with my shirt, I push it off as I kiss her throat. "What do you mean, love?"

June gasps as I pull out and then thrust into her. Her hands move over my ass, then she manages to wiggle my clothes off of me — *fucking minx.* I grin as she moans, wrapping her legs fully around my hips, lost for a moment as she pants out, "The heat ebbs. I feel like *myself* when you're inside me."

I'd read as much as I could on the flight back — about omegas, heats, and what helped the most. There had been a few vague mentions that when a pack was involved, the prime, or pack alpha, would be the best suited to keep the omega satisfied. The entire dynamic apparently revolves around everyone deferring to *me.* It's a lot of weight, sometimes, juggling Theo's moods, Bennett's cool sensibility, and Seth's impulses.

It all fades as I brace above her, finally naked, one hand on the mattress and the other on the meat of her thigh. Kissing her deeply, I give in and *fuck* her. My omega — the woman who trusts me enough to be here with her, to have embraced our pack in a time of chaos and need.

I nip at her lips, sliding my fingers through her hair, my voice rougher as I push deeper, grinding myself against her clit, teasing her with my knot.

"*Arin*, please knot me. I need it. I need you so —"

Her gasp makes me even harder as I jerk her head to the side, biting softly at her neck, not breaking the skin. She clenches around me, and then she comes, flooding me with her orgasm as I suck softly, slipping my knot into her. The feeling of her strangling me is otherworldly and I come with a strangled moan, breathing out against her skin.

She writhes under me, nails in my shoulders as she comes down, making little satisfied sounds. I shift us, buried and locked inside of her, lifting her into my arms and settling back to sit with her draped across me.

June turns her head, smiling at me with flushed cheeks and bee-stung lips.

I grab the mug of risotto and put some on the spoon for her. "Open."

She complies, and I feed her, leaving her to rest tucked against me as I focus on getting some energy back into her tired body. Wrapping a blanket around her shoulders, I settle in to be here for as long as she needs me — even if someone has to carry my corpse out later.

CHAPTER FOUR

THEO

BENNETT LOOKS *WRUNG out* when he walks into the kitchen.

Three days.

It's been three straight days of June in the nest and me staying as far as fucking possible. Except for the one time I felt trapped like a wild animal watching Seth fuck her as she whimpered *my* name.

Bennett walks to the fridge, pulling out various ingredients as he speaks. "I'm making soup to see if she'll eat it. We finished the risotto last night."

I've been existing solely on wine and take-out, I wouldn't know.

Any of the hard liquors we have around the townhouse are from Bennett and Seth's brand, and I didn't relish the thought of getting so drunk that I found myself stumbling upstairs to beg for forgiveness. I've also been sleeping on the couch, folding my huge ass body into a pretzel to do it.

I nod at him, stepping out of his way. It does nothing to stop the smell of his orange perfume wafting over to me, covered in honey, like it's drizzled on him. I'm not one hundred percent sure he was in the nest last night — but Arin's barely left since he got home.

Bennett grabs a rotisserie chicken from the fridge, shredding it onto a plate, separating it from the bone. "I'm making my own stock, it'll take some time."

"I can help," I offer, shifting closer.

He levels me with a look. "Seth will be down soon. Any particular reason you've been sleeping in the living room instead of in your room?"

I cringe, grabbing my glass of wine. My room shares the same floor as the nest above us, that's reason enough. "Giving you all space."

"She doesn't want space, Theo." Bennett picks the chicken apart with deft fingers. "Arin won't hold up by himself, I'm still tired, and Seth is doing what he can *as a beta*."

"I think I've done enough."

Bennett raises his head, staring at me. "I don't know... *what* this is." He motions up and down, encompassing me. "But it's getting really fucking old."

I still. "I don't know what you mean. I've been helping where I can."

He drops the chicken onto the plate before wiping his hands and staring up at me, his voice low. "I'm glad that's what you're telling yourself, because she was a *mess* when we got home. And I'm not talking about the way you covered her in marks, or the way you were the *first* of us to have her in the nest. I'm talking about the way her eyes have been swollen for days because when we finish doting on her, *loving* her, she asks if you're okay — if you're coming upstairs."

His anger makes his voice break. "And I can't tell her one more time that you need time to adjust. Either step the fuck up and recognize that you have to sort your own shit out, or *leave*."

I think if he'd plunged a knife into my chest, it would hurt less.

Seth rounds the corner into the kitchen, long hair damp. He freezes, eyes darting between the two of us.

Bennett looks back at the ravaged chicken. "Oh, and Theo?"

I give him a wary look.

He swipes the bones into the stock pot. "Seth is an adult and can consent to whatever he wants with anyone he wants in this pack, but if you bark at my beta again and keep making my omega cry, I'll fucking kill you." He grabs two bottles of water and shoves them at me. "Take those upstairs to Arin and see if he's going to come out anytime soon."

I take the bottles, stunned speechless as I pass Seth. Regret tastes bitter on my tongue, but Seth flashes me a weak smile, patting my shoulder. "He's just a little prickly. I'm not mad at you."

The simple words and smile ease the tightness in my chest as I head toward the stairs. *I can do this.* I inhale, focusing on heading to the nest, ignoring my room and hesitating just a moment outside the door, making sure I can't hear any gasping or moaning. When I don't, I turn the knob, glancing inside.

Arin looks *tired.* His eyes are closed with his hand on June's head, curled up against his side, her head on a pillow. For once, she looks like she's actually sleeping deeply.

Arin's head raises sharply before he lets out a breath. "You can just leave them at the door, I'll get up in a moment." His rough voice is barely above a whisper, and he winces as he sits up, careful of June next to him.

I take in his bare body, deep tanned skin pulling over his lean muscles as my prime, my oldest friend, climbs out of the nest. He stands, naked, getting his feet under him before he steps toward me. I've seen everything of my pack mates in the last seventy-two hours, but it's never bothered me. There are other, more pressing matters taking up my mental bandwidth.

"You look like shit."

He grimaces, moving slowly with a groan. "I won't lie, she's wearing me down." Taking a bottle from me, Arin drinks deeply before his eyes meet mine. "She won't let us take her into the bathroom to clean her up. She keeps saying she doesn't want to lose your scent on her. We've been reduced to washcloths only."

My eyes fall on her, drawn like a magnet. She's partially covered by one of the fuzzy blankets I panic bought for her — the same one that I'm sure was bunched under us days ago when I found myself in here with her, finally giving in.

My mouth goes dry. "Bennett is making soup. Seth is helping him."

Arin's stare sears my skin. It's all out psychological warfare. I want to spill my fucking soul in the doorway of June's nest like I'm a young alpha who can't keep his shit together.

"You look like you need rest." I blurt the words at him, desperate to break the tension.

Arin pushes a hand through his wild curls, nodding. "Yeah, I think this is the first time she's slept more than an hour. It might mean she's close to the end, we could be lucky and it's only five days, not seven or eight."

I step to the side, glancing at her again. "Go get cleaned up. I'll... I can just sit out here and if she wakes up, I'll come get whoever she wants."

Arin brushes past me, then pauses, looking at me and then back at her. "She wants *you*, Theo."

He leaves me with those words.

Slowly, I sink to the floor outside the door, leaning against the frame. From this angle, I can't really see much other than the nest wall, and I fidget with one of the water bottles. The room smells like a mix of all of us — my own scent lingering. Rain, with warm mint tea full of honey, pieces of chocolate fudge and oranges — like the perfect early morning breakfast back home in the States.

Closing my eyes, I breathe in and out, letting it coat my senses. I was so *panicked* when I couldn't find her the other day, so frantic at the thought that something had happened to her while I was hiding in my room. I'd been trying to figure out how to leave during the heat — but not leave Bennett and Arin and Seth to fill in the gaps and exhaust themselves.

I should have known it was an impossible feat.

Heats should be easier to navigate. Where's the instinctual feeling in me that wants to give in? Why can I fight it so easily? Why does this all just remind me of hearing my mother fight with my fathers, flinching memories of them barking at her to '*shut the fuck up*' and watching her take under the counter heat suppressants so she didn't have to spend weeks at a time out of her mind at their mercy.

She's never told me the full story — if there was love there once, or if it's always been this tumultuous. I swear she used to have more fight in her, but the older I got, the more she just gave in to their ire.

A whimper from the nest makes me jolt.

June sits up, looking around frantically, her eyes wide, the blanket falling off of her. "Arin?"

I push up. "It's okay, Arin just went to shower."

Her head whips to the side, her eyes finding mine, red-rimmed, just like Bennett said. She hiccups, her voice shaking, her pink lips parted as she breathes out. "Theo?"

She doesn't *sound* totally out of it, not as dazed as before, and I perk up. "Yeah, it's me, June. Bennett's making you some soup with Seth. You gonna eat for us?"

"Why are you over there?" She shifts, her hands reaching toward me. Her hair is a *wreck* around her neck and I find myself standing, almost stepping closer, freezing so I don't cross the line into her nest. June frowns at me. "Why aren't you over here?"

"Do you want me?" I stare at her, swallowing. "Are you sure?"

She nods, reaching for me again. "Theo —" June pauses, clearing her raspy throat.

I crunch the water bottle in my hand and sprint across the threshold, letting the door slam shut behind me as I stride over to her. Dropping down on one knee, I open the bottle and cradle the back of her head, holding it to her mouth. "Drink, then talk."

She looks up at me, and this close I see how shiny her eyes are with unshed tears. June listens, letting me tip the water into her mouth. I watch her drink until she sighs, her hand reaching out to wrap around my tattooed forearm.

Her voice is barely a whisper. "I'm so tired. Everything hurts." She swallows thickly. "Nothing stops the cramping unless I'm coming. I think my fever is finally lower, though." Her voice breaks, and I'm not sure I can stand here and listen to her cry as her lower lip trembles. "I don't know what I did to make you leave, but I'm *sorry*. I'm sorry that I even came here, that you don't want me, but everything in me wants you, Theo. I want your stupid, stubborn, mean self, because at least you made me consider whether I should have stayed here or not — if I only picked this because it was the easiest option."

My heart falls out of my stomach as I stare at her. "June..."

She shakes her head, grasping my arm harder, clinging to me. "I like that you didn't ask me what I wanted — that you just *bought* me things for this nest. I like that you and I can't seem to figure out if we hate each other, or if it's something more complicated. I like that you don't make me admit what I'm thinking like Arin does, or know what you're doing like Bennett always seems to."

June sucks in a breath.

"And I *love* that you told me not to listen to my mother. I want you all. I'm tired of pretending like I don't."

I let the water bottle drop to the floor as I lean in, cupping her face.

June's lashes flutter, tears brimming. "We'll figure it all out, whatever it is between us. Even if it's a nightmare to do it, because I don't feel *right* unless you're a part of this too."

Dropping my forehead against hers, I exhale, closing my eyes, unable to look at her. "I have completely fucked this up. I should be begging you for forgiveness and groveling. You have nothing to apologize for."

Her fingers drag up my arm. "Fix it. I... I did something, my presence did something, and I want you to fix it."

I sigh, pulling her closer for a moment before I bend down and swing her up into my arms. Her soft, full curves fill my arms as I lift her effortlessly out of the nest and step around the edge, carrying her to the bathroom door.

June lets out a noise of surprise.

"You should *not* have to hear my bullshit in the middle of your heat." I place her down on a bench inside the bathroom and turn on the taps for the huge tub to let it fill, my shoulders tightening. "That's unbelievably selfish of me."

When I glance back at her, she pulls her knees to her chest, covering herself as she rests her chin on them. "I think we're past that." Her voice is gentle, even though her words are punctuated by a teasing smile. "I've had four separate dicks in me for the past few days, *and* I've been begging for it. We've reached the appropriate time to trauma-bond."

I shoot her a look, failing to hide my smile. "You must be feeling better if you're making an orgy joke, princess."

She scoffs, turning her head away, but I catch a glimpse of her cheeks as they flush a light pink. "Trust me, I still feel like shit, but at least you've all been polite enough to ignore it."

I look at her for a solid moment, taking in the bare curves of her body, hunched over, her skin soft and smooth, but flushed and marked with various bites — she's been kissed, sucked, and fucked during the past few days. She'll probably bruise, but the memories of being buried between her legs come back to me in flashes — my lips wrapped around her skin, wanting desperately to leave a lasting impression of myself on her.

Pathetic desire claws at my chest. The urge to fall to my knees, to *prostrate* myself, is so strong that I have to swallow it back. This isn't about me. None of this is. It should all be about her.

I step around her, rummaging in a cabinet and pulling

out some bubble bath I bought the other day. Pouring it into the tub, I check the temperature as I swirl my hand through it, looking over at her. "Want me in with you?"

"What kind of question is that?" She arches an eyebrow at me, her pout delightfully bratty.

Rolling my eyes, I tug my t-shirt off, dropping it onto the bench next to her. Her answering smile makes my chest warm as her eyes drag over my skin. They pause a few times on various art pieces, before she hums and watches me push my sweats down.

When her eyes come back to mine, her pupils are larger, lips parted. "I like how you make me feel small."

Bending down, I scoop her up from the bench, easing us into the tub, grateful it's just steps into the water, like a pool. The warm, scented water embraces us as I murmur, "What do you mean?"

She grumbles, but lets me pull her back against my chest, content to work on the tangle of her hair at the nape of her neck until she's ready to explain herself.

"It's stupid." June swirls her fingertips through the bubbles as I start to work soap into her hair. "It's probably some kind of omega hindbrain *'big alpha, small omega'* bull-shit." Leaning her head back while I massage the shampoo in, she sighs. "But you're *big*, you're all muscle and have a soft stomach, and I like it."

June doesn't turn her head, but her hand does move under the water, stroking my side as she sits in my lap. "Arin, Bennett, and Seth are all thin. You and I are fat. It's simple fact — even if both words are charged with too many negative connotations. Seth's shirts would never fit me if he didn't buy them so oversized."

I hum, abandoning her hair for a moment to dip my hand

under the water, caressing her round stomach as I press a kiss to her bare shoulder. "I love the way you look, June. I have since I saw you that first night, curled up outside my bedroom."

She'd been crying and I'd only made it worse out of sheer stupidity, but it doesn't change the way I've wanted her since that very moment.

I touch her, just lightly, letting my fingers brush over the swells of her skin, down to the fullness of her inner thighs. "You're beautiful just as you are."

She turns her head, her eyes soft. "Will you tell me your bullshit, please?"

Sighing, I guide her back around, focusing on untangling her hair as I speak.

"It's always weirded me out when alphas my age have been focused on finding omegas who are barely eighteen. It makes my skin crawl." I rub the strands between my fingers, lathering them and untangling piece by piece. "I don't know if there's much to the story. My mother came from a traditionalist family, who wanted her with alphas who held the same belief. I think she emerged at sixteen and was married by seventeen to my two fathers."

Scrubbing her scalp, she relaxes back into me, her breathing evening out. "I was ten before I realized how fucking weird it was that they treated her like a walking incubator, because at that time I realized that she was useless to them — having me nearly killed her, they had to give her an emergency hysterectomy immediately after I was born."

She stops breathing in my arms, her hand dropping to my thigh to hold onto me, solidifying me. She's right — we're both full-bodied, but the weight of her on my lap feels right.

We're perfectly matched, like the world was just waiting for us to collide — two dying stars creating a cataclysm.

"I don't think my fathers wanted to save her." I whisper the words to her back. "But they also didn't want to raise me alone, so they made the life-saving call, even though they both wanted a litter-full of alphas to command and groom to be just like them. By saving her, they lost that chance — and I was never what they wanted."

I work out a particularly nasty tangle, bringing her head lower to rinse the soap clear before switching to conditioner. It slicks up my palms as I stroke her hair, careful to get each strand.

"Needless to say, my fathers are pieces of shit. They think everything should be handed to them because they're alphas, and it doesn't matter who it is, they lash out if they feel like they're being mistreated."

Maybe there's some kind of special conditioner for omegas. I focus on her hair for a moment, letting the words hang. It's a mess — and I don't want her to have to go through this process every single heat.

I could braid it.

"Theo?" she prompts me softly.

Clearing my throat, I blink. "I just didn't know better until I met Arin. When we were just kids, I saw that his parents actually *loved* each other. I realized people who love each other don't scream and break things, or hit their partners."

Her voice is gentle as she speaks. "My parents are betas, but they believe what your fathers do. All of their friends believe that one day they'll do the ultimate service and pop out an omega, and give them to the 'right' type of alpha. The kind of alpha who doesn't believe in packs, who will keep an omega in the house, locked up, barefoot and pregnant." June's tone turns scathing. "Alphas do *so* much, you know, they should be on the top of society, the most powerful positions, and come home every night to a warm meal and a willing cunt."

I make a noise in the back of my throat, half a growl, half guiding her to be quiet as I rinse her hair again, working my fingers through it so the conditioner washes out.

"I told myself to never bond to an omega, because I didn't want to become them, that's my bullshit. I'm fucking terrified of you." I go quiet, letting her sit in my lap as I survey the back of her hair to make sure I didn't miss a single tangle. "When Arin finally said he wanted to form a pack with me, I panicked because I thought he'd found someone to bond, and that was the last thing I ever wanted."

She turns her head. "What about the alpha urges? Don't you want to take care of someone, want to be there for them? I feel like I've been losing my mind with the emotional back and forth the last two weeks, how have you ignored it?"

I shrug, giving her a forced smile. "When it gets bad I just reorganize Arin's sock drawer and piss him off by doing housework until I earn my place here — until I'm useful."

She slides in the water, sloshing it up on the sides of the tub as she turns in my lap, her knees moving to the sides of my thighs, looking at me seriously as she cups my face. "You don't need to earn your place in this pack, Theo."

"And you don't have to give up your freedom to have your own place here."

The bathroom is silent as we stare at each other.

I run my thumb over the side of her jaw, my voice barely audible as I break the silence, stroking a bruise. "I really did a fucking number on you, I'm sorry."

She leans closer, shaking her head as she makes me meet her eyes. "Yeah, well, I seem to have come into your life and set fire to all your childhood insecurities, so we're even."

I snort, leaning up as I lift her in the water, letting her fully straddle me as I slide my hands over her back, warm skin under mine, my throat raw.

"Maybe it was time for me to get over my shit."

"Maybe it was time for me to let someone in" — June tilts her head — "or four someones."

Smiling up at her, I cup the back of her neck, watching her eyes flare with heat in the split second before I pull her to me, kissing her slowly, our noses nudging as I stand with her in my arms. As I climb out of the tub, I grab a warm towel, slinging it over her and drying her off before placing her on the counter, my hands palming her thighs.

"Can we be adults about this, or are we going to keep fighting like animals? Do you..." I swallow around the weight on my tongue, my brain spinning as I try to find the right words. "I promise you right here, right now, that I will prove my worth to you every second of every day."

She hums, her hands moving up my back, her voice breathy. "I don't need your fealty, Theo. I kind of like having someone to scream at when I feel a little crazy. As long as you don't mind. I'm tired of running, but if I do, will you promise to catch me?"

"I promise." I pull her to the edge of the counter by her thighs, rewarded with a little gasp as her perfume blooms, soft and fragrant honey coating me from head to toe. "I will *always* catch you." Dropping one of my hands from her thigh, I run my fingers through her slit, gathering the slick there before I slip them between her folds, parting her for me.

"This is how tonight will go, princess." I toy with her, thumbing her clit as I lift her again, letting her cling to me as I turn toward the nest. "You're going to come until your slick is dripping down your thighs, and then I'm going to fuck you until you shake, until you just can't take it anymore."

Dropping her in the nest, I land on top of her, bending down to bite her lower lip, careful not to break skin. "And then, only then, will I give your sweet little honey-flavored cunt my knot."

June's lips part, her eyes hooded as she stares up at me, breathing harshly. She whines a little, lifting her hips, but I pin her down with a hand, smiling. "And then I'll fuck you into the pillows while you're stuffed full of me, and then fuck you some more until there's nowhere else for my cum to go but seep out between us."

She moans, changing tactics and grabbing my hair by the fistful, her nails scoring my scalp as she tries to tug me down to kiss her.

I resist.

"Finally, I'll hold you until my knot goes down and do it all again until your heat breaks." I relent, letting her drag my face to hers, kissing her deeply as I whisper, "There won't be an alpha who exists that won't know you're mine. They'll be able to smell me dripping out of you."

June gasps as I drop a hand, opening her thighs to me before I press myself at her entrance and thrust into her in one smooth stroke. She nods, her head tilting back, exposing her throat to me as she whines, "*Please*, Theo."

I groan as my lips fall to her neck, holding her against me as I thrust deeper. "Whatever you want, it's yours. I've caught you and you're *mine* now."

CHAPTER FIVE

JUNE

"GOD."

I gasp, clenching around Theo's fingers as he looks up at me from between my thighs. His thick tongue slides over my clit repeatedly, making me whine while I tug on his hair and arch into him. His fingers curl *just so*, and I feel my body wind itself tight, all thought leaving me in lieu of mindless pleasure.

He grins, and I swear it makes him harder when I can't think — can't *function*.

Shrieking, I throw an arm over my face as I come *again*, his fingers stroking the spot that Seth showed him hours ago. My body shakes as slick drips out of me, breathless as Theo sucks it up and then peppers small kisses across my lower stomach.

"More, princess?"

"No," I moan, shivering from the rush. "For the first time in *days*, please no more."

Theo laughs as he works his way up my body, his lips grazing a breast as he hums, "Hear that, Seth?"

"I do," Seth murmurs lazily, running his fingers over my shoulders as I sink into his warmth behind me. "I guess you finally hit your limit, which is good for us, I was about to die between your thighs, June. They were going to have to pull my carcass away with my tongue still fluttering inside you."

I laugh, turning my face into his skin, inhaling lungfuls of fudge as I sigh, "God, I'm so tired."

Theo's hands glide over my thighs. "But you feel better?"

I nod, pulling my head back just enough to glance down at him, taking in his mussed blond hair, his own soft and concerned smile. "I do, it only took the thousandth orgasm to break it."

Theo grins. "Or just little old me."

"Shut up." I plant my hand on his forehead, pushing him away halfheartedly, breaking out into laughter when Seth holds me down and Theo grabs onto my legs, tangling us together as he kisses every inch of skin his lips can find.

The door to the nest creaks, and I turn my head, smiling wide when Arin appears, Bennett half a step behind him, both laden with bags of take-out. I remember eating soup sometime yesterday, in a haze with Bennett spoon-feeding me, but my stomach rumbles finally with true *hunger*. The lucid moment with Theo didn't last long, just long enough for him to drag me back into the nest and knot me and fuck me and then knot me again, just like he promised. I'd passed out and slept like the dead for a handful of hours, waking up enough to eat, before sliding my lips down Seth's chest to seek out the taste of him.

Honestly, I don't remember much, just filthy flashes. Every bit of research warned me that it would be like this — but I'm grateful that I felt safe the entire time.

Fidgeting between Seth's legs, I try to ignore the dull

ache of *want* that thrums through me at the sight of the other two alphas.

Arin's eyes find mine. "How are you?"

Licking my lips, I focus on him. "I'm finally hungry."

Bennett smiles wide. "Good, because we ordered the whole fucking menu."

Seth shifts, resting a hand on my side as he perks up. "Did you get extra spring rolls?"

"Always." Bennett shuffles the bags as he climbs into the nest with Arin, holding out a take-out container.

I laugh, shuffling to the side as Seth scrambles out from behind me to crawl across the nest and grab the spring rolls for himself. My eyes fall over his semi-naked body, heat crawling across my skin as Theo leans in, wrapping a blanket around my shoulders. He kisses the side of my head, adjusting me so I can sit up comfortably against him, my braid flopping over one shoulder.

He did that for me — and even though it's a wreck with strands falling out, my hair is nowhere near the mess it was before he washed it. Pulling the blanket closer, I hide my grin against the palm of his hand, kissing the skin there that smells like petrichor and honey.

Bennett settles across from us with Seth by his side, pulling items out of the bags as Arin lingers outside the nest. I pat the empty spot next to me.

Arin's smile is gentle. "You want me over there?"

"Yes, always." Seth offers a spring roll to me across the nest, stretching his arm out. Plucking it from his fingers, I take a bite, groaning loudly as my eyes widen. "Oh my *god*, that's so good." Covering my mouth, I chew fast, shoving the rest in as Arin sinks into the empty place. The nausea is gone. Every bite is better than the last as Bennett hands me a fork and roots through the boxes.

"Go slow, you don't want to get sick." Theo's hand on my back makes me ease up from my little goblin crouch over the spring roll container. My arm brushes Arin's as I settle between the pair of them, taking a container of fried rice from Bennett and digging into it like an animal.

Seth laughs loudly, shoving his own spring roll into his mouth as he leans into Bennett's side. "I told you she'd like this place." His happiness is infectious. "We eat it nonstop when we're here in London."

"*You* eat it nonstop." Bennett shakes his head. "And Arin. Theo can at least make himself dinner if he's hungry instead of ordering enough takeout for an army."

"I'm fine with takeout," I mutter through a mouthful of rice, shrugging. "I mean your cooking is delicious, Bennett, but this is *so* good. What the fuck did they put in it?"

Arin chuckles, rubbing my arm. "Juniper, you're starving. You've barely eaten for a week."

"No, it's definitely the food." I shoot Seth a look. "You're right, it's the best."

The beta's grin widens, splitting his face. "See? She's saying I'm right, listen to our omega."

"Great, now there's two of them." Theo mutters the words under his breath as I laugh, watching Arin pick up his own food.

Bennett rolls his eyes at our antics, but there's a little smile lifting the edges of his lips as he looks between Seth and I. A pang rocks my chest. Bennett *knows* how Seth is feeling right now, intrinsically, from the silver scarred bite on Seth's neck that I've brushed my lips over multiple times in the last few days.

Vulnerability rears its ugly head as I survey the four men around me.

They let me stay here. No forced bonds, no following the standard expectation that I would be *theirs* — other than my single promise to Arin that I'd let myself be open. It wasn't a hard vow to make, because it meant having *this*.

Arin glances over at me, putting his fork down. His hand rests on my forearm as I clutch the takeout container with white knuckles. "Are you alright?"

I sink back into Theo's chest, seeking its comfort and warmth. Something about him eases the tangle of anxiety, making the words easier to utter. "I was just thinking." Swallowing, I let the food rest in my lap. "I'm really happy this is where I am. Thank you for being nice to me and letting me stay."

"*June.*" Bennett's voice cracks as he puts his food to the side, leaning over the middle of the nest just to grab my hand. "There was no other option, you were leaving with us that day at the center. Seth will agree."

Seth's shiny hazel eyes find mine. "I wasn't leaving you there for one more damn minute. You know that, baby."

One of Theo's thick arms wraps around my waist from behind and I glance up as his head tilts slightly, his expression serious. "This is the *bare* minimum that you deserve. Do you hear me?"

My mouth goes dry as I risk a glance at Arin. He clears his throat, putting his food to the side, plucking mine out of my lap as his stern eyes find mine. "What did I say, Juniper?"

A shiver crawls over me, feeling scolded and small.

"You are *safe* with this pack." His stare is unwavering. "No running, because none of this is temporary. Nothing that has happened in the last few days has changed my mind."

Theo's hand tightens on my stomach.

"I don't think we made it clear enough, alpha." His voice makes me tremble as my chin jerks to look back at the man behind me. Hearing *alpha* from him reignites the ache between my thighs. Theo runs his tongue over his lips. "I think we need to prove it to her."

Bennett clears the food from the center of the nest, catching my eye as he makes a noise of agreement. "We must have not done our job to satisfy her if she's questioning all *three* of her alphas."

Heat licks up my spine as every eye in the nest focuses on me, but mine find Seth, breathing out in a sharp exhale when I find him staring at the blanket haphazardly hanging on my naked body, like he can see right through it.

"What do you say, June?" Seth rubs a thumb over his lower lip. "Are you going to let us all show you how much you belong here?"

The air pulls tight, like a rubber band about to snap, and my heart kicks. *Yes.*

My lips part, eyes locking on Seth's. "How do you want me?"

Seth's answering grin is wicked. "Bend over for me, baby. I want to look my fill while Theo and Arin fuck you senseless."

I gasp as Theo turns me, cupping my face with a wide palm as he kisses me deeply. Movement behind me is my only warning before Arin's hands tugs the blanket away, baring me to them. I scramble, free from the fabric to straddle Theo, my nose brushing his as I kiss him harder, breathing out as I tangle my fingers in his hair. He's so *solid,* stacked muscle hidden under layers of soft skin that feels like a cushion.

Sinking lower, my lips pull away from his as I move down, kissing and puffing out little breaths across his chest, lower and lower until my nose nudges his erection tenting the front of his sweatpants. It would make me a bad omega to leave him wanting.

Theo's hand slides over the braid, and then slips the tie free. The rest of my hair falls free, joining the strands already around my face. He tangles his fingers in it, his voice low. "You don't like any of this and you dig your nails into me, okay?" His nails press against my scalp, a tease. "I'll stop it and kick them all out."

I smile as I kiss over his erection, glancing up from under my lashes. "Yes, alpha."

Lips brush the curve of my ass as I bend over, my eyes fluttering as I push back into the touch. Soft, long fingers open me up until a tongue finds the slick dripping between my thighs. Moaning, I focus on Theo in front of me, pulling his sweatpants down far enough for my lips to find the soft skin of him, kissing and running my tongue over the length of his cock.

The tongue behind me teases until I wrap my lips around the head of Theo's dick, and only then does it pull back. I feel Arin notch at my entrance, already wet and ready. Theo's hand in my hair guides my mouth as I take him down my throat, moaning around him as Arin thrusts in from behind, making my legs shake from the full feeling of having two holes filled.

Single-minded, I use my hand to grip Theo's base, strangling his knot as I bob up and down, clenching around Arin as he slowly pushes into me, then stops. Pulling back with a little gasp, I glance to the side, searching for what I already know I'll find.

Seth is leaned back against the nest wall, lounging like a goddamn king. His hand wraps around his cock, stroking lazily, eyes hooded as Bennett sheds his pajama pants beside him. Seth's lips twitch, tongue running over them as he watches me. "You shouldn't ignore Theo, baby, he needs your mouth."

Just as I return to my task, my skin heats with the thought of being watched. It's filthy, but it makes me suck harder as spit suddenly hits me from behind, mixing with slick. Arin's hips rock into me deep, plunging roughly as his spit trickles over my ass. I cry out around Theo as Arin's finger teases the tight hole, opening me up.

"Who should have you here, Juniper? I'll be a good prime and let you pick."

Fuck.

I switch to flattening my tongue along Theo's length as I whine and press back against Arin, my head blanking as I say the first name that comes to mind, "Theo."

The alpha in question lets out a groan so loud it shakes over my skin. He's so thick my fingers don't even meet around his swollen knot, but the idea of him buried inside me makes me want to climb on top of him and sink my teeth into his throat.

Before I can ask him if it's okay, he tugs me up and away from his lap. Theo kisses me heatedly as Arin slips out of me. The alpha in front of me manhandles me for a moment, lifting me with two hands, pure strength as he tugs me against his chest, feverish in his touches. Gasping, I cling to him, clenching on nothing as I just let him throw me around.

"Turn around." Theo's voice is hoarse as he pulls back. "And bend the fuck over."

I squeak, scrambling with a little laugh as I pull away from him and do as he says. Arin's lips twitch as he looks down at me, gloriously naked in front of me as I bend over for Theo, reversing our positions. Arin's dick shines with my slick and I reach out for him, whining when I'm immediately pulled back, just shy of touching.

Theo's hand rubs over my hip, his voice softer. "Gotta get myself wet with you, princess. I don't want to hurt you." He thrusts in without preamble and my eyes close as I suck in a breath, the stretch and difference from Arin making my brain go fuzzy as a hand strokes through my hair.

"He's going to start fucking you." Arin's voice is gentle, but firm, baring no argument. "And when he's ready, he'll take your ass and then I'll lift you onto me."

Just as he says it, Theo pulls out and switches to rubbing his head against my ass. My body relaxes, almost instinctively, and I exhale as he breaches the entrance with only slight resistance. *I was made for this.*

Theo's moan cuts off, partially strangled as his hands grip my hips. "*Fuck*, she's so tight, oh fuck, such a good omega taking me here."

Pleasure whites out my brain as he bottoms out. We both exhale, the sound of heavy breathing echoing in the nest. Arin's hand stills on my head, murmuring softly, "Are you okay, Juniper?"

"Yes," I slur the word, nodding as I look up at my prime, eyes only for him. "Please, I want you too."

Arin's hair is slightly mussed, his eyes dark as he strokes my head once before leaning down and lifting me up just enough to push me back against Theo's chest. When he does,

Theo's hands spread my legs wide, my ass sinking back against him, feeling full as Arin drops to his chest in front of me, his mouth attaching itself to my clit as Theo thrusts up lazily from behind.

"You're doing so well for us, omega, you deserve an orgasm."

I cry out, clinging to Theo's arms banded around me as I clench on nothing, Arin's beard grazes my thighs as he eats me out while Theo thrusts. Seth strokes himself across from us, Bennett palming himself and caressing his own knot, his eyes focused on the sight between my legs.

Arin thrusts a finger into me, wiggling it slowly, his voice dripping sin. "Are you ready for me, Juniper? Do you want us both?"

"Yes." I gasp as he lingers on my clit, suckling it before Theo shifts me to lean back a little more. His large hands move, cupping handfuls of my chest, palms wide enough to hold most of my breasts, making the sight obscene when I glance down and see my cleavage spilling out over the top of his fingers.

My back bows as Arin leans up, one hand landing near Theo's shoulder on the nest wall as he bends closer, capturing my lips and thrusting into me in one firm stroke.

I see *stars*.

Crying out, I hold onto Arin's shoulder with one hand, my other dropping to Theo's thigh, clinging to him as the fullness takes the air right out of my lungs. The stretch makes me curse, gasping as Arin kisses me, Theo's knot bumping against Arin's.

Theo moans as Arin rocks forward, breathless as he grunts. "Fuck, I can feel you, alpha." I shiver as his hips punch up under me, bouncing me once. Theo's voice slurs in my ear. "I can feel you clenching around him, princess. I can feel Arin's knot rubbing mine."

It's all I can do to cling to them both as they take turns thrusting into me, fucking me back and forth, rocking my overstimulated body between them. A quiet gasp makes my eyes flutter as I'm rewarded with the sight of Bennett bent into Seth's lap, sucking on his cock messily, spit dripping off his lips as he pulls back just enough to ask. "Do they feel good, darling?"

I sob out an unintelligible confirmation as Arin rocks forward, his knot teasing me again. One of Theo's hands stops massaging my chest, toying with my nipples. It drops to my clit, rubbing in tight little circles. My head drops back against Theo's shoulder as I bite my tongue, trying to hold in my shriek as I come without warning, my body shaking between the two of them as I clench and flutter around Arin.

Arin curses, his head dropping to my chest, his lips running over my bare breast before he rocks deeper, his bark powerful as he commands, *"Don't stop coming."*

The *feeling* of it rocks through my body, all my muscles shaking as I keep spasming around him, it wringing out the orgasm until I can't think, just feel as I clench rhythmically. Theo shakes under me, and then thrusts up harder, chasing his own orgasm before I feel him explode, filling me.

Arin snarls, his teeth just barely grazing my nipple as he slams into me hard enough that his knot breaches me, even with my ass full of Theo. As he comes with a ragged shout, I twitch, my muscles giving out as I sink back into Theo's solid embrace, heart pounding as I take it, punch-drunk from the pleasure.

After a moment, Arin's head lifts as he kisses me deeply, making sparks ricochet over my skin. His fingers press between us, then a finger carefully pushes where we're joined — slipping into me despite his knot. I let out a shocked breath as he releases himself from me, knot sliding free, leaving a mess between my thighs as he lifts me off Theo's spent chest.

"Bennett, she's yours."

There's a small part of my brain that doesn't know if I can take it, but the forefront of my mind moves faster, *needing* Bennett too, needing Seth to hold onto me as his own alpha takes me after I'm already covered and used.

Bennett lifts away from Seth's cock, his grin feral as Arin's hand cups my cunt, two fingers pushing his cum back into me before he guides me over to Bennett and Seth.

Seth's eyes lock on mine, a flicker of concern for a brief moment. "Still okay?"

"Mhm." I drop down, replacing Bennett's mouth with my own as I suck Seth down my throat, having a much easier time taking him all the way until my nose brushes his pelvis. Seth curses above me, his hand grabbing the back of my head as Bennett rubs against me from behind.

I moan, lifting up in an unspoken beg for him to take me. Bennett's hand braces on my hip before he thrusts into the mess Arin made of me, the length of him stroking every inch of me from inside, his knot slipping into me with ease before he pulls it right back out and begins to fuck me steadily, knotting and unknotting me.

Holy shit. I didn't know my body could feel this good, but I never want it to *stop.*

Crying out around Seth, his hand tugs on my hair, his hips punching up into my mouth as Bennett sets a brutal pace, grabbing handfuls of my ass. "I'm not going to last, I need you to come again for us, darling. Can you give us one more? I bet Arin would make you give it to us."

My veins are pure fire as Arin's voice makes my head spin. "You heard him, Juniper." He pauses long enough for my eyes to meet his before his bark grabs ahold of the last shreds of my sanity. "*Come.*"

My body gives out, the orgasm overtaking my senses as I hold onto Seth, feeling him release into the back of my throat at the same time Bennett slams into me, his knot swelling as he falls apart.

Slumping, I do my best to swallow, but Seth lifts me off him, letting me breathe raggedly as my cheek drops to rest against his thigh.

"Do you believe us now?" Arin's voice is soft as he runs a hand over my back. Bennett slips free after a moment, and my body is so well-used that I can't think, I just let Theo lift me up into his arms. Someone wraps a blanket around me, and then I'm tucked into Arin's chest, his hand idly stroking my sweaty hair back from my forehead as he stares at me. A damp washcloth smoothes over my skin and my eyes water as I stare up at Arin. He wipes my face off with a look of pure devotion.

"You're ours. No running."

My heart rests heavy in my throat, finding Theo's warm gaze just to the side, Bennett's hooded eyes meeting mine. Finally, I meet Seth's gaze full of so much affection, it chokes me.

Emotion clogs my throat as I rasp the promise, "No running."

PART TWO

CHAPTER SIX

JUNE

My new passport is dark navy and stamped with the American seal. The cover and spine are uncreased, save for the earmarked page at the very front. My face stares back at me, unsmiling, my hair behind my ears, showing my bare neck to the camera.

The nice beta at the embassy said it was a requirement to expose my throat, even without a bond mark.

"It's protocol, unfortunately. Just remember to head to the DMV when you get home and get settled." He flashed me a kind smile as I adjusted in the chair and stared down the lens of the little camera. "Have your prime sign off on the documents before you leave today."

Under my name is a small Greek symbol, denoting me as an omega.

Heathrow buzzes around us, just as overwhelming as every other time I've had the misfortune of being here — but this time, the pack room off to the side of the gate is quieter, dimming the chaotic nature of the airport and providing respite.

Theo's arm around my shoulders is definitely helping too.

He sits next to me in one of the cushioned seats, one leg crossed over the other, an open paperback in his lap as he flips a page.

"We should be boarding soon." His voice is soft as he turns his head slightly toward mine, rubbing my shoulder absent-mindedly. "It'll be quieter in first class."

Clinging to my passport, I glance at the counter visible just in front of the hall that will take us to the plane. It's not *just* first class — our tickets all specify it's first class for *packs*. The ultimate experience for any omega who flies, where there are clusters of seats together, forming little pods where an omega can have their entire pack surrounding them, instead of being separated throughout the plane.

Shifting slightly, I dip my chin, muttering under my breath. "I'm okay."

Theo side eyes me.

I feel weird, like I don't quite know what to do with myself. My carry-on was checked with the rest of the bags, and Seth helped me pack up the clothes he and Bennett bought me, plus some of the nesting material that I found myself unable to leave at the townhouse. I felt a little ridiculous asking for blankets to be brought back to the States with us — but Arin's mushy smile made the decision for me.

"I like that you want them."

So much said in so few words.

"Coffee!" Seth rounds the corner into the pack area, placing a large to-go cup in front of Theo and then a smaller one in front of me. "Tea for you, no caffeine."

My lips twitch as I glance up at the beta, his hair pulled back into a messy bun. "Thank you."

Seth drops into the seat next to me, leaning over to peck my forehead as Arin and Bennett step around the partition, holding their own cups from the small convenience store near our gate.

"No problem." Seth grabs my hand, casually threading his fingers with mine.

"You'll connect from JFK to Ronald Reagan." Arin perches on the edge of the chair across from us, leaning over as he shuffles tickets in his hand, holding two out to Seth. "I have the rental agreement for the moving company, Seth, and I've forwarded it to your phone. I couldn't put June's name on the documents because of the ID situation."

I glance up at him as he fidgets, my heart kicking in my throat. There's a tidiness to his normally mussed dark curls, and Arin's gaze lifts behind his glasses, offering me a slightly disgruntled look. "We'll head to the DMV the second you arrive in Rochester. I'm sorry there are so many legal hoops because of the designation switch. I'll take care of it all for you."

"It's okay." I give him a weak smile, clutching Seth's hand a little tighter. "It shouldn't take Seth and I long to pack up my apartment. I don't have much."

"The movers will be there to do the irritating work." Arin sits back, crossing one long leg over the other. "They'll arrive the day after you get home. I made sure they agreed to carry off anything you don't want to bring to Rochester. Don't hesitate to let them do it all. I don't want you to hurt yourself or feel rushed."

My pulse echoes in my ears as I nod at him.

Something shifted when my heat ended.

It wasn't subtle. Suddenly, I was lucid enough to realize that everything had changed from the nerves and anxiety leading up to the heat, replaced with Arin acting like I'm already a cemented part of their pack, even though I don't have a single bond to show for it.

It's not how this is supposed to go. Most omegas have an alpha who bonds them immediately during their first heat, or even before it. Most omegas have no choice — it's the way for anyone else to tell that they're taken, that their alpha is wholly devoted to them. Yet the passport in my hand proves that none of them forced me into a bond, adhering to the normal expectations.

I push up from the chair, not touching my tea as I mumble, "Bathroom, sorry." Darting away, I avoid Bennett's startled look after me as I find the private bathrooms to the side, meant for omegas. Everything is labeled — seats, areas, sections, tickets, passports — my heart pounds as the door clicks shut behind me, the noise of the airport dampening.

Sucking in a deep breath, I stand in front of the sink, clutching the edges of the porcelain as I try to calm myself down. I fumble for a moment to get the cold water turned on, running my wrists under it, trying to shock the rising nausea from my body. I've never been a great flier, but this anxious feeling isn't *just* that — it's a crawling, sinking reminder that everything that's happened in the vacuum of the last month is suddenly *real*. No longer is every action with the men outside hidden behind the walls of their London townhouse — there are official *documents*, I'm *moving in*.

Seth is only coming with me because everyone else had tasks to take care of at their pack house in upstate New York. The house where I'm supposed to be moving into — taking everything I've known for the last six years, all the books and memories from my apartment where I've worked and *lived* —

Just to go to New York.

A state I try to avoid at every cost because it's loud, obnoxious, and overstimulating.

I've never been to Rochester — in its defense — and Bennett told me last night that the house is quiet and set apart from the city itself, but that isn't helping the clammy feeling coating my skin.

A light knock on the door startles me as I jerk my eyes away from my own reflection, watching the door to the bathroom slowly open.

"June?" Seth steps in, one hand over his eyes, hesitating in the doorway. "Are you alone in here?"

"Yeah." I glance around the single-stall room as he drops his hand and lets the door shut.

"Well" — Seth glances down at the knob — "there's no lock, so don't get any ideas." He flashes me a grin that falls quickly as he takes me in. "What's wrong?"

I laugh, but it comes out mildly hysterical as I look back at the mirror. "I *think* I'm panicking."

"Oh." Seth mutters the word, then he comes over, appearing in the mirror before his hands run over my back soothingly. His lips brush the back of my head, one hand rising to rest over my heart. "I could probably change our tickets and kidnap you. Where do you want to go? Montréal? Bora Bora? Mexico?"

"Why Montréal?"

"Oh, I would *kill* for some poutine, and Bennett would be so mad if we were there without him. He loves it." He grins at me in the mirror. "Is it the flight, or everything else?"

"Everything else." I lean back into him, closing my eyes as his hand, warm on my heart, rests for a moment, just holding me. The smell of his light fudge fragrance eases the panicked sprinting of my mind.

"Arin means well, but his constant plans and organization is enough to make a nun curse."

I snort as Seth turns me carefully, kissing my forehead as he wraps his arms around me, sighing and muttering. "And, well, you know Theo's a neurotic mess most of the time." He rocks us for a moment, holding me with no pretense. "Bennett would never admit it, but flying does scare the shit out of him. He does it out of obligation."

I hunch slightly, just to bury my face in his chest, my lips twitching. "And you? What's your fault?"

"Me?" Seth snorts and I glance up to see him smile easily down at me. "I'm *flawless*, baby, don't you know that by now?"

I laugh, soft enough that his eyes crinkle around the edges. Resting my chin on his shoulder, I tuck my face into his throat, whispering my fears to the man who's been steadfast in his support since the very beginning. "It feels like I'm waiting for the other shoe to drop. My heat is over. The reason I'm even with all of you is done."

Seth's hands tighten on me. "I don't know how to sugarcoat this one, sorry." He clears his throat. "But you're fucking *insane* if you think I'm going to let you walk out of my life after the last few weeks. You think those three assholes are territorial?" He shoots a look at the door, raising an eyebrow at me. "I don't even have *biology* to blame, baby, I'm serious. I'll lock you in a bedroom with me until we both waste away and die."

I let out a barking laugh, staring at him. "Yeah? What if they break down the door?"

Seth scoffs. "They couldn't drag me away from you. I'm stuck to you." He grins even wider, hugging me tighter. "Like *glue*."

I wrap my arms around his neck, turning my head to kiss him softly, nuzzling his face with mine. "Thank you. For everything."

He hums against my lips, rubbing my back. "You're welcome. I have no idea how I could say no to such a demanding, needy, *annoying* omega." Sarcasm drips off the words as he rolls his eyes.

I'm smiling when we step out of the bathroom into the small seating area. We catch a few glances from the others on our flight, but I ignore them, squeezing Seth's fingers in mine as he drags me over to our seats. Let them talk — we would have been a hell of a lot louder if we'd gotten up to anything *fun* in there.

Arin stands up quickly when we get closer, and I put my free hand on his chest, tilting my head up to him. "I'm okay." This time when I say it, I mean it.

His eyes soften as he takes me in, reaching out to touch my cheek. "I can still change my connecting flight and come with you and Seth to Virginia."

"No, you can't," Theo mutters, catching my eye. He finally closes the book in his lap and I freeze — the pink cover, the illustrations of the characters — it's *mine*. It's *my fucking book*. The first one I ever published — the catalyst for the book tour, my heat, and meeting *them*.

Theo levels Arin with a look. "We have shit to do. I'm making you clean out that junk room."

"Theo." I stare at the book.

He looks over at me innocently. "It's not mine, it's Bennett's."

My head whips to the side, laser focused on the quiet alpha as he clears his throat, readjusting in his seat. Bennett scrubs a hand over his head, his eyes darting away. "I read all three of them last week."

I drop back into my seat next to Theo, feeling my cheeks warm. "I don't want to hear a single *word* on what you all think."

"I loved them." Seth flashes me a smile, not listening, per usual. "I'm excited to see what the author writes next."

Grumbling, I knock into him half-heartedly as I reach for my tea, taking a long drink. Theo shifts, putting his arm back around my shoulders as he leans in, his lips caressing the shell of my ear. "I do have some thoughts. I think the next book should have an alpha who's kind of an asshole, but he's hot. *So* hot, with tattoos."

I can't help it, I nearly spit my tea out as I laugh, turning to look up at him.

Theo's blue eyes spark as he stares down at me.

Stupid fucking *alphas* — but they're *my* stupid alphas.

A FINE LAYER of sweat and dust covers me as I finally grimace at Seth, sitting in the middle of a pile of books as he packs them into various boxes. He's even got bubble wrap for the special editions.

"I'm tired."

He looks up, laughing as he puts the book in his hand into a box. "Me too, how long have we been doing this?"

My eyes find the clock. Our flight landed *early* this morning, a red eye that ended with a driver dropping us both off at my apartment. I let us into the building of mostly betas, nodding at the early morning desk attendant as Seth and I slumped against each other, making it to the elevator before echoing twin yawns.

Arin really thought of everything, because there were moving boxes already in front of my apartment door when we arrived. Not that we did anything with them but drag them into the small entryway. I was too tired to function, and ended up face-down on my bed, ignoring the slightly musty smell in the air from the apartment being abandoned for an entire month in lieu of falling almost immediately asleep the second Seth's warmth dropped down beside me, one arm slinging over my back.

We'd woken up to three frantic calls from Arin asking if we got in safely, which made me feel extremely guilty because we'd *promised* to call and promptly forgotten. Seth called him back while I'd wandered into my kitchen, taking stock of the expired food and a single dead plant on the counter.

I wasn't lying when I told them I don't own much.

I'd forgotten how sparse I'd kept my place. With nothing on the walls, the bare bones quality shines through, and I see it with new eyes every time I look up from packing another box. Seth's taken the bulk of packing my prized possessions — my book collection.

"I don't know." I squint at the clock. "At least forever."

He laughs again, shaking his head at me. "Forever, huh?"

The furniture I have has already been labeled with sticky notes that all read DONATE. I have no attachment to the manufactured pressboard I bought on a budget just after college. We'd jumped into organizing everything into piles because of the imminence of the movers coming, and now I just feel tired — like I'm packing up someone else's home.

The only thing that tugged on my heart was seeing my

laptop on my shitty little used desk, still waiting for me like I left it before going on tour — when I thought I'd be home in a week.

Seth pulls his phone out. "We should eat. What sounds good?"

I press my lips together, pausing as my eyes catch on the boxes in my bedroom. Most of them are clothes that I unceremoniously grabbed handfuls of and dropped into the cardboard without folding.

Seth's eyes follow mine. "Theo will be horrified if he helps you unpack those." He groans as he stands up, looking around the room. "Nothing else is organized except your books."

I shrug as I grunt to stand, stretching. "Nothing else is important."

"Except the books?"

"Except the books." I grin at him, stepping over and wrapping my arms around his waist, happy to peck his lips, our heights so even that it makes it easy to wrap myself around him. "I know it's ridiculous to have so many, but I like them, and I like having the proof copies of my *own* books. It's a reminder of all the steps it took to get where I am."

He wraps his arms around me, smiling gently. "It's not ridiculous, but I do think I should tell Bennett that you apparently spent all your grocery money on special editions."

I mockingly gasp at him. "You wouldn't."

Seth laughs, kissing my head as his stomach grumbles. "I wouldn't."

I give him what I'm sure is a dopey look, moving closer as I kiss his jaw. With my lips on his ear, I drag my nails over the back of his neck, relishing in the way he shivers as I whisper in his ear. "Pizza?"

"God yes, give me the greasiest, shittiest American pizza we can find." He pulls back, shoving his feet into his sneakers. "And we should stop for ice cream, before we have to tackle cleaning out your kitchen cabinets and decide what you want to bring home."

Staring at him, I slow as I finish putting my own shoes on.

Seth pauses with my keys in his hand, glancing back at me. "What?"

"You said home."

"Yeah, *home*. I can't wait until you get to see the pack home." Seth jingles the keys, lingering by the door, a grin splitting his face. "Come on, let's *go*."

I laugh, sinking into his side as he locks up my apartment and leads me downstairs. We find my car, and I'm pleasantly surprised and happy when it starts up after sitting idle for so long. I elect to drive, taking us to a small pizza place that's in a shopping center right next to a grocery store.

Seth twists the dial for the radio, turning it up. "You know, you could practically draw a line up from your place to our house." He makes a motion with his hand, coupling it with a zipping noise. "We'll be there in no time when we finish packing. Arin said the movers will take care of all the donations first. Then they'll come back Sunday and pack it all up in the truck. You and I can head up to Rochester on Monday morning."

I had stipulated that the donation boxes, bags, and furniture went to an omega donation center when Arin said he was booking a moving company — and the paperwork confirmed they'll be taking it all off to the one nearest to my apartment. Maybe no one will get any use from it — but if it helps even *one* person, then it's worthwhile.

Pulling into a parking spot, I grip the steering wheel for a moment before turning to Seth, my voice softer. "I'm glad I don't have much. I'm glad we'll be back with them in only a couple of days."

Seth stops, his hand on the door. "I miss them too, baby."

The unfamiliar tightness in my chest loosens when he verbalizes it. Laughing, I let go of the wheel, grimacing. "Sorry, I think I just had to say that out loud."

He tilts his head at me, then gets out, moving around to open my door for me. When I slide out, he tips his chin down and kisses my cheek. "When Bennett bit me and our bond snapped into place, I wouldn't leave his side for a month. I kept bursting into these board meetings and just *sitting* next to him. No one was supposed to know we'd bonded, but I wasn't subtle."

I smile over at him as we head toward the hole-in-the-wall pizza place. "That's cute."

"You'd think he would be the clingy one, but it's really me." Seth shrugs as he opens the door for me, the smell of basil hitting us both, an old rattling heater knocking the chill from the air. "I was *beside* myself when one of the distributors flirted with him in front of me. He had to drag me to a supply closet and tell me to get me shit together."

I laugh as I grab us a menu. "And nothing else happened in that closet?"

Seth shoots me a look, a wry smile lifting the edges of his lips. "You can fill in the blanks."

We settle on a large pizza and Seth digs his wallet out, placing it as a to-go order with cheese sticks, stepping back out into the cold twilight just to walk the couple paces to the grocery store.

"I'm going to grab water bottles for the movers." I glance at him, pointing toward the back of the store. "I'll meet you in the ice cream?"

He drops a kiss to my forehead just before I pull away. The store is quiet this late, and almost empty. I pass aisles full of product, but devoid of people, making it to the back of the store where the pallets of plastic water bottles are stacked on top of each other. Picking one, I heave it up.

I should have gotten a cart —

The moment I turn with it in my arms, I run directly into someone standing just behind me.

The tang of chemical suppressants hits me first and I look up sharply, wobbling with the weight of the water. The guy reacts, reaching out to steady me, the waves of chemical, acidic smell coming off him and his clothes. My brain recoils at the same time my body does.

"Whoa, careful."

I take a half step back, swallowing back bile. He's rail-thin, but wearing multiple bulky layers, including the collar of a sweater that covers part of his face. He's bundled up like there's a blizzard outside, not just a slight chill in the air. His black, stringy hair falls out of the darkness of his hood. I'd think it was rain — but I know for a fact it isn't, and that makes my stomach churn, recognizing the unkempt nature and the fact it's probably *grease*. His eyes pinch at the corners, focused on me.

Dizziness hits me, the antiseptic smell so similar to hospital cleaner.

Shaking my head, I dodge his hand as he reaches for me again, flashing him a polite smile. "Sorry, I didn't see you."

"Let me help." I can't see his features, and it's unsettling.

"No, I'm good." I take another step away, hesitant to turn my back on him before I lift the waters and hold them closer. "Have a good night." Darting around him instead, I leave the aisle with my skin prickling.

I head straight for the freezer section, scanning the rows until I see Seth standing alone in front of a display of ice cream pints.

Throwing myself at him, I catch his wide-eyed look before he takes the waters and plops them into an abandoned cart near the freezers. "When you said water, I thought you were getting two bottles, not an entire *case*." He moves toward me, then pauses, his nose wrinkling. "What's that smell?"

My skin crawls as I glance behind myself, wrapping my arms around my torso, swearing I still feel eyes on me as I lean into him. "Some guy ran into me. He smelled."

"Yeah." Seth wraps an arm around me, pressing his cheek against the top of my head, his voice lower. "You smell like someone sprayed you with perfume cover. It's harsh, like there's not even a hint of Bennett or Arin or Theo on you anymore."

The way Seth touches me, one hand on the back of my neck, the other on my side, grounds me. His fingers tighten just below my hairline and I watch his jaw flex as he looks from one side of the aisle to the other, hazel eyes narrowed.

Frowning, I press closer to his taut body, my voice shaking. "I don't like that."

"Me either." Seth's voice drops. He refocuses on my face, nodding toward the ice cream. "Come on, let's go back to your place. Pick your favorite flavor, baby."

I suck in a breath, scanning the options until I spy a blue pint. "That one."

Seth opens the door, his chest rumbling as he laughs, pulling the chocolate pudding ice cream out and turning the logo to me. "Fudge Remedy?"

I shrug, fighting a small smile. "Yeah, it's my favorite."

"I'll give you a fudge remedy." His hand dips on my back, grazing my ass.

I jolt, laughing loudly. "*Seth.*" The tension breaks, like nothing happened as he grabs a second pint of the same flavor, chucking them into the cart on top of the water.

"We should take a photo of our dinner and give Bennett a heart attack."

Snorting as he directs us toward the check-out, I can't help but glance over my shoulder. Just in case. "Wait until we get the pizza, he'll stroke out that there isn't a vegetable in sight."

"Genius." Seth kisses my head, laughing into my hair.

CHAPTER SEVEN

JUNE

I MIGHT THROW UP.

The closer we get to the house, the more I feel unprepared for what awaits me.

It only took two days for Seth and I to finish packing my apartment. True to Arin's word, the movers carried off the haphazardly boxed items for donation. I only packed what I absolutely loved. Everything else felt... unnecessary.

It served its purpose, and now, hopefully, another omega might find some use with it.

The medium sized truck was only a third of the way full by the time it pulled away from the building in Virginia, and I turned in my keys the moment the landlord's office opened. Seth and I packed the bare essentials into the backseat of my car — my favorite books, my laptop, and the single cardboard box of sentimental items I've managed to keep from childhood.

We stopped once for lunch, Seth getting out of the car with a dramatic groan before we shoved our faces with diner burgers and set off on the endless interstate leading up the

East Coast. The bulk of our drive has been navigating from one end of Pennsylvania to the other.

"June," Seth mutters my name, reaching over blindly and covering my hand with his. He squeezes my fingers once. "I say this with love, but please chill the fuck out."

He's been a champion. At the barest hint of anxiety, he seeks me out, chasing it away with a kiss and a soft reassurance that everything will be alright.

I fidget again, tugging on the seatbelt strap and glancing over at him with a soft groan. "Sorry." Sinking back into the seat, I try to reorient my spiraled thoughts, and fail miserably. "I don't know if it's *me* or the biology making me antsy."

"You *are* the biology." He glances over at me for the briefest of moments, the road a quiet two-lane highway. "The biology is you? I don't know how else to say it — but you might have *lived* as a beta for almost thirty years, but you've always been *you*. Nothing that has happened in the last month has changed that. If you're worried about seeing the house that's one thing, but if you're nervous you're somehow disrupting us, or will be unwelcome — that's just not true."

His lips twitch at the edges as he looks back at the empty road.

"You should know that they've texted me *fifteen* times since we left the diner. Arin reminded me that you need to *eat*. They don't just miss you, they're clawing their own eyes out waiting."

I stare over at him, a laugh spilling out. "But we were barely alone for forty-eight hours."

Seth shrugs. "They care about you." His hand squeezes mine once more before it returns to the steering wheel.

I press my lips together, watching trees and fields pass

by. "I guess it's just intrinsically *me* that I'm nervous to move in after a month of knowing you."

"A month and six days, but who's counting?" Seth shoots me a sarcastic look before taking an exit. "Don't you know anyone else would be totally and completely normal about the breakneck speed of all of this?"

I grumble, sinking down further into the passenger seat.

"If it helps, you have your own space." His voice is softer, soothing. "Apart from the nest, you have your own room, and the freedom to do whatever you want. I don't want you to feel trapped there, but I do hope..."

He trails off and I turn my head.

"I hope you enjoy it." His eyes flicker to mine. "I hope you don't regret any of the choices you've made, because I don't."

My heart tugs and I reach over, sliding my hand over his shoulder before bending down to kiss it, resting my cheek there for a moment.

"I don't." I whisper the words. "I don't regret a single thing."

"Good."

This close, his smell is vibrant, sugary sweet like walking into a patisserie. I press my lips against the curve of his shoulder one more time before leaning away and looking out the front window. "I'm nervous about seeing the house. Is it big?"

He barks out a laugh, then pauses when I don't join him. "Oh you weren't joking."

At my panicked expression, a line forms between his brows, almost sheepish.

"Arin doesn't do anything half-assed. We all have our own rooms, plus a few offices — mostly for Arin and myself.

Bennett and I have a headquarters inside the city where we take meetings. I'll take you over there one day and you can try some of our rum."

Wringing my sweater in my lap, I suck in a breath. "So... take the townhouse and double it?"

Seth makes a noise. "Maybe triple it?"

"*Jesus.*" I lean back, laughing nervously. I only brought my car because Seth and I needed a way to get here — but now I'm very aware that the almost decade-old rust-bucket is probably the *last* thing that will fit in with this new lifestyle. "No big deal." I try for levity. "It's not like I'm going from a two hundred square foot apartment to a mansion."

Seth's lips quirk. "Is this a bad time to tell you we have a butler?"

"*What?*"

He drums his fingers on the steering wheel. "We travel a lot, so Arin hired Charles. He oversees the house when we're gone and keeps an eye on our security system. He's nice, and an older beta." He shrugs at my open mouth. "He doesn't *live* with us or anything — there's a small house for him on the edge of our property. It went up for sale and Arin bought it. It makes Arin feel better to know the house isn't sitting empty when Bennett and I are off, he's gone signing contracts, and Theo's off investing in whatever the fuck he's decided sounds cool."

I blink. "Alright."

Seth chews on his lip, glancing over at me again.

"I don't know how to process any of that information, so I'm just going to go with it."

"Probably for the best." Seth takes another turn, then muses. "I wonder which one of them is going to rush you first? Arin's been clawing at the walls according to Bennett, but Theo's handsy. Bennett's anxious." He reaches a hand up, rubbing his chest almost subconsciously. "We're close enough I can feel it in the bond, but I think it's just nerves. They just want you to be happy."

"I am." I look over at him again, my voice softening. "I'm happy wherever you are, Seth."

His eyes flicker to me, his hand easing from his chest and seeking mine out. Twining our fingers together, he nods toward the road ahead, where trees lining the long drive suddenly stop.

"Take a look at our home then, baby."

My eyes widen as mature firs fade behind the car. Seth pulls us down the gravel road, slowing to a stop in front of a house — a *manor* — more like, because it's huge and sprawling. It's a brown brick monstrosity that goes out on both ends, hiding the rest of the property behind it with its berth. It looks like something plucked from the English countryside and plopped down here.

Where the townhouse was white, with clean lines and a traditional look that matched London, this place feels rustic. It oozes comfort with ivy trailing up the brick and flower beds around the front containing a medley of wildflowers, all thriving even though the air still has a sharp chill.

"*Wow.*"

Seth glances at me, his hand still firmly in mine. His smile is only for me as he nods toward the wooden front door. "Wait until you see the view from the backyard."

I shove the passenger door open and step out, the wind cutting me from the side as I stare up at the house. The ivy rustles in the breeze, fluttering against the brick. There are so many windows I can't wrap my head around it — not to mention an entire side to the right that I swear looks like a greenhouse.

Just as I turn toward to it, the front door bursts open.

Theo is a blur of blond muscle as he bolts out of the house. With his long legs, he eats up the space between us in no time and I let out a soft *oof* when he practically tackles me. His warmth wraps me up, arms winding around my waist as he presses his head against my shoulder and *lifts* me from the gravel drive, swinging me around in a small circle.

"God, I *missed* you."

My heart clenches as I bend into him, tangling my fingers in his slightly long hair and inhaling the sharp smell of rainwater. Humming, I let out a little laugh as he responds in kind. Theo's hands slide over my back, pulling me closer just to take a deep inhale of my throat.

"I missed you too." My voice sounds thick when I pull back, smiling down at him as he holds me in the air, his muscles straining against his t-shirt. Cupping his face with a hand, I lean in just as he tips his chin up. Theo's blue eyes catalogue me before he pulls me flush against his chest and kisses me firmly.

Laughing into the kiss, I slide down in his arms until my feet touch the ground again as he devours my mouth.

"Times up, Theo. *Move.*"

Bennett's voice curls around us as I pull back from Theo's embrace. My head turns sharply as hands tug me from Theo's arms unceremoniously.

Theo lets out a little growl at the other alpha, but it doesn't phase Bennett at all as he cups my face with two large hands, brushing my hair away as he leans our foreheads together.

"Please, *please*, tell me you ate more than pizza and ice cream while you were gone."

My nose scrunches as I grin. "If I did, I would be lying. Seth and I are eighty percent pizza and shitty drive-thru burgers right now. Not a vegetable in sight."

Bennett grimaces, but his brown eyes spark with delight as he leans in closer, his nose grazing mine. "What do you want tonight for dinner, darling? What can I make you that you'll enjoy and that has some kind of substance?"

I press my lips together, trying to hide my sheer elation at seeing him again as I shrug, pretending to think. "A kiss sounds good?"

He pauses, one eyebrow raising. "That has *no* nutritional value, but suddenly I don't care about your health in the slightest."

A laugh bubbles up, but it turns into a shriek as Bennett dips me, kissing me with a fervor that surpasses Theo by a thousand. I cling to his shoulders, breathless as he sweeps me back up, his excited movements turning sweet and loving as his lips part against mine. He tastes like fresh orange juice, and the familiarity makes my chest warm as a hand slides across my back.

"Leave the bags, Seth, we'll get them after." Theo barks the words, but they're half-amused instead of actually angry. His fingers toy with my sweater and I smile against Bennett's lips, pulling back just enough to bump my nose against his.

"Sorry I left you with the grumps."

Bennett takes me in, his lips lifting. "I survived."

"I was only grumpy because you were gone." Theo's voice is pure silk as he leans into me from behind, caging me up against Bennett. A flush of heat crawls up my skin and I glance back at him, moving a hand to touch his jaw as he pouts.

"Poor baby." I rub my fingers over the slight stubble on his cheek, glancing back at Bennett to catch his eyes dragging between Theo and I. There's a hint of restrained hunger behind his normally cool demeanor and I bite my tongue, my stomach clenching.

"I was only gone for two days." I peck them both on the cheek, trapped between them happily. "And I'm here now."

Theo tips his head down and kisses my brow. "It felt like forever. I can't wait to show you everything."

My heart crawls up my throat to rest on my tongue. I've missed this, I've missed *them* — being showered with so much love and affection is overwhelming in the best of ways. But there's someone missing.

"Juniper."

Arin steps out of the front door, his hands buried in the pockets of his slacks, like he's *trying* to appear relaxed. But I can see the tension in his shoulders as he holds himself back, letting the others have their moments with me first.

The instinct to drop everything and go to him fills me up. It's been too *long*. I need his scent on me, his arms around me — I need my prime.

Untangling myself from Theo and Bennett, I bolt forward, momentarily uncaring about our audience as I throw myself at Arin. He catches me at the last second, his hands firm on my hips as I bury myself against his chest. Our lips find each other, magnetized.

The smell of mint burns through my body, invading my senses as I cling to him, pressing closer as his hands rub up and down, fingers crushing me.

I'm going to bruise.

85

He kisses me harder, and even though there's no bite on my skin from him, I can *feel* how much the brief separation killed him. I could let him slam me against the door, steal every breath from my lungs with a thousand kisses.

I don't care if he does. Let him mark me.

"Welcome home, love." Arin leans back just enough to clear my hair from my face, his voice soft and his glasses askew. His dark thumb brushes against the swell of my left cheek as he smiles, brown eyes taking me in like he'll find a freckle out of place.

My throat closes as my smile wobbles. Blinking rapidly up at him, I touch his jaw, my voice rawer than I expect as I whisper, "Wow, I didn't realize just how much I missed you."

His answering smile crinkles the edges of his shiny eyes. Arin tugs me against him, tucking me into his chest as he rubs his cheek against the crown of my head, muttering softly. "I wish I could say the same. I missed you every second you were gone, Juniper. It felt like we were missing parts of us." His throat works as he kisses my hairline, then pulls back.

My eyes fall on Seth, leaning into Bennett, the other alpha's hand on Seth's shoulder, thumb rubbing Seth's bond mark absentmindedly as they watch us. Theo lingers near them, his lips tipped up in the tiniest of smiles.

Arin clears his throat. "Two very integral parts of our pack were gone."

My eyes dart back to him and I sniffle a little, pressing a hand to my eyes. "God, sorry."

I don't know why I was worried about coming here — about moving at all. I was meant to be here, with them.

Arin makes a soft cooing sound then tips my head up, kissing me sweetly. "Don't cry." His hands smooth over my back, pulling me into another tight hug before he clicks his tongue and guides me toward the door. "Let's go inside. It's cold out here and there's a lot of rooms we'd like you to see. It doesn't have to all be done today."

"Yes it does." Theo's heavy footfalls are quick to join us. "What'd you do to make her *cry*?" He lets out a frantic noise and then bends closer. "*June*. He's already on thin ice, what did he say?"

"Theo." I let out a choked laugh, the emotions getting the better of me as I tug him to me and kiss him solidly once, making him stutter as I pull back. "Stop. They're happy and overwhelmed and good tears. I promise."

He blinks down at me, looking half-dazed before his eyes fall to Arin, narrowing. "Are you sure —"

"Theo." Arin's voice is dry, dripping with humor. "You're only upset because I wouldn't let you do whatever you wanted. Let her go."

Theo's hands slide away from me, leaving lingering touches on my back as I look through the open wooden doors at the foyer. I feel utterly dwarfed by the size of the space, in between Theo and Arin with Seth and Bennett bringing up the rear.

It's *stunning*.

The walls are all dark wood paneling, setting off warm tones in the decor scattered around. This entire place *looks* like my alphas — Arin's stability, Bennett's sensibility, and Theo's masculinity. There are small touches of jewel tones that pop, from a green hand-blown glass lamp to a purple shock of flowers on a table that scream Seth, like he's sprinkled everywhere my eyes land.

Arin slides his hand into mine and I look up at him, my lips parting. "It's so pretty."

"You can thank Bennett for that."

I glance over my shoulder, beaming. "I should have known."

Bennett smiles at me as Seth leans into him, the beta eyeing Arin. "Whisk us away, I'm ready to see this place through June's eyes."

Arin's hand squeezes mine before he pulls me carefully to the left, past a set of wooden stairs that lead up to the other floors. I glance around at the walls and doors as he points to them. "The kitchen is just through here, but we're passing my office right now, it's behind that door."

"He kept forgetting to eat dinner and Bennett was about to throttle him," Theo mutters from beside me.

I laugh as we all step through an archway, but the sound dies in my throat as my eyes widen. The kitchen is *huge*, one room with walnut wood everywhere, and a *stained glass window* above the kitchen sink. The design is simple, jewel tones to match the rest of the decor, a rose inlaid to the center. I gasp as I pull away from Arin, taking in the table pushed to the side, just like the townhouse's breakfast nook.

Spinning in a little circle, I try to catalogue it all, my eyes running over every detail. "I love it."

Arin smiles, nodding toward a door just past the kitchen, in the sight-line of the archway we just entered through. "We just started." Stepping over, he opens the door and motions me forward.

"Someone better get a photo of her face," Seth pipes up from behind us.

I stagger to a stop in the doorway, rendered breathless.

It's a library. A *massive* library.

Wooden shelves extend up and up, spanning two levels. There's a scattering of comfortable couches and chairs in front of a large gray stone fireplace, with picture windows on either side looking out to the back of the property, a great expanse of grass leading to water. I breeze past Arin in the doorway, going immediately to one of the shelves to skim the titles.

A spiraling staircase in the corner leads up to the next level, allowing access to the other books above us, but my heart stops at the sight of it all. I feel like I'm in *Beauty and the Beasts* — just a girl suddenly finding herself trapped in a magical castle with multiple surly alphas.

Giddy laughter bursts out of my mouth as I run my fingers over the titles on the shelves, running the length of the shelf to see what they have. There's fiction and mysteries and thrillers, all meticulously organized by genre and then by author's last name. It screams of Theo's neuroses.

Darting to another shelf, I find a mixture of nonfiction and cookbooks, some of the pages worn and stained around the edges, and I just *know* that Bennett has used them while in the kitchen behind us.

"Oh my god."

I stop short, my eyes finding the shelf at the end of one of the rows.

The spines are the most colorful in the library, by far. A bright spot in the room. Three paperbacks sit in a line — green, yellow, and pink spines facing out. *My* books. My silly and hopeful romances shelved so carefully, having their own home in this space.

I choke on a sob as I stare at them.

Arin's suddenly beside me, his hand soothing on the small of my back as he whispers, "You're a part of this pack, Juniper. I had to put all your hard work on display in our library. I can't tell you how *proud* I am that you've made a career out of something you love."

The tears pour out, and I don't even try to hold them back, letting myself become an utter wreck as I turn into him and bury my face in his chest. *Years* of being told by my mother that my work amounted to nothing — that low-quality love stories were a waste — years of writing, breaking my fingers, trying to get my name out there and create things that made me proud even if no one else cared —

And, yet, Arin is proud of me.

It doesn't fix the lingering hurt, but it eases the painful memories. Just to know they are is enough. I know the action isn't hollow, nothing Arin does is superficial or only a means to an end. To have my books *here* means I have my own place here.

He pulls me close, rocking us back and forth, his lips on my forehead. "Don't cry, sweet omega. I didn't mean to upset you."

"You didn't." I gasp the words as I try to sort through the sucker punch of emotions. Arin's chest begins to rumble, the soft start of a purr humming through us both as he rubs my back until I can catch my breath.

"There's more." He strokes my hair. "Let me show you your nest, love."

I walk with him, tucked into his side with his arm around me, and for a moment, I almost expect Theo to overreact, or Bennett to rush toward us, but they both just give me heart-breakingly kind looks, deferring to Arin as his purr echoes. They lead me back to the kitchen and to another door on the opposite side.

The wood is thicker, even I can tell as Arin shoves it open. As it swings shut behind all of us, the noise dampens in this hallway, plush carpet underfoot. Arin slows in front of an archway with a pocket door and slides it open with his free hand.

"This is the nest bathroom." He motions to the dimly lit room, more spa than bathroom, and I spot a large shower big enough for ten, a sunken tub, and another door that's on the far wall.

"When we sketched out the renovations after we bought the house, we thought it would be better to have the nest suite on the main level, near the kitchen." Bennett's voice is gentle as he moves forward, looking down at me. "At that point, we didn't know if we'd ever have a use for it, but I hope it's acceptable."

The sheer thought that it *wouldn't* be is staggering as I blink at it all. "It's perfect."

Arin lets out a contented noise before he eases away and takes the couple steps to the door at the end of the hall. He pushes it open, stepping to the side as I drift forward, sucking in a little hiccuped breath.

The room is dark, but not pitch black. Instead, filtered, colorful light drifts in through a skylight made entirely of stained glass. It's similar to the one in the kitchen, casting rainbows onto the floor. From wall to wood-paneled wall, thick, lush carpet spans, save for the mattress area in the dead center that's double the size of the nest in London.

The mattress is *huge*, and will give us all enough space to stretch out, compared to the one at the townhouse. My eyes take in the bare mattress, the dark green paint on the upper third of the walls above the wooden wainscoting, and the stacks of boxes carefully stashed against one wall.

It smells faintly of them. All of them, save for Seth. Mint, orange, and rain linger in the air like they tried not to be in here too much, but the scents stuck, burrowing themselves into the walls anyway.

I turn slowly, partially inside, just to see all four of them in the wide doorway, not a toe over the line.

"We briefly stepped in to put your things down from London." Arin clears his throat. "I hope you don't mind. I thought we could take you into the city and properly shop — all of us if you'd like. We will pick up whatever would make this space feel like yours — permanently."

I'm so touched I feel a little lightheaded. "Thank you."

Arin's smile makes my heart lurch. "I'm supposed to end my portion of this tour. I was bullied into it, really."

A grin spreads across Theo's face as he holds his hand out to me. "Come here, princess. You can't sleep in the nest all the time, let me show you to your *actual* room."

I reach for him and let out a breathless laugh as he snags my hand and tugs me back down the hallway, rushing us through the kitchen and toward the foyer stairs. Arin, Bennett, and Seth follow us, but they can't keep up as Theo bolts upstairs, past the second floor, throwing words over his shoulder, half-breathless. "We don't have to look at this floor, it's just Bennett and Seth's rooms."

"Wait!" I laugh louder as Theo drags me up to the next landing, his grin lighting him up from the inside as he stops and points at the end of a hall.

"My room is right there." He whirls and then nods toward the arch we're next to. "And *yours*, June, is here."

Excitement races through my veins as I stare at the wooden door, classically ornate. As the rest of them finally reach us, I glance over at them, chewing my lower lip. "Can I open it?"

"I wish you would" — Theo nudges me forward — "I worked really fucking hard on it for you."

I flash him a little smile before I eagerly shove the door open, pausing in surprise.

The room, aesthetically, matches the rest of the house with its dark wood tones and classic design, but it's almost a perfect mirror to the library downstairs. There's a lofted area that extends high above our heads, doubling the height of the floor to ceiling shelves spanning one wall, a window set in the middle of them that has a small walkway in front of it to the shelves in the corner. Under the walkway, there's a reading nook with a large, comfortable, and familiar looking leather chair.

It takes me a moment to realize *why* it looks familiar, but my brain conjures up the shopping day with Seth weeks ago, and the random furniture store he dragged me into. It's from *London* — they shipped a *chair for me from London*.

My heart goes wild in my chest as I take it all in, every shelf empty and more than enough room to house my personal book collection, plus space to expand.

On the other side of the room is a huge four poster bed, set against a dark green wall that matches the color of the nest. It also reminds me of the drive up to the manor — with dark pines and earthy browns.

"I hope you like it." Theo's voice is soft as he shuffles in the doorway. "I didn't add art, I thought you'd want to add your own personal touch. Seth helped with the color palette after he got to your apartment." He gives me a sheepish look, his eyes darting to the green wall. "I wanted to make sure the colors were right. You know... because your couch was green."

I turn toward him and throw my arms around his neck,

kissing him multiple times on the lips as I murmur, "I love it. I love everything. It's perfect. Let's pick out art together and fill the shelves. Thank you."

He clears his throat awkwardly, but pulls me closer all the same, crushing me as he does. "When we go into the city to get your nest supplies, we'll get you some decor — really make it your own. Whatever you want — or we can order it online. I'll give you my card."

I shake my head at him, unable to wrap my head around it all. "Is this why you came back here instead of coming with Seth and I?"

"Yes." Theo finally smiles. "I had to make sure it was perfect."

Pulling back, I kiss his jaw one last time before I wander toward another door. Inside, the closet spans an entire separate room, shelves, displays, and drawers all ready to be filled and organized. I step out and over to the other door, exploring an uncannily similar bathroom to the nest downstairs. Instead of a sunken tub, however, it has a golden clawfoot antique, freestanding in front of a stained glass window.

"Thank you." I whisper the words when I turn to look at the four of them, laughing because I feel like a broken record, but what in the world is there else to say? It's not enough. Nothing will ever be enough.

Bennett squeezes Seth's side. "One more space, darling. Humor me."

I can't even fathom what could be left, but I let him lead me downstairs, turning us in the opposite direction to the kitchen. The space opens up to a massive living room with three couches pointed toward a huge TV. On the entire back wall, windows span, looking out into the backyard where I can see a pool, hedges, and then nothing but *water*.

"Lake Ontario," Arin supplies, slowing to a stop next to me. "You don't even realize the property is right on the water until you see the back. It's private, we enjoy being able to come home here after so much traveling."

I just stare, dumbfounded. "I can understand why."

"Do you like it?" Arin reaches out, winding a strand of my hair around one of his fingers. "Will you let me know if there's anything at all you need to feel comfortable here with us?"

Without the haze of the heat that made my mind so cloudy and decisions so difficult, I can see him for what he is. Undeniably *alpha*, well suited to head an entire pack, kind and considerate.

And *mine*.

My hindbrain nearly snarls the word, making my throat go dry as I reach up to touch his jaw, running my fingers over his coarse beard before I whisper, "I would be happy anywhere with you."

And I mean it. Deep in my bones. The anxiety of moving my life, coming here, ebbs. There's no reason for me to even *be* nervous when I've found myself, somehow, inconceivably, becoming the luckiest woman in the world. I don't have one alpha, I have *three* incredibly considerate alphas and a beta who would do anything for me, including making one of the scariest times in my life into something that feels like a dream.

Arin smiles down at me, a gentle expression crossing his features.

"June?"

I turn, looking over at Bennett as he lingers in another doorway, leading to another maze in this place. Pulling away from Arin, I move over to the other alpha, taking his offered hand as he guides me into a hallway behind the living room.

"This was an addition we made a few years ago." His voice is soft as he pushes open a door. "This is Seth's office." Bennett motions inside to a tidy room with a mildly messy desk. "But I wanted you to have your own space here, not just the library, or the nest, or your bedroom. You deserve a place where you can write and work, but walk away from it when you need a break."

My breath catches as he moves down a door, hesitating in front of it.

"I moved my own office to our headquarters in downtown Rochester. I don't work much from home anyway, and what needs to be done can be handled in Seth's office." He gives me a little smile, then opens the door that begins as part of the house, wooden parquet flooring transitioning to gray stone at the back half that's covered by a glass, greenhouse ceiling. Large panes expose the room to the light and the view to the backyard, giving it a stunning view of the nature surrounding the property.

I gasp, squeezing Bennett's hand, my eyes landing on a huge oak desk near the door and an armchair on the stone tiles. They're the only two pieces in the entire room.

He squeezes my hand back. "I cleared out most of my things, but I thought you could use a desk and a chair to relax in. If you don't like them, or the room, we can find something else that you'd be happy with."

"Bennett." My voice breaks and I stare up at him, truly touched.

He touches his forehead to mine. "It's a little far from the kitchen, but I'd be happy to bring you lunch every day."

I wrap an arm around his neck, tugging him to me just to

kiss his jaw, smiling against his skin, inhaling the zest of orange I find there. "You've rendered me speechless."

He touches my back, then tilts his head to brush his lips against mine. "Maybe after you're settled in, I could take you out in your brown dress."

My heart flutters as I nod quickly, my eyes dragging over his face. This alpha — *my* alpha if I wanted him to be. If I asked, I think he would.

Seth claps his hands. "Okay, let's go grab your things from the car and eat, because I'm starving and the movers should be driving up tomorrow. Then we get to start the long process of Theo micromanaging us all."

I glance over at the beta, my lips twitching as I take in the office, the air warm from the greenhouse side. There's a light trickle of bird song coming in through an open window, coupled with the sound of the lake rushing up on the shore behind the house.

If this is a dream, I never want to wake up.

CHAPTER EIGHT

BENNETT

THIS HOUSE WASN'T a home until she moved in.

June being here has brought a different kind of light and joy to the house. Sometimes I wonder how the four of us existed before her. Sure, Seth and I have a sincere love for each other, but oftentimes it felt like we were just roommates with Arin and Theo. Four people, each with separate lives that occasionally crossed paths for dinners or the rare moment we all happened to be home together.

But with her, it's changed.

She's only been sleeping here for a little over a week — but already I can see the ways the house feels more cohesive. The truck arrived with the rest of her clothing and her personal items, and I found her and Theo upstairs, sitting in the middle of her bedroom floor, sorting everything. Theo griped at her while he folded everything precisely how he wanted it, telling her how best to organize her own closet. When she caught sight of me in the doorway, she'd rolled her eyes and given me a little smile.

The next day I'd found her in the library, sprawled out

on one of our leather couches, half draped over Arin as he held a book in one hand and played with her hair with the other. His soft voice had echoed off the walls, reading aloud to her while resting.

She's already made a seat out of the surface of Seth's desk. I'd walked down the hall two nights ago and found her perched on the edge of it, swinging her legs back and forth as he leaned back in his office chair, beaming up at her with bright eyes, laughing loudly.

June bridges the road between us all, connecting us in ways that I didn't even realize we were missing. She's the effortless thread keeping us tied together.

And I love her.

I've never had to think about my feelings this much. Through the years I've never paid attention to them — I've been attracted to who I'm attracted to. Seth and I orbit each other, a symbiotic relationship from the start. I also come from a family that doesn't have the same issues that Theo's upbringing had. I have two absolutely wonderful alpha mothers and an omega father who love each other more and more every single day that passes. I've always been able to do whatever I've wanted in life — if that meant college, great, if that meant traveling the world, I could choose that as well.

Falling in love with Seth was as natural as breathing.

June hit me like a train.

June in her well-worn sweater in the elevator, smelling of green tea and honey. June curled in on herself at the Designation Center, so uncertain on what to do. June finally relaxing in the townhouse, letting herself be open to us. June in her nest, rosy skinned and flushed, whispering sweet nothings against my skin while Seth slept next to us in the middle of her heat.

I step around the kitchen counter, washing my hands. There's an entire meal ready in the fridge for Arin, Theo, and Seth — I didn't plan on making it, but my brain has been going nonstop since this morning. I don't mind leaving it for them, it makes me feel good — the providing aspect makes my alpha settle in my chest.

Walking down the hall, I push Arin's door open and stick my head in his office. "Have you seen June?"

Arin looks up, hair mussed and eyes dark underneath. "Uh..." He squints at me, adjusting his glasses as they slide down the bridge of his nose. "No, but didn't Seth just take her food?"

I blink at him. "Arin, that was three hours ago."

He grimaces at me and then looks back down at the paperwork on his desk. "I've been combing through this contract. I haven't — seen her, that is." He mutters the words as he shuffles the pages. "Check her office, or find Theo — he can't seem to leave her alone."

I pull back, quietly shutting the door to leave him be. Shaking my head, I hold in a snort at the fact there's *two* of them now. Arin's inability to pull away from work will be the death of him, and I already know where I'll likely find our omega.

Passing the foyer and living room, I glance out the back windows briefly to the pool and patio, seeing Theo swimming laps. Seth sits on the side, feet in the water as he yells out random numbers — trying to make Theo lose track of what number he's on.

I step past Seth's office to the door that used to be mine. Truthfully, it was wasted on me. I like to keep work separate from home life, the antithesis to Arin's constant drive to be productive.

Just like someone else I know.

Bracing against the doorframe, I smile softly as I gaze inside.

June sits at the desk, her laptop set up with nothing but a mug and an empty plate next to her as she types away. She's told Theo multiple times that she doesn't want a new set up for writing yet — that the old laptop will do — but I have a feeling that Theo's about to go wild with buying. Arin and I had to rein him in the second we stepped off the plane in Rochester, because otherwise Theo was prepared to do a full scale house renovation before June moved in.

She flicks her hair back, wearing oversized headphones over her ears as she focuses on the screen, slightly hunched over and chewing on her bottom lip. I think she had a call with her agent a couple days ago, but I don't know the specifics about her deadlines and the rescheduled tour dates yet. I imagine with everything in London her planning time took a hit.

But I'm determined to make sure she never has to worry about anything ever again. If it's up to me — she'll be able to live out the rest of her days spending them doing anything she wants.

"June." I murmur her name, testing to see if she has her headphones on noise cancelling mode. When she doesn't react, I push away from the door and step over to her, embracing the cloud of perfume that hangs around her like pure temptation.

My fingers glide over the back of her shoulders, brushing her hair from her neck before I bend down to kiss the crown of her head.

She startles, then tips her head up, relaxing back into me as she flashes me a smile and takes her headphones off.

"Hi." Her hazel eyes brighten as she tilts her chin up.

"Hi." I glance at the clock on her laptop. "You've been at this desk for five hours, darling."

"I know, I know." She laughs, licking her lips, her cheeks darkening. "I just got started on something and the words were flowing."

"Come on." I bring my other hand up to touch her other shoulder, squeezing my hands. "We have plans tonight, you should go get ready."

"Oh?" June drops her headphones to the desktop, her mouth opening in a little 'o' as she glances at the unfinished work on her screen. "We do?"

"We do," I confirm softly, taking her in. Her nose is adorable — maybe my favorite part of her features — a perfect little button in the center of her face. "You have plenty of time to get ready if you go upstairs now. I wouldn't spring this on you if I wasn't sure you did."

June pushes back from the desk, standing up after shutting the lid to her laptop. She makes a little squeaking noise as she stretches out her back, and I make a mental note to get her a better desk chair if she's going to insist on sitting in it without moving.

Her warm little hands slide over my shirt, bracing on my chest as she stands on her tip-toes. "Okay." She bites her lower lip. "Just us tonight?"

My lips twitch. "Yes, just us."

June gifts me a smile that lights up her entire face.

I've had tonight planned since Seth brought her to Rochester.

After calling in a few favors, I hope she enjoys herself, but I'm really fucking nervous.

For the first time in years, I'm cautious that she'll let me down softly. We've had small moments together, mostly before her heat, and I *do* understand there's a draw between her and Seth, and her and Arin — even her and Theo have something.

But she could just want to be casual with me. Courting her could go nowhere.

I fidget in the foyer, glancing at the tiling and sucking in a breath as I look back at the stairs again. I steam-pressed my button up, and the cufflinks on my wrists are shaped like little oranges — a gift from Seth ages ago.

Footsteps on the stairs make me straighten, holding my breath as I wait for her to appear.

When she does, my heart stops.

The brown dress elicits memories of London, of the dressing room, and being bombarded by her scent when everything was so new between us.

Her body is elongated as she takes the steps slow, heels clicking as the hem swirls just below her knees. The silken fabric hugs her curves with its bodice before skimming over her full hips into a skirt that makes me want to fist it and crawl under it. At the end of the day — I'm only a man, and I would give up the world to be on my knees for her.

Her hair is pulled back, up in a complicated swirl at the base of her head, softly curled strands hanging around her face as she walks down to the foyer to meet me. My heart only starts beating again when she gives me a hesitant smile.

"I had Theo zip me up this time."

She takes another step and I catch a whiff of the rain-water scent, but mostly it's just *her* — just honey, mixed with tea leaves.

I reach for her instinctively, sliding my hand over her right arm, grasping her hand. "You are stunning."

June flushes, red flooding her cheeks as she glances at the door. "Are you going to tell me where we're going?"

"In a minute." I step closer, careful of her makeup as I cup her jaw and lean in, my voice softening. "I said I'd court you before your heat, and I'm sorry it took me this long to take you out properly. Arin got his moment, Seth has had his time, and I'm sure Theo will keep fighting for all your attention — but I want to make sure you know I'm serious, June."

Her eyes brighten, crinkling as she stares up at me. "You don't have to court me, Bennett. I mean..." Her lips part as she glances over my face. "I *live* here now, it's not like I'm going anywhere."

I catch her eye, raising my brow. "I know that. But I'd like for us to have something of our own. Do you understand?"

Her expression softens as she nods, and my chest suddenly feels tight. "Then we better leave before we pick up a stray." June's lips twitch.

I whisk her out of the door, rewarded with her laugh as I tug her toward my car. It's far easier to have a driver when we're in London — but it's extravagant and *fun* to have my own car at home. I open the passenger door of my 1965 Ford convertible for her, the dark green of it reminds me of the house, of Seth, of *her*.

Her eyes widen as she gets in. I hop in after her, turning the car around in the drive, the top down and the loose strands of her hair flying everywhere.

"I feel like there's so much I don't even know about you!"

A grin overtakes my face. "We have time to learn."

In under thirty minutes we're in downtown Rochester, pulling into the back lot of the restaurant. June's eyes glance from me to the building as I grab her hand and help her out.

"Dinner?"

"Oh no." I pull her with me to the door to the kitchen, trying to suppress the giddy feeling in my chest. It took some finagling, but the entire restaurant is ours for the evening.

The moment I open the door, Ashley turns sharply from the prep counter, her eyes bright and her smile wide. Her pin-straight black hair is pulled back into a sleek bun, angular eyes taking in June before they land on me.

"You're here!"

She steps over, the faint smell of thyme coming with her as she embraces me first, then tilts her head down to look at June. "I'm Ashley." I have to give her credit, the other alpha doesn't reach for June — and I'd guess it's because I can't seem to let her hand out of my death grip.

"Did he even tell you where you were coming tonight?"

"No, he didn't." June shoots me a wry smile.

Ashley jumps right into it, grabbing June by the arm. I have to pry my fingers off her to let her go as Ashley leads her to the prep table, rambling away.

"Mr. Romantic wanted me to teach you how to make fresh pasta." She grins. "So that's what we'll be doing this evening. But first, you have to tell me which sauce you want." She waves her hand over a plethora of ingredients. "We can do white sauce, or I can teach you how to do a crushed tomato red sauce."

June stands in front of the table, her mouth dropping

open as she looks back at me. "I shouldn't have worn this dress. We're *cooking*?"

Sliding my hands into my trouser pockets, I tilt my head at her. "Ash has aprons. Pick your sauce, June."

Ashley bounces for a moment, and I'm thrown back to childhood when she'd drag me around the yard while my mothers assumed we were having a nice playdate — it often involved Ashley getting into trouble and me figuring out how to get us *both* out of it.

June stares from me to the tomatoes, then laughs loudly. "Fuck it. Let's learn the red, it sounds delicious."

"Love it." Ashley throws open the industrial fridge, pulling more ingredients out and spinning around the kitchen with an air of familiarity — which is no surprise, considering the entire restaurant is like her child.

June shyly creeps back over to me, sliding her fingers into mine, speaking under her breath. "She's an alpha?"

"Oh yeah," I mutter back, watching Ashley turn into a tornado. "We grew up together. My mothers know her family. It was a stroke of luck that she decided to set up a restaurant here in Rochester instead of New York City."

"It's quiet." Ashley shoots us a sly grin, all teeth as she smiles. "*And* my girlfriend is a music teacher at a private school here. Bennett just likes to leave that little fact out that I'm a massive softie who'd follow her anywhere." She drops flour and eggs onto the prep table, rolling up the sleeves up on her chef's jacket. "You both ready to work for your dinner?"

June grins, her eyes lighting up as she grabs an apron off a hook on the wall, tying it around herself. "I'm ready."

CHAPTER NINE

JUNE

I THROW my head back in a loud laugh as semolina flour scatters across the front of my apron.

Never did I think that I'd be in a restaurant kitchen, rolling dough, forming it into neat little yellow lines, just to messily cut it into homemade pasta. Nor did I expect to have Bennett behind me, laughing as he tries to guide my cuts to be a little more precise instead of utterly inconsistent.

"It's embarrassing how bad I am at this."

He grins down at me, planting a kiss on the side of my temple. "It doesn't matter what it looks like as long as it tastes good."

I smile back at him as Ashley reemerges from a side room, a bundle of basil in her hands and a small ceramic container of tiny red tomatoes. They look so fresh, I could believe she has a garden somewhere in the maze of this old building.

"Looks good!" She throws us both the praise before turning to the stovetop. "June, let him finish that and come over here. Let me show you how to get the *most* flavor out of these tomatoes."

I brush my hands off on my apron, turning in Bennett's arms. He leans down, muttering, "You're going to listen to *another alpha* right in front of me, June?"

A shiver crawls up my spine at his teasing look and I bite my tongue. "She's hard to say no to."

He grumbles for a moment before relenting and letting me slide out from under his arm. I move over to the stove, in front of a searing hot pan already waiting. Olive oil, basil, and tomatoes sit in a neat grouping nearby. Ashley glances at me, nudging me with her hip, her eyes crinkling at the edges.

"I've never seen him this relaxed with anyone other than Seth."

My heart warms as I look over my shoulder at Bennett standing in front of the prep table, meticulously cutting the pasta dough into neat lines so we'll have actual noodles in our dinner instead of the misshapen chunks I hacked off.

Ashley grabs the basil, finely chopping it as the pan heats with oil. "His mothers, both alphas, are friends with one of my mothers. She's also an alpha." She hovers her hand over the pan, staring at it as she mumbles, "Female alphas aren't... rare, per se, but less likely, as I'm sure you know. We really stick together, know each other. It's a weird place to be when you turn eighteen and, instead of emerging as glorified property, you've got more power in the world than you or anyone else knows what to do with."

I tilt my head at her and she glances over at me.

"No offense at the property thing. It's fucked."

I shrug, she's not *wrong*.

"It was weird," I say as Ashley scoops the tomatoes into the pan, sizzling immediately. As they begin to cook, she smashes some of them with a wooden spoon. "Being suddenly not in control of my own choices was an adjustment. The center didn't know what to do with me. They gave me a bunch of information on packs they couldn't find other placements for. Those were the ones that were rejected for obvious reasons — or the ones with female alphas as the prime. They were the ones that didn't want kids —" I flinch when one of the tomatoes explodes, splattering our aprons.

"Sorry!" Ashley laughs loudly, giving me a sheepish look. "I should have warned you. Go on?"

I grin back at her. "Don't mind me, I'm just rambling about how they asked me to remove my IUD before even saying hello."

"*Ugh.*" She makes a face, shivering next to me. "Basil goes in last, so it doesn't wilt. You like garlic? Of course you do." Ashley turns sharply, striding away. "Bennett, this is your warning that I'm putting an *ungodly* amount of garlic into this sauce."

He looks up as he wipes up the remaining flour from the workstation, glancing over at me. "I don't think it matters as long as we both smell and taste like it."

"Good man." Ashley comes back with a bowl of garlic cloves, the skin already removed. She throws it onto the plate with the basil, finely chopping it before adding it to the pan with the tomatoes.

As she does, her gaze darts to me.

"You know, for as much progress as the world has made, the centers and the government still struggle to see any reason why some omegas might not want kids. But it's the same as anyone else, sometimes that's just not what you want for your future, and that's alright."

I chew on my tongue, my eyes finding Bennett. "Yeah, but it worked out."

Ashley nudges me with a little grin. "It did. And at least you smell *divine*, some people get the short end of the stick, or scents only a mother could love."

Inhaling deeply, I breathe in the comforting scent of thyme from the alpha next to me, slightly twinged with bitterness. "From an omega perspective, I think you smell lovely — like coming home to a warm dinner, a huge smile, and a good hug."

Ashley's gaze softens as she stirs the tomatoes. "Thank you."

Nudging her back with my own hip, I smile. "No problem."

She quietly talks me through the steps of the sauce, what to look for, and how to know when to pull it — before the garlic gets too fragrant, and before the strands of fresh basil wilt. Ashley steps back and waves at me with a towel. "Okay, get out of here. Bennett can take you to the table and I'll be out in a second with your final dishes."

Bennett's hand slides into mine, tugging me away from the stove. He takes my apron off of me, then pulls me into the main restaurant. It's all exposed brick and soft lighting. At the center of the room, a table meant for four only has two chairs, side by side. We walk over to it together, hand in hand, my heart rising to my throat as I see the bouquet of wildflowers at the center of the table, surrounded by candles.

He pulls a chair out for me and I turn to him the moment he sits down, taking his hand again, hoping I sound as earnest as I feel. "I love this. Thank you."

His brown eyes rove over my face, his thumb stroking my hand. "I'm glad. I wanted to do something different for you."

Leaning into him, I press my lips against his cheek, whispering against his orange-scented skin. "And you wanted to make sure I could at least make *one* meal for myself when you're out of town."

His rumbling chuckle echoes through me as he reaches up and cups my face, pulling my lips to his. The kiss is deep and makes my toes curl in my low heels, his words getting lost against my lips. "That's the other half, yes."

Humming, I nudge his nose with my own. "Just remember, that's your last kiss from me sans garlic breath."

Bennett's loud laugh bounces off the wall before he pulls me closer and bites my lower lip, tugging it between his teeth. My breath catches as heat creeps up my skin. The orange scent *rolls* off him in waves that threaten to drag me under — I know it's partially biology, but my heart sings its praises for how much this man has wormed his way into the organ.

The door to the kitchen opens and I pull away just as Ashley comes out, brandishing two plates with a wide smile. "Alright, lovebirds!" She slides the pasta in front of each of us, picking up a block of cheese from a side table, holding it up to a grater. "This evening, I have for you *two* expertly made plates of pasta, honestly, my chefs did such a good job."

I flush at the praise, looking down at my plate. I can't deny that it looks delicious — albeit rustic. When she grates the cheese on it, it helps cover up some of the more freeform noodles I cut.

"*Bon appétit*, you two."

She whisks away and Bennett grabs a bottle of wine from the side table. He uncorks it, pouring the white wine into each of our glasses before lifting his own.

"To us."

I stare at him, clinking my glass with his. "To us."

ASHLEY'S HUG is crushing as I say goodbye.

"Thank you again for tonight."

The female alpha flashes me a huge smile. "Anytime you want a dinner away from that chaotic pack of yours, you come here — no reservation required."

I grin back at her. "I might have to take you up on that."

Dusk hangs, darkening the air, and my feet ache, my stomach comfortably full as Bennett pulls me over to his vintage car. I glance up at the sky, leaning into his touch as his eyes flicker over my face.

"Happy?"

"Yes," I answer honestly.

His body crowds mine against the side of his car. Sparks crawl up my skin as he leans down, pressing a hot kiss against my jaw, moving to my cheek, then grazing my lips.

Closing my eyes, I fist my fingers in his shirt. "If we go home, will we be able to have a night to ourselves?"

He pauses, his hands on my hips. "I hope you know that you will always have a say in who joins you in bed." He squeezes me once. "There is no open door policy if you don't want it. They'll respect that. They'll respect *you*. And if you want something with just one of us, or multiple, or want us to leave you entirely alone, that is *perfectly* acceptable."

Sucking in a deep breath, I nod, my hands roaming his chest as I drop my forehead slightly, his lips brushing it. "I just know it might be different after my heat —"

"June." Bennett stops me, making my eyes flutter open as

he growls, "One moment of your consent does not mean we have consent in perpetuity."

"Okay." My lips part, throat suddenly dry as I tip my chin, breathing out, "Because I want you tonight. Just you, alpha."

Bennett's smile is *devastating*. I can see the spark of desire in his eyes, the way that he probably drew Seth to himself unknowingly. He's not broad like Theo, or enticing like Arin — he's entirely different — alluring and earnest. *Mine.*

As he cups my face, his voice lowers. "I can't wait to fill you and fuck you so much the others won't be able to smell you without smelling *me* inside you."

I gasp as he drags me into another kiss, nodding, "I like that. More of that."

His answering growl rolls over my skin as he pushes me back against the car, hands moving all over me, touching my face, my arms, my hips, sliding the dress up almost to the point of exposing me to the night air. "You'll learn quickly, darling, that I *love* to share. I love to watch. But making them all wild because I'm the one who gets to fuck you? I love that too. We could tie them all up, force them to sit and watch while I make you come over and over and *over* again." His voice sounds raw as he groans against my lips. "And then maybe one day you can do that to me."

Fuck yes.

I scramble to hold onto his shirt, needing him closer, but knowing we can't risk anything in this stupid parking lot. "Take me home — take me home before I need you right here, right now."

He grabs the car door and jerks it open.

I dip down and climb into the seat, turning to watch as

he drops into the driver's side. We're both breathing a little hard as we buckle and he tears out of the lot. I make it to the outskirts of town before my hands drop to my legs, stretching in the passenger seat as I ruck up my dress slowly, but surely.

Bennett glances over at me, his eyes laser focused as his nostrils flare. "What are you doing?"

"I can't promise they'll watch us tonight, but *you* can watch me as we drive home." I lift my hips up, enthralled by the way he keeps glancing between the road and me, like he can't bear to miss it as I slide my fingers up my skirt and slip my underwear off. Bracing one foot on the dash, I spread my thighs as wide as I can, my fingers dipping into the slick already gathering at my entrance.

He curses and the car jerks. Gasping, I glance up at the empty road, toying with my clit. "Eyes ahead, alpha, or I won't let you see me come."

Bennett's strangled moan sends a shiver up my spine as I giggle and angle my hips so he can see what my hands are doing a little easier. I'm not used to this, but I roll against my hand as I draw a whimper from my own mouth, whispering, "I'm so wet, Bennett." As my fingers circle my slippery clit, my eyelids droop. "I'm so ready for you. I could come just like this, knowing you're stuck driving while I'm so fucking close."

His eyes deviate from the road for a breath, his knuckles whiting out on the steering wheel. "You're going to fuck yourself on your little fingers for me, June. I know they won't feel as good as my cock, but I'm going to get us home safely and give that to you as soon as I can."

Biting my tongue, I lower my fingers, teasing my entrance. The sound it makes is swept away in the air of the open top as I thrust two fingers into myself and whine, heat flashing on my skin. With my other hand, I throw my underwear into his lap and mutter, "There's your consolation prize."

He grunts, pressing them against the front of his trousers, where his bulge looks painful. "You're going to fucking kill me."

I laugh, tilting my head back as I gasp, fucking myself with two fingers, keeping them steady as I spasm around them. Clinging to the armrest with my other hand, I arch off the seat. "Fuck, you're right, alpha. They're not thick enough. I need you. I need your knot in and out of me, filling me and then pulling back out. I'm so empty."

Bennett's answering laugh is hoarse. "You started this, darling. Finish it before we get back home and I give you *exactly* what you just asked for."

Moaning again, I curl my fingers, but it's a poor imitation of how *good* Seth is at it. I can't reach my own g-spot and I push down in the seat, moving my fingers faster as I turn my head to stare open-mouthed at Bennett, my eyes tracking over the tension in his shoulders. Something about the way he looks near-feral makes me whine, my omega going insane as I try to play with my clit at the same time as I fuck myself.

"I keep thinking about them watching us, about me leaning back on your bed and fucking myself while you just have to sit there and take it. You couldn't even touch yourself — I'd tie you up. Would you like that?"

His eyes dart to mine as he takes a turn a little too quickly. "Would *you*? Because it sounds like you would." Bennett inhales, his eyes tracking my fingers as I try to find the right angle. "Smells like you like it. Do you want to put on shows for me, darling? Do you want to make me near-crazy by the time I can touch you properly? Because this is getting me close."

I thrust my fingers faster, riding my hand as I spread my thighs wider. After a moment, I abandon finger-fucking myself just to rub my clit as fast and hard as I can, gasping, "What if I fucked Theo in front of you?" I don't know *where* it comes from, but I can feel all my muscles tightening at the thought. Heat builds at the base of my spine, coiling in my stomach as I whimper, "What if he took me hard and fast while you had to sit there and know he was getting to fuck me and you weren't? Would you try to replace his scent with yours?"

"*Fuck*, I love it." Bennett snarls the words and then one of his hands lashes out, grabbing my chin and pushing a thumb into my mouth. "You have five minutes to come for me before we're in the driveway and I take you how *I* want you."

I cry out, my fingers slipping and sliding all over my clit, unable to get the proper pressure as I suck on his thumb, writhing against the seat as I gasp his name. The orgasm comes, but it's tepid at best, not enough to make me lose my mind.

The car bounces on gravel before skidding to a stop. My body jerks against the seat as Bennett throws his door open and stalks around, opening mine. His arms encircle me, then he picks me up like I weigh nothing, striding into the house and straight to the stairs.

I shriek, turning in his arms and pressing my face against his neck, kissing the skin there as I wiggle in his hold. "I want you to knot me," I whine as we reach the second landing. "I only want to feel you. Leave your impression on me wherever and however you can."

"That's a given, darling." He kicks a door open and I briefly see his room from the light in the hallway before he drops me onto his bed and crawls overtop of me, kissing me heatedly.

I moan into the kiss, uncaring about the dress as he pushes it up to my waist and drops between my legs, his tongue sliding over my messy thighs.

"Door open tonight, or closed?" He looks up, voice ragged.

I glance at the open door, chewing on my lip. "Closed, please."

It must take all his self-control to leave me, because he groans as he pulls away, staggering to the door only to slam it shut. Bennett pointedly turns away from it and strides back over to me, unbuttoning his shirt as he does.

"I want to fuck you in front of an audience, June."

Heat lashes up my spine as he drops on top of me, his chest exposed, his lips suctioning to my throat. His fingers work their way under me, and then he unclasps the dress, jerking the zipper down. The fabric sags, exposing my bare chest as he kisses down my pale skin, sucking and licking as he moans.

"I want everyone to see how fucking *good* I make you feel, omega."

My mind spirals as I lift my hips, letting him tug the dress off of me and throw it to the floor. *It's way too expensive to be treating it like this* — but the thought flies out of my mind as Bennett kneels between my legs, in just his slacks. His hands capture my thighs, and then he pushes them *wide*, my muscles burning as he grins up at me.

"I want everyone to see how fucking pretty, shiny, slick,

and swollen this little pink pussy gets, and know they can never, *ever* touch it."

He thrusts two fingers into me, and it makes a wet noise as he curls them. They're thicker than my own, and I push off the bed with a cry as he grunts and moves his wrist at a steady pace. Bennett leans up, kissing my stomach and sucking on my skin, his voice raw. "I need to mark you up, need everyone to know you're *mine*." The possessiveness in his tone just makes my breathing come quicker.

"I want to put little clamps on those gorgeous breasts of yours, make your skin all red for me, and then give you more and more until you can't take it." A third finger thrusts into me and I see stars, sawing in a ragged breath as he stares up at me.

"You can take my knot, but can you take my fist, darling? Do you want to try?"

I let out an unintelligible noise, clenching around him, somehow still feeling so goddamn *empty*, and I tell him as much. "God, yes." Cupping my breasts, I flutter as he starts to press a fourth finger into me, stretching me, breathing through the slight burn as I push my hips into it. It only hurts for a moment, before my body adjusts to it like it's craving it — delicious and mind-blowing as I writhe on his bed.

There's going to be a wet spot.

The sounds are obscene as he thrusts his four fingers in and out, slick dripping around his hand, making their movements easier. He fills me so fucking good that I'm not sure he'll be able to fit the last one.

But then he does.

I must black out for a moment, because suddenly his entire hand is disappearing between my thighs, *in* me as I stare down, open-mouthed. *Being an omega suddenly has its perks.* My body was *made* to take knots, to be stretched and filled and fucked, and it's proving it. Bennett's grin is wild as he looks up at me, his fingers all pinched together as he slides his fist into me before he suddenly *flexes* them, splaying them out inside me.

The movement of his wrist — the way his fingers graze every spot — the pressure explodes. I bend over, coming off the bed with a scream that shakes the house as I come. Slick gushes out around his hand as I shiver, the euphoria crashing as my body flushes and drops back to the mattress in an instant.

Bennett slides his hand out, licking it as he pushes his pants off, fisting himself with the same hand and pumping his erection as he crawls over me. "Good fucking girl. I would have *paid* to have a recording of that."

All I can muster is a moan as I tug him to my lips, kissing him roughly as I taste myself on his mouth, on his tongue. Pushing my hips up, I rub against the head of his cock. "God, please fuck me."

He cups my hip with a hand, pinning me to the bed before lining us up. Bennett's hips hold mine down as he slams into me, all the way to the hilt. Knot and all fill me as he grunts, not an ounce of resistance as he bites my lips and rocks into me. In the next breath — I'm *empty*. He pulls all the way out, knot popping as I keen and press my chest against his. It's a delicious pull, but it doesn't hurt — more a tease than anything to have the pressure I crave given and taken in a single pump of his hips.

"*More.*" I sound drunk as I writhe under him and it's *so fucking good.* Better than the heat — because I'll have memories of this as he fucks me roughly, punching his hips into mine, knotting and unknotting me with each thrust.

Bennett chuckles and the sound is so dark that my skin prickles in warning. His hand on my hip moves between us while his hips thrust steadily. It's my only warning before he pinches my clit so hard that I clench, locking his knot into place for a thrust. I squeak as he sets a brutalizing pace, pinching and toying with my clit, tugging on it as he fucks me into the bed.

"Like this, darling? Do you like it a little rough? Do you like it when it's a little too much?"

Pain and pleasure blur together as my mouth drops open, finding purchase on his throat, sucking and licking. My tongue slides against his skin as I shriek, "So good —" My words cut off as he moves faster, his hips rocking into mine, my head bouncing against the comforter.

I clench again, and then it hits me.

His knot slips in, and his thumb and forefinger pinch my clit while his knot swells, rubbing my g-spot. The orgasm is indescribable as I come apart around him, gushing and blubbering nonsense as every muscle in my body tenses before releasing.

My body gives out as Bennett comes with a roar. He fills me, breathing hard as he holds onto my hip, one elbow near my head, his upper arm tense as he stops himself from dropping on top of me.

After a moment, he moves his face, his eyes searching mine. "Fuck, are you alright?"

I moan as I kiss his jaw, slurring my words. "Keep the fucking door shut and give me another, alpha. I'm all yours tonight."

He breathes out harshly, half a laugh, half a groan as he pulls out, a mess dripping between my thighs before he thrusts right back in. Bennett cups my face as he kisses me. "You're so insatiable, and I love it."

CHAPTER TEN
JUNE

BENNETT'S ARMS are warm as they firmly hold me to his chest. Filtered sunlight drifts in through the large window on the far wall, and I feel his head buried against the nape of my neck, breathing in and out softly against my hair.

I hum, turning in his grasp so I can nuzzle into him, closing my eyes tightly as I savor the quiet. With our heads together, I feel his lips lift, a smile gracing his sleepy features as he moves his nose to my jaw, murmuring, "Morning."

"Morning." I smile back, pulling back just enough to take him in. His expression is slack, brown eyes still shut to me and the world. His dark skin is flawless, lashes brushing his cheeks as his broad nose nudges my cheek again.

I lost count how many times we fell into each other last night. The final time, his knot slipped free and I collapsed back onto a pillow, half delirious and unable to stop giggling. He'd bundled his arms around me and kissed me until sleep took us both.

And that was that.

Drowsily, I look around his room. It's painted in a lovely,

rich shade of blue that reminds me of the night sky, with little accents of yellow and orange that scream of Seth. At the thought of him, my chest aches, an emptiness in the bed that yawns open like a void.

"I should get up and brush my teeth."

Arin wants us to go to the nesting stores tomorrow, he's been talking about the plans since I moved in — but the urge to stay in bed keeps me from moving away from Bennett's grasp immediately. Still, I should be *working*, not languishing in one man's arms while I think of another —

"Give me five more minutes with you, darling." Bennett kisses me suddenly, morning breath and all. "Do you think I care" — his hands wind around my bare waist, holding me steadfast — "at *all* how your breath smells in the morning? Because, I can assure you, I don't give a single fuck about it."

"I *care*," I laugh, devolving into little snorts as he peppers my face with kisses. Sliding closer, I bend into him, trying to ignore reality creeping into my subconscious, darkening the edges of this happy moment. It slides in anyway.

"I need to finish what I was working on yesterday. If I go down now, I could have enough time to wrap it up and then look it over before we leave tomorrow. My agent called a few days ago and I'm ahead enough that I could still make my original deadline for this fall for my manuscript, but she wanted to talk seriously about rescheduling the signing dates — but that means flying *back* to the UK. There might be openings if she can —"

Bennett shuts me up with another kiss, his lips firm on mine. His hands rise, grasping my face as he sinks into me. "We've been awake for *five* minutes, June." His voice goes a little raw as he strokes my hair, leaning his head back to stare at me. "I want both your body *and* your brain in my bed — not just one."

I peek up at him, my heart resting in my throat. "Sorry."

He pecks my forehead, rubbing my cheeks with his thumbs. "Don't apologize. But you're going to give Arin a run for his money. You might even be worse than Theo and his early morning training schedule." Bennett leans in closer and his orange perfume wafts over me, settling like a blanket. "Maybe even worse than Seth, because he leaves *everything* to the last possible second, then completes it flawlessly, making it infuriating to everyone involved."

My lips twitch at the mention of Seth and I turn into Bennett's touch, pressing a kiss against the palm of his hand.

"You know how you could keep me and my brain in bed?"

"Tell me and it's yours." Bennett slides an arm down, winding it around my middle.

My tongue feels heavy, and I glance away, focused on his hand as I kiss the soft skin there, pressing my nose against his wrist where a scent gland releases concentrated orange perfume. It's not like Arin's mint — clarifying — or like Theo's — calming. Bennett is as steady as my own heartbeat, he's comforting.

"I..." The words get caught as I try to force myself to vocalize what it is.

What if he thinks you're rejecting him? What if he thinks you can't stand to spend time alone with him? What kind of person are you to want someone else while you have it all right now?

Bennett's fingers graze my cheek, holding my face to his wrist. "I'll tell you what I want."

I glance up at him, biting my tongue.

"Well, *who* I want."

Hesitating for a moment, I meet his bright look as he reaches for his phone, thrown carelessly onto the nightstand. Bennett drags it between us and types something before he flashes the screen at me.

An unsent text fills the message box of his and Seth's thread.

BENNETT

Would you be interested in coming to bed with June and I?

Simple.

"Can I send this?" He catches my eyes again, holding my gaze for a heartbeat. "Do you want him to join us?"

I nod.

He presses the send button and then chucks his phone off to the side.

"Come here." Bennett drags me back into his arms, chest to chest as he kisses my forehead and murmurs, "Stop second guessing when you want one of us — or more."

My eyes flutter shut as he dotes on me, sinking into the feeling. I never understood the way everyone spoke about the biology between alpha and omegas — but now I think I do. My body feels calmer than it ever has been when Bennett is touching me. The general anxiety, the inconsistencies in my own *brain* come to heel when his fingertips are on my skin.

His thumbs smooth out the line between my brows.

"I think any of the others would agree with me in saying that we'd love if you'd ask for *more*, June." His voice is gentle, contemplative. "But, I won't lie to you. I can't imagine what it was like to be raised by parents who said you didn't matter because you were assumed to be a beta. I can't imagine being told that you were inherently worthless unless you helped find an alpha their omega."

I open my eyes, staring up at him with my nose against his. Confusion and sadness mar his features.

"It's bizarre to me to think that the world could exist as it is, but there can only be one perfect person for every one of us. That just seems statistically ridiculous to me. What about the people that feel like soulmates, but platonically? What about the ones that are only there for a season, but very much exactly what you need in that moment of time? Are those not people you're also fated to be with? Why is there supposed to be one, singular, magical person that is a fix-all? That's a lot to saddle another person with."

My throat tightens as I stare at him.

"Besides" — Bennett hugs me, rubbing my back — "I love Seth. I've loved him for over a decade and it transformed in that time, from a friendship to something more." His eyes flicker, catching on mine.

The unspoken other half of the sentence hangs between us. My mind spins as the air thickens.

Does he want me to say it first? Or is he holding back because of me?

A loud *BANG* startles us both as the bedroom door slams open.

Seth stands in the doorway, chest heaving like he bolted from downstairs. His eyes light up when he sees us, a grin splitting his face.

"God, it smells like you two didn't sleep at *all*."

I flush, head to toe, rolling away from Bennett and covering my face.

Seth's laughter fills the room as I hear the door shut. The bed dips, and then hands tug at mine. Seth manages to pry my fingers away enough that I can see him hanging over me, beaming wildly.

"And garlic. It smells like *so* much garlic."

I shriek as I bend away from him. He's not deterred as he tries to grab my other hand from covering my mouth. His lips land on my eyes, on my nose — and as Seth pries my fingers away from my mouth, he kisses me squarely on the lips, pulling me partially into an arch off the bed.

I giggle, making a face at him. "I need to brush my *teeth* —"

"Yeah, you probably do." Seth's gaze softens as he holds onto me. "But it's not going to stop me because I love you."

The room goes quiet as we just stare at each other. My heart pounds wildly, threatening to break out of my chest. I was so *stupid* to think I could get away from any of this without falling completely head over heels for him — for them *both* —

His expression falls as he leans away, letting me sink slowly back to the bed. "I'll let you go."

"*No.*" My voice cracks as I scramble to hold onto his forearms, sitting up under him as panic lances through me.

You took too long and now he thinks you don't love him too, you fucking idiot — how are you this inept of a human —

I swivel my eyes to Bennett, so aware of his presence next to us as I fumble, kneeling on his bed. He shifts to sit up, his eyes flickering from me to Seth. Swinging my head back around, I stare at Seth, sucking in a breath.

"I should have told you *weeks* ago."

The hopeful expression that rises breaks my fucking heart. One of his hands finds mine, squeezing my fingers as he pauses, his voice shaking slightly. "June, you don't *have* to —"

Fuck it. No running.

I grab Seth by the face, uncaring as I lunge forward, nearly knocking him off the bed as I kiss him hard, whispering against his lips. "I love you too."

His arms wrap around me as he suddenly bends us forward, pinning me to the bed in one movement as he presses between my legs, his voice raw as he kisses me back. "Thank *fuck*."

I'm not made of flesh and bone — my entire body is anxious heartbeats and butterflies as Seth pulls his head back, his brown eyes roving over me, like he's questioning that this is really happening. I reach up, touching his chest, palm to the skin over his heart.

"I *love* you, Seth."

He exhales sharply, dropping his forehead to mine as his hands shake, grasping my waist. "I love you." Seth kisses me again and the scent of fudge encircles me. "I *love* you, June. You don't know how many times I've almost fucking said it."

His smile shatters me as I lean up with him, turning to stare at Bennett.

The alpha in the room looks between us, his eyes soft, full of unsaid emotion. They're shiny when he focuses on me. I reach out, one hand on Seth's chest, the other touching Bennett's shoulder.

My voice is softer, but infinitely stronger than before.

"I love you, Bennett."

He surges forward, grasping my face and staring at me with a surety that I can't fully deserve.

"I not only love you, Juniper Walden, but I am *in* love with you. I am in love with you in the exact same way that I am in love with Seth." His thumb scores over my jaw. "If you question everything else in your life, please never question that."

Seth's arms tighten around me from behind, his lips against my head. "She won't."

My lips tremble. "If I ever do, I have two people who will remind me."

"Damn right." Seth kisses the back of my neck, then the side of my throat, his hands sliding down until they find my bare hips. I sink back against him, suddenly cognizant that Bennett and I are still fully naked from last night, muscles happily aching. I can't stop myself from resting against Seth as Bennett moves forward, caging me against the beta, his hands moving to the fronts of my thighs as I kneel on the bed.

He kisses me first, then pulls back with a breath to turn his head and kiss Seth behind me.

Stuck between them, I've never felt safer, or more *loved*. I tilt my head, kissing Bennett's throat as I reach behind me to rub Seth's side, whispering. "I need you both. Right now."

Seth's hands coast up, cupping my breasts as Bennett's head drops to lavish them with kisses. Sparks echo behind each touch, until I gasp when he sucks on one nipple, then the other, gazing up at us both.

"How, darling?"

The question should give me pause, but I'm speaking before I fully wrap my head around it. "In me at the same time, filling me. I want you both feeling me and each other."

"*Fuck.*" Seth mutters the curse as he nips at my jaw, making a shiver crawl up my spine as he presses closer to me from behind. "Sweet girl, you're all *ours*," he breathes out, grinding against me as he groans. "I wish I was an alpha, so I could sink my teeth into you and make sure everyone else knew that you were *mine* from one glance." His hands squeeze my chest again and I press into his touch, my breathing growing labored.

"But I can bite you."

He pauses behind me, his breath hot on my skin as he grabs a handful of my hair and jerks my head so we can gaze at each other.

I stare at him, feeling Bennett's teeth drag over my nipple. "I love you, Seth Harding" — licking my lips, I stare at the beta — "and I want everyone to know it too. Can I bond you? Can I mark you as mine?"

He curses under his breath again, and it's the only warning I get before he kisses me roughly, holding my head by my hair as he grinds up against me. "*Yes*, June."

I lose myself in the sensation of his lips, the feeling of his hardness through his sweats, bare chest against his arm as Bennett's hands drop from roving over my skin. They land on my thighs as he then pulls them wider, making me splay out in a kneel as one hand snakes between them, teasing and touching.

"You're so fucking slick for us, omega. You'll take us both so well."

I whine, gasping as I pull away from Seth's lips for a moment. Bennett helps me turn until my back is resting against his chest, in his lap with my legs spread out, thighs parted as his cock rests against me. Seth shuffles back, only enough to shed himself of his clothes as he stares, watching Bennett's hips roll up, teasing my entrance each time.

"You're going to take us both while I bite you, darling?" Bennett's voice drips into my ear as he nips at my earlobe, nudging at me. "Seth can put me in you."

A shiver crawls up my spine as I nod.

Seth jerks forward, naked and reaching for Bennett, wrapping a hand around him and pushing the head of his cock into me. Biting my lip, I throw my head back, bracing against Bennett as I writhe, the fullness making me clench down as he guides his hips up, nudging into me as Seth watches. Seth's fingers reach between my thighs, holding one open to keep me splayed out as he circles my clit. Finally, I relax, panting out softly as Bennett sinks in, his knot nudging against me.

"That's a good girl." Bennett kisses my throat. "Stay relaxed, let your beta join me in that sweet tight cunt."

Seth whimpers, moving closer until he's crowding us, hovering over me as he slides his hand over me, feeling where Bennett and I are joined. I'm so wound up, I feel the way slick drips down my thighs and he gathers it, using it as lube on himself as he presses the head of his dick against my entrance, over Bennett's.

"I'll be so gentle for you." Seth leans in, kissing me as a distraction. He pushes his hips forward. "Focus on me, baby, focus on how good it's going to fucking feel to have both Bennett and I filling you."

I try to hold myself back from thrashing from the pleasure, the stretch taking the air out of my lungs as I dig my nails into Bennett's arm banded around my middle. The alpha behind me hums, staying perfectly still as he whispers filth to both of us. "You should see yourself, June. He's just fucking slipping right into you, filling you up, but you can take it, can't you? I lost count how many times I knotted her sweet pussy last night, Seth, it was over and *over* again. She even took my fist — so I know she can take us both."

Seth's hips punch forward and I scream as his lips clamp down on mine, swallowing the noise as he kisses me hungrily, fisting my hair in his hand again, his voice raw. "Adjust to us, baby, and then tell us when we can make you feel as good as you're making us feel."

Breathing hard, I try to focus on unclenching my muscles, held up between them. At some point it goes from overly full to a mind-numbing sense that I need to *feel*. More, both of them, movement, friction — *something*. My hips rock down and I make us all suck in breath as I clench on them both, experimentally, letting out a keening moan.

Bennett kisses my throat, just over my hammering pulse. "She's ready. Seth, fuck her."

"Yes, alpha." His words melt me as he hooks my legs over his arms, spreading me as wide as I can go as he pulls out and thrusts back in. The movement rocks Bennett and I — and the sensation of fullness goes from blinding to heady craving. Every time Seth pulls out, Bennett punches up, almost filling me with his knot, stretching me impossibly wider as I gasp and fist Seth's hair in one hand, my nails breaking the skin of Bennett's arm.

"*God,* I love feeling you both." Seth's voice sounds like it's coming from a fishbowl as my mind focuses on the point of sheer pleasure between all three of us.

Rocking between them, I buck into the movement as much as I can, pliant and needy and overwhelmed. My mouth waters and Bennett's tongue roves over my jugular. I drag Seth's head closer, mirroring the movement on his throat, brushing up against his existing silver bond mark, already faded from Bennett's bite years ago. The raised skin runs over my tongue, and I nudge it as my teeth scrape over the skin just next to it.

There isn't much information in the world about betas and bonds. It's generally understood that it's a weaker connection than what forges between an alpha and an omega — but it's *instinctual* how much I want to sink myself into him, to make him bear my mark like he already shows off Bennett's.

He's fucking *mine.*

I bare my teeth, and feel Seth's cock twitch inside me just as I rear back, striking at his throat, nudging up against his existing mark as I break skin. Seth lets out a little howl, and his hips kick as he does, clinging to my legs as Bennett's snarl reaches us both.

"I'm going to make sure that if anyone looks at either one of you, they'll know without a shadow of a doubt that you both belong to *me.*" He strikes at my neck, unexpectedly sinking his teeth into my jugular at the same place.

I come with a scream, mouth against Seth's throat as I convulse around them both — but I'm not alone in the feeling. A rush of emotions hit me in the same moment, my chest exploding with the orgasm and the unshakable gravity of both bonds locking into my heart at the same time.

Three heartbeats echo — mine, with two others, like I'm listening to everything in stereo. I'm no longer *alone* in myself as a flood of emotions drags me under — pure love shining through the brightest. The power of the bond stops my breath as I try to reconcile the feeling, my body shaking between them.

"Breathe, darling, breathe." Bennett's voice pulls me back, his lips moving over my throat, licking and sucking the wound he just gave me.

I gasp, swearing I taste oranges and chocolate as I look up at Seth, finding him staring at me wide-eyed and in awe as he touches his chest.

"God... I can..." Tears well as his lips part, his fingers

pressing into his breastbone, over his heart. "I can *feel* you here, baby."

Bennett is the only thing holding me up, strong and solid as I gasp over and over again, my body coming down from the orgasm while adjusting to the feeling of the bond. It feels like a taut string, leading both to the beta in front of me and the alpha behind me, golden — vibrant — tying us together, binding the three of us in ways I don't even have the words to describe.

Seth touches my cheek as he slips out of me, kissing me slowly, the blood on his neck pooling as he does. Bennett presses us all closer, and the second a flare of doubt ignites in my mind, both of them growl. As Bennett stiffens, Seth grabs my chin roughly. "Don't you fucking dare doubt that I want this, want *you*. For *life*."

My throat closes as I stare at him, touching his chest, one hand moving behind me to grab at Bennett's head and pull him to the side so I can kiss him messily while I draw Seth into it. The kiss is a confusion of tongues, lip, teeth — three breathes intermingling — but it's *us*.

"You're both mine." I nip at Bennett's lower lip, catching it and breaking skin. The bond flares even brighter between the three of us as I hold onto them both. My alpha brushes his nose against mine, flooding the bond with certainty and affection.

"And you're ours," Seth murmurs in agreement, crowding closer, joining Bennett in feeding the bond with pure adoration.

I give it right back to them.

CHAPTER ELEVEN

JUNE

My hair is getting really long.

I didn't have time to get it cut before I left for London, and between the heat and the move, it's down to my collarbone, in wispy waves of auburn. I push my fingers through it, trying to make it look like something instead of limp and frizzy, fidgeting as I pull it all to the side, exposing the silver bond mark at the junction of my neck and shoulder.

It thrums when my fingers glide over it, like a second and third heartbeat.

Seth's impatience sings through the bond, quickly followed by Bennett's amusement.

It's a foreign feeling, having such an unobscured idea of what both of them are experiencing at any moment, but I love it. Unabashedly — I can't get enough of feeling both of them inside my chest, as clear as I feel my own emotions.

We only dampened it slightly this morning after I finally crawled out of bed from between them. I don't think Bennett meant to keep me in his room for another twenty-four hours, but after the bonding, it was like I couldn't settle unless my lips and hands were on them both. I had to lick Seth's neck and shoulders, I had to feel Bennett's body against mine, his knot in me while Seth pressed into him from behind. We were limbs, raw emotions, and endless desire.

Maybe with enough time I can understand every little nuance of the connection, but for now, it just feels like I'm constantly being wrapped in their arms.

I'll never be alone again.

Turning my head, I eye the bathroom door one more time. It took a lot to leave them, but I knew Arin wanted me to do this — to go into New York City with every one of them and shop for the nest downstairs that they've given to me. And I should feel *happy* and grateful and some level of excitement.

Should.

Sweeping my hair back down, I leave it pushed to one side and step out of my bathroom, dressed warmly for the still-cool spring weather. My hands find my phone, leaving everything else except it and my ID in my room — I don't really *need* anything when I'm with them all, and my brain doesn't know how to function this way.

I also don't know how Arin and Theo will react to the giant fucking bite on my throat.

My hand rises, touching it, and a spark of pleasure hums through my skin. Seth and Bennett echo in my chest, joy and love, patience and impatience. Shoving my feet into my boots, I reach for the door, lighting up when I see Seth leaning against the wall just outside.

Rushing toward him, I wrap my arms around his torso, kissing his throat again, even though it's only been two hours at most since I was underneath him, squirming and gasping. My tongue nudges the fresh golden bite on his throat, soothing it as he cups the back of my head with a hand. I like seeing my bite next to Bennett's — an alpha's bite scars silver, an omega's golden — perfect compliments to each other on my beta's tanned skin.

"Keep doing that and we won't make it downstairs, baby."

Bennett said that bond marks heal unexplainably quickly, especially when constantly tended. I've been using that as an excuse to cling to him and I press an extra kiss to Seth's throat, my nose nudging his skin as I breathe in, humming softly.

"Sorry."

Seth nudges me back until I'm the one against the wall, then pulls my head up and kisses me softly, sweetly, his lips twitching against mine. "Don't apologize. It's cute when you're territorial and loving."

I give him a look before dragging him back to me, assaulting the mark on his neck and making his knees falter. Seth falls forward, a hand on the wall by me as he groans, lust and heat flashing over the bond.

He grunts as I suck on it. "Arin will *kill* me if we don't go downstairs."

Flashing him a smile, I grab onto his free hand and pull away, licking my lips. "I won't let him. You're mine now."

His lips graze over my knuckles as he lifts my hand to his face, mumbling against my skin. "Bennett's downstairs with them, since he's the only one not totally chewed up."

Save for his lip. That didn't swell for very long, though. There's two little golden marks where my teeth broke skin, only visible if you pull his lip down.

My eyes meet Seth's as he tilts his head at me. "Want to go show them you're not running?"

I smile back, my heart aching as I nod. He tugs me away from the wall and to the stairs, winding down them with me as our shoulders brush, fingers intertwining. My hand clutches his a little tighter, my voice soft as I chew on my tongue. "What if they're mad?"

"They won't be." Seth stops us, squeezing my hand tightly and looking at me seriously, repeating the words, softer this time. "They won't be mad, baby. I love you."

Sucking in a breath, I close my eyes before I nod and whisper back. "I love you."

Anxiety wraps itself around me, familiar but unwelcome as I let him tug me down the last few stairs. My eyes find Arin first, lingering near the front door, entranced in a conversation with Theo. I move toward Bennett instinctively, wrapping my arms around his neck and leaning into him with a little sigh, trying to gather myself before I confront the two other alphas in the room.

I'm not worried about the way I smell like Bennett and Seth — there is no denying that I've spent time with them both. That's ebbed — it's the worry that somehow, I've done this wrong. *Should I have bonded Arin first? Should I have proven that Theo and I are better than we were in London and let him bite me?*

Bennett kisses the side of my temple, muttering in my ear. "I prefer you in dresses." His hands slide down my sweater, cupping my hips in the jeans I threw on. "But these make me want to take you back upstairs."

I flush, my mind pulled back to him.

Bennett's lips twitch, his nose brushing mine. "Oh, I felt you toying with our poor beta upstairs. Sucking on his mark?" His voice lowers to a growl, speaking directly into my ear. "Naughty, Juniper. Almost as naughty as you in a dress, covered in flour, pushing it up your thighs and fucking your-self on your fingers —"

I shove his chest, feeling my cheeks flame as I jerk back, clearing my throat.

He laughs loudly as I try to stop the flustered way my perfume blooms in the foyer. It fills the air with honey and tea and I glance over at Arin and Theo, pushing my hair back without thinking.

Arin's eyes, dark and hungry, find mine before he stops mid-sentence with Theo — both their gazes landing on my exposed neck. My heartbeat picks up, reverberating in my ears as I stand still, Bennett at my back providing warmth and strength to retreat to — but I don't need it.

Theo's face *lights* up. He takes a step forward, then another, before he darts across the foyer to me, shoving my hair entirely out of the way and bending down to look at the bite for himself, his voice hoarse. "You..." He straightens, looking behind me at Seth and Bennett.

I bite my lip, tilting my chin up to stare at Theo, so tall and broad and strong. His blond hair has grown out, almost coming to his ears, and as I reach up to card my fingers through it, his thumb presses against the raw mark on my throat, making me jolt into his chest.

"I love them, I..." I gasp the words, looking behind Theo at Arin, trying to make sure they both hear me. "I wanted everyone to know that I had a pack."

Theo pulls me closer, his arms wrapping around me in a tight hug, crushing me for a moment as he whispers, "You *do*, June. You do have us. I'm so happy, I'm jealous, and it's going to take everything in my power not to drag you into my room and —"

I flush again, pressing my lips against his slightly stubbled jaw as I giggle at the feeling of him lifting me, spinning me in a little circle. When he puts me back down, my eyes find Arin, nervous as he smiles gently.

"I see you made sure you had your claim to Seth, too."

Seth grins as he strides toward the front door confidently, baring the mark on his throat proudly. "She could chew me up and spit me out and I'd say thank you."

"Me too," Theo mutters in my ear, nipping at the other side of my throat, making me shiver.

"*Theo.*" Arin says the other alpha's name and I squirm a little, trying to fight my smile.

Theo ignores him, grabbing my chin and kissing me. He devours my mouth, making my brain blank as his lips and teeth tug at my lips. "I wanna drag you into my room and push you up against the window so you can look at the pretty lake while I fill you over and over again until your legs give out. Then I'll just hold you up and do it again because I like when you smell like them, but I love it when you only smell like *me*."

A whimper drags itself out of my throat as my knees wobble. *Yes*, a *thousand* times yes — but instead of giving in, I gasp out, "You're so fucking possessive."

"You love it."

I do, and I don't even have to say the words. Theo eyes me knowingly as he lets me go. Arin holds out a hand to me, his eyes roving over my outfit, coming to rest again on my throat. "We should leave now if we want to finish our errands in the city before it's too late."

Stepping closer, I reach for his hand, but it evades mine. His fingers flick my hair back, dragging over the bare side of my neck, collaring it and squeezing just slightly, cutting airflow for the briefest of seconds. His voice is gentle, but a possessive growl hums just underneath. "You look so pretty with that bite on you, omega."

I stare up at him, my lips parting. "You're not upset?"

Arin's eyes flash as he shakes his head, smiling. "I would never be upset about this. I'm more upset Bennett took the side I wanted. But I'm already considering other places."

My heart stops, unable to comprehend his words as he drags me outside, the rest of them following us.

I MET Charles the day the movers arrived with my things from Virginia. The nice beta is easily twenty-five years senior to Arin, and is the one who drives us to a small airfield not ten minutes away from the pack house.

The private flight barely took an hour to get us from Rochester to New York City.

Clutching Theo's hand, I glance out the windows of the town car that picked us up, taking in the busy streets, flashing lights, and constant noise. His other hand swallows mine, soothing my white knuckles as I suck in little breath after little breath, anxiety overtaking me.

Across from us, Bennett and Seth shoot me worrying glances, sending as much calm and reassurance as they can through the bond, but it all bounces off the wall of panic like paper planes, crumpled and weak.

The car slows as we near Fifth Avenue and Theo pulls me into his side, forcing me to press my nose against his chest.

"Shh" — he strokes my hair — "the stores will be quieter." His chest vibrates as he growls aloud to Arin. "I *told* you we shouldn't have come into the city — what the *fuck* were you thinking —"

I fight away from his chest, flinching away from the way he's snarling at Arin, turning to shoot our prime a wide-eyed look. "I'm okay."

Arin's expression shatters. "We can just go home, I'm sorry, I didn't realize it would be this distressing —"

"No, we're here." I glance at the door, trying to steel myself. In the process, I feel almost a wall come down, cutting off the support and dimming the emotions down the bond from both Seth and Bennett. It's isolating, but it shoves the shaking away — the same process I used to do to get through painful dinners with my parents or meetings with my publishing team.

Suppress it. It's fine. I can be fucking *normal* for one second.

"Let's go in."

Theo gets out first, and his bulk helps shield me from the chaos of the street as I slide out of the car, pressing against his chest. People walk quickly, split in two different directions as they move with the hustle and bustle. His hand curls around my hip, turning me toward the white brick storefront the car is idling in front of.

The sign above the awning reads *RETREAT* in white neon script, and I stay plastered to him as he splits the flow of the people walking, charging directly through them and bringing me with him to the door of the nesting store.

Bennett, Seth, and Arin follow behind us, with Seth jogging to join Theo and I, grabbing my hand just to squeeze it.

"This looks too fancy." I mutter the words as we step

inside, the noise of the city quieting the moment the door clicks shut.

Theo looks down at me, scowling. "Nothing is too much for you."

I scowl right back, rearing up to glare at him. "Theo —"

"No." He bends down, getting in my face. "You're going to pick out anything you want and not question it when I buy it all for you."

I bite my tongue to hold off my snarky response as Seth tugs me away, tension sparking and fizzling out in the same moment between Theo and I.

"I think we've had enough of alphas." Seth guides me over to a random display of flameless candles, and his scent comes off him in waves. I swear it's more powerful since I bit him, the fudge melting on my tongue as he picks up a box and waves it at me. "I *do* agree with him, you should grab what you want while we're here."

Inhaling his perfume, I let it carry away the mixed emotions, turning to focus on the candle he's holding.

"Nothing has a price, Seth."

"I know." His lip twitches. "If you start to feel overwhelmed, we'll go home. Bennett *did* try to talk Arin out of a trip here, but he's a little narrow-sighted sometimes. Arin just wants you to have whatever you need, baby."

Letting out a breath, I lean into him, muttering against his shoulder. "Fucking alphas."

He ruffles my hair. "Thank god I'm not one, right?"

Snorting, I kiss his shoulder before pulling away, noticing a worker as she strides toward us, her eyes brightening.

"Hi!" She slows to a stop, wringing her hands together, brown hair swept back in a sleek ponytail as her eyes dart to my neck, then Seth next to me. "Welcome to Retreat!" She hesitates, then steps a little closer, her voice lowering. "I'm sorry, my boss said that someone reserved the store for a new omega, but I didn't know it was *you*." She squeaks. "I literally have my paperback of *The Pack and I* in my bag to read at lunch. Will you sign it? Please?"

All the anxiety in my body gets shoved away as I smile at her, practiced and gentle. "Of course. I don't mind at all."

She gives me a wide-eyed look before turning sharply, then whirling back, blurting out, "Please look around and let me know if you or your pack need anything!" With that, she's gone.

My smile falls slightly, barely masking my discomfort as I suck in a little breath, reminding myself to look like I'm enjoying myself.

Seth's hand slides over my side, and warmth presses against the wall blocking off the bond. I lower it just enough to feel Bennett's pride in me as Seth leans in, whispering, "Go shop. The store is yours for the afternoon."

I go into a meditative state as I step over to a display of blankets. It almost reminds me of writing — of sinking into a scene and just knowing what the words will be next, even if I've not fully planned it out yet. Wandering in circles, I touch samples and displays, picking things up when I'm drawn to them, but putting a lot back. The lack of price tags is too strange. How can I buy anything if I don't know if it's too expensive?

People flicker around me, but all on the cusp of my vision, like they're all hesitant to break the omega haze over me. The only thing that startles me is when the worker returns, paperback to her chest. I can see the cover is creased, the spine folded multiple times as she gives me a hesitant smile.

"Sorry it's kind of beat-up, it's my third time reading it and I dropped it on the train a few times."

I take it and a pen from her, running my fingers over the illustration on the front. I never expected it to become my most popular — but Janet reminded me on the call a couple days ago that she always believed in my stories — even if it took a few years for others to find their love for them too. My heart warms as I stare at the book that got me out of my parents' house, into my own apartment, into a career that, for all its pitfalls, fills me with joy even on the bad days.

"What's your name?"

The worker grins at me, stuttering, "L-Libby."

I flip the cover open and sign my name under the title, adding *LIBBY, FIND YOUR HAPPINESS* to the top with a flourish. Handing both the book and pen back to Libby, I glance around the store, offering softly, "I'm sure this won't be my last time at Retreat, if you'd ever like the other books signed."

She nods rapidly, her eyes comically round. "Yes! I mean — yes, absolutely. I had tickets for your NYC stop for the last book, but I couldn't make it. I know you had to cancel the UK dates, but I'm so excited that I even get to *meet* you. I just love the story. I love that Katie found her pack *and* her happiness in it. It means a lot. It makes me remember not to take things for granted, to say *yes* more."

I feel a presence at my back and I lean into it, letting Theo's soft perfume curl around me as I nod at Libby. "You should say yes more — let yourself have the good, unexpected experiences."

Her eyes brighten, but then they dart behind me. Libby

clutches her book to her chest. "Please flag me down if there's anything you need." She runs off before I can thank her just as Theo's hand curls protectively around my hip, fingers spanning across to the curve of my ass.

He bends down, kissing my head. "Sound advice." Theo nudges my hair with his nose. "Arin thought we could go get food next, but it's your choice if you're hungry after we finish here." His voice grows a little darker, fingers tightening, sending a jolt of dangerous pleasure through me. "You haven't picked out much, do you not like this store, princess?"

My eyes flicker around the soft colors, the fabrics that fit with what seems *right* for my nest — but I can't stop thinking about the fact that everyone's focus is on *me*, waiting for *my* choice. I fidget as I stare at a wedge-shaped body pillow, made out of a cool fabric for heats, but supportive for *other* activities.

"I don't know how to be an omega," I blurt out. "I don't deserve all this special attention, time, or energy. I should be more normal. I shouldn't panic because we're in a busy city, especially not since I have the *entire* store to ourselves. I'm *broken*."

I freeze, unable to believe the words hanging in the air came out of *me*.

Theo's voice is low, barely audible as he turns me by the shoulders, bending to look at me, his face against mine. "Yeah?"

I blink up at him, licking my suddenly dry lips. "Yes?"

His eyes drag over me, lingering on my hips, then my chest, then my neck. Each look feels like a caress, a groping grab that sets my skin on fire. This isn't Bennett or Arin —

this is *Theo*, and the unrestrained lust in his gaze makes me squirm.

"What are you doing?" I hiss as he pulls me closer.

"I was trying to figure out what part of you doesn't deserve this." His nose touches mine, the soft touch juxtaposed with a growl. "I *know* it's not your throat, with that pretty bond mark on it now, connecting you to those two assholes over there." He throws a glance to Bennett and Seth, engrossed in a display of cooling sheets meant for nest mattresses.

Theo's eyes snare mine, the blue *dark*.

"And it's not your pretty little pussy that takes my knot so fucking well."

It's *embarrassing* how quickly my heart rate rises, my perfume blooming.

"*Theo*."

He hums, shaking his head as he eyes me. "No, I don't know *what* kind of bullshit rules you think you're not adhering to, and frankly, I don't give a fuck about them." He pauses, sucking in a breath. "Because I spent *years* telling myself I could fold laundry to satisfy the *need* in me to care for someone, instead of accepting that I needed someone in my life to throw my entire fucking weight and love into — so I don't really like it when you tell me you think you don't deserve all of me, all of my *alpha* that wants to satisfy you. Whether satisfying you means buying a goddamn blanket or burying my cock in your cunt."

I fluster, my hands grabbing onto his biceps as he drags me closer, whispering against my lips.

"Because I sure as shit didn't spend your entire heat fucking you out of the kindness of my own heart. You're *it* for me, June. You're *mine*. My *omega*." He snarls the words, kissing me heatedly and taking my breath away as he nips at my lips. "Hearing all this kind of makes me want to punish you, make you see reason and sense while you come so hard you can't function."

My breathing is ragged when he pulls his lips away from mine. Theo glances around the store, his nostrils flaring.

"This is no longer an optional trip, princess. You're going to pick up every goddamn thing you like in this store, then we're going to the next one and we're doing the same, and I'm going to feed you while the rest of the pack ignores the fact that you're going to be constantly squirming closer to me, wishing I'd touch you. You say you don't know how to be an omega? Fine, I'll make you accept the spoiling, the court-ing, the presents, *and* whatever else I feel like giving you. If that's my fucking knot in public at the dinner table, so be it."

My lips part in surprise, and his eyes zero in on my tongue.

"And maybe after that, I won't even make you come. I'll just let you go back to Bennett and Seth's bed, with the explicit instructions that neither of them ease the ache between your legs that makes you want *me*."

He leans closer, brushing a kiss along my flushed skin. "So pick out some fucking blankets, omega, because you want to do a good job for me and get a reward later instead of being punished, don't you?"

"Yes, alpha." My hindbrain *buzzes* as I nod, my eyes locked on him as he lets me go.

"And June?"

I stare at him, my heart in my throat as he crosses his arms over his wide chest.

"If you question *one more time* if you deserve all of this, I'll let Arin turn your ass so red you can't sit for a week. And I'll enjoy choking my cock in my fist to the sight of him doing it."

CHAPTER TWELVE

JUNE

THEO'S WORDS have echoed in my mind for *two* days.

And it's my own damn fault that I didn't get to reap all the rewards and promises he made.

I'd taken another walk around *RETREAT* like a good little omega, and this time I'd actually *looked* at all the items, instead of being skeptical about their cost. Pointing out the few I wanted was a little painful, but I forced myself to walk away when it was time to pay, instead letting Arin lay down a black card and sinking into Seth's chest.

Then we did it all over again in the next store.

Theo's eyes tracked my every movement, making the hair raise on my arms, but by the time we got to dinner, the crash hit me. All the anxiety and forced pleasantries hit me like a tidal wave, dragging me into exhaustion. One second I was leaning on Bennett's shoulder at the dinner table, and the next I was cradled in Theo's arms as he carried me from the town car to the plane, buckling me into a seat.

I'd whined and grabbed his hand so he would sit next to

me, but I'd fallen back asleep curled up against his side, my face buried in his shirt that smelled like a summer rainstorm.

I would give anything to go back to two days ago.

My phone trills next to me again. I don't know how she managed to do it, but muting my mother's texts to me doesn't work anymore. The notifications still come through — the messages lighting up my screen as I stare at my laptop, sitting in the office that I've still yet to decorate that Bennett gifted to me. Impermanence staring back at me.

This draft was *almost* there a month ago. I made it past the sixty percent mark, where the middle was dragging both me and the pacing down. But then I had to leave it — to go to London, only to be surprised by the heat, my own designation, and everything else falling apart around me. Now I just feel like I'm spinning my wheels when I stare at the screen, trying to reconcile the differences in my life.

There's always one constant though.

DO NOT ANSWER

> Juniper, you cannot keep ignoring me.

DO NOT ANSWER

> Juniper Walden, when I address you, I expect a response. I raised you better than this. Are you still in London? We've lost touch with the alpha that was willing to get you.

DO NOT ANSWER

> If you stayed with that pack during your heat, I'll never forgive you.

DO NOT ANSWER

> You're an embarrassment. You're not even the daughter I love anymore.

I glance away from the messages, one after another, bile rising in my throat as I blink rapidly at the email Janet sent this morning. It was so positive. I'm *on pace* for the deadline — but on pace is practically behind, because I need to be *ahead* of all of this. It reads almost cajoling. On pace isn't good enough, because what if I want to spend more time on one part and I don't have a cushion built in? Why can't I do literally anything right? I should have known that something was wrong before London. I should be able to adjust to everything faster, be *better* — not a fucking disappointment —

DO NOT ANSWER lights up the screen, this time as a phone call.

I shove my hands through my hair again, getting my fingers caught on the tangles as I knock my phone to the very edge of the desk. It's not a good day to work — but if I want to get ahead, I need to. I *have* to push myself, despite the clawing feeling in my stomach, and growing headache from not eating this morning. I have to get words down.

Forcing everything else aside, I bend my head and focus on the manuscript, skimming the paragraph I just wrote and making changes. It's not where I want it. And it's just too fucking late to delete it all and rewrite.

I have to make this book good because if my next release is a disappointment after *everything* else that's happened, my career will be over before it's even begun.

I have to be perfect.

My phone goes silent as I sink into typing, forcing myself to work on paragraph after paragraph. Line by line, I manage to make it three more pages before my phone screen lights up again.

DO NOT ANSWER

Your apartment is empty? Where are you,
Juniper. This is the last time I ask before I
report you as a missing omega and get the
authorities involved.

Fear, deep and unsettling, strikes through me. I reach for my phone just as another call comes through. Sucking in a breath, I clutch it in a shaking hand.

What's one more crisis?

I answer it.

"Hi, Mom."

"Juniper Walden!" Her voice is sharp, shrill and piercing. "I'm here in front of your apartment building and the landlord said you don't even *live* here anymore?"

I stare straight ahead, my eyes tracking the water lapping on the lakeshore just outside. I could probably make it waist deep before one of my alphas rushed out and stopped me from drowning myself to avoid this conversation.

"I moved."

"You —" My mother cuts herself off, making a strangled noise. "You're back *home* and you didn't *stop by*? You didn't tell your father and I you were back in America. We *need* you to come home so we can start the process of setting you up with a suitable alpha —"

"No."

She stops mid-sentence.

"This is *not* the time, Juniper. God help me, do not start in on your nonsense about how packs are natural. Do *not* tell me you spent your heat in London with whatever disgusting men took one look at you — my sweet, innocent daughter — and just took advantage of you."

I flinch, dragging my eyes away from the water. "They

made me feel safe." My voice is barely a whisper, and I try to find the strength to fight back, to do *something*, but I choke.

"Is that some kind of code for something?" She spits the words out, then laughs. "Never mind, I don't want to know. Where are you? Your father will come get you." My father — always doing my mother's bidding, even in the most inopportune or hare-brained moments — of course she'd push this task off on him instead of just confronting me herself.

Running my tongue over my teeth, I make a fist with my free hand, trying to stop it from shaking. "I'm in Rochester, New York, in my new house." When she doesn't speak, I add, "With my pack."

It takes long enough for her to respond that I think maybe the call disconnected, or she hung up — but there's not a chance in hell she'd give up the fact she managed to get me on the phone after hundreds of messages in the span of a month.

"Your pack." She clears her throat, half-strangled. "Let me make sure I'm understanding you correctly. You stayed with those men. You let them defile you? You do realize that you're no better than a common whore now? What did I do to make my own daughter hate me so much? What misstep did I make in raising you? Tell me, please, because we did so much to make you be successful, we paid for your schooling, we fed, clothed, and housed you — we made sure you could have friends in the club, we told everyone that it didn't matter to us when we thought you were just a beta."

Each sentence chips away at me, a tiny chisel taking layers off.

"You met them in London only a *month* ago. I *told* you that we could send someone. We *had* an alpha who reached out to us there and said he would take you. We know a *very* nice boy here who was so looking forward to meeting you —"

"Stop," I cut her off, my throat working. "I don't hate you — I've never hated you and Dad, but you don't — you *can't* —" Closing my eyes, I try to make the words come out, but it's useless. I'm crumbling and I'm not even face to face with her.

"This is *it*. Your father and I are coming up there."

"Mom —"

"*No,* Juniper," she snarls and I flinch as I clutch my phone against my ear.

"This is enough. You've acted out enough. I should have known from the beginning you were an omega, because this is just another in a *long* series of times you've completely disregarded how we've raised you to act better, ignoring what's right and what's the proper way to conduct yourself. This is *ridiculous*. I'm so disappointed that you've compromised yourself and put this meeting at risk with an alpha *right* for you. You're being too emotional right now, you're overreacting. We'll be there by the weekend. And I want us to have dinner without... these distractions you've suddenly saddled yourself with. We'll figure out something. God can only hope that the alpha we picked might be kind enough to overlook all this."

This isn't happening.

"You can't —"

"I will see you Saturday, Juniper. Please stop talking before you upset me even more." Her words echo as the call goes quiet, and when I finally pull the phone back, I look down at the screen to see that she *hung up on me*.

My hand shakes as I stare at the messages, the end call screen closing just to reopen the litany of texts she's sent me in the last thirty days. I've done my *best* to ignore them. I was *so* fucking good at pretending they didn't exist. I was *so* good at acting like nothing was wrong, but now the nausea and panic rises in my body, overwhelming and horrifying. I can feel Bennett's spark of worry, an echo of alarm from Seth through our bond as I totally fucking *unravel*.

Sucking in a breath, I let out a scream that nearly rattles the greenhouse windows, before I reel my arm back and throw my phone. I don't *care* where it lands — I don't *care* anymore because this is all over. I should have known this would happen. I can't have anything good. I can't be *happy*.

I shove away from my desk.

She wants to see reactive? She wants me angry and emotional?

I'll give it to her.

Throwing open my office door, I charge out, nearly running straight into Seth as he exits his office quickly, reaching for me. "What's wrong? What's going on? Junie?"

I dodge him, charging down the hallway and into the living room. Theo jerks up from his position on the couch at the sight of me, his eyes widening.

"What the fuck is going on?"

Ignoring them both, I make it through the foyer and stalk through the archway, shoving Arin's office door open. Bennett jumps, halfway to the door with a hand on his chest. Fury, devastation, and terror fight each other, my emotions welling the second I see Arin behind his desk. His black hair is messy, glasses perched on his nose.

"I need you to bite me, right *now*." The words come out broken, pleading as I rush into the room, bypassing Bennett and staring at our prime instead. "I need you to claim me because you're the prime in this stupid pack and if you don't they're going to *take* me away and I don't *want* to leave." My voice cracks, and the fury bubbles into blubbering tears as my shoulders start to shake.

"I don't want to go, please don't let them take me. Please don't let them put me with someone I don't know and make me have kids and move back to Virginia. Because they won't let me keep writing. They won't let me keep doing what I love. They already tried it once and that's why I moved out. But if I have to marry whoever they want me to, he's probably not going to let me either, and I'll be *trapped* —"

"*June.*" Bennett's voice cracks and when I feel his hand on my shoulder, it completely breaks me.

Putting my head in my hands, I sob, shaking in the middle of the room like a leaf. Maybe she's been right all along. Maybe I'm just a stupid omega, too blinded by my emotions to make rational decisions about my own life. Maybe I'm just a whore, thinking it's right to want all these men in my life. Maybe I'm destined to never have what I want because it's not what I *need*.

But for the first time in my life, I felt like I could finally have it *all* and now it's all going to be taken away. A bond with Bennett won't mean a single fucking thing to my mother — she'll rip me away faster than I could even fight back, and bonds can be broken if the next alpha is cruel enough to do it.

Bennett drags me into his arms, enveloping me in a tight hug, holding me into his chest. I hear Theo enter the room, making a distressed noise, but it's muffled by the way Bennett rubs my back, shushing me. "You're going to hyperventilate, June, you need to breathe with me."

"This was in her office."

Seth crosses by us and then something clinks onto Arin's

desk. I cringe into Bennett's touch, knowing what he found — praying that I shattered my phone so much that they can't read the messages for themselves.

I'm such a fucking embarrassment —

"Did your mother call again? Did you *pick up?*" Theo growls the question, crowding against my side. He *told* me not to answer her again before my heat and I was so good, I didn't —

"Theo, that is not helpful." Arin's voice cuts through the office, silencing everyone except my wracking breaths.

Bennett strokes my hair, holding onto me tighter as he whispers, "Arin, what the hell is on that phone?" Panicked worry spikes in the bond, before he manages to tamp it down, pressing his lips against the top of my head, murmuring, "Deep breaths, June, whatever it is, we'll handle it. You're not alone."

Seth's hand wraps around the back of my neck, just under Bennett's. Both their touches scorch me. It isn't healing, but the support and love they both flood our bonds with quiets the reeling of my own thoughts as I try to figure out what I'm supposed to tell them. I've been keeping this from them since the beginning, they're going to be upset with me, maybe even more than my mother was. If they left me, I would deserve it.

I lift my eyes, finding Bennett's concerned gaze as I suck in little hiccuping breaths. He strokes my hair again, then moves his hands so he can cup my face, wiping away tears with his thumbs.

"There you are. Let's take a deep breath together."

I force myself to suck in a deep breath with him, reaching up to scrub at my face. Seth presses his lips to the back of my head, unwavering and solid as he presses me between him and Bennett. Shame crawls up my spine, and I glance down at the nice rug in Arin's office, unable to meet any of their eyes.

Theo doesn't let me get away with it.

He moves closer, grabbing onto my chin, "Was it her?"

"Theo —" Arin's voice is a warning.

"Yes." I stare up at him, tears filling my eyes all over again. "She never stopped."

He snarls, and I watch as he tugs away and snatches my phone off Arin's desk. The screen is shattered, but still lights up. I sink into Bennett's chest, closing my eyes because I *know* what he's going to find as Arin steps closer to read with Theo. It would be better if a black hole just opened up and swallowed me.

Theo curses under his breath, and worry comes through from Seth as he pulls away too. Bennett doesn't leave me, he just holds me closer, pressing his lips against my cheek. "It's okay." His voice shakes. "Whatever it is, it'll be okay."

"There are *hundreds* of messages," Theo whispers. "All from your mother, all calling you things I can't... I..." His voice breaks and I glance up at him, watching his jaw clench. His blue eyes shine, a soured, muddy scent coming off him in waves, stress permeating the air.

I did this to him. I'm the worst omega in the entire world.

Arin takes the phone from Theo, putting it onto the surface of his desk. His shoulders roll, body straightening. Then he stares at me, cutting me to the quick with the determination and pain in his brown eyes.

"I am not biting you, Juniper."

I flinch into Bennett, and the alpha holding me starts to growl.

Arin holds up a hand. "I am not going to bite you

because you're begging me to do it just to..." His voice catches, and then he tugs his glasses off, pressing a hand against his eyes. "Just because you're trying to prove something to your parents, to whoever will come along and question the genuine joy and light you've brought to all of us. That is no reason to bond you."

A low, wounded sound bubbles up from my throat, and Theo's eyes find mine, haunted as a tear slips down his cheek. "*June.*"

This *hurt* is bone-deep, like my marrow is being scooped out. My omega, the deep part of me, feels so undeserving and rejected, I want to dig a hole and crawl into it to die. I have to explain myself, because if Arin never bites me, if we never have a bond, then I'll know I truly ruined *all* of this —

"I thought if I never answered that she'd stop, but then she didn't. I thought if I moved, then she'd just go back to ignoring me. I thought it wouldn't get to this point —"

Arin steps forward, touch gentle. He holds my face as he bends his head down. "I want to make one thing clear; I am not mad at you, Juniper."

I wait for the 'but.'

His eyes don't leave mine.

It doesn't come.

Floundering, I grasp at straws. "But you should be."

"Why?"

"Because..." The world crashes around me, my breath coming too fast, chest rising in panicked heaves. "Because..."

"Because you're mad at yourself?" Theo speaks up and I wince as he wipes at his own tears. "Fuck, you should *not* be putting the blame on anyone but the two people who are supposed to love, protect, and support you, and instead one of them called you a *filthy used whore.*"

A whimper catches in my throat. That had been the first text I'd seen after my heat, staring at my phone just showered, about to leave for the embassy so I could get a temporary ID.

"They aren't welcome here." Bennett's words are so quiet, so unnervingly calm that it sends a bolt of fear through me.

"Of course they aren't." Arin's thumb rests above my pulse point, on the unmarked side of my neck. "This is our home, and I'm not going to invite them here."

Seth makes a distressed noise. "But could they take her away from here? From us?"

"No," Theo growls. "No, you're not going anywhere. I won't let them. You're ours." He shoves Arin away from me and I squeak as he wraps his arms around me, burying his face in the top of my head, crushing me to his chest. His scent still has a bitter edge to it, but the rainwater rushes over me, dragging me under as I cling to him, my knuckles tightening as I fist his shirt in my hands. My strong alpha — so big and unyielding.

I believe him.

"I'm sorry." I let out a strangled sound. "I'm so sorry I didn't say anything —"

Arin's hands rub my back, then Bennett's touch presses against the bond mark, Seth crowding in. It's too many arms, hands, and slightly stressed perfumes, but it's overwhelming in a way that grounds me. This is my *pack*, these men are all mine.

Arin kisses the side of my head, his voice softer.

"When I bite you, it will be because we've come to the same point you did with Bennett, with Seth — not on anyone else's timeline. And I will *not* let your parents believe they have any kind of claim over you, other than the most base, biological notion that they contributed to your DNA."

He turns me in Theo's arms, staring down at me seriously. "You are a part of this pack, which means you are *ours*, just like Theo said. I will facilitate it from here." Arin's eyes narrow. "We will be civil, we will meet them for dinner, but we will also not welcome any untoward comments, nor suggestions or concerns about the way we love each other or the way we love *you*."

My heart stops as he cups my face, reverent and kind, eyes only for me.

"And you are, June, you are so loved."

Tears overflow, blurring him as I choke out, "No running."

He leans in, pressing his forehead to mine. "That's right, no running, love."

CHAPTER THIRTEEN

JUNE

"Ashley said that we'll be in the private dining room."

Bennett looks up from his phone, the car rumbling down the road as Arin points us toward the heart of Rochester. I run my tongue over my teeth, sitting in the center of the backseat, Seth on my right, Theo on my left.

I feel like I'm about to walk in front of a firing squad.

"That was very kind of her, please thank her for us." Arin's voice is deadly calm as I reach for Seth's hand. Intertwining our fingers, I lean in the opposite direction, nuzzling into Theo's side. He's been unnervingly quiet for days, and the atmosphere at the house has been on edge, like we're all waiting to see what tonight brings — what my parents could possibly say or do.

Theo scoops an arm around my back, his hand landing on my hip and rubbing the fabric of my dress. I didn't know what to possibly wear until Bennett walked in earlier and calmly pulled the dress out of a bag, laying it on the bed for me. He even reminded me to wear shoes I'll be comfortable in, instead of trying to impress people we shouldn't care about.

I love him, but the crux of the issue is that I *do* care, even if I shouldn't.

Arin hasn't mentioned anything about the conversation in his office. Nothing about the fact he told me I was loved, or that he would handle this. I've not been able to stand sleeping alone, so I've either been curled up between Bennett and Seth, or laying on the couch with Theo against me, trying to find what pieces of solace I can.

I've missed Arin. He said he wasn't mad at me, but he has to be. What kind of person doesn't admit to the harassment that's been thrown at them for almost two months?

I've only gotten one single text from my mother, confirming tonight's dinner. I found a new phone on my bed two days ago, replacing my shattered, older model, and the cream color is gorgeous. It didn't help much when I read the addition to the thread.

DO NOT ANSWER

> Arin Mohan contacted your father and I.
> The three of us will see you at the
> restaurant on Friday evening. Look
> presentable, Juniper.

So I put on the dress Bennett left for me and tried to be okay that Arin *handled* it.

Smoothing my hands over the white fabric, I glance down at the intricate fitted bodice. It hugs my upper body like it was made for me, before the fabric dramatically flares out around my hips, the corset top covering my stomach but not uncomfortably. The skirt, itself, matches the same white as the rest of the dress, save for the very bottom, which looks dipped in ink, staining the hem.

I love it — I have no idea where he bought it, or how he found the time to get it for me — but it makes me feel like an adult, squished between Theo in his button up, and Seth in a blazer. Arin's in a full suit in the front, with Bennett in a nice shirt, covered in an overcoat.

"I could fight the other alpha for you." Theo murmurs the words, rubbing my hip again. "I bet they picked some dickhead who thinks he could just waltz out with you. His name is probably... Braeden or Jaxton or some shit."

I snort. "I don't think Ashley would like it if you started a bar brawl in her five star restaurant."

He hums, glancing down at me. "Would *you* like it, though?"

Stuttering for a second, my perfume gives me away before I can make an excuse. It's not that the idea of Theo beating someone to a bloody pulp is attractive — *except it is.* The tiny voice in the back of my mind that is all omega is damn near giddy at the thought.

Theo's eyes rove over my rising chest, making me squirm a little.

From the front, Bennett curses softly. "*Theo*, leave her *alone.*" An echo of want, unrestrained and needy, comes down the bond, and I squeeze Seth's hand a little tighter, pressing my lips together to suppress a silly giggle at the way they're all reacting to me.

I suck in a breath as Theo dips down, kissing my collarbone and nudging his nose against my skin. It takes my brain a moment to catch up with his actions as his breath fans out across my throat, then I *do* giggle.

"You possessive asshole, are you scent-marking me?"

"Yes." He doesn't even try to hide his grin, pressing it into my skin as his tongue darts out, licking a stripe up my throat. "Bennett gets to show off his bite on you, it's only fair."

My eyes flutter, and I feel breathless as he marks me with his rainwater smell, drenching me in it like I was caught in a storm. "*Oh.*" His teeth drag over my mark, and I clench my thighs together as Seth fidgets beside me. His squirming draws my gaze, and I watch him as his hand carefully tries to readjust the tented front of his trousers. I lift my palm to my mouth, barking out a loud laugh as Seth gives me a tortured look.

"This is *why* Bennett and I tamp shit down, fucking hell, I can't go to dinner with a hard-on."

I laugh harder, it exploding out of me as Theo shakes against my side, laughing even with his head pressed into my throat.

"Want to make me rock hard, princess? I'll walk in like a total degenerate, really play it up in front of them."

"Can none of you behave?" Arin's laugh drifts back to us as I peek up to see him shaking his head with a smile in the rearview mirror.

"Theo has a point."

The car is quiet for a moment, then Bennett shifts, glancing back at me. "What do you mean?"

Biting my tongue, I look to the side at Theo as he finally pulls back from lavishing my neck. "If you all smell like me and I smell like you, maybe they'll realize I do care — maybe they'll accept my choice... Maybe they'll accept that we're a pack."

Theo's brows pinch as he looks down at me, sighing softly. "You could walk in smelling like an entirely different pack and they should still respect *your* decision about *your* life."

Seth's hand drifts over to mine, drawing my gaze as he squeezes my fingers. "At the end of the day, their approval of us doesn't matter, as long as you're happy, June bug."

"I know." And I *do* — but the silence hangs and I can't help but add, "But I still, selfishly, want everyone to know you're all mine, as much as I'm yours."

Seth flashes me a smile. "Want to bite me again?"

"Maybe." I lean forward, brushing my lips over his as I sigh. "But maybe I just *do* want you all to indulge me and let me mark you up with my scent. Even if it's just selfish, wishful thinking that they'd respect me."

He leans in closer, pulling me into a deeper kiss as Theo's hand slides slightly to the side, touching my thigh over the dress instead of my hip. From the front, Bennett lets out a little groan, his voice a warning as he growls, "Arin, they're not behaving."

"They're *your* bonded."

I laugh, but it's not very loud, transforming into a wanton moan as Seth's tongue slips into my mouth, toying with mine. Covering Theo's hand with my own, I press his touch further into me, breathing out as I kiss Seth messily. "This dress *sucks* for easy access." Theo makes a noise as I turn, capturing his lips next as Seth's touch moves to my jaw and throat. I reach up, shimmying the top of the bodice slightly, moaning softly. "I might be able to get my tits out."

"*June*, please keep your clothes on," Bennett admonishes me from the front, but it's through pained laughter, lust zinging up and down the bond as he's subjected to both mine and Seth's antics.

After a moment, Theo takes mercy on us all, pulling

away and grabbing my chin. "Behave. No more, little omega, or we'll never make it through this god-awful dinner."

That doesn't sound like much of a threat to me. I'll take a fivesome with my pack over a pained dinner conversation with my parents any day.

Whining, I let Theo go, but pout while he pulls back. Maybe I am projecting, or maybe I just am a horny omega with no other desire than to be railed — but the small voice inside my mind gives me pause.

Why wouldn't I want to constantly be surrounded by the love of these men? Why wouldn't I want to stay in their arms, soaking up the fact that time and time again they have proven I am worth more than what my parents always insisted. I'm worth more than a passing glance, or an unsatisfying relationship.

I deserve to be happy.

The thought is sobering as I glance over at Theo. His eyes flicker to mine, the softest blue that makes my heart flutter every time they light up.

"What's that look for?"

I smile at him, my throat tightening. "I'm just really lucky to have all of you."

"No, we're lucky to have you," Seth whispers as he kisses my shoulder.

The car slows and turns into a familiar parking lot behind Ashley's restaurant, the same one where I kissed Bennett senseless just before we bonded. Trepidation builds as Arin parks the car, and we all get out.

Fussing with my skirts, I smooth them out as best as I can, then reach up, trying to adjust the way my hair has fallen out of its updo with all of Theo and Seth's touches, but Bennett steps over. He slides the pin keeping it in place free, letting my hair tumble down as he guides me to stand in front of him.

"Let me." His deft fingers scoop it off my neck, kissing my nape before he twists my hair up and pins it back into place. "You definitely smell like Theo and Seth, it's not overwhelming, despite how much you tried, but it's there." Bennett turns me around and I reach up with a little smile, smoothing out the nonexistent wrinkles in his shirt, my fingers skimming under his overcoat.

"I guess I'm just missing a bit of mint and some orange."

Bennett smiles back at me, his thumb brushing over the silver-scarred bond mark he left on my throat. It thrums with heat, with *love*, before he bends down and kisses me senseless. Every painful moment of edging in the car compacts into the touch as he devours me, pulling me close and sipping from my mouth like he's drinking the finest of wines.

I'm breathless and a little dizzy when he pulls back, thumb idly toying with the bond scar as he smirks. "There. That will have to do. As much as I want to bend you over and fill you with my cum, I don't want a public indecency charge. You're plenty marked by me with my bite and my kiss, darling."

I take a dazed step back, immediately stopped as I bump into Arin. Bennett's eyes flash from my face to Arin behind me, before his chin dips and he steps away. I watch him for a moment, transfixed as he takes Seth's hand, kissing the beta's knuckles before they walk toward the building with Theo.

Arin's touch slides over my hip, his mint perfume clearing my mind as the ghost touch of his lips linger on my throat, then my jaw, then my ear.

"Where do you suppose I mark you, Juniper? You're drenched in their scents, so much rain and orange and chocolate I can just *barely* smell you, sweet and honeyed under-neath it all."

I make a little noise as his hand curls into mine, fingers tangling, and it's the only invitation I need to turn around.

He looks *devastatingly* handsome in his full suit. The jacket fits him like a glove, the perfect black to match to the ink-stained hem of my dress. My free hand lands on the lapels, smoothing them as I whisper, "I'm so scared."

"I will never let them do anything. No matter what's said tonight, you belong in this pack." He frowns at me, then lifts his hand to touch my jaw, tipping my head up as he leans in. "I am so proud of you — for being here, for your bravery, for it all."

My eyes sting as I take him in, relishing his touch as my mind races.

"I don't want you to see me as a reflection of them. I don't want you to ever think for a moment that I held their beliefs. I'm *embarrassed*, Arin. I don't want you to see that this is where I came from, what I grew up with because..." I flounder, my mouth opening and closing as I choke out, "Because I can't stand the thought of you thinking that I said yes to Seth because I saw you as only a line of dollar signs."

His palm, so warm, slides down, before he holds the side of my throat, steady and calm as his brown eyes sear into me.

"I wish I could crawl into your mind and reorganize it. I wish I could leave notes on the mirrors inside it and let you have them as a reminder every single time you believe these things, because *they're not true*." He whispers the words, pulling me a step closer by my throat. "I would never think that you accepted help from Seth or Bennett because of money, or some perceived notion that you grew up with that all your worth is tied to your designation and ability to bear children."

He licks his lips, then sighs.

"Maybe I've not made it abundantly clear, Juniper."

My confusion must show on my face because he presses his forehead against mine, overwhelming me with his perfume.

"I'd like to spend the rest of my life making you incandescently happy. I'd like your cheeks to hurt just from smiling by the end of the days we spend together. I'd like the moments you dream about to pale in comparison to the time you spend with myself, with Theo, with Bennett, and with Seth. The people inside this building do not reflect you or your sweet heart. The words that may be said tonight are not yours. I know that. Do you?"

Tears prick in my eyes as the sheer weight of tonight rests on my chest like an anvil. Arin's lips twist as he kisses the top of my forehead, ruffling my hair with his breath — his own version of drenching me in the essence of him.

"I know now." My voice breaks. "I believe you, and I'm so in love with you, I could be sick over it, Arin."

He gives up on keeping it chaste the instant the words leave my mouth. Arin cups my face in his wide hands, then kisses me passionately, pulling me against him as the world teeters for a moment. One hand drops, and then he grasps my hip, lifting me just to spin us in a circle, my skirt swirling around us as he does.

He only slows when he mutters, "I am so enamored with you, Juniper. I'd let the world fall to ruin and still be caught in your eyes." Arin pulls back, so handsome, so *perfect*, his eyes crinkling as he smiles at me. "I love you."

Reaching up, I tangle my fingers in his hair, uncaring as I

laugh and kiss him hard. He stumbles, but then twists us, pinning me against the side of our SUV as I lose myself in *him*. My prime — this man who has done everything in his power to make this entire process magical in so many ways.

His beard scratches against my jaw as his nose rubs against my throat. "No one better *look* at you, you're *mine*." With that, he sucks on the skin and I whine, pressing up against him. His teeth grab hold of my skin and sparks race through my veins. Arin doesn't fully bite and he curses as he exhales sharply, letting my skin go. "You're my omega, my love, *my* Juniper."

All the air leaves my lungs as his hands run up the corset, sliding over my upper arms, his tongue darting out to taste me, humming in sheer satisfaction.

"There, no one will question that I've left my mark on you."

I stare up at him, my heart beating wildly as he kisses me one more time, just a brief caress, then pulls us away from the car.

"We should go in." I cling to his arm, staring at the door as I hesitate in the parking lot.

Arin grimaces. "We should, but there's still time to text Seth and Theo to cause a distraction. We could run." Arin pauses, squinting up at the dusky sky. "I have property in Germany. Have you ever been?"

A laugh bubbles up as I turn into him, sucking in another lungful of his scent before I whisper, "No, but take me another night. Let's just get through this one."

My alpha holds onto me as he leads us forward. His gentle voice is a promise only for me as he murmurs, "Of course. It'll be something to look forward to."

CHAPTER FOURTEEN

JUNE

Lukas Peterson is very handsome.

He's built like a linebacker, with a dusting of blond hair at the top of his head. The second I enter the dining room, I'm hit with the smell of apples, fresh from the tree, crisp and juicy. I don't feel *drawn* to the scent, but it's not offensive like some alphas I've encountered.

Lukas stands immediately, manners and propriety winning out as he looks at me the same way I'm sure I'm looking at him — sizing me up.

The painfully tight set of his shoulders doesn't ease as his gaze flickers to Arin briefly. Theo, Seth, and Bennett all stand too, waiting for me to decide which empty chair to go to — one at the head of the table and next to my still-seated father, and the other sandwiched between my seated mother and the unfamiliar alpha.

I don't *relish* the thought of being trapped between them, but Seth is positioned across from that chair, and I'd rather be there than at the head. Everyone will already be looking at me tonight, I don't want to make it even worse.

Arin catches my hand as I step toward the chair between my mother and Lukas, stopping me briefly to kiss my cheek sweetly. He pointedly turns his cheek, rubbing the stubble along his jaw against my skin, making me flush as he adds an extra, unnecessary layer of his scent to my skin.

Lukas fumbles, the smell of apple taking on a vinegar tang as he pulls my chair out for me, giving me a hesitant smile. I force a small one back, smoothing out my dress before taking my seat.

The moment I do, my mother adjusts her fork and hisses, "What in the *world* are you wearing, Juniper?"

My fingers freeze as they skim the expertly folded napkin resting on the charger plate. The table is quiet — too quiet — and my mother's shrill voice rings in the air. Her whispers have never been subtle.

Finally, I raise my head, pulling the napkin into my lap carefully as I offer her a tight-lipped smile. "Do you like it? Bennett, my alpha, bought it for me as a bonding gift."

Here we go.

She sucks in a shocked breath, staring at me like I have three heads and just announced to the room I'm carrying Satan's illegitimate baby. Her eyes fall, skimming my neck, fixating on the fully exposed bond mark. Sudden gratefulness hits me that Bennett was the one to pull my hair back, fixing it to make sure she and everyone else could see the way he marked me as his own.

My father won't meet my eyes, sitting on my mother's other side.

Arin watches us at the end of the table. Seth fidgets across from me. Bennett stares next to him. Theo's lips twitch, fighting a scowl. Lukas looks like he'd rather be shot than be here.

"Congratulations on the bond." Lukas says it so softly, it takes me a moment to register it.

Smiling, I turn toward him, genuine. "Thank you." My eyes dart to Bennett for half a second, catching his smile as the bond warms, a hot coil around my heart. "Bennett isn't my only bonded." I reach my hand across the table toward Seth, sliding our fingers together.

"*Two* alphas." My mother squeaks the words, sounding like a leaky balloon.

I catch Theo's eyes on my mother, barely restrained anger rolling off him in waves, daring her to say something about any of us.

"Actually." I let Seth go, picking up my water. "Bennett is both mine and Seth's alpha." The glass clinks as I accidentally hit the charger plate, and I lick my lips. "Bonding will happen when it's time with the rest of my pack."

My mother puts a hand over her chest, sucking in a breath and opening her red-smeared mouth.

Harriet Walden is a lot of things, but unopinionated is not one of them.

I can't remember a time in my life where she hasn't offered unsolicited thoughts or advice on everything I've done. From who I should have been friends with as a child, to the degree I chose to pursue as a college student, to the career that got me out of her house. Sometimes I wonder if my father ever even proposed — or if she just *told* him it was time to get married and he went along with it.

"Three alphas and a *beta*." She says Seth's designation like it's a curse, and I know to her, it is. "And you stayed with them during your *heat*?" Her hands flutter, her face flushing. "I have never — I mean it's just — how could you bring this up to us? How could you make me think of you in this way? I can't even imagine strangers making this decision, but my own *daughter* —"

She cuts herself off, making a strangled noise as she looks around me at Lukas. "Alpha, I am *so* sorry, I sincerely apologize for my daughter's actions, the fact that she's *bonded* one of these..." Her eyes flicker across the table and she suddenly trails off when Theo's lip curls.

Lukas has the good graces to look mortified that she even *brought* up my heat.

I just feel... nothing.

Nothing for the fact she's trying to embarrass me. Nothing for the woman next to me who is so similar in so many ways, but so different in others. We share the same almost-red hair. Our faces are rounded — something she could never diet away, even though her limbs and body are stripped of as much fat as she could starve off. She's a shell of a person, and it's never been clearer to me than it is now.

It's both devastating, and horrifying.

"I know I raised you better than being passed around a group of men like a toy." She pivots, her eyes finding mine, pinched at the edges. "What happened to saving yourself for a *nice* alpha? There was an option in London right *there* for you, but you were too *stupid* to take it. We never should have allowed you to move out or write those pack books you do —" She shoves away from the table, shaking her head. "All of this is just — oh, I feel faint. I can't —" She cuts herself off again, then walks straight out of the room.

All before the first course.

I feel like I'm floating outside my body for a moment as my father swallows. His eyes dart to the door, then back to me. In the split second, I see a thousand emotions, but mostly sadness.

"She just needs a minute." He stands. "We'll be back."

And then he runs after her — like he always does.

No one moves. The door clicks shut.

It's all so *dramatic*.

I turn and meet Lukas' eyes, bursting into guffawing laughter at the same moment he does. We both bend halfway over the table, tears springing to our eyes as we shake, howling with it as the rest of my pack stares at us.

"What did —"

"I don't —"

"The club had to —"

"Oh, there's no way it didn't —"

We talk over each other until we both manage to catch our breaths. I press my hands against my cheeks, staring at him in a new light as Lukas leans back in his chair and sinks down, groaning softly.

"I'm so sorry they dragged you up here," I mutter, shaking my head at him.

His face falls as he scrubs a hand over it. "No, *I'm* sorry, about all of this. I think both our parents decided they could... force some weird matchmaking, but it's clear you're happy. I tried to tell mine no, but there was no arguing. It was all so last minute, they only told me you existed last week."

I grimace at him, chewing on my lower lip. "You shouldn't have been roped into this."

He shrugs, glancing at Arin. "I tried to tell them if there was already a pack in place *and* with a prime, then there wasn't any point, but they —"

"— don't see any type of reason," Arin finishes, his eyes on *me*. "Yes, I see that now."

Lukas makes a face. "At least you all aren't too far away. I can still make it home tonight if I take a late flight."

My heart tugs. "Are... will you be okay?" I know what it feels like to be monitored, forced and coerced, all under the guide of parents thinking it's the *right* thing to do. And there's a biological part inside me, purely platonic and omega, that just wants to make sure this alpha next to me is happy. He deserves to be. It doesn't need to be *me* that makes him that, but I want it all the same for him.

Lukas fidgets in his seat. "I've spent the last six months trying to figure out how to tell my parents that I have a pack of my own."

"Oh."

A soft smile brightens his features. "Yeah. I mean... well it's not traditional, in any way that they'd like." His features are that kind of all-American handsome that I can see anyone else melting over. "But there's a beta and she's amazing. We met another alpha when we were out one night and there might not be an omega in the picture but the three of us together, we just *work*... and both of them..."

"You're happy." I whisper the words, recognizing the look of yearning.

Lukas nods. "Yeah, I'm happy."

The worry that the alpha that they were bringing to tonight's dinner would be a cartoon villain dies in my chest, replaced by aching sadness. He should be home with his pack, not suffering through tonight because of a group of disillusioned betas who insist that biology trumps sense.

I glance across the table at Bennett and Seth, before my eyes find Theo, then Arin. "I guess if you're here, you should at least stay for dinner. Ashley is a wonderful chef."

"Maybe if we're lucky, they won't come back to the table." Theo picks up his napkin, shooting me a teasing look.

I smile at him, but I know it doesn't reach my eyes. This is too simple and the night is young. Something else will ruin it.

MY PARENTS RETURN minutes before Ashley sweeps in with plates piled high. She happily serves us all, throwing a few flirty comments my way, much to my mother's shock and horror. I try not to let it bother me as I eat the tart salad and rich soup.

But as the main arrives, I can't keep it at bay any longer.

"You should be full, Juniper."

A stunning plate of pasta sits in front of me, but I can't bring myself to pick up my fork as my mother speaks.

"You had all of the salad *and* all of the soup. You should be finished with dinner." She barely glances down at her plate as she picks it up and leans around me. "Lukas, *alpha*, would you like mine? I couldn't possibly eat it, and you need it."

The way she says his designation makes my skin crawl. At the end of the day we aren't people around a dinner table — we're predetermined roles meant to play the exact parts she's already mentally cast us in.

"Uh" — Lukas fumbles with his fork — "no, I'm fine, thank you Mrs. Walden."

A sour taste fills my mouth. Anger — hot and fiery — strikes through the bond and I jolt, looking up at Seth as he

179

glares daggers at my mother next to me. Just as he opens his mouth, Bennett lays a hand on his arm.

"We should ask Ashley for this pasta sauce recipe, June." Bennett says the words casually. "We'll make it together next week. It's delicious this time."

I glance back at my untouched fork, haunted by memories of growing up with family dinners always ending the same. My mother in the kitchen, scraping her full plate into the trash, sipping water through the meal to make herself feel full.

"Sure." I look away from the fork, forcing a smile in Bennett's direction.

He tries to catch my eyes, concern flooding our bond, but I glance back down as Lukas stutters in Seth's direction. "You — uh — have a liquor company?"

Seth takes the opening and the conversation shifts, but I feel eyes on me as I keep my head down, staring at the full plate as my mind swirls.

I should be embarrassed. Not only did my parents already cause a scene, but now I'm doing it too. Pick up the fork. Eat. You haven't been like this since college. Eat. You're just going to make them ask questions. Fucking eat something.

A waitress comes in, clearing other dishes, before hesitating next to me. "I'll box this for you." She picks it up, then whisks it away with the rest.

Just as I pick up my napkin from my lap, my mother leans into me. My skin prickles, the familiar light scent of her natural perfume punched up uncomfortably with enhancers. She used to smell of tart cherry, oddly comforting, but now it has a sugared, faux edge to the scent.

"If you intend to keep these alphas' eyes from wandering, it's time to take care of yourself, Juniper."

I swallow, blinking rapidly as I try to keep my eyes from straying to her, one ear on the conversation going on between Lukas and everyone else. It's mundane — Seth gives him recommendations of restaurants in London, because apparently Lukas has never been.

"I am taking care of myself."

My mother makes a noise of discontent, and the sound draws my attention. Her eyes flicker down, over my full chest in the dress, and then the skirt bunched in my lap. "Are you?" She leans back in her chair, shaking her head at me. "Don't expect me to facilitate another meeting with a suitable alpha when this all falls apart. They won't stay with you if you let yourself go anymore. I'm sure you've already exhausted Lukas' good graces with this evening, and with that bite, it would be a hard sell. I suppose the alpha in London decided to cut his losses too — he probably knew you'd roll over and give it up for these alphas."

I open my mouth, my throat going dry as I just stare at her.

"You need to stop writing, immediately. Clearly you can't focus on your health and your alphas while also working. Your alphas should find you a personal trainer and put you on a diet. I'll make sure I send over recommendations. Remember the lime diet in high school? You lost so much, you looked so good."

The sound of a fork clanging against the table makes my eyes dart around her. My father sits, stock-still, as Arin glares at my mother from the end of the table, like he can burn a hole through the side of her face from sheer will alone.

Undeterred, my mother smooths out her napkin, whipping her head to the side.

"I assume you'll provide for my daughter accordingly?"

She snips the words, cutting off the conversation around the rest of the table. "Omegas should not be expected to work, they're too fragile and their conditions are too unstable. The stress isn't good, and if you've chosen to saddle yourself with my daughter, then I expect she'll have what she needs." She pauses, then motions to my father, "As will we, per tradition."

"Fuck tradition."

Theo's rough voice travels across the table as Seth's jaw drops. Nausea roils as bile burns the back of my throat.

"*Excuse —*"

"You're excused." Theo stares at her, his fists white-knuckled on the table, barely restrained. "You have spent this entire fucking evening doing your best to upset June, while belittling *our* pack." His tone doesn't waver as he stares her down. "Arin might be our prime, he might be convinced he needs to play nice with you, but I sure as shit don't. Shut the *fuck* up."

She gasps, floundering for a moment as her eyes dart to my father, like he'll do anything. He just sinks lower in his chair. *At least someone is capable of feeling ashamed.*

Theo's eyes find mine, blazing like blue fire. "I need to make one thing *very* clear. Not only will I not place boundaries on what June wants to do with her life, but I won't even entertain the thought of providing for you." His gaze flies back to my mother. "You're a cruel, vicious woman who thinks designation overrides decency. June will *always* be loved and provided for, but that same kindness does not, and will not ever be extended to *you*."

The table goes quiet, my ears ringing — torn between elation that *Theo* spoke up, that he said what I can't seem to get out of my mouth, and the utter horror of realizing this evening went exactly how I expected it to.

"We understand." My father finally speaks, clearing his throat as he stands up, pointedly avoiding my gaze as he looks at Arin. "It's time for my wife and I to return to our hotel room —"

"I'm leaving. I won't sit idly and be disrespected." My mother jumps up, grabbing her clutch like it was her idea in the first place, storming out without looking back once. My father takes one last look at me, echoes of my own features reflected in his face. In the span of a heartbeat, his hazel eyes soften before he turns and follows after my mother at a slower pace.

I blink down at the uneaten dessert in front of me as Lukas quietly places his napkin on the table.

"I should go too." He clears his throat and I feel his eyes on me. The pity makes my skin crawl. "Are you —"

"Go back to your pack." I force the words out.

"I am." He hesitates, brief as his gaze moves to Arin. Something unspoken passes between them, before he mutters, "Thank you for tolerating this entire fucking night. I don't think I could ever be as calm as you've been, but now I'm realizing that I don't give a shit what anyone else says — I love my girls, and we don't need anyone else's approval. And they both deserve to know that."

In a flash, he strides out.

I just sit for a moment, the room feeling smaller and smaller as Bennett reaches out through the bond, Seth's emotions brushing against mine.

"June?" Bennett extends a hand across the table.

I shove them both away from my chest, building a wall

they can't get through around my heart as I stand, looking at Arin. "Can we go home now?"

He nods once, his face pulled tight. "Absolutely. What can —"

"I just want to go home." My chest fractures wider.

This was all wrong. This was exactly what my mother wanted to happen. She proved every point she wanted to. She peeled me open and showed them all who I really am. How am I supposed to take care of them if I can't even take care of myself?

"Bennett, thank Ashley for the lovely dinner." I wrap my arms around myself, unable to look at the table as I walk away from it, trying to keep it together long enough to make it back to the car.

CHAPTER FIFTEEN

JUNE

ASHLEY PULLS me into a hug in the back parking lot, her scent warm and inviting, like a kitchen full of fresh herbs. "I sent home extra food, in case you get hungry later." As Seth shoves *bags* of leftovers into the back of the SUV, an amount I can't even fathom, I know that she noticed my portions went uneaten.

"Thank you." I make sure she hears me, but I don't really feel *present* in myself as I climb into the back of the car. Bennett takes the driver's seat, leaving Seth to climb into the passenger beside him. The bond between the three of us is still blocked from my side, but I don't need it to see their worried glances in the rearview mirror.

Arin and Theo are motionless beside me in the backseat — or maybe it's all me. I don't know. I stay quiet, staring out the front window until we get to the house. Arin lets me out and as I walk in, I hear him mutter to the rest of them. "Give her space."

"*What in the world are you wearing, Juniper?*"

My mother's voice echoes in my mind as I mechanically take myself upstairs, shedding the dress, putting up my jewelry into a small box, and walking into the bathroom — avoiding every mirror I can.

"How could you make me think of you in this way?"

I fill the clawfoot tub with water, dumping some kind of lavender scented bubble bath into it before climbing in. Knees to my chest, I rest my chin on them, staring at the stained glass window casting rainbows on the marble tile. The light is dying outside, and the water heats my skin quickly, almost uncomfortable as I try to wrap my head around tonight.

None of what happened feels real.

Nothing feels real.

This house — moving — being surrounded by Arin, Theo, Bennett, and Seth — I love it, but it also feels intangible, like it could be ripped away at any moment. Tonight should have proven that it can't be, but I can't shake the feeling that my mother was right. I will do something to lose all of this, and in that, I'll have to go crawling back to my old life. I'll scrape by with taking care of myself, back to what I can tolerate, with the added issue of being an omega.

I'll be miserable. I won't want anyone but the four men downstairs who crawled past my defenses — but it'll be deserved. They'll realize their mistakes in caring for me.

Rubbing my chest, I hunch forward, my breaths coming short and quick.

A surge of concern — worry from two ends of the bond — makes me jerk in the water, slamming the wall back up where it slipped. I mentally shove the bond down, tighter, so small that my emotions go with it.

And with their absence, I'm just left grieving.

Why would any of them stay with me after tonight? What good am I to them? She was right, I have a job, I love it, and I want to keep doing it. I don't want children, I don't plan on spending my life doting on them or providing what every other alpha wants — a family. They should want alpha babies and an omega entirely focused on them.

A harsh knock startles me, the water sloshing as I turn toward the door, scrubbing my burning eyes.

"Yeah?" My voice breaks, and I clear it. "I'll be out in a minute —"

"Can I come in?" Theo's voice is gruff from the other side and my heart jolts. Glancing around the semi-dark bathroom, I panic at the thought of him seeing me like this.

"June" — his voice cracks as he pleads with me — "*please.*"

I suck in a ragged breath, then pull my knees back up, folding in on myself as I call out, "Come in."

The door eases open, and then Theo appears, still dressed for dinner. The only thing that's changed is that his button up is rolled at the sleeves, exposing the tattoos crawling up his forearms. He lingers in the doorway for a moment, taking stock of me, before he steps in. His hands immediately rise to the buttons of his shirt.

I startle. "Theo?"

He makes a noise that he heard me, but strides over to the side of the tub anyway, pulling his belt out of the loops of his trousers with one hand as he braces the other on the porcelain.

"What are you —" I stop myself as he pushes his shirt open, exposing his chest, before he gives up and just climbs in, still mostly clothed. *"Theo."* I make a noise of shock as water overflows over the sides, his big body crowding mine.

He dips, cupping my face before kissing me hard, forcing my silence as he mutters against my lips. "Arin said not to bother you." He talks as he kisses me harsher, like he's branding me, his hands sliding over my bare shoulders, kneeling in the water, his clothes sodden. "I decided he was making the wrong call."

My breath catches as his nose nuzzles my throat.

"Bennett and Seth said you suppressed the bond."

I swallow, my eyes darting back to the stained glass, wishing I could see the backyard through it as his hands slide into the water, touching me, clinging to my skin.

"Please don't shut us out. I know how fucking ironic it is for *me* of all the people in this house to beg you not to, but please don't do it," he rasps as he kisses the top of my shoulder. "I can't stand the thought of you taking anything they said tonight to heart. If I overstepped, I'm *sorry* —"

"You didn't." Closing my eyes, I try to keep my breathing steady as I pull my knees closer. The weight of his hands on me is just shy of uncomfortable. "My mother was never going to accept this. She's never taken *no* as an acceptable answer. At least this means it'll take a few months before she licks her wounds enough to pretend like tonight never happened."

The bathroom is silent as I finally raise my head and look up at Theo's broken expression.

"Who knows, I could be back in Virginia by then."

He rocks back like I sucker punched him. The water in the tub goes cold as he sits back on his heels, choking out, "What are you *talking* about, June?"

His hands drop from me the second I pull away. "She

was right." Swallowing back the bile in my throat, I barrel forward. "I have no idea what I'm doing here. There's no *reason* to keep me around. I'm *nothing* like the omegas that packs normally choose. The entire point is to have children, and to be a support point. What do I even offer except constant issues? You've all shifted your entire lives around me, and there's no reason for it. You will find the time to resent me. It might not be tomorrow, or next week, or next month even — but in a few *years?*"

Theo's expression shatters, his mouth opening as his brow furrows. I can't take it.

My voice cracks as I look away. "Years from now you'll wonder why you agreed to this. I should have gone to a heat hotel, or gotten through it myself. I'm a biological mistake. You were right in London."

When he doesn't speak, I shift, feeling too vulnerable, all too aware that I'm completely naked. "I should get a towel."

"Stop." His hand darts out, touching my arm. Freezing, I look down at his fingers as they curl over my skin, encompassing so much space, the starkness of his tattoos creeping down to his wrist and brushing against the paleness of my skin.

This is only going to hurt worse if I keep thinking it won't end.

"Tell me you don't believe any of what you just said." He shakes his head, speaking softly, but angrily. "Tell me that you're just upset and you'll wake up tomorrow and not even entertain the idea that we'd come to... resent you." His eyes find mine, shiny. "Please, I'm begging you, tell me that you know I don't think of you as an object. I've never thought that, I —"

The look on his face makes me nauseous as his hand grasps my wet arm.

"You haven't!" I break. Snapping at him, I jerk away. "Not since before the heat." The weight of the words settles as my voice softens. "It'll come back. All those feelings will come *back* and you'll start to hate me again and Bennett and Seth will regret me and *Arin —*"

"I don't fucking *want* children," Theo snaps right back at me, getting in my face as he spits out. "I told you I can't stand alphas who leer at eighteen-year-old omegas like they're breeding stock. I don't *want* any other life but the one I see with *you.*"

He's near-desperate as he grabs my face, forcing my head to tip up, to *look* at him.

"You want to write until your fingers fall off? You want to travel around the entire world and never have kids? You want to do whatever you want? Fuck it — do it — I'll be right there beside you. You want to just lay on the couch until your ass fuses with the fabric? Move over, I'll rot with you." He clutches me, pressing our foreheads together. "But don't you fucking *dare* start making decisions based on what you *think* I want, because they're *wrong.* The voice in your head isn't yours — it's not logical, not *right* — it's the voice of a woman who is deeply unhappy with who she is and passed it right down to you."

My throat works, too tight to form a sentence as tears well in my eyes.

"*You —*" Theo stutters, our lips nearly touching. "You, June, are the only goddamn thing I care about in this life. If you're happy, I'm happy. If you're upset, I want to make it better. You might have a bond with Bennett and Seth, but I need you to know that even if my teeth never grace your skin,

I'll love you until the day I die. You're the woman who crawled past every stupid wall I put up. You're the woman I want to care for the rest of my life. You're *my* omega. You're the love of my life."

My entire body feels raw. I'm flayed open in front of him, unsure what to say as tears overflow, dripping down my cheeks. Just as I open my mouth, making a choked, whining sound, Theo shakes his head.

"No." His voice is just as ragged as I feel. I'm coming apart at the fucking seams.

"I should have said this months ago. I regret every second of my actions when Seth and Bennett brought you to the townhouse. I should have been on my knees begging for your forgiveness before you ever let me into your nest." He scans my face, hands scrambling to brush away my tears. "I'm fucking terrified that your mother isn't the only voice in your head saying these things. I'm terrified you're hearing *mine* too."

I gasp as I stumble over my words, rambling. "It's *not* yours — but some days it's so easy to ignore and then some days I'm too tired and it creeps back in and she's *there*, and tonight all I kept thinking was that you all were putting a fucking lot of effort in to keep *me* — to *love* me."

"You are worth it." His stare doesn't waver as he clutches me. "Juniper Walden, you are worth *loving*."

I can't hold it back. Dissolving into gasping, heaving sobs, I fold into his chest, sinking down in the tub as his legs extend. Theo lifts me, pulling me into his lap, the wet fabric of his pants clinging to my bare thighs as he wraps his arms around me tightly, rocking me back and forth.

He shushes me, holding me with a hand against the back of my wet hair. "Let it out. It's okay. I've got you." His perfume curls around us, mixing with the lavender from the long-gone bubbles, and I clutch him, pressing my nose against the skin over his heart.

Theo's chest starts to shake.

A purr, unused and cautious, raggedly echoes out of him and into me. I dig my fingers into his shoulders, shaking as he squeezes me tighter, rubbing my back as he nuzzles the top of my head with a strangled laugh.

"I've never purred before. I didn't think I could." His face buries in my hair as he holds me tighter, bruising strength a solid comfort. "I love you. I love you now. I'll love you when you're old and gray. I'll love you forever, at any body size, at any designation. Like calls to like, and you're it for me."

I lift my head, moving my hand to touch his wet cheek, clearing the tears there as I whisper, "I'm so sorry." I don't know what I'm apologizing for. Maybe for my parents, for being who I am, for the mess we make together, for making him love me — maybe for it all.

"Stop." Theo shakes his head. "No apologizing. I understand more than I wish that I did. But if that helps me understand the bad days with the good ones, then I'm glad."

Readjusting to straddle him, I tangle my fingers in his blond hair, marveling at how long it's gotten. My burly, standoffish alpha — it was near-buzzed when we first met, and now I can card my fingers through the growth.

"Theo." I search his face. He terrified and infuriated me only a couple months ago. He's right. Like called to like and I see so much of myself in him — so much pressure of expectations, so much baggage coming with designations.

His eyes meet mine, and the blue of them is like crystal clear ocean water.

"I love you."

His smile is devastating. He leans in, kissing me slowly and softly as his hands run up and down my back, whispering. "I love you." He kisses my jaw, pressing searing butterfly kisses all over my skin. "I love you so much. Please let me be your voice of reason. You can be mine."

Winding my arms around his neck, I kiss him back with a nod. The water splashes as I push against him, losing myself in the feeling. The soft rattle of his purr shakes through me and the smell of his perfume permeates the air, clearing out the soured anxiety of my own scent.

"Water's cold, baby, let's get you out of here."

A shiver crawls up my spine as he stands, lifting me effortlessly. The cool air hits me as Theo's arms lock, pressing me against his wet clothes.

I tuck my head into his throat as he steps out of the tub, my voice soft. "You're all wet."

Theo tilts his head toward me as I pull back enough to look up. He grins, but it doesn't quite meet his eyes. "Good thing I have a sweet little omega to keep me warm."

A blush crawls up my chest as he places me on the counter, shedding the rest of his wet clothes and standing in front of me naked. He snags two towels from the warming rack in the corner, wrapping one around my shoulders as my eyes flicker over his body.

He's so *big*. Stocky muscle layers under his skin, his belly slightly rounded like mine — except the bulk on him speaks to how truly strong he is. I can tell how much he works out, every movement of his body careful and precise. The tattoos stretch, criss-crossing over his skin as he barely swipes the water off himself.

His eyes catch mine, smiling lopsidedly. "What's that look for?"

Heat tangles with adoration. My lip wobbles as I mumble, "I really do love you."

Theo drops his towel before sliding between my thighs, rubbing his hands over them as he kisses me again, his voice rough. "I want to hear that for the rest of my life, understand?"

I nod as my towel falls, wrapping myself around him. I let him pick me up and carry me into the bedroom. My chest tightens as he lies me back on my bed, crawling on top of me and pulling the blankets up around us. His hands explore my skin, teasing as he lays on his side, pulling me with him as one hand cups my hip, hitching my leg over his and opening me up to him.

My nose brushes his as I breathe out, feeling his hips roll forward, his length sliding against me as my fingers tangle in his hair. "*Theo.*"

He shushes me, guiding my hips up and rubbing against me in slow circles. One hand rests on my ass, cupping it before pulling us flush together as we kiss and grind together. Emotions rise in my throat, a sob crawling out as he finally reaches between us and glides his fingers through the slick dripping from me, moaning into the kiss.

We don't talk. Heavy exhales mix as he slicks himself up, notching before pushing forward and thrusting into me. The strokes are slow and long as I cling to him, climbing up his body as the heat surrounds us.

I come with a soft cry, burying my head against his as he fucks me deep. Our cheeks smash together as I clench down, his knot almost breaching me. "*Please,*" I beg as I push my hips down, nails scoring his scalp. "I want to feel closer to you."

He groans, then cups the back of my head, kissing me passionately as he thrusts *hard*, just once. His knot locks inside me as he comes with a broken grunt, breathing against my lips.

I bury myself against his chest, fingers in his hair, clinging to him and refusing to let go as I let sleep take everything else away but him.

CHAPTER SIXTEEN

ARIN

"What would you do if I was feral?"

"Well, I'd tolerate you, but you'd be a hell of a lot less mouthy."

"Theo!" June's loud laugh echoes as she slaps his chest. Theo wraps his arms around her, rocking them back and forth as she sprawls overtop him on one of our huge couches. She bends down, her nose scrunching with her smile as she murmurs, "I'd bite you."

His grin is wicked, eyes flashing with unrestrained hunger. "That's okay. I can do that too, princess."

"Get a room, you two." Seth throws a pillow at them.

June shrieks, dodging it as her face lights up with a thousand-watt smile.

Then her hazel eyes lock on mine.

My stomach flips — it's been two weeks since the dinner with her parents. I did everything in my power to make the night as painless as possible. I oversaw where we met. I coordinated with Ashley to ensure the food was all of June's favorites. I thought I planned for everything.

But I still failed.

She's grown closer to Theo than I ever expected, something soft blossoming between them. I've been witness to it. Theo didn't listen the night of the dinner when I instructed everyone to leave her alone.

Whatever happened means she is finally back to her level of comfort she felt with us after the heat.

I'd never intimately dealt with an omega's heat before June — for *obvious reasons* — but I certainly read a lot about it in preparation before she decided to stay with us. I'd poured over books all hours of the day, trying to puzzle out what *good* alphas provide, what's expected from a prime — and I still completely ruined it.

It's clear to me now that her closeness with Bennett and Seth is for a reason. Their three-way bond is unbreakable. Maybe this all means I'm just not suited to head a pack. If everyone else can understand June's emotional needs better than me, who's to say that I should even be prime anymore?

"Arin?"

June stands in front of me when I look up sharply.

A tiny frown tugs on her lips as she reaches out, palm meeting my cheek. "Where'd you go?"

Exhaling, I turn into her palm. The warmth of her skin makes her perfume brighter, sweetened syrup soothing the back of my throat.

"I was thinking about work, I'm sorry." The lie rests heavy on my tongue as I blink. "What were you saying, Juniper?"

The frown doesn't quite leave her face. Her thumb rubs against the edge of my beard as she glances over her shoulder, her eyes finding Seth. "We were trying to decide on a movie tonight. And I was going to get us all snacks. Do you want popcorn?"

"Popcorn is good." I breathe in her scent one last time, my lips brushing the inner skin of her wrist, letting my nose graze the gland there as her perfume thickens. Her touch is like a hit of the best drugs in the entire world, and I hum softly, regretful to let her pull back.

Her lips lift, only a hair, before she bends down and kisses the crown of my head. My stomach flips as she bounces over to Seth, grabbing his arm. "Let's go, then."

The beta beams at her, and I feel hollow at their shared excitement, echoed by Bennett when June gives him the briefest peck on the lips before laughing and running out of the living room. The room suddenly feels a lot emptier.

I shift in my chair, reaching for my phone as it vibrates in my pocket.

Theo's voice stops me. "What's eating at you?"

I glance up, finding both Theo and Bennett's focus on me, scrutinizing in two wildly different ways. Bennett looks pensive, brows pulled together and a tight frown on his face. Theo's too relaxed for that — sprawled out on the couch where June left him, but his glance is cutting, like he can read my thoughts.

"What do you mean?" I brush him off as I pull my phone out.

Bennett scoffs. "You seem off."

Theo grunts in agreement, shifting to stare at me harder, his head tilting. "Is something going on that we need to know as a pack?"

"No," I answer him firmly, looking between the two of them. They're annoying separately, but *god*, when their focus combines, it's maddening. Bennett and I don't butt heads like Theo and I do. The give and take has always been a careful coexistence — at least until June entered the picture.

Now I'm not sure where the three of us stand.

"Is it work?"

"Is it June?"

They ask two questions at the same time.

I rub my nose, pushing my glasses askew as I grumble and close my eyes. Bennett *would* jump to assume that my mind is on work — I said as much. While Theo manages to worm to the heart of the issue, as always.

A part of me, content to wait, no matter how long it takes, settles. I do *want* to be here for June, but in the weeks she's lived with us, her energy and attention have been spent with everyone else.

My chest pangs.

I told her frankly that I loved her — and she said it back. I don't regret it, and I'm *trying* not to be hurt. She needed to hear it both the day she burst into my office, and then again before the dinner. It doesn't make it any easier to know that her time is being spent in Bennett, Seth, and Theo's beds. Maybe the kind of love she gave back to me wasn't the same as the love in my heart. Maybe it's more akin to the yearning to have someone *in* your life — not being the center of their world.

Maybe I've pushed her too much.

I don't know how to reconcile it. I *want* her to be the center of my everything. Yet, somehow, I find myself standing at the edges of my own pack — looking in at the rest of them developing, loving, and *being* with each other.

"Hey," Theo barks, throwing a pillow at me.

It hits me in the side of the head and I snarl, whirling on him. "*What?* What could you *possibly* need from me?"

One of his eyebrows arches. "Damn, don't rip my throat out."

"You zoned out again," Bennett supplies.

My eye twitches.

Readjusting my glasses, I throw the pillow onto the floor. My skin feels tight, my heart constricting in my chest. Maybe *this* is what it means to be a prime — taking whatever the fuck I can get — as long as everyone else is happy.

"Bennett, we're out of *peanut butter cups* —" June whines as she walks through the archway, arms laden with multi-colored bags of candy.

Seth nearly bumps into her when she stops short. Her eyes flicker from Theo to Bennett before they narrow on me. My heart stops when she inhales, then whips around to Bennett.

"Hold these." She dumps the candy into his lap and strides across the room.

I want to *run*. She's fucking terrifying when her laser focus is on *me*. My phone vibrates in my hand and June's eyes dart to it before becoming slits. "Don't you *dare* answer that."

I freeze as Theo guffaws.

A snarl rises in my throat that June cuts off as she fists my shirt and drags me up. I follow her mindlessly, around the chair and to the back hallway. The sounds of the living room fade when the double doors shut behind us.

Extracting myself, I shove my phone back into my pocket as I stop in front of the door to Seth's office.

"Why do you smell like that?" June's question draws my gaze. Fading light streams in from the wall of windows looking out at the front of the property. Her face pinches as she touches my chest. "Are you stressed? Is something wrong?"

Swallowing, I clear my throat. "It's nothing — just work." I ease her hand off, making it easier to think. Her close proximity is still dizzying, a twisted sweetness that invades my soul as I'm thrown back to London. Memories of her sweet body against mine, soft whines at dinner when I'd pushed her against the table and snuck my hand up her skirt.

Has she ever wanted me? Or did she just go along with it because that was expected?

June's head tips as she shrinks back, curling her arms around herself. "You don't have to tell me." Her soft voice twinges with hurt and I refocus on her.

God damn it.

I can't do anything bloody right.

"But I'm worried." She licks her lips, and I just stare at her. Golden light cascades over the side of her face, highlighting the red in her hair, catching on her long lashes and soft, round features. She's a fucking piece of *art* — even in a pair of leggings and one of Theo's old shirts. I can see the raised bite on her throat from Bennett, her hair swept up into a messy pile at the top of her head. Even though she's spent time with Theo, they've not bonded. Maybe it's not been the right time, but it has to be coming sooner rather than later. Then I'll be the only one *left* —

"Arin Mohan." June steps closer, but she doesn't reach for me again. "Where do you keep going in that head of yours?"

My hand rises, and I adjust a strand of her hair, pushing it behind the curve of her ear. I shouldn't — this should stay at the pace *she* wants it to be at — but *god* I want to drop to my knees and beg her to love me in the same way she seems to love everyone else.

Her eyes dart over my face, like she's reading the urge from the pages of one of her books. Her lips thin as she whispers, "No running, remember?"

The words hit me like a punch to the gut. I pull my hand back, but she catches it, threading our fingers together as my head hangs, defeated.

No running.

June squeezes my hand, then leans up to kiss my cheek, her nose against my skin as she murmurs, "I'll be here when you're ready. You've been patient with me, I can be patient with you." As she pulls back, her gentle eyes catch mine, offering the ghost of a smile as she leads us back into the living room where a movie is already paused on the TV.

She takes me back to my chair, leaving me to resume lying on top of Theo. He leans in and whispers something in her ear, which makes her shake her head, running her fingers over his face before his hands smooth over her curved form. Theo kisses the side of her temple.

Seth clears his throat. "We good?"

"Yes," June confirms. "Start the movie."

He unpauses it as I fish my phone back out, glancing down at a series of texts from Charles. Our security system has been on the fritz since June moved in — randomly alerting when nothing is on the monitors. We've never had this issue before, and I feel like I need to switch the company we use — the house needs to be monitored when we're all traveling, or preoccupied with June's next heat.

Rubbing the bridge of my nose again, I resolve to call the company and see what's going on this week. I can at least do *that*, even if I can't seem to do anything else correctly.

CHAPTER SEVENTEEN

THEO

Arin is being weird.

And it's making all my alarm bells ring.

It started with his weird behavior during our last movie night, but for the past few days, he's only pulled further and further away from the rest of us. I even found him *doing his own laundry*.

Which is a fucking war crime because he doesn't know how to use my natural detergent properly — it keeps us all smelling fresh without adding microplastics to the environment.

He excused his behavior by saying it was just a small load, but that's *bullshit*. He's been eating at odd times, closing his office door, and not reciprocating June's touches. That pisses me off almost as much as the laundry.

Turning my head, I blow out a breath as I cut through the water. The pool is almost too cold to be out here this early, but I refuse to turn on the heated function when I'm swimming my morning laps. The sound of the back door sliding open makes my focus waver as I reach the far end, shifting upright to shake water out of my hair.

June walks out barefoot, dancing across stone pavers on her tip-toes with a blanket slung over her shoulders. Her nose is slightly red as she catches my eye. Last night I slept alone for the first time in a handful of days, but only because Seth and Bennett are going into New York City for the day.

My little omega plops down on the side of the pool, sticking her bare legs out from the blanket and into the water. They kick as I swim over, grabbing her left calf and squeezing it. The smell of honey and orange compote covered fudge comes off her in waves as she giggles down at me.

"Charles just took Seth and Bennett to the airport. I thought you'd be up."

"I'm always up." I murmur the words, bracing my hands on either side of her hips as I hoist my upper half out of the water, capturing her lips in a kiss. She's so goddamn *sweet*. Her body molds to mine on instinct, and I have to resist every urge to climb out on top of her and take her at the side of the pool.

Not that I won't reconsider doing that when it's summer.

She laughs harder, pressing her palms against my wet chest as she wiggles. "*Stop*, you're getting me all wet."

"Up and wet?" I brush my lips over hers, nipping at her. "We're a match made in heaven."

She shoves me and I fall back into the water with a massive splash. It gets the exact reaction I hoped for — she shrieks, flinching away from the water as I splash her. June huffs, scolding me as she wags a finger. "*Theo*, you're such an *asshole*."

My dick twitches. It shouldn't when she calls me names, but I'm harder than fucking steel.

Dunking my head under the water, I come up and smooth my longer hair back. I'm hesitant to cut it. She keeps letting me lay in her lap, fingers twisting it idly at night when we're in my bed, up on *our* shared floor, away from everyone else.

I grin at her. "Born and raised."

She rolls her eyes, but dips her hand into the pool, splashing me half-heartedly. On one of the deck chairs, my phone starts to vibrate. June jumps up, leaving wet footprints as she pads over to it. "I'll get it for you."

I float backwards, closing my eyes as I call out. "It's probably just my financial advisor."

My childhood goal of never having to work felt stupid — until I actually managed it. A few careful investments and friendships made during college turned into early stakes in booming industries. I have my hands in everything from tech to medicine. When I realized I could live off a fraction of the interest my various investments make, I knew I had *made* it. Some of my favorite companies to invest in are the private resource centers for omegas who want to get *out* of bonds.

I'm still waiting for the day my mom lets me help her like I've helped strangers.

And I'm obviously a key player in Seth and Bennett's liquor company — I threw money at them the moment we were a pack. I'll never regret that decision because it's what brought us the cute little omega standing on the pool deck, frowning down at my phone.

"The contact says it's *Dick #1*." June raises an eyebrow. "I'm going to assume it's not someone named Richard."

"Shit." I reach the edge in seconds, lifting myself out of

the pool with my arms. June's eyes widen, flaring as she stares at me and the water sloshing off my body, but I can't indulge her lust-blown pupils as I snag my phone from her and answer it.

Peter never calls.

"Hello?"

I don't even sound like myself, half gruff, but mostly panicked. If this asshole is calling me to say something happened to *Mom* I'm going to kill him myself. I reach out to her weekly hoping that she'll meet with me without my fathers in tow.

"Theodore." Peter's voice rings across the call. "Glad I caught you — I was about to go into a meeting."

June gives me a concerned look, then grabs my towel and wipes off my back and stomach. Her arms wrap around me as she presses her lips against my sternum. The feeling of her body against mine makes my heart rate slow as I clutch the phone.

"Is Mom okay?"

"Your mother is fine." I can hear him rolling his eyes, his words clipped. "George spoke with Dev and Laila Mohan yesterday evening and they said they were visiting Rochester — that you have an *omega* living with the pack now? Why is this the first time we've heard about this?"

My throat swells. I unconsciously drag June closer, squeezing her hard enough that she squeaks. Her hands smooth over my back, rubbing my muscles as I bite out, "I wasn't aware that Arin's parents were visiting."

"It's his entire brood, apparently," Peter states. "We'll be there. Especially since the last time we spoke, you insisted that you'd *never* take an omega." I bristle, but I don't get a chance to respond as my father continues. "My meeting is about to begin. See you then, Theodore."

I pull the phone away, staring at it blankly as the call ends. June touches me gently. Arin's *family* is coming? And he just... didn't tell any of us? I want to see Mom, but *god* — I can't even imagine June meeting my fathers. It'll be a repeat of the dinner with her parents.

"Hey." She blinks up at me, eyelashes fluttering.

I discard my phone on the deck chair, cupping her full cheeks. Bending down to kiss her forehead, I whisper, "I need to go talk to Arin."

"Oh." She gives me a puzzled look when I pull back, frowning softly. "Okay?"

"I promise we'll do something today." I catch her gaze, finishing drying off as best as I can. "What if we went into Rochester and finally visited that bakery you found?"

Her lips twitch. She showed me no less than twenty social media posts from some small business near us, *oohing* and *ahhing* over their various cupcake flavors.

"Yeah, we can do that today." June brushes our fingers together. "I sent the first draft off last night of the new manuscript, so I'm free for a *few* days."

Chuckling, I brush back her hair. "You work too much." I say it with affection as we step into the living room. She rolls her eyes, crashing onto the couch.

"You say that now, but you also begged me to print out the draft the other day."

I walk past her, heading for the foyer as I call over my shoulder, "I contain multitudes!"

Her laughter follows me, easing the tightness in my chest as I reach Arin's office door, shoving it open. Arin looks up from his desk, pausing in the middle of writing something, his hair messy and his expression taut.

Sucking in a deep breath, I attempt to keep my temper measured as I grind out, "Why the hell did Peter just call me and tell me that your entire family is visiting?"

Arin has the good graces to look guilty. He rubs his nose, a nervous tick that he's had his entire life. Arin glances at the door, like he's worried someone else will pop up behind me — and I just *know* he's hoping it won't be June.

"Meena texted and it spiraled," he admits. "I barely let Bennett know before they left this morning, you were my next stop. I didn't think my parents would call yours."

"Well they did." I throw my hands up. "I don't want a repeat of June's parents —"

"We won't have that, my parents would *never* —"

"I *know* they wouldn't, but *mine* will."

Arin grimaces. "My hands are tied, Theo. I cannot let only my family visit without extending the invite to Bennett's parents and Seth's —"

I cut him off again. "Seth's parents don't care. They're probably in Antartica studying penguins fucking. His brother calls him once a year. I don't even know anything about the rest of his family. Bennett's dad is a *saint* and will *want* to meet June. My fathers will just make our lives hell."

His face twists, anger rolling off him in waves as he slams his pen down. "I don't know what you want me to say. They're all coming, and we will deal with it all as it happens."

My lip curls as I lean away from him, snarling, "What the *fuck* crawled up your ass and died? You've been a prick for weeks. Don't think I haven't noticed you pulling away from June —"

"That's rich, considering you made it your sole purpose to make her cry when she was in London with us."

My blood runs cold.

I stare at him, my body vibrating with a growl. "Don't come to *me* when you end up isolating yourself so much that she won't even *look* at you. Don't think I don't see it, Arin '*the martyr*' Mohan. You've always been so concerned about everyone else, and that makes you blind to your own self-sacrificing nature, even when it's harming other people." I step closer, fisting my hands at my sides. "You're doing a fucking *spectacular* job being prime — any other information you're keeping from us?"

The office goes quiet.

"Just leave, Theo. I don't have time for this right now."

I don't dignify him with a response, but I *do* slam the door behind me as I stalk back toward the living room — back to *June*. Because Arin's right, I did make her life hell, but I've apologized, and she forgave me.

We love each other.

That's enough.

CHAPTER EIGHTEEN

JUNE

"THEO!" I cackle, leaning back in the cafe chair as he walks over with another *six* cupcakes. The pink tray looks comically small in his huge hands as he balances it, switching it for the empty one on our little table.

"You said these flavors looked good too."

I beam up at him, my heart warming as he carries the empty tray away. I found the random bakery one night while scrolling through social media, curled up with Theo's head in my lap. Then I might have proceeded to show him twenty separate posts while he was captive, just to talk about their flavors and the decorations.

He came out of Arin's office determined and angry this morning, his normally soothing scent tinged with bitterness. The call from his father had clearly upset him — but whatever Arin said must have only made it worse. I'm not sure what's going on with our prime, the last few weeks have felt like he's pulling the rope taut between himself and the rest of us, from eating dinner separately to spending all hours in his office.

I miss him, but he'll talk when he's ready, just like Theo will. Communication doesn't work when it's forced.

I was worried, initially, when Bennett, Seth, and I bonded. Tension is the last thing I want to cause, but now it feels unnatural that I ever existed without their bonds in my heart, thrumming softly even with them hours away in New York City today. They've also been very understanding that what Theo and I have is different from what the three of us have.

Each relationship looks different.

Bennett and I *really* enjoy torturing Seth through the bond. Seth is so in tune with me sometimes I think he can read my mind. But Theo is the one that I can whisper my worst thoughts to in the middle of the night and let them melt away the next morning.

Theo sits back down next to me, snagging a bite of the double chocolate cupcake in front of me with a plastic fork, holding it up to my mouth.

I smile over at him. His blond hair is slightly waved from the pool this morning and the black henley he has on is stretched across his wide shoulders. His blue eyes cut into me as he dips his chin down.

"Try it."

"Theo, I'm so *full*."

"Come on." His lips twitch, a devilish smirk lifting them as his eyes dart down to my lips. "Be a good girl for me."

Heat races up my spine. Spoiling me seems to make his mood brighten considerably — especially when taking care of me means being in control. As much as he wanted to fight it, it's never been clearer that he's *happier* when he's able to dote on me and be a giant sap.

The omega in me is extremely smug that no one else has ever gotten this treatment.

Flushing, I shake my head. "You should have gotten those to go. This is too much sugar, Theo."

He pouts, but glances back at the register. "Do I need to go get another box? I was going to get us another dozen to take home, plus whatever flavors were your favorites so you'd have snacks."

I stare at him. "I am *not* eating a dozen cupcakes."

His eyes narrow. "You won't even take *one* bite for me before we go to the nest store?"

The lines have blurred, this trip has turned into one for *him*, not me.

Leaning forward, I glare back at him. "I already said I don't *need* to go —" I nearly choke as his other hand rises, collaring the back of my throat. My words die as I stare up at him, mouth dropping open.

Theo stares down at me, eyes hooded. "Tongue out. Taste it, June."

My breath catches as I open my mouth wider for him. He slips the fork into my mouth and my lips close around it. An unrestrained moan bubbles up as the chocolate melts on my tongue, the food version of Seth's scent and taste.

"*God.*" I cover my mouth as I chew, glancing down at the cupcake.

He smirks. "Just Theo is fine."

I roll my eyes at him and then steal the fork, stabbing the cupcake to get another bite.

"Did you just *roll* your eyes at me?" Theo leans in, his voice lowering so the other tables can't overhear. "Don't be a brat, June. Let me spoil you like you deserve."

Pausing with the fork on my tongue, I stare up at him before smiling slowly. Licking the prongs, I watch his nostrils flare, savoring the taste of chocolate before I tilt my head at him and whisper, "No."

Theo's eyes twinkle with danger. "No?"

"No, I'm not going to let you spoil me."

He nods, then stands up. I nearly drop the fork as he bends over me, one hand on the table, trapping me in the chair. My heart flutters as his lips graze my earlobe. "I'm getting a box and we're leaving." His eyes darken, flickering over my face as they dip to my lips, but he doesn't move.

"Are we going home?" I hate how breathy I sound, but I'd shove him to the floor of this bakery right now and fuck him in front of the pink glitter cupcakes if he'd let me.

Not a bad idea, either. I should make sure everyone else knows he's mine.

Just as I tamp down *that* unhinged omega thought, he walks away without giving me an answer. I stare at him as he returns to the counter, pointing at various cupcakes behind the glass and ordering a box. My eyes catch on his back, my tongue rolling over my teeth as he takes up so much *space*. He's an *alpha* in every sense of the word.

I love our quiet moments together, but the tension makes me goddamn feral.

Theo returns a moment later with two boxes of cupcakes and one empty container. He packs up the half dozen on the table, his tone casual. "We have a nesting store to get to." Theo glances over at me, and the dark look in his eyes makes me grin, tossing my hair over my shoulder.

He's just as affected as I am. We're barely going to make it home. I'm so excited to fucking *ruin* him for anyone else.

⚛

THERE'S ONLY one nesting store in Rochester and it's significantly different from the two luxury ones that I've been in. I *do* like this one a lot, though my focus is totally shot.

"Add a spank every time you put something back."

Theo walks behind me, his voice hot against my neck. My brain is fucking *fried* as I touch a candle, having to wait a second for it reset itself. Then I pick up the candle, hum, and put it back, repeating the motion four more times with the same exact scent, before I walk away.

I don't know *where* the sudden confidence comes from — but I've been waiting for this since our little New York shopping trip. I have his attention all to myself and I'm damn well going to savor it.

His hand comes down on the side of my hip, one quick crack that makes me jump as I whirl on him, wide-eyed and blushing. Theo just tilts his head down at me, backing me up against one of the displays.

"You can either wait in the car while I check out, or you can behave. Which one?"

I choose neither.

Something in me flares. Maybe it's my own desire to show him how bratty I can be — or it's the omega in the back of my mind that craves every bit of attention I can get, but I dart under his arm and walk away.

At the back of the store are all the aisles and displays for heat items, ranging from crotchless underwear to anatomical toys in a range of sizes, lengths, and knot swells. I feel his eyes on me as I browse, humming until I stop short at a little box.

With a slow smile, I grab the clit suction toy. The information on the back is straightforward — all the hands-free orgasms I could ever want in one tiny little package.

Turning on a dime, I flounce back over to him at the counter and drop the box next to the other items I collected. "This too, please." I give the beta behind the register a pleasant smile, then make the mistake of beaming up at Theo.

The look on his face nearly knocks me on my *ass*.

I'm so screwed.

Giddiness floods my veins as he stares down at me, eyes dark and lips parted as he looks from me to the toy. Fuck, I should have grabbed a paddle or flogger too.

The poor cashier clears her throat. "The card reader is ready whenever you — oh okay." She squeaks the word as Theo taps his card, eyes on me.

He takes the bags and turns toward the door without a word. I slide my hand onto his elbow, holding onto him with a gleeful wiggle as we walk outside. Theo throws everything into the back of our SUV before he whirls us, pinning me with a hand on my hip to the side of the car before he kisses me roughly.

I moan as I push up against him, the grind of his body against mine making my hands drop to the hem of my sweater. I'm not *totally bare* under it — a bralette isn't public indecency.

"You are so fucking *bad*," he hisses as he nips at my mouth. "What'd you get that for? Trying to replace me?" I groan when his hands push mine down, stopping me from rucking my sweater up. "Stop trying to undress yourself and get in the fucking car."

Squeaking, I dissolve into giggles as he manhandles me into the passenger seat. Theo tugs the seatbelt down and buckles me in, raising an eyebrow as I squirm.

"You shouldn't be getting princess treatment when you're being such a brat, but I'm a sucker."

Biting my lip, I grin up at him as my perfume blooms between us. With one hand on the top of the car, Theo leans in. His nose brushes mine as I murmur, "But you love me, and you know you get me all to yourself the rest of the day. Think about how good I'm going to look in your lap, riding your big, fat alpha c —"

He pulls away, giving me a scathing look. "*Behave*, June."

I huff as he shuts the door, getting into the driver's side and pulling away from the store. With a whine, I fling myself back into the seat, staring out of the front window. "You could have fucked me in the backseat. No one would have known."

"No," he snaps, merging onto the highway. "You've never been quiet a day in your life, they would have heard you screaming across town. Keep popping off with that shit and you won't be able to sit for a week."

"I dare you." I turn to give him a mocking glare, crossing my arms.

Theo's eyes cut to me for the barest of moments, heating my blood as he mutters, "You're being a *brat*, princess. Do you know what brats get?"

"Not fucked, apparently," I scoff, staring back out the window. What's the point of having an alpha wrapped around my finger if I can't goad him into giving me what I want?

I've spent my entire damn life doing everything I'm supposed to — from the clothes I wore when I was a teenager, to the excelling grades and scholarships I won. I have tried and tried and *tried* to appease everyone else, to not stand out for the wrong reasons, not to be on anyone's bad side — and I'm sick of it. I *want* to be bad. I've earned it.

His smile is dangerous as he takes a turn, and the car bumps as it eases up the driveway to the pack house. Warning bells echo in my mind as I glance at him, but then *I* smile as I reach for my seatbelt.

He glances at me as I touch the release, the car stopping in front of the house.

"We wouldn't want the cupcakes to melt, so I'll leave you to take care of those for me, *alpha*. Good thing I got that toy, since you'll be too busy to help me!" Diving into the back-seat, I find the right bag and wrap my fingers around the box before flinging myself out of the car. "See you later!"

"June!"

His snarl follows me as I take off with a cackle, scrambling through the front doors and into the foyer. Theo curses behind me as I make a beeline for the stairs, glancing to the side and stopping short when I see Arin in the hall to the kitchen.

Hesitating on the steps, I flash him a hesitant smile. "Don't tell him you saw me?" Theo will know — regardless — but if Arin can delay him for even a *few* seconds, it would be nice.

Arin's lips twitch *just* so before he nods.

Grinning, I turn and *bolt*. The sounds of Theo bursting

into the foyer behind me makes me scramble up the stairs even faster, passing the floor with Bennett and Seth's rooms and stopping on the one with mine and Theo's. I go straight to his room, kicking off my boots, stumbling and tripping on his plush carpet as I run into his bathroom.

Everything is decorated simply in a dusty blue color palette, calming and peaceful. The entire space is *coated* in his rain perfume, and it feels like I'm wrapping myself in a warm blanket most days, but right now I just want to drive him as off the rails as I feel.

I rip into the box, pulling out the toy and plunging it into the sink to wash it, giggling as I try to tug my sweater off while I multi-task. Footsteps stomp up the stairs and I move faster, leaving my sweater on the bathroom floor as I race back into his room, throwing the toy onto the bed and reaching to get my jeans off.

The door behind me slams open before I can even touch the button.

"*Stop.*"

My hands drop as I whirl. Theo *fills* the doorway, shoulders broad and heaving as he takes me in, eyes catching on my gray lace bralette. It's comfortable, but so thin it does nothing to hide my nipples pebbling through it or support my heaving chest.

"Turn back around, omega. Bend the fuck over."

Biting my tongue, I grin despite myself and do exactly what he says. With a wiggle, I stick my ass out, chest to his bed as his hands drop to grasp my hips.

"Is this what you wanted?" He bends, whispering as he massages my hips through fabric. "To drive me insane today? Every day? I see you and I can't think straight. I want you, in so many different ways, it's like my brain isn't even my own. I could spend every waking hour with you and still crave you when I'm asleep."

I suck in a little breath as one of his hands leaves me, only to crack across my hip with a slap. Moaning, my heart flutters as I reach back, grabbing his wrist as I whine and press against him. *"Theo, please."*

The new omega gynecologist I saw warned me that keeping the IUD in might lead to more and more heat spikes as my body tries to fight it and adjust to the supplemental hormones. I really should have believed her — I want him. I *need* him.

"Please what?" He nips at my ear, twisting his hand to free his wrist as he reaches around to unbutton my jeans. "*Theo* please fuck me? *Theo* please spank me? *Theo* please make me come?" he taunts me as he drags my jeans down, leaving me in the gray underwear that match my bra.

As he drops to his knees behind me, I shiver, feeling his lips graze my calf. *I'm going to die. This is what's going to kill me.* I want him so much I can't think as he pulls my pants off and throws them to the side.

"You make me want to drive you insane." He whispers the words as his hands slide over my bare skin, kissing up until his lips land on my lower back. "You make me want to edge you until you're crying just so you can feel the fraction of frustration I do."

"I love it." I gasp as his hand slides into my hair. Our eyes connect when he pulls my head back, my lips popping open as I moan, "I know you'd never actually hurt me."

His eyes soften, burning with unspoken desire as his fingers tighten in my hair. "We still need a safe word if I'm actually going to spank you, baby."

"Cupcake." My lips twitch as I wiggle my hips, pressing

back against his jeans just to feel the length of him. "There, now you can fuck — *me!*" My voice goes up a pitch when he spins me around, making me gasp as he deadlifts me with one hand, guiding my legs around his torso. With one hand on my ass and the other in my hair, he drags me into a soul-searing kiss, making my veins thrum as the scent of him sends my head spinning.

Theo drops us to the bed, crawling on top of me as my hands land on his chest, running down to grab the hem of his shirt. He stops me, pinning my hands to my sides as he kisses my jaw, groaning, "No, I'm in control here."

"Are you?"

He smacks my bare hip and I shriek, it turning into a strangled moan as he grinds his jeans against my core, the friction making me shiver.

His low, dark laugh crawls over my skin as he kisses me again, fingers rubbing the raw skin he just slapped. There's love in the motion as Theo lifts up and looks down at me, breathing harder. "Look at you."

"I know." I bite my lip as I smile up at him, spreading my thighs wider for him. My underwear is soaked. "And I'm all yours, alpha."

He leans down, voice a near growl as he takes my lips again. "I don't own you any other time, June." Biting my lips, he just barely pulls back before breaking the skin, running his hands all over me as he grinds into me. "But when you're in my bed, your body belongs to me, omega."

As his teeth drag over my throat, he grabs me by the hips and flips me, pushing my head into the bedspread to make my back arch.

"When you get on your knees and present for me, you're *mine.*" Theo's hand cups me over my underwear, his breath catching. "And I'm going to fuck you and bite you to prove it."

Sparks alight on my skin as I push back against him. *Yes, God yes.*

"But first —"

He pulls his hand away and grabs the toy near my head. With one flick, the motor hums, silicone nub suckling the air. Theo rips my panties to the side. "You need to be punished."

He suctions the toy to my clit and I *scream*. Burying my face into his bed, my back bows as the sudden tugging pressure zaps every thought from my body. Everything was already heightened — on a hairpin trigger since my heat — but now I know it's not me, or the biology, it's *them*.

It's Bennett. It's Seth. It's Arin. It's *Theo*. I just want them. I want to be surrounded by them, touched by them, absolutely drowning in our love for each other until there's nothing left of me.

I sob out a gasp as the toy does exactly what the box promised — sucking and never letting go. He can have his way with me because there's something completely freeing to have my brain off and my body reduced to just *feeling*.

Theo spreads my legs wider, rubbing my ass cheeks. "Tell me, June. How many spanks did you earn today?"

I arch my back a little more, my head spinning. "I don't know."

Clicking his tongue, his hand smoothes over my skin before pulling back. He hits me across the hip and ass and I clench down on nothing as the toy thrums and thrums, suctioning until I feel my thighs shake.

"One." He counts, rubbing the skin before alternating to the other side. "Two..." A moan leaves him as he stands behind me. "God you should see yourself. You're fucking *soaked.* Let's make it to five. Count with me, can you do that before you come?"

Three more. I nod, fisting the bedspread as he rubs my hip.

"Good girl." His hand comes down again and I squeal.

Slick drips down my thighs as he rubs my heated skin. "Three!" I whine out the number as he rears back and repeats it on the other side, but between the teasing this morning and the toy, I can't function. My knees wobble as I try to hold myself up, his hand sliding between my thighs and gliding through the mess there.

"Are you sure you haven't already come? Do you like it when I punish you, princess? Are you just my little toy to tease and do whatever I want?"

Is this coming? My body feels electric as I push back into him on instinct. He flicks the button, turning the suction up to the next setting. Stars burst behind my eyes as I flutter around nothing. One hand cups me as his other raises.

"Last one. I think you *are* coming already. I think you can't fucking stop yourself. You look so pretty too, your ass all red, your body begging for what you need — release. Take it from me."

His thumb flicks the button one more time, cycling to the third and highest setting as his other hand comes down across my ass. My mouth opens, but no sound comes out as my back arches, my legs giving out as all my muscles clench, release dripping down the insides of my thighs.

But Theo is right there. His arms band around me, jerking the toy away and throwing it somewhere as he picks me up and readjusts us so I'm laying on top of him on the bed. My heart pounds in my ears as his hands soothe over my skin, pushing the bra and underwear away along with his clothes.

When my cheek finally touches his bare chest, I sink into him, body trembling.

"You did so well for me." Sweet nothings pepper my consciousness between kisses as I splay out on top of him. It takes my brain a second to reboot as I unconsciously grind down against him.

Theo grunts as I cup his face, kissing him heatedly as I whine, "I love you. I love you so much. Bite me. I want you. I want *this*. I need you —"

He shushes me, pulling me closer as he kisses me, his voice just as raw. "I love you too." One hand pulls my hair back, exposing the bite on my neck as his eyes find mine. "You're sure? You want me like that?"

"Bond me, Theo." I stare at him, my heart in my hands, ready to give it to him if he'll accept it.

Theo flips up, putting me on my back with a gruff noise. His head drops to my throat, kissing over the existing mark with reverence before he moves lower, his voice growing strangled. "I've had so much time to think about where I'd do it." Theo's lips wrap around a nipple and as he sucks, I hook a leg around him, dragging his hips to mine.

"I don't care where you do it, just *bond me*."

One of his hands slides up, bracing the back of my neck, holding me still as he suckles on my chest. Then his fingers shift and tangle in my hair, fisting it and jerking my head in the same motion, making my back arch and baring my chest to him. He strikes without warning. His teeth bury into the side of my left breast the same moment he slams into me, knot and all.

It's instantaneous.

One moment it's just the faint awareness of Bennett and Seth at the edge of my consciousness, and in the next *he's* there. Love, lust, uncertainty, yearning, acceptance, admiration, adoration, sheer *want* — every emotion hits me as I clench down on him, coming unexpectedly with a cry.

Tears streak down my cheeks as he pulls back, his tongue lavishing the mark on my breast, breathing hard as his voice wobbles.

"Let it out." He sucks on my skin again, emotions wracking through me as his voice breaks. "Be a brat with me. Fight with me. Play with me. Because at the end of the night, when your ass is red from my palms, and your thighs are sticky with my release, you're still mine. I will still love you, even at your worst, even at your nastiest, angriest, unyieldingly stubborn — I will love you."

The bond snaps into place, like it was always meant to be a rope around my heart, ensnaring it, enrobing *me* with the feeling of love emanating from the man on top of me.

Bending down, I pull him by the hair away from the mark and kiss him hard enough that he groans. Theo's hips pump, shallow thrusts as he twitches, and I don't give him a second before I snag his lower lip in mine and bite it harshly, breaking the skin and making the bond sing between us.

He comes with a shout, bracing himself overtop of me as I breathe hard under him. I'm a total fucking wreck — but it doesn't matter as we claw at each other, him locked inside me. I giggle, almost drunk on the feeling of his amusement rocketing through me. The connection is so strong I catch his lip again and run my tongue over it, getting a hit of his endless arousal.

Theo tangles a hand in my hair, his voice thick. "God, I love you."

I lean up as much as I can, kissing him slower, softer as I roll against him, the knot tugging as we both moan. "And now you know just how much I love you."

He grabs me by my reddened hips and grinds us together, pinning me down as we lose ourselves in each other.

CHAPTER NINETEEN

JUNE

THE BITE on my tit itches and I'm sweating.

I only picked a turtleneck because the back wall of the living room is open to the pool deck and yard, letting in the cool air coming off the lake.

Not because my entire body is covered in purple bruises from Theo.

The hickeys wouldn't even disappear with make-up, and the bonding bite keeps brushing against the edge of my bra, sending little teasing sparks through my body as I try to look normal at this ridiculous party that Arin seemed to plan overnight.

Chewing on my lower lip, I glance around the living room. So far the only people here are Arin's parents — Dev and Laila, who are two of the kindest people I've ever met. Laila is tall, equal to Arin's height, but Dev only comes to their shoulders. Both of them gave me the biggest smile when they arrived, and yet, I'm still terrified to meet all four of his sisters with their packs and significant others.

Seth's family couldn't make it. He said his parents work

in remote areas — and then changed the conversation. I reach out to him with the bond and with a hand, grabbing onto him. As I turn to kiss his cheek, I whisper, "I'm really nervous."

His fingers intertwine with mine as he takes another swig of the spiked lemonade in his hand. The unmarked cans are scattered amongst the other drink options sitting out — because who better to test his and Bennett's new products than family?

"I hope you know that Bennett's parents won't leave you alone when they get here. His dad *loves* hugs. It'll be fine, Junie." He kisses the side of my head. "Deep breaths."

I can tell he isn't lying to me because the bond is so relaxed and open between us, but still, I nudge the bites on his throat and sigh. "What about Theo's?"

He grumbles, taking another drink. "They'll behave or I'll drown his fathers in our pool."

"Seth!"

He doesn't *sound* teasing.

"What are we talking about?" Bennett strides over, wrapping an arm around each of us before wiggling between. He turns his head, kissing me, then Seth. "Because the vibes from the bond are murderous, but you both seem far too happy right now."

Leaning into him, I breathe in his freshly showered skin, rubbing my nose against his neck. He smells so fucking *good*, like peeling an orange on a hot summer day and licking the juices off your fingers.

"June's nervous," Seth supplies, then pauses, raising an eyebrow at me. "Well, she *was*, until you walked over and apparently made her horny."

Bennett turns, his hand rising on my side, thumb skimming over my sweater. "I promise this evening will be okay. Arin's sisters will adore you, my dad can't wait to finally meet you, and Theo's mother is very kind."

The mention of Theo's family sobers me. The third bond in my chest is quiet, almost somber, and Theo's *still* not in the living room. He and Arin were coordinating the catering. It already takes a lot to feed our pack of five, and it takes a lot more to supply enough food for almost twenty more people that will be in the house tonight.

My skin feels itchy as I pull back. Arin and Theo step into the living room just as Arin's father looks up from chatting with his wife.

"Theresa just texted! She's almost here with Keelan."

Arin steps over, planting a kiss on his mother's cheek. "I'm sure Vera isn't far behind, or the twins for that matter."

"Juniper!" Laila turns, waving me over. "Come here, I need to see you next to my son and Theo."

The doorbell goes off as I take a step and Bennett pivots toward it. Seth drops his drink on a table, kissing the back of my head. "We'll grab it."

I give Bennett a panicked look, but he just responds by flooding the bond between us with warmth. Theo's bond opens up and his nerves mix with mine, tangling until Seth leans in, squeezing my hand tightly. The support from both of them is a bleed of reassurance, calming both Theo and I. As Bennett and Seth leave the living room, Seth touches Theo's arm, casting him a little smile.

I step over, finding myself between Arin and Theo, tipping my head up. Poking the bond between Theo and I, I graze his hand with my own. He glances down, and then the rest of the walls he has up fall — nerves, resentment, anger, worry — I take it without wavering, pushing love back at him as he holds my hand.

"Look at you three." Laila beams at us, her eyes misty. "Arin." She clicks her tongue, waving her hands at him. "Move closer, why are you standing there so awkwardly?"

"Amma, he was born awkward."

Arin jolts, turning sharply. My eyes follow his, finding the spitting image of Laila walking into the room. The tall, leggy Indian woman has a wild mane of black curly hair around her head, and she gives me a wide smile, her eyes falling on Theo.

"There you are." She wraps her arms around him, almost nose to nose with him — taller than Arin as she pulls back and gives her parents hugs too. "I see the steroids are still working."

Theo flips her off.

"Theresa," Arin grumbles.

Her grin widens. "Shut up, prat." Her focus darts to me. "He didn't even *tell* us about you until last week."

I glance at Arin, gasping out, "I've lived here for *two* months."

Arin stares back at me, swallowing. "I didn't want to invite any unnecessary comments. It's our private pack business."

I'm oddly touched, but a huge part of my heart fractures a little. He didn't even tell his *family* about me. I'm already *bonded* with three of the people in this pack and Arin couldn't even find time to tell his parents that I was living with him?

Laila fawns over Theresa for a moment before letting her go and embracing the next person who walks into the living room, beer in hand. "Keelan, look at you." She squeezes their shoulders, cooing over them. "You look so thin, is my daughter not feeding you well?"

"Oh my god." Theresa mutters the words, rubbing her forehead. "I swear she loves them more than she loves any of us. If Keelan and I broke up, she'd pick them to keep and toss me to the curb."

My lips twitch. "Do you think she'd keep me or Arin?"

"She'd keep Theo, he's not as boring as our son," Dev pipes up and I bark out a laugh at Arin's father. He smiles back at me. "But I'll keep you, Juniper, you're sweet."

"*Great.*" Arin drawls out the word, looking more and more uncomfortable. "Thank you. I'm so glad you'd all leave me destitute."

"I'll make room in my refrigerator box for you." Theresa bumps his hip with her own. "I can't let my baby brother work the street corner."

Theo chokes on his beer as I laugh loudly.

Theresa lets out a strangled noise. "*Ay, Amma!*" she shouts at her mother, storming over to make her stop poking at Keelan's shoulder, questioning them about their job and when they're planning on proposing.

"Oh no," Dev mutters, putting his drink down. "I need to get your mother before she starts showing Keelan engagement rings again." He squeezes Arin's shoulder as he passes by.

"We're *here!*"

"They know, you were so *fucking* loud outside, the whole state probably knows —"

My head spins as twin, spitting images of Arin's entire bloodline, bicker and walk into the living room. One of them is Meena — the other Mila. Meena has her long, curly hair pulled back into a ponytail, trailed by two men. The impression of one of them hits me like a gut-punch — *alpha*. His angular eyes roll as he leans into the other man and mutters something under his breath.

"*Don't*" — Meena stops short, snarling at them — "side with her."

Mila flashes her twin's pack a grin.

I only know the barest amount about Arin's family, snippets learned while prepping for this last minute party. The twins both have established packs of three, while Arin's youngest sister has three alphas.

Mila's short curly hair brushes her chin as she looks around. "Where's Greta and —"

"Here, love." A willowy blonde woman enters the room and immediately goes to her side, kissing her cheek. "Bennett was showing Rose and I his new car."

My throat feels a little tight, all the new scents and sounds assaulting me as I suck in a deep breath. Even with the wall open to the outside, the living room feels *small*. A hand on my jaw turns my head and I inhale mint, breathing in deep as Arin pulls me into his arms.

"It's okay." His voice is soft, only for me as his other arm wraps around me, putting my back to the party. "Theo just stepped away to get another drink, but let me go get him —"

"No." I cling to him, frantic for a moment. I bury my nose against his chest, my hands shaking as I fist his shirt. "Don't leave me."

"Okay." He sounds a little panicked, but he pulls me closer and moves my head to his throat, pressing my nose against his scent gland. My eyes flutter, embarrassed and overwhelmed as tears spring to my eyes. My throat burns. I should be able to handle a few people in the house, but it hits me out of nowhere. There's too many voices, too many scents. *Where is Seth? Bennett? Theo?*

Arin's hand cups the back of my head, his bark rocking me to my core. "Juniper, *breathe*."

I suck in a breath, inhaling his perfume. It swipes my spiraled thoughts away, until he straightens and growls, "I'm kicking them all out."

"No!" I grab onto him, mortified that he would send everyone away when it's already started. "I can be okay. I'm okay."

His eyes flash to mine, and this close, I see the gold flecks amongst the brown. Arin's gaze narrows. "You've never been around other packs like this. I shouldn't have — I mean —" He sucks in a breath, stopping himself. "I read it's very over-stimulating for an omega to be around other alphas when a pack is new. I did this all wrong, and now it's upsetting you. I should have waited for you to be settled with Theo, Bennett, and Seth."

My heart clenches. "And you?"

Arin pulls away. "We don't have a bond, Juniper."

Pain lances through my chest. Taking a step back, I force myself not to cry as I separate from the once-safety of his arms. "You're right. We don't."

His face breaks, just *so*, and as I open my mouth to ask him what he means by that — why he's throwing this in my face *now* of all the times — Laila grabs my arm excitedly, making me jump.

"Come meet Meena and Mila!"

I don't look back at Arin as I let his mother drag me away.

The Mohans take up half the party guests.

Laila introduces me to multiple people, and each time, I plaster a smile on my face like I'm not viewing the entire evening from outside my own body. There's Meena, and her two bonded, an alpha and beta — then Mila and her two female alphas.

"Vera is pregnant," Laila chatters excitedly as she whirls us around the room. "Come meet her and her alphas."

She steers me toward one of the couches and I glance at the three alphas standing behind the couch like guard dogs. One is *huge* — broad and dark-skinned. Another has red hair — my brain struggles to catch up as my eyes flicker to the omega, still seated.

The moment we connect eyes, we both say, "*Oh my god.*"

"It's you!" Vera flings herself up from the couch, ignoring her small, rounded belly to throw herself at me, smelling of blueberries. Same dark skin, silky black hair — she's the omega I spoke to months ago in the airport who knew my own fucking designation before it hit me the next night at my signing.

The three alphas behind the couch all leap forward, and I flinch, partially away from her but mostly away from *them* — three massive bodies all trying to stop Vera from hurting herself.

She turns, murder radiating off her. "If you don't get *back* right now." Vera whirls, grabbing my arm. "You want to go outside? Let's go outside." Her other hand buffs her alphas back, grabbing me and pivoting us toward the open air.

I suck in lungfuls of it as she rubs my shoulder, leading us over to the deck chairs.

"It's okay, just breathe." She sounds so solid, comforting and familiar to my body as she murmurs, "I can tell you're one second from losing it. I fucking *freaked* when I emerged. I don't know if Arin ever told you —"

"He did."

She pushes me into a chair, plopping down next to me.

"Well he's an idiot for letting all of us invade your space right now, you're still trying to adjust to everything and we should *not* be here. You and I are just going to sit out here for a tip until you stop hyperventilating. What can I ramble about —" She glances at me, squinting. "Oh! Okay, so my big alpha? That's Aata, he's Kiwi and plays rugby in England. The first time I saw him I squeaked because — I mean, did you even know men came that *big*? What are you supposed to do with a man that huge? Well, I figured that out, clearly." She motions to her stomach, and the utter ridiculousness of her words clears my brain as I focus on the sound of the lake behind us and the cool air on my oversensitive skin.

"Keep going," I rasp at her, blinking rapidly to stop myself from crying.

"Right." Her British accent is crisp. "Well Aata will make sure none of your alphas come bother us, because you know what *doesn't* help when you're having a little omega freak-out? When one of them goes all territorial for no reason."

Pressing my hands against my eyes, I whisper, "Fuck being an omega."

"It's awful, isn't it?" Vera chirps, then she rubs my arm.

"Anyway, I met Aata three weeks after I emerged. He was an exchange student and I was already at uni and it all went tits up."

I lower my hands, staring at her.

She smiles back. "You stopped shaking. I didn't even get to Ollie's bisexual awakening."

Sniffling, I swallow back bile. "How am I supposed to do any of this?"

Her expression softens. "You survive, and you're already doing a bloody good job at it." Vera's hand pulls away as she glances back at the house. "Not that my brother seems keen to help you adjust properly. Prick."

"I don't think he likes me."

She rears back, barking out a laugh. "*What?*" At my blank look, she shakes her head. "June, my brother *fought off* our entire Indian family, aunties and all, who wanted to come to this party tonight. I think he waited as long as he could to tell any of us — and honestly, he made it longer than I expected. Still doesn't save him from actually letting anyone into your home, but it does give him a few brownie points."

The tears spring right back to my eyes as I glance at the house, my voice shaking as I rub my arms. "I feel like I'm losing my mind sometimes."

She makes a sympathetic noise, touching her stomach. "I think a lot of us do. I've never felt more understood than when I've been venting to my omega friends. It's a lot to handle, and no one else will understand every moment of it except for *us.*"

Her eyes flicker to Aata, standing in the doorway, tattoos winding up his thick arms as he keeps an eye on us. "Aata introduced me to a friend on his rugby team — he'd emerged as an omega just after he turned twenty-one. We can talk shit about our designations *and* Aata at the same time." Her hand lifts and she points to the red-haired alpha, then the blond man next to him. "Ollie and Quinton kind of fell into our pack, but I can't imagine having a beta too, that seems like a lot."

"Seth is..." My voice trails off as I find him. His tanned hands raise, pulling his hair up into a scrunchie as he laughs at something Keelan says. "I love him." Touching the bond mark on my throat, my composure shatters, tears overflowing. "I love them all. God, why can't I stop *crying*?"

Vera rubs my back. "Are you bonded with all of them?"

"No" — I look up at her through tears — "not with Arin."

Her mouth pulls down into a frown before she embraces me, hugging me tightly. "I don't pretend to understand every dynamic or how it works with our biologies, but I do know it's hard when you don't have a bond with the prime." Vera squeezes me. "I thought Aata was the prime, but then I met Quinton."

I look over at him as she pulls back.

"He was my last bond." Her lips twitch at the memory. "Everything felt *right* after he bit me. He's like a salve." Vera looks back at me, pushing her hair behind her ears. "Can I ask why you and Arin...?"

I hesitate, pulling a leg up into the chair and resting my chin on my knee.

"I didn't know what I was doing before my heat." I swallow back the lump in my throat. "It was enough to make sure I was somewhere safe in London... it was enough to be scared of how quickly it all moved. I had to trust that I would come out the other side okay." My eyes scan the back of the house, finding the window for my bedroom. "Bennett was my first bond, along with Seth..."

Vera nudges me with her elbow. "When you know, you know."

"Yeah." I glance at her, smiling softly. "Theo happened this week."

"It sounds like that you just haven't had your moment yet with my stupid brother, but if I know anything about him, he's probably terrified to cross a line that he's arbitrarily drawn in the sand." She leans back in her chair. "And he's probably convinced himself that he's doing everything wrong — which is right, because he's stupid."

I open my mouth to defend him, but then my bond with Bennett flares with love. Looking back at the house, I find him wrapped in the arms of two women and one man. His father pulls away first, cupping Bennett's cheeks and kissing his son's forehead, their skin-tone identical in its richness. One of his mothers is also dark-skinned, her head shaved, the other olive-toned with short brown hair.

Seth darts over to them and Bennett's father tugs him into a tight hug. An echo of the love comes through and I blink back to myself, realizing I'm touching my chest.

Vera is quiet beside me as I process it. "Want to head in?" She offers me a hand after standing up. "I'd lend you one of my alphas as a bodyguard, but you seem to have your own waiting for you."

Arin lingers near the open doors, standing next to Vera's alphas, Oliver and Quinton. Her alphas talk to him, drinks in hand, eyes casting out to us occasionally.

Pushing up, I brush my hands off on my jeans, my eyes finding Arin's like a magnet. My chest tugs, harsh and uncomfortable and for a moment I think it's my own emotions toward him, until Theo charges toward the foyer.

I feel torn for a moment — wanting to go to Seth and Bennett — but having a feeling that Theo's parents are finally here — but Arin is right *there* —

Vera takes my arm, tilting her head toward me, her voice soft. "What do you need?"

"I need to meet Bennett's family, and I need to be with Theo."

"Got it." She nods, sharply. "Aata can trap Arin in a conversation. Go meet Marcus, Yasmin, and Kary —" She tugs us around the pool and to the house. "Bennett's parents are lovely. Theo's... on the other hand..." She makes a face.

"Yeah. That's what I'm worried about."

The bond already feels muddled again, like Theo's suppressing it.

Aata suddenly appears, like Vera summoned him from thin air. The huge alpha tugs Arin into a boisterous hug, allowing Vera and I to slip past them and into the house. I mouth a *thank you* at her before I dart across the living room.

Bennett snags me, one arm coming around my waist as he swings me into his arms, his smile splitting his face. "There you are." He bends his head, kissing me out of the blue.

I flush, but his expression is soft when he pulls back, pushing my hair away from my face as he pivots us toward the three adults in front of us. "Meet my parents." Tugging me a half-step closer, Bennett preens next to me. I glance at them, seeing the uncanny resemblance between Bennett and his father, Marcus.

Marcus is nose to nose with his son in height, and his face lights up.

"I'm so glad to finally meet you, Juniper." He pauses before he shifts forward. "I'd love to give you a hug, but not if it's too much."

My heart warms at the omega man. Letting Bennett go, I eagerly step forward, embracing him, a wave of sweetness wafting over me. Blood orange — Marcus squeezes me, then motions to the dark-skinned woman to his left. "Yasmin." He looks to his right. "And Kary, my wives."

Yasmin's expression is gentle. "It's so nice to meet you, Juniper."

Kary echoes her sentiment, then opens her arms. "It's been *months* since Bennett told us you were with him in London."

I hug her too, getting hit with a punch of a spicy perfume. It's so vibrant it throws me for a loop — but when Yasmin squeezes my arm, a scent of lime chases it away. The three of them together smell like a spritzer.

Pulling back, I feel Bennett move behind me, his hand coming to cup my hip. "I didn't know he told you all." I tilt my head back, glancing at him.

He looks sheepish. "Well —"

"He had no chill." Seth mutters the words next to us, wrapping his arms around us both. "But it was adorable and it all worked out."

Smiling at Bennett, I lean against his shoulder, feeling soothed by both of them around me. "It is cute."

Bennett scoffs, but his lips twitch. "Quit, you two."

Marcus beams at us. "I want to hear all about your work, June. An author —"

Kary shifts, her eyes widening. "I read your first book on the flight here, it was wonderful!"

Blushing, I sink into Bennett's embrace, warmth and

kindness radiating from his family. Just as I promise to give Kary an advanced copy of my next release, a jolt of anger punches through me.

Two men stalk into the room, thick shouldered and scowling.

One of them, a blond, snaps, "Keep up, Grace."

The blonde woman behind him has her head slightly bowed, hands together in front of her as Theo rushes to catch up, reaching out for his mother. Devastation floods the bond from him just as both of Theo's fathers scan the room.

Their eyes lock on me.

CHAPTER TWENTY

ARIN

MEENA TAKES a long drink from her beer, eyeing me. "You've never been the stupid one in the family, but you're *really* giving Mila a run for her fucking money tonight."

I've been trapped by every single *bloody* person in this house in the span of twenty minutes. First, I'd felt like an ass when June stepped away from me — but the comment about us not having a bond slipped out. I only wanted to remind her that she didn't have to prioritize me, or include me in the list of people that she needed.

And then she'd given me a look like I'd slapped her.

After I tracked her down, finding her with Vera on the porch — Vera's alphas cornered me and did everything but explicitly tell me I wasn't welcome outside my own goddamn home. June was clearly *upset* and I caused it.

Now I'm trapped with Meena ragging on me while June stands between Bennett and Seth, talking to the Lawrences.

"Shut up." I grimace at the burn of the alcohol as it races down my throat.

My sister snorts. "*Okay.*" Her voice drips with sarcasm as

her alpha — Jakob — bends down to whisper in her ear. She barks out a laugh, glancing over at me with her eyes twinkling. "A little birdie just told me something, dear brother."

Jakob's lips twitch and it takes everything in me not to lay the other alpha flat on his ass. His bleached, buzzed hair shines under the light, leather jacket whispering as he wraps an arm around my sister. I've never had a *problem* with him, per se, but sometimes this many alphas in a room makes the one inside *me* want to come out.

It doesn't rise often, but the power simmers under my skin. I'm stronger than anyone in this room — maybe not physically — but in *designation* — *yes*. I could bring everyone to heel, pick June up and throw her over my shoulder, commanding everyone else to stay as I carried her off.

Get a fucking grip. You're not a fucking neanderthal.

It's *very* disrespectful to do that, so I just finish my drink as Meena gives me a shit-eating grin.

"Vera's spread it across the party that you're not allowed to talk to your omega anymore." She sing-songs the words, glancing back at Jakob with a cackle. "Someone's in the *doghouse*."

I give them both a disgruntled look. I'd *never* growl at her — but I'm considering it. My eyes flicker to June. Bennett's hand rests on the full curve of her hip, which fills out the jeans she has on. I've never seen her in them before — they're painted on her.

I allotted part of the pack finances to an account for her. Though she probably doesn't know about it. These, however, look like something Bennett would choose. Theo likes to buy her decor — Seth is a renegade.

They perfectly cup her ass.

Clenching my fist, I blow out a breath, my nostrils flaring. Once again, I'm standing on the outside, staring at them as June leans forward, nodding enthusiastically at Kary. She has the Lawrences wrapped around her little finger, just like she does with everyone, lighting up the fucking room, making it smell like honey and tea, comforting and saccharine sweet.

Commotion from the foyer reaches Jakob and I at the same time. Every alpha in the room prickles, our hearing picking up the sounds of the argument before everyone else. Theo sounds one step away from losing it.

"You can stay for twenty minutes."

Peter's rough voice snaps back. *"We'll stay for as long as we damn well please, until we can see this omega you've apparently taken in. I hope, for her sake, you've broken her in and finally laid claim. Maybe you'll finally be the prime of this shamble of a pack."*

Theo snarls, but then a soft whisper calms him. *"Theodore, just introduce your fathers and I to her."*

"We don't need his permission." George speaks as I watch him stalk through the door. *"Keep up, Grace."*

June's head jerks in alarm and I jolt, taking a half-step toward her as Theo stumbles into the room behind his parents. He looks shaken and upset, and Meena makes a low noise in the back of her throat — we all *know* what Theo's fathers are like — every one of us has had firsthand experience with either Peter or George pretending they're the most powerful men in the room.

Peter's stocky form stops, his eyes narrowing on Juniper. George straightens — bringing him a *hair* taller than Bennett and Yasmin. As his shoulders move back, he puffs his chest.

"This is her?" George's voice drips with disdain, his eyes roving over *my* omega, catching on the neck of her sweater. It covers her entirely — including the bite from Bennett on her throat and wherever Theo bit her — I've not seen that yet.

"She doesn't look like an omega." Peter looks back at Theo. "No wonder you didn't let us know you'd taken an omega, where did you find her? She's *old*, Theodore. How do you expect to have strong alphas with someone already at the end of their birthing years?" His eyes cut back to June, a sneer on his face. "Clearly you haven't put her on a diet, either."

The party goes quiet.

Noise rushes in my ears, blood thrumming hot in my veins as a snarl builds in my chest.

June's jaw clicks, her eyes narrowing as she twists. "The appropriate greeting is, 'Hello, June, we're Theo's fathers. It's nice to meet you.'" Her lip curls, her eyes darting between the two older alphas. "Being *fat* and *old* is better than over-compensating for your tiny alpha energy by immediately jumping to petty pot-shot insults."

Peter's lips purse. "A lot of bite for such a little bitch."

June sucks in a breath, and then she *smiles*.

My blood runs cold. I've only seen that look once — before her heat — when Theo was goading her into fighting. Now, framed in this context, panic lances through me that she'll say something that will make Peter and George lash out at her physically. I've seen it with Grace — the other omega is dressed demurely in a button up shirt, not a hair out of place, covered entirely save for the green bruising along her neck, just under her collar.

Theo snarls from behind his fathers. "Don't you dare —"

"It's okay." June steps away from Bennett, moving closer to Peter and George. "What is it that you want to see from me? Would you like to see the proof that your son could overpower me if he wanted to? Is that what gets you off? You really believe you're better than anyone else in every room you enter? Does it make you feel better about yourselves when you make everyone else feel inferior?"

George looks down his nose at her. "Theo, control this omega, or I will."

June *laughs.* "I'd love to see you try. I have a *name*, by the way. It's June, and I'm not just an omega, I'm the bitch your son *bit* and *bonded.* Want me to talk about his knot, too?"

Peter recoils at her words. "You should be heeled and collared by now. Our son's bite clearly didn't take, because you're running your nasty mouth —"

"Oh it took." She spits the words out and then tugs the hem up on her turtleneck, flashing her pale stomach, covered in love bites. The shine of the scar on her neck catches the light — silver, undeniable — and the one on the side of her breast draws my eye, half-hidden by the red lace of her bralette, matching the swollen, angry, freshly bitten skin.

My head spins. My omega is *topless —*

"Believe me now?" She smiles innocently, fluttering her eyelashes. "Or do I need to take more clothes off?"

"Cover yourself up, you're an *embarrassment* to our son —" George reaches out.

I see *red.*

"*Don't touch her.*" My bark echoes across the living room, making everyone flinch. George's hand stops mid-air, and he looks at it in shock as I stride forward, snarling so loud that Peter rocks back on his heels.

June shifts, tugging her top back on, a flush across the tops of her cheeks. "Arin —"

My alpha is secretly pleased she's clothed again, only so its entire focus can pivot to the scum in front of me. Peter and George stand side by side, shorter than me — *pathetic*. Grace's blue eyes are round behind them, the spitting image of her son. Theo's hand rests on his mother's arm, holding her.

It's been *years* of this — no one standing up so the careful balance was never upset and Grace never caught the after-math. That's *over*.

"This is *done*." I bark the words. "You both are no longer welcome in this house, in the same *space* as my omega and my pack."

George scoffs, but it's wobbly. "You can't *bark* at us, we're alphas too — it won't —"

"*Shut the fuck up.*"

His lips clam shut, mid-sentence.

Power — heady, thick — races through me. I'm *the* alpha, not just June's, but Theo's, Bennett's, Seth's — they're all mine to protect, and that extends to Theo's mother, to Bennett's family.

Peter has the audacity to laugh. "Maybe you're not as powerful as you thought, George." The cheap shot makes him smirk, an *air* around him, like he thinks he's impervious to my ire.

Before I can open my mouth, June jerks forward.

"Neither of you are." She glares from beside me. "You're *nothing*, just two pathetic men who think your designation means you can get away with every shitty thing you've ever done. I love your son, despite your attempts to turn him into a monster. He cares about me, about our pack. He *loves* us — a feeling I'm not sure either of you have experienced." Her voice breaks. "Love isn't fear, love is safe and *kind*."

"How charming," Peter sneers. "Grace, it's time to go. Your son has embarrassed us enough tonight. He's a mockery of how we raised him. He was a mistake from the moment I forgot to use a condom. We should have let you both die on the operating table."

June snarls, and it's so jarring it makes me flinch.

Peter's head turns as she steps forward, pointing her finger at him, stabbing him right in the center of his chest.

"Let me be very *clear*." Her eyes flash, pure, murderous fury in them. "*You* are leaving right now, and that's a fucking *order*."

The bark hits me, shocking me to the core, my own alpha reacting to it. I've never heard an omega bark — only rumors of it, when they're 'feral' or without bonds, meaning their biology finds its own protection. This is different than my own, it's like shackles falling from the air, unbreakable.

George's eyebrows raise, while Peter takes a step back from her, paling.

Pride rushes through me at this omega — *mine* — barking to stand up for us all.

CHAPTER TWENTY-ONE

JUNE

"LET ME BE VERY CLEAR." I'm so angry, I'm shaking. "*You* are leaving right now, and that's a fucking *order*."

I don't recognize the feeling deep in my chest, but the biological side of my brain does. The omega in me is snarling, hackles raised, poised. If I strike, it'll be to kill. Theo's fathers jerk away from me, Peter turning on a dime to follow my bark, too quickly for it to be his own choice.

"Grace —"

"No." Theo's mother whispers the word, shifting to shield her son. "I should have said that years ago, even if neither of you would have listened." Her eyes find mine, a clear, crystal blue, just like her son's. "This bond is over. I'll have a bond dissolution lawyer reach out with the official documents."

"*Grace —*" George opens his mouth.

"*No,*" I snarl, taking another step forward. "Get the *hell* out of here and don't look at her again."

His shoulders raise, a snarl building in his chest before

he barrels past Grace and Theo, knocking into his son's shoulder. Peter storms past on the other side, unable to look at Grace, even though his neck twitches like he wants to.

All the air leaves the room with them, the front door slamming.

Next to me, Arin breathes in, pulling out his phone and lifting it to his ear. "Charles — yes, make sure they leave and don't double back."

Rushing forward, I touch Theo's chest, a little frantic. Even though I *know* they didn't hurt him, I check him over, his arms, his chest, *him*, just to make sure. "I —"

I don't know what came over me. Unlike my own parents, the blatant abuse and the way both of Theo's fathers smelled like layered scent enhancers, finally broke me. They were pretending to be the biggest, baddest alpha in any room — when really, all their power was built on a foundation of sand.

Theo wraps his arms around me, his voice soft. "Thank you."

My heart cracks as I squeeze him tightly, the bond between us flooding with a mix of gratitude, awe, and love. I look at Theo's mother, giving Grace a smile. "Hi, we've not been introduced yet."

She looks even more like Theo this close. They have the same nose, and their mouths flatten naturally in the same way. Mostly though, it's the *feeling* I get when I look at her — like she's stronger than anyone else could ever guess.

"I won't be here long, I'm sure there's an omega hotel in the city —"

"Absolutely not," I whisper, shaking my head at her. "We have room in the guest house as long as you need it. I'm sure

Charles will be happy to have someone else to talk to other than us."

Laila cautiously approaches. "Grace?" Theo's mother turns, her shoulders falling, eyes filling with tears as Arin's mother grabs her, hugging her tightly — decades of history vast between them.

Stepping back, I look up at Theo, checking him again. His eyes flicker behind me.

"Juniper."

I turn to Arin, certain he's about to lay into me for the entire ordeal, but instead, he nods toward the foyer, leaving the living room. I catch Bennett's eye, Seth shrugging beside him as I bite my tongue and rush after our prime.

"Arin —"

He throws his phone onto the console table near the front door, shoulders tight.

"I don't know what came over me — I just kept thinking *no one deserves to be spoken to like that* and I lost it a little bit. I didn't even *know* I could bark —"

He whirls, nearing me as I ramble. My words cut off as his face twists, broken beyond repair.

"Juniper Walden, I am in *love* with you." Arin looks like he's being tortured as he talks. "I know that you've chosen to have bonds with, and I accept that, but I need you to know that this goes beyond my duty as a prime. I *love* you and I can't keep standing to the side. I *need* you in my life, in my *heart*. I wanted you from the moment you walked into my office, and I warned you of this and I'm sorry I couldn't hold it back, that I couldn't *wait* —"

I throw myself at him, interrupting with a kiss. Climbing up his body, I drag his face to mine, a low groan echoing through his lips and into mine as he kisses me back, his hands coming around to pull me flush against him.

He feels so *good*. His hands comb through my hair, mint searing me and resetting my brain. Every moment between the two of us flashes through my mind — falling asleep on his chest, our dinner, my heat — I grab him by the hair, breathless. "I love you, you stupid alpha. I was waiting for *you*."

"No more waiting." He clings to me. "I was too *dense* to realize what I had in front of me —"

"We have years to make up for the lost time." I pull away, on my toes so we can kiss, pressed against his chest. Sliding my fingers down, I brush them over his scraggly beard, my heart fluttering. His soft brown eyes find mine, every second we've not been touching since I moved in, distilling to nothing, as I whisper, "Take me upstairs, alpha."

He stares at me for a heartbeat, then bends down and grasps me by the backs of my thighs. I squeak as he lifts me up, walking us toward the stairs, his hot mouth searing mine. "I don't think I can make it up all three flights, but I can at least make sure we're far enough away that no one else hears you come but me."

I laugh, pulling him into another kiss. He stumbles up the stairs as I slide down his body, fumbling past the second and third floors. Arin grabs me by the hips, slamming me against the wall on the final flight, his voice a growl.

"We're far enough."

His kiss is heated and determined as he tears my turtleneck off, kissing across the mark from Bennett before he switches to the other side, sucking on my skin. My eyes flutter as I hold him to me, gasping as his teeth scrape. His hands deftly slide up my bare stomach, cupping my breasts as his head drops lower, burying between them as his palms squeeze and knead.

"You're going to come so well for me, right on my knot." His words make me squirm as his tongue drags over a nipple through the lace, thumb pressing against Theo's bite, making me slick from touch alone. "You'll be mine. How does that sound, my love? Will you let me keep you forever?"

He rips my bra down the middle, shredding it as he looks up at me, lips swollen.

"Yes." I can't breathe. "Make me yours, Arin."

His smile is dangerous, breathtaking — he lifts me again, kissing me as he carries me to his room on the final floor. It's a suite, his space expanding across the entire floor — but I don't see much of it as I wrap my legs around him, the door slamming shut behind us.

Arin steps down and I pull back, taking in his bedroom, almost an echo of the nest. His bed is on a massive platform, set partially into the floor, covered in silky black sheets as he drops me onto it, leaning over me to undo my jeans. His hands rest for a moment, throat working and nostrils flaring before he peels them off my legs, baring me to him.

"I've been staring at your hips all night. These" — he grabs my thighs, spreading me open — "are so fucking biteable."

I moan, lifting my hips as he bends down, kissing my lower stomach. Arin pushes his sleeves up, then cups my face, eyes searching mine.

"Are you going to be good for me?" His thumb presses against my lower lip. "Should I beg for forgiveness for making you wait so long? That was so rude of me. You lost out on so many orgasms. I'll have to make up for them all."

Biting the tip of his thumb, my tongue drags over his skin. "Just make love to me."

His smile widens. "Anything for you, my love." Arin's head drops, kissing me briefly before his lips score down my body, pausing at my chest to tease and touch, fingers and tongue exploring. As they graze Theo's bite, I cry out, feeling a flare of lust echoed threefold in the bond, knowing our pack is downstairs, knowing they *feel* what I do.

I clench on nothing, gasping as Arin chuckles. "So slick and wet for your prime." His fingers hook in my underwear, but instead of removing them, he jerks it up, holding it tight against me as he sucks my clit through the fabric. Clinging to his messy hair, I wrap my legs around his head, crying out louder as I roll my hips against him.

Pleading his name is all I can do as he pulls back to blow cool air over me. Every time he touches me I remember the torturous way he wound me up before my heat. He pushes my thighs open wider, my muscles burning as he drags my underwear off with his teeth. He nips at my sensitive skin, teeth leaving red lines.

He's *feral* and I love it.

His nose brushes against my mound before he dives in, arms keeping me wide as he eats me out messily. A flash fire burns under my skin, his tongue talented enough that I feel another gush of slick leave me, struggling against him, unsure if I want to pull him closer or push him away. If this is him begging for forgiveness, I'll let him get on his knees any time he likes.

One of my hands lands on the bed, fisting the sheets as my muscles tense, my thighs shaking as I start to arch from the bed. Pulling him by the hair, I guide him until his lips suction around my clit.

I come with a scream, biting my tongue as Arin sucks, groaning the entire time. He licks me up, his beard shiny as he leans back just enough to suckle on my thigh, his voice soft.

"I'm so sorry it took me this long."

My head spins, the orgasm aftershocks making me twitch as I look down at him. Arin's touch softens as he moves to my other thigh, giving them both equal attention.

"I should have done this the morning after we woke up together in my office. I knew then that you'd never leave my life. I knew then that I wanted you with us — with *me* — forever." His eyes dart up as he opens his mouth and buries his teeth in the flesh of my inner thigh.

I gasp, the bond cracking into place. My heart nearly explodes — it feels so *full* — Bennett's stability, Seth's assurance, Theo's strength, and Arin's *love*. The others felt like strings on my heart, but Arin — Arin feels like a gilded gold path from my soul to his.

His emotions trickle into me like rain, sheer love overwhelming as his tongue soothes the bite. His voice is ragged, the only thing giving away the shock of emotions. "I'm not done with you yet. Tell me you can take more."

The air sparks as I grab him by the shoulders and drag him on top of me, tasting myself as I kiss him. He settles between my legs, still fully clothed, and I take care of them quickly, grabbing his ass and grinding his bare skin against mine.

Biting at his jaw, I moan into his ear. "It feels so *right* with you."

Arin braces himself with a hand next to my head, rocking into me. His cock nudges my clit, making my mind spin as lust echoes between us. My teeth drag up and down his throat, and my breathing is labored without him even inside me yet. Pulling him closer, I hook a leg around him as his other hand holds my thigh open, thumb touching the fresh bite mark.

We both gasp as he notches at my entrance and I raise my eyes, licking my lips as he slams into me, his knot already partially swollen and grazing my clit.

As his head tilts, I strike. Burying my teeth in his throat, I rip his head to the side by the hair, the bond resonating like a humming chord between us. Arin thrusts at a steady pace, his knot kissing me with each movement as he gasps.

"I had resigned myself to understanding that my happiness and satisfaction would come from other avenues." Arin's voice is raw as he thrusts faster, grasping my chin when I pull back from the bite on his throat. "I can work a job I love. I can do hobbies that fulfill me."

I stare at him, my lips parting as his knot slips in, and then out. The stretch makes me keen, the noise almost inhuman as he pins me down with his body and gaze.

"But you" — he bends closer, the bite on his neck bloody and shimmering gold like firelight — "my sweet Juniper, bring a joy to my heart that can't be replaced by some paltry imitation. You bring me warmth. You fill me with light. I love you."

I kiss him, unable to hold back the wave of emotions as I pant against his lips. He slams into me fully, his knot locking as I clench down, coming with a sob, holding him to me as I feel him jerk and then fill me.

Arin presses his head against mine, kissing me until both our lungs are begging for breath. Our hips keep rocking as he drags us onto our sides, our limbs tangling as his *awe* overtakes me. I pepper kisses over his face, then return to the bite, sucking and licking it as I murmur, "I love you too, Arin Mohan — my alpha, my prime."

He cups the back of my head, holding me in place as he lifts my thigh higher on his hip. Arin's palm covers his silver bond mark on my skin, pressing into it as my muscles clench down on him and his knot, losing myself in finally having all my bonds.

CHAPTER TWENTY-TWO

JUNE

I CHEW on the edge of my thumbnail, staring down at my phone.

The house has been in utter chaos since the night of the party. Arin and I didn't emerge for almost forty-eight hours after the bond — and no one interrupted us, save for leaving food outside the door. It felt like a mini-heat, the sheer high of his touch sending me to heaven.

Then life came knocking.

The reality of Grace actually separating from Theo's fathers ricocheted. I watched Bennett and Seth rally behind her, agreeing to take her into Rochester to meet with an omega rights group and lawyer specializing in pack dissolutions. Theo even reached out to a medical facility working on a way to destroy bonds safely.

All of it has been very busy, and now I'm staring at an email from my *publicist* — because I have one of those now. My next book will be out in a few months, with a rescheduled book tour for next year — and it would apparently *behoove* me to also sit down for an interview with my pack to discuss my journey from beta to omega.

I do my best to stay away from the chatter online. I don't touch social media unless it's to look at food or cute animals. The idea of sitting in front of a camera makes my skin crawl.

Looking up at the living room, I chew on my nail even harder, knowing I need to go talk to Arin. He'll have the right thing to say, and he can always make the feeling of anxiety ebb into something quieter and manageable.

I shake out my hands as I stand up. *It wouldn't be bad, just different.* An interview is a huge public step — we all deserve our privacy — I never wanted to be subjected to spotlights. But... maybe it would be worthwhile. Maybe it would help someone.

Hesitating outside Arin's office, I nudge at the bond. Bennett and Seth are dull, but Theo is louder than I expect. I push the door open, shocked to find Theo lounging in a chair, Arin behind his desk, raising his head.

"I thought you were with your mom." I stare at Theo, my heart jumping.

"I got told I'd be a distraction." Theo sulks, then frowns. "Why are you nervous?"

"Uh —"

"Juniper."

My eyes dart to Arin and everything comes out in a rush. "My publicist wants us to do a news interview. All of us, I mean. The entire pack. But mostly just to see me and talk about me? And the omega thing. *My* being an omega. Not another omega —"

He blinks at me as I clasp my hands behind my back.

"I think we should do it."

Arin's eyebrows rise, he nudges his glasses up. "You do?"

I look from him to Theo, nodding, suddenly certain. "I do. I think that in the past few months, a lot of things have been said about me. It's high time people realize how shitty my situation was in London. If talking about it can change it for even *one* person, it will be worth it."

They're both quiet before Theo leans forward in his seat. "Are you going to be comfortable sharing that story and having it air on TV, baby?" He's stolen Seth's nickname for me and it's the cutest thing I've ever heard.

"I think..." I lick my lips, staring up at the ceiling as I try to organize my thoughts. "I can't be the *only* person on the entire planet to emerge late. If there are other betas who spent their entire lives separate from the designation system and suddenly find themselves in my position — I want them to have an easier time than I did." Looking back down at them, I breathe out. "Isn't that worth the temporary anxiety?"

Pride floods my chest from both of them. Arin's bond flares as Theo stares at me, so openly full of love that I feel my cheeks heat. Wrapping my arms around myself, I shrug. "I know we need to talk about it as a pack, but I think it would make a statement if we were all there — all five of us." Glancing at Arin, I whisper, "Because it'll say that even though all these people in the world think alphas and omegas should just be paired off, it's more nuanced than that. In our pack it looks different and that isn't a bad thing." The more I talk, the more certain I am. "And I think that Seth will say yes, and with Seth comes Bennett, so it's really just up to you."

My eyes lock with Arin's. "Because you're the prime. You make the rules."

He leans back in his chair. "Is that right?"

Tension crackles as my blood heats. "I mean, I like to do what you tell me." *That's an understatement.* Looking over at Theo, I smile. "Don't you, alpha?"

Theo raises an eyebrow.

"Will you at least give me a maybe?" I address Arin again. "I should reply to the email."

He inhales and then nods. "We should do it. We'll talk to Bennett and Seth when they get home. But we will be holding the interview here, not in New York." Arin reaches for his cufflinks as he speaks, undoing them and folding his shirt sleeves up.

I watch enraptured as my brain tries to comprehend his words.

"Here in the house?"

"You're uncomfortable in the city." He eyes me. "We should lessen our time spent there as much as we can. I still regret taking you to the nesting stores. I don't like it when you ignore your own anxiety in lieu of making someone else comfortable, Juniper."

Huffing, I roll my eyes. "It would be inconvenient to make them bring an entire film crew to the house, not to mention it would interrupt your work. The nesting stores are old news, you were trying to be helpful. I wasn't going to say no — that's rude."

Arin stares at me as Theo chokes on a laugh.

"Am I wrong?" I cross my arms, turning sharply to Theo. "Am I?"

His eyes blaze. He undresses me with his eyes alone. I don't know what it is about leggings and a sweater that keeps falling off one shoulder that makes lust burn from him through the bond.

I keep having stupid hot flashes because of my dumb

birth control — even though my next heat isn't for another couple months. It's irritating me so much I've already considered getting it removed, but that would mean we can't keep sleeping together without protection.

I'm not giving that up.

My skin warms under both of their gazes.

I *really* like being trapped on top of my alphas' knots, whimpering and shaking.

Biting my lip, I try to stay focused, turning back to Arin.

"This discussion is tabled." He speaks before I can, crossing one leg over the other as he lounges back in his chair, running his thumb over his lips. "Right now, there are other pressing matters." His nostrils flare and I fidget.

"You've been working too hard." Theo's voice jolts me as he rubs his palms across his jean-clad thighs, staring at me hungrily. "I think you need to relax."

"I agree," Arin mutters, making my focus snap back to him. "Will you let us help you relax, Juniper? We'll all talk about the interview this evening and decide the next step."

Standing in the middle of his office, I raise my chin. "What did you have in mind?"

"On your knees, omega."

My heart lurches in my chest and I have to remind myself not to give in *too* quickly, even though I'm already bending in front of his desk. On my knees on the rug, I stare up at Theo, since I can still see him, flashing him a wicked grin.

His eyes spark, leaning forward in his chair. We both feed off each other, and I already know that whatever Arin has planned will be incredible — and also *very* fun to derail.

"Good girl." Arin stands, stepping around his desk to stand in front of me. "Submission looks so beautiful on you, love." He taps my chin once, stroking my hair before he glances at Theo. "Don't you think? Isn't she pretty when she listens well?"

Hunger rolls off Theo in waves, crawling down our bond, entangling with my own as he grunts. "She's always pretty."

Arin laughs, then pushes my hair to one side. "Lift your arms for us, love."

I do as he says, letting him pull the sweater off. It leaves me topless, and goosebumps prickle over my skin as he folds the piece of clothing carefully, placing it to the side. Theo's nearly out of his chair, and I *feel* his impatience — but Arin's power keeps us both from moving as he returns to his office chair, making a neat stack of the papers on his desk before moving them to a drawer.

"How about now, Theo? Still pretty with her tits out and your bite on display?"

"*Yes.*" Theo sounds almost strangled as he speaks.

Arin smiles at me. "Stand back up, Juniper. Why don't you play with yourself? Take those leggings off and show your alphas all your bites."

Leaning up, I stand in front of his desk again, staring at him as I wiggle my leggings off, shimmering them off my hips and bending over as I do it. Theo groans behind me and Arin's eyes cut to him, barking. "Theo, *stay.*"

He moans and flops back in his chair as I tug my underwear off too. A soft whine leaves Theo's throat as I hold my clothes in one fist.

"Give them to him, Juniper. He needs something to do and he's so good at folding clothes. Focus on making yourself feel good for us."

I follow his instructions, stepping forward entirely

naked. The soft rug gives under my feet as I drop my clothes into Theo's lap, his hard-on already visible in his jeans. He stares at me as he lifts my underwear to his nose and inhales with a broken groan, not reaching for me, but looking like he's fighting himself every second I back away. Sliding my hands over my chest, I lick my lips as I eye him, the thrill of being watched by them both making my heart pound as I graze his bond mark, widening my stance to show Arin's silver bite on my inner thigh.

"That's a good girl." Arin says the words softly, drawing my gaze as I touch his bite, then moan, swiping my fingers through the slick already gathering between my legs.

My eyes flutter shut as I toy with myself, barely touching, whimpering as I flick my clit, trying to make sure my shaking knees stay stable so I can be on display for them.

"Would you like help?" Arin's dark voice curls around me, full of unspoken promises.

I shiver and nod, reaching with my other hand to pinch at my nipples. "Please, alpha."

"Theo, be a good boy and eat our omega out."

My big alpha is suddenly *there*, his presence overwhelming as my eyes open to see Theo kneeling in front of me. The sight makes me breathe harder as he pulls me closer by the hips, grabbing a thigh, pressing into Arin's mark. The pressure makes me gasp and Arin grunt. Theo arches my leg over his shoulder, his other hand supporting my ass as he dives between my thighs, tongue thrusting into me without warning, messy and enthusiastic.

I squeak, it turning shrill as I grab onto his blond hair to steady myself, staring at Arin. Theo makes ungodly noises between my thighs, sucking and licking.

Arin's chin tilts down, a small smile on his lips as he rubs himself overtop his trousers. "You can eat her, but don't let her come."

I gasp, whining as Theo pulls back, circling my clit with his tongue. I drag him closer by the hair, arching my back as I lose the edge immediately, cursing wildly as I stare at Arin. "Theo, *please*," I whine as I rub my chest, stimulating his bite as I rock against his face. "Please let me come, don't listen to him."

Theo groans and the vibrations make me flutter as he holds me up. He latches his lips to my clit again, then alternates between sucking and flicking it. The orgasm barrels toward me as I gasp over and over again, bowing partially over him, my eyes on Arin as I beg Theo.

"Don't stop," I gasp. "Right there." *God.* "*Fuck!*"

"Theo..." Arin's voice is a warning, but there's no bark. The thought of him watching the two of us go against his command gets me to the edge quicker than ever. Theo's lips suction onto me, nails dragging over my bond mark as I scream with my climax, my bones turning into liquid.

Theo is there, licking a stripe up my stomach, muscles straining against his shirt as he lifts me, standing up with me in his arms, his voice ragged. "We're in so much fucking trouble."

I lick my lips and pull him to me, kissing him hungrily. "I don't care."

He laughs. Writhing against him, I wrap my legs around him, the orgasm high too good not to chase again as I hear the office chair creak.

"Bring her over here. Do *not* make me stand up."

A shiver crawls up my spine as Theo turns us, then lays me out on Arin's desk like a fucking feast. I turn my head, grinning up at our prime, arching my chest.

"You're not mad at me. You like seeing me come." I coo the words, reaching for him.

Arin threads his fingers with mine, kissing my hand. "You're right. You look so pretty all flushed for us. Maybe this punishment is for Theo." Theo's hands still on my body as he kisses my stomach. Glancing down at him, his eyes flash as Arin mutters, "I'm not sure he's earned the right to come anymore."

I let out a shriek as Theo jerks me lower on the desk, growling against my stomach as he grinds his erection between my thighs. "I'm not going to last if you try to edge me."

Arching up, I drag my nails through Theo's hair, looking over at Arin again. "I can take the punishment for him, alpha." Licking my lips, Theo grinds into me again, slow enough that I can feel my slick already soaking the front of his pants. "It's not fair to make him stop." I pout.

Arin shrugs, leaning back in his chair. "I don't operate by fair terms. I do, however, want to watch him turn that pretty little ass red — maybe a few spanks will teach you both a lesson."

I wiggle as Theo bends down, kissing my throat. "How's that sound, cupcake?"

Grinning up at him, I drag him into another kiss before he extracts himself and then flips me like a rag doll. I land, my feet spread, on the tips of my toes as I lean over Arin's desk, naked and pliant as Theo stands behind me, hands all over my ass, squeezing and grabbing it.

"Look at this, Arin. She's so fucking *pretty*."

Arin smiles at me. "Prettier with your hands on her, Theo." There's a slight dark spot on the front of his trousers and I lick my lips as he rubs it with a palm again. "Spank her as many times as you'd like, you can even stroke yourself, but when you come, it better be all over her. That's the only rule. Make her messy for me."

Theo eagerly unzips his jeans, and I *know* he doesn't even push them down, just pulls his cock out as he uses one hand to plunge three fingers into me, making me squeal as he gathers my slick to pump himself. With his other hand, he smacks my hip. "Stop wiggling your ass at me and be still."

Dropping my forehead to Arin's desk, I can't help the delirious smile that creeps up my face as Theo finds his own rhythm in the movements. He spanks me, alternating between each hip, making my skin sting, my cheeks reddening. I writhe back against him, the pressure between my legs growing as he starts to pump one hand faster, the smacks getting quicker.

Arin leans in, one hand reaching out before he grabs the side of my ass and forces me to lift higher on my toes. "Present for him, let him cover you before we take both your holes and remind you who you belong to."

I gasp as Theo's hand comes down on my ass one final time, so hard that I clench before he spreads my cheeks and comes with a broken grunt. I feel his cum as he covers me, the mess dripping down over my ass and cunt as I bite my tongue, my thighs shaking.

Arin pulls away and I watch him stand and pull himself out of his trousers. His cock strains in his hand, knot already partially swollen. My mouth fills with saliva as he jerks himself once before he mutters, "Get her up, Theo. Put yourself on my desk so she can ride you while I take her ass."

Yes.

I almost move faster than Theo, turning and dragging him against me, kissing him as we switch positions. While

Theo gets settled, I turn to Arin and grab him by the collar, shoving his hand away from himself and wrapping my fist around him. I kiss him as I pump my hand once, then twice. "I love you, you wicked man."

He laughs against my lips, a shocked sound leaving him before he pushes me into Theo's waiting hands. Theo drags me on top of him and the desk groans under the weight of us, making us pause. Arin's chest brushes my back as he cups my pussy.

"The desk will hold," he mutters, half-amused. "But next time we should do this in a bed."

I can't help the laugh that bubbles up as Theo spreads my thighs wide, notching at my slick entrance. He grabs the back of my neck, holding me on top of him before slamming me down on top of his cock, the angle making me spasm as his knot slips right into me, Arin solid behind me.

Arin's lips land on my throat, hands around my stomach as he rocks against me, moving me on top of Theo in a slow grind, making us both hiss. Arin chuckles darkly. "My good pets, already so eager. I could keep you both naked for me day-in and day-out, just waiting to be used." He pushes me further down, forcing me chest to chest with Theo. "Let me get her in position so I can fuck her right into you, Theo."

The praise from him is sinful, my body and bond with Theo sparking as we both react to our prime. He rubs himself against my ass, using Theo's cum and my slick as lube as Theo and I breathe hard.

Then Arin punches his hips forward and he's *in.*

I feel so full my head spins. The room dims, everything else fading except for the pleasure. Arin grabs my arms, then bands them behind my back, making me entirely beholden to both of them as he forces my spine to arch. Both of the alphas rock and move, Theo from underneath, and Arin from behind, his knot slamming against me. I can't take it just yet, but the burn and build makes me cry out.

"That's it, love, strangle his knot while you take me. Theo, don't ignore her pretty tits."

Theo moans at Arin, his lips landing on my breasts.

"*Fuck.*" Arin snarls the word, using his other hand to wrap it around my throat, holding my head in place, squeezing lightly. "Rub her clit, Theo, I'm busy."

The moment Theo's fingers fall between my legs, I *come.*

I don't know my own name. Sight and sound fade, my body alight with the electricity between the three of us as Arin slides deeper, his knot breaching me as I clench around them both. He snarls into my ear, using my body for his own pleasure as Theo ruts up faster, both of them filling me.

My thighs shake, my breathing coming in short gasps as I tremble. The drop is so intense I choke on my next breath, and Arin pulls out, letting go of my neck and making soft noises as he rubs his hands over my overstimulated skin, kissing the backs of my shoulders.

"Good girl. Such a good omega for us. You did so well."

The sound of wetness between us makes me whimper as Arin helps Theo's knot release, then he cups my pussy, pushing the cum back in. I shiver as Theo leans up, kissing my jaw, rubbing my hips and lifting me into his arms like a blushing bride.

Arin and Theo exchange a look. Arin stares at the other alpha, his voice softer. "Good boy. Let's get you both cleaned up."

I feel almost drunk as I reach for Arin, tangling our fingers together as Theo carries me out of the wrecked office and to the nearest bathroom.

CHAPTER TWENTY-THREE

JUNE

TUGGING on the skirt of my dress, I smooth my fingers over the deep brown fabric for the millionth time. The house is full of equipment and a camera crew. I only picked this outfit because it reminds me of Bennett — and I step over cords, moving to his side on instinct just to slide my hand into his, leaning on his shoulder.

Theo was right. I'm a nervous *wreck* — and this is not the time for Arin to send me into subspace with a handful of orgasms to make the anxiety abate.

"Hey." Bennett kisses the crown of my head, squeezing my hand.

"Hi." I glance around the room. The crew moved one of our couches, placing it in a way that the camera will have a view of it and the beautiful backyard in the same shot, while the interviewer sits across from us. Clinging to Bennett, I mutter, "Who's sitting where?"

"I think you'll be on the couch." He pulls into a hug. "Probably in the middle, since you *are* the focus of this interview."

I make a disgruntled noise, eyeing the two chairs behind the couch. That makes sense — but does it mean something if Arin stands behind me, or sits next to me? What if they try to shove Seth in the back because he's not an alpha? My omega prickles at that, ready for a fight.

I take a deep breath of Bennett's perfume, trying to calm down.

"S'cuse me, ma'am." One of the audio guys brushes past us, laying the final cords. I shuffle away, sucking in a breath as Arin walks in with the interviewer a step behind him. She's a leggy blonde, eyes bright but no-nonsense as she nods at my prime.

"Let's get you all settled to make sure the framing is how we want it." She turns, looking at me first. "Will you sit in the center of the couch, Miss Walden?"

I let Bennett go, taking a deep breath before I sit. The interviewer comes over, her cream colored silk blouse fluttering as she hums and points to the two spots behind me. "I think I'd like the prime, Arin, behind June's left shoulder." As Arin takes his place, I look back at him. He reaches out, touching my shoulder gently.

"And..." The woman speaks again, looking around the room. "Seth. I think you should sit on Juniper's right. Bennett can be behind you, next to Arin." She looks back at me. "Is that alright with you?"

It leaves the spot on the couch next to me for Theo and I nod, smiling at her. Theo squeezes Grace's hands. His mother remains standing next to Charles — the older beta's black hair peppered with gray, smile lines around his kind eyes as he looks over at her softly.

All of us are in our best, looking polished and coordinated, and it makes my heart flutter as Theo takes his spot, my hands darting to each side, taking one of Theo's hands in mine and Seth's in the other. They both squeeze my fingers as the interviewer checks the monitor, giving the cameraman a thumbs up before she takes her seat across from us. She pulls out a pad of paper full of scribbled notations and my stomach swoops.

"Okay." Her smile is kind as her eyes find me. "The *Designation News Network* said we could film as much as we'd like, but the story will probably only have a medium time slot. Don't worry about being polished, it'll be cut down, and I've already told your prime that he can view the final footage before it airs."

The largest news conglomerate will air our pack for the world to see — no big deal.

Theo's thumb smoothes over my skin and Seth turns to me, muttering under his breath. "They'll probably cut us down to a sixty second puff piece."

I snort, giving him a dry look. "I doubt that."

Seth grins. "You're right. They'll probably double the air time, just so everyone can see how hot you look."

I flush, fidgeting as I scowl at him, but it just makes his grin widen.

"I'll be asking a few pre-approved questions, but some will be clarifying based on your answers." The interviewer draws my attention. "It shouldn't take us long, and it'll be a conversation at the end of the day. This is a way for you to tell your story, Juniper. We're all very excited to hear it."

I swallow, forcing myself to smile and nod while I remind myself *why* I'm doing this. Grace and Charles on the side draw my eyes — an omega who just left everything she knew and a beta who's only ever brushed up against designation politics.

I'm doing it for them. I'm doing it for *me*.

"Are we ready?" The interviewer looks up from the notes in her lap.

"We're ready," I confirm, setting off a flurry of activity. The producer swings around to signal that the audio recording should begin, cameras trained on us.

The interviewer finds her camera, flashing a smile.

"Good morning, I'm Florence Miller and it's my sincere pleasure to introduce the world to bestselling author, June Wald — or Juniper Walden — who shocked everyone when she cancelled a string of book signings in Europe after discovering that her designation wasn't actually that of a beta — and instead was an omega. Biologists have weighed in on the possibilities, world leaders have questioned if omega responsibility laws need to change, but it's only right that those *affected* be the voices who receive a platform in this heated designation discussion."

WE BREEZE PAST INTRODUCTIONS, discussing Arin's job, Seth and Bennett's business, and Theo's work, before ending on me. When Florence asks me about the sales boost, I feel so awkward that I mumble something about not expecting my books to sell out.

"I don't find that bizarre, with omegas electing not to work, it makes sense that the public would have a vested interest in reading your books, as they were written from a beta's perspective on omega life. Were you heavily involved in designation politics prior to emerging?"

"No," I answer softly, shaking my head. "I stayed away

from it. My family — my parents —" My voice catches as Theo's hand grounds me, touching my thigh. "They're both betas and believe in alpha supremacy. They think that everyone should defer to alphas, that alphas should be the only ones in power, and each one deserves a single omega who serves them."

Florence hums, her eyes sparking with interest. "And how did they feel about your choice of pack life? The London Designation Center didn't pair you, correct?"

"No." My voice gets a little stronger. "They provided *no* help. I wasn't covered by their existing policies and many of the packs refused to meet me because of my age. I would have been in a very poor situation had Seth and I not met by chance. The Designation Center only facilitated pack meetings when a handful of alphas reached out in concern. I was made to sleep in an office for multiple nights, turned away from my hotel, *and* from flying back to the states, because I wasn't bonded and considered high risk."

Florence's eyes widen, almost imperceptibly. "Let me clarify, you were *trapped* inside the center for multiple nights, refused agency, and told to pick a pack of alphas from total strangers?"

"That's exactly what I'm saying." My eyes find the camera as I hold Seth's hand. "But Seth came in, he demanded to see me. I understand their policies exist to protect omegas, but I went in as a grown woman with free will — and I could only leave because an alpha signed that he would *oversee* me."

Florence shakes her head, looking briefly at her notes. "The alpha that signed you out — Bennett Lawrence — you were already bonded to Seth Harding?"

Bennett clears his throat. "Yes, Seth and I are bonded.

And yes, it was me that signed June out." He pauses and I glance back to see his face twist. "It made me vastly uncomfortable to sign documents that essentially signaled *ownership* of Juniper. The center wanted to wash its hands of her, and wanted to claim that she was no longer their responsibility. She was exhausted." He reaches forward and his hand brushes my hair back, voice softer. "She was hungry, scared, and forced to meet a revolving door of alphas that were unmatched for a variety of reasons. It wasn't right, that was *no* way to treat another human being."

"And" — Seth pipes up beside me — "they didn't respect me either, just because I'm a beta doesn't mean I love her any less." He shifts on the couch, leaning forward, voice passionate as he squeezes my hand. "I was not leaving her there, the poor treatment of omegas has to stop. It's not right to have the majority of the world turn a blind eye to the designation system that affects us *all* at the end of the day. There are omegas as young as *sixteen*, being paired off by their guardians to packs, just because that's how it's always been done — but what does that mean for people like June? For older omegas who grow into themselves and end up with a pack or bonds that are more like shackles?"

"And what would you suggest be the policy, Mr. Harding?"

"It's fine if the world wants to act like omegas can't think for themselves, or live by themselves — but the proof is that they very well can. There's no point in forcing bites and bonds on young omegas, or stripping people of their own choice in the matter." Seth's voice goes soft, eyes on me. "Don't get me wrong, I'm very grateful that June could go to a center, but having them function as places that make money off the buying and selling of an omega's rights is wrong on a humanitarian level. She deserved to feel safe, not like a burden during a terrifying, life-changing moment."

The room is quiet as I lean in and kiss his cheek, whispering against his skin. "I love you."

He turns his head, brushing his lips against my cheek in return.

After we part, Florence speaks. "This just brings us back to the heart of the issue. It's unprecedented, an omega emerging this late — how did you feel about it, as pack alpha and prime, Mr. Mohan?"

Arin's voice is clear as he speaks up. "It doesn't matter to me what *age* an omega figures out their designation, but much like the rest of my pack, I was appalled at the treatment June received during a high stress moment. The entire reason she found herself with our pack was that we provided a safe place for her to process the change while preparing for her upcoming heat."

I flush, sitting up a little straighter.

Florence doesn't look at all ruffled at the mention of my heat. "It's said that heats set in two weeks after a designation emerges. Juniper, did you consider, or were you given the option of a hired heat help service? There have been many discussions recently on their safety and efficacy."

My skin flushes as I open my mouth, floundering. Theo's palm on my leg rests heavy, a reminder I'm not alone.

"Not officially." I settle on the words. "Even if I had chosen a service, I would have had to pay for it out of pocket. I wasn't sure if I could afford a reputable option. Suppressants weren't a choice, because the heat broke through so quickly. The option of help during a heat might work for omegas who come from well-off families who have the funds, but for someone like me — I was in a foreign country, I was told I was a risk and that my only option was finding a pack of strangers that I could feel safe enough spending a solid week with, needing their care and attention."

"I'm sure the options presented to you were not your first choice. Can I ask —" She pauses, then looks away from her notes, leaving them in her lap. Her eyes meet mine — woman to woman. "Did you feel *unsafe* around any of the alphas that you met? Before you left with Pack Mohan?"

The use of Arin's surname throws me — but politics elect that packs take the surname of the prime. I frown as I glance at Seth, then Florence.

"Well, actually, yes. I did feel unsafe." I steel myself. "The alphas I met were mostly nice, but there were a few instances where I felt I wasn't protected. Someone called claiming to be family, I guess to circumvent the process and protections the center had in place — but I was glad to already be with Seth and Bennett by then. Nothing ever came from it."

Florence looks a little pallid as she mutters, "That's interesting. I'll have to reach out to the center to see if they have phone records. I find it very concerning they were willing to let someone see you without validating if they were telling the truth."

"Me too." Theo finally speaks and I move my free hand overtop his on my thigh.

He clears his throat, looking at me. His eyes are so gentle that I feel my chest throb.

"I wasn't happy when June first came to our home in London. I didn't understand the levels of difficulty she'd already experienced, and the vast changes happening in such a short amount of time to her. I regret that every single day."

"Theo." I say his name softly, frowning.

He gives me a little smile. "I'm just telling the truth. And it's opened my eyes in the ways the world refuses to help omegas who find themselves in terrible situations." The unspoken words about his family make my throat tighten.

Theo looks at Florence and the cameras. "I think I can speak for us when I say that I can only hope June's story and experience usher in a change for any other omegas who find themselves in this situation. The way the current system works is flawed, inherently, and no one deserves to go through what she did. We can't continue treating omegas like property. They deserve to make their own, *informed* decisions, at every step of the process."

Pride for him swells in me — I just *know* his words will echo for weeks across news stations.

"Well." Florence clears her throat. "I have greatly enjoyed meeting and speaking with you all, Pack Mohan. Thank you so much for your time."

Arin shifts behind me. "Thank you, Florence. But I've never enjoyed the tradition of packs taking the surname of the prime. That isn't my place, I am not the heart of this pack. We are not Pack Mohan — we are Pack Walden."

Tears spring to my eyes as I look back at him.

Arin smiles, touching my cheek. "Juniper is the heart of us, she is our world, and the world deserves to know it. I'm so honored, every day, to know my future will be spent with her."

CHAPTER TWENTY-FOUR

SETH

"Do I want to ask why you're wiggling so much?"

June glances at me, giving me a disgruntled look as she crosses her arms and huffs in the passenger seat. She's *cute* when Bennett works her up and then leaves her on edge. It's damn time she got a taste of her own medicine — considering how often she does it to *me*.

"You know why." She turns partially in the seat, pouting. The back of my SUV is stacked with boxes, every single one is full of enamel pins, bookmarks, and signed bookplates. We sat up for hours, watching movies while she signed them all. I'm not sure how I keep getting so lucky to spend hours uninterrupted with her, but I'm not going to look a gift horse in the mouth.

Her first signing sold so many tickets that the independent bookstore hosting the event had to change the location from their store to the New York Public Library.

"Are you sure we have time?"

"Yes," I answer her immediately, easing her anxiety as I merge onto the highway, slinging my arm across the back of her seat. "There's a reason we're leaving a day early. We have a nice hotel room for the night and we'll take it easy after we drop these boxes off. You will *rest* before tomorrow."

She hums, her hazel eyes vulnerable. "Arin keeps fielding interview requests."

I shake my head at her, glancing at the road. The DNN interview aired, and as Florence said, it *ignited* a conversation about omega rights, putting June right in the center of it. I'm proud of her, but I don't like the extra eyes on our pack. I've spent years making sure that the Seth Harding that others meet is the affable, goofy beta who is glued to his alpha's side.

"If you want to do another, we will." I brush my knuckles over her shoulder. "But if not, we can tell everyone to fuck off and move to Antartica." My parents probably have room somewhere down there between their biological research into penguin fucking — *or species retention*. I know my mother genuinely loves it, but it also brings her the furthest place possible from New York City.

June snorts and my heart warms as she flings back against the seat, reaching for my hand. "We can't tell people to *fuck off*. Well, maybe we can, but it has to sound professional."

I grin. "Bennett would phrase it as, '*We are no longer choosing to speak publicly about our pack's private lives.*'"

She makes a little noise. "That's good, you should write that down." June toys with my fingers, fidgeting before she whispers, "Can I ask you something?"

"Always." I twist my wrist, threading our fingers together as I split my focus between the road and her. "What's on your mind, beautiful?"

"Why weren't your parents at the party?"

"The party you skipped out on to get fucked by Arin for two days straight?"

"*Seth.*"

I laugh loudly, pulling my hand away and watching her cheeks light up. My mind spins as I try to come up with an acceptable answer. Bennett is the only one who knows everything about my past, and it was only right for him to know as one of my oldest friends and my bonded — I don't want June to be entangled in it.

She deserves the goofy beta side of me, not the other side.

"They've never been hands-on with my brother and I." I shrug. "We're all betas, so we did our own things, chose our own paths in life. They sent a congratulations card when Bennett and I bonded. I'll tell them about you whenever you want."

"Oh." Her expression softens.

"Not a big deal, they're biologists. But the boring kind, not the kind that looks up designations and figures out how all that works." I run my tongue over my teeth, tasting the bitter lie and carefully hiding it from the bond between us. "I have a cousin in the city, but we don't talk much anymore."

Not since I left the family business.

She doesn't question anything. The conversation moves on, but I still feel a nudge of guilt for not being forthright. She doesn't know — Arin and Theo don't either.

It's history and it can stay buried.

THE DRIVE PASSES IN A BLUR, between singing loudly to the radio and a couple gas station stops for snacks. I smile as June presses her nose to the window, her eyes lighting up at the sight of New York City through the car.

"You know, I used to think I'd just never travel" — her breath fogs the glass — "because of the anxiety." The word sounds like a curse and the urge to *murder* her mother jolts through me. I'd have her in the Long Island Sound, never to resurface.

June keeps going, blithely unaware of the restraint I'm showing. "It was easier for a long time to not do anything. I moved out as quickly as I could, first to dorms and then again when I left college. I think I got really lucky that I could even get out, you know? Still, I just let my life be paused because I was scared for so long at their reaction to what I wanted to do, what I wanted to write."

I glide the car into the traffic trying to get into the city, headed toward Brooklyn.

June pulls away from the window.

"Not very many people can sell their first piece. I had an English professor who really loved romance books and got me in contact with an agent, and from there it was a lot of back and forth, but she believed in me. I guess I should be thankful."

I stay quiet as she shrugs her shoulders, her eyes sparking a little when she sees the water. "Arin was right, I really don't like the city." I have *no* idea when Arin said that, but I don't dare interrupt her as she sighs, almost wistful. "But I think I could be happy going around the world as long as you're right beside me. You make me feel safe."

My heart shouts in joy. The way she settled so comfortably into our pack, into my *life*, just wrecks me. She deserves to be this happy, vibrant and stunning, all the time.

I get us into Brooklyn and then flick the hazard lights on, parking in front of the bookstore as I turn to her.

"June." She flushes when I grab her hand and kiss the back of it. "I love you *so* fucking much, it's physically painful when you're not around. Never forget that. I'd do anything for you."

She smiles at me and then leans in, brushing her lips with mine. "I know. London proved that."

Twenty minutes later all the boxes are out of the car with some help from the booksellers at BOOKS AND BOND-MARKS. June waves at them excitedly from the window, beaming at me as we drive off. "Tomorrow will be fun."

"I'll remind you that you said that when you're freaking out before going on stage."

She grimaces at me. "You're an asshole, don't remind me I'm supposed to do a *Q and A*." She shudders, glancing out the window. "I'm hungry and you promised me shitty pizza. Where are we staying tonight?"

I stay quiet and her eyebrow raises. "Seth?"

Miming zipping my lips shut, I turn the car down another road, headed toward the Brooklyn bridge. June gasps when we reach the throng of people, the sun setting on New York City, lighting it up gold. It takes us some time to cross the bridge, but once we do, I pull into our hotel in the financial district, the building spanning multiple blocks.

June makes a noise when someone opens her door and I jump out, rounding the car to help her out. She looks down at her jeans and sweater, hissing at me, "Seth this place is *fancy*."

"Baby." I lean down, wrapping my arm around her as I let them get our bags. "I'm *rich*." She squeaks when I drag her inside around a group of men in suits. Striding up to the desk, I tug out my card, confirming it with the receptionist. Bennett and I have stayed here a few times, but seeing the space through June's eyes makes me appreciate the sprawling gold decor, the lobby open to the floors above us, shops and restaurants all on the main floor.

"Mr. Harding," the receptionist greets me. "Welcome back to the *Signa*, we're so happy you chose to stay with us again. Your room is ready and your bags should be upstairs when you arrive. Please don't hesitate to call the front desk if there's anything else we can help you with."

I snag our keys, flashing her a smile before I look down at June. Her head swivels like an owl, and it's adorable as I mutter, "Come on, let's get upstairs and get settled."

"*Oh my god that fountain has ducks.*"

Her words come out in a rush as she twists my arm, looking behind us at the huge fountain in the center of the lobby — where, yes — there are multiple water fowl swimming and washing themselves. I'm not sure I've ever noticed it.

"This is not the kind of place we can order shitty pizza to the front lobby, *Seth*."

Snorting, I drag her into the elevator with me and flash the attendant our card. He presses the button to unlock the higher floors and June stares out the glass, passing multiple floors full of amenities, giving her a peek at the pools, a restaurant, and part of one of the spas.

She clings to my arm, dragging me closer. "I want a massage."

I smile at her excitement. "We could extend our stay. Or I could take you to one of the spas that Arin is a shareholder of in the Alps." Her lips pop open in a little 'o' as I lean closer and whisper, "We'll take a pack trip."

"Okay." Her soft voice is full of awe as the doors open. This floor is limited access, with only a handful of doors leading to suites, and I thank the elevator attendant with a nod and a tip slipped from my palm to his as I guide June toward our room. Swiping my card, the lock turns green and I let her in.

"Go explore. Be feral."

June throws herself past me, squeaking as she races into the suite, gasping over and over again each time she finds something new. Her words race together, one long sentence of excitement — "Seth! The view! We have three couches! There's *pizza*!" The last one has her the most excited and I close my eyes, grinning as I shake my head and lock the door.

Love radiates through me. Sometimes I forget that all of this isn't normal. Not all the time — but especially not *now*, not seeing June's reaction firsthand to the way Bennett and I have lived for years, and the way we plan to spoil her forever.

Pushing away from the door, I step into the living area. There's two New York style pizzas waiting for us — pepperoni and sausage — her favorite. All hot and fresh because I made sure the hotel knew we were coming the second we left the bookstore.

The expression on her face is worth it.

She barrels into me and I grunt, catching her as she drags me down to kiss me senseless. My brain short-circuits. I might not be an alpha, but the feeling of her wrapped around me is enough to make me feel as dumb as one.

Humming against her lips, I walk her backwards until we reach one of the three couches and then push her onto it. She laughs, pulling me with her as her fingers card through my hair, untangling it from being tied back into a bun.

She makes a little noise, frowning at the scrunchie in her hand.

"This is mine."

"Yup." I grin. "Sure is."

June scowls. "Are you the one who's been stealing all my scrunchies?"

I shrug, holding onto her hips as I kiss down her neck and throat. "I like them. They're like little pieces of you that I get to keep with me all day."

"Oh." She lets out a breath, melting under me. "That's so *cute.*"

Her legs wrap around me as I lean up and kiss her, slowly pushing at her sweater so I can reach her stomach. The skin is so pliant and *soft*, it makes me groan as I whisper, "I wanna eat you out, baby. I want to dig my tongue in your sweet little cunt."

She moans, nodding rapidly under me. "Okay. You should do that."

Her giggle is like music to my ears as I work at her clothes, getting her pants off and running my hands up and down her legs. With one palm on her knee, I spread her open for me, snorting. "I am so fucking lucky all those idiots couldn't come with us. I get you all to myself."

June grins, her eyes bright. "That's right, I'm all yours."

Dropping lower, I kiss her through her underwear, muttering as I pull it to the side. "Eating out, then pizza, then more sex, then bedtime."

She makes a cute little noise as I slide my tongue through her slick. June's fingers tangle in my hair as she gasps out, "Sounds good."

All I can do is give her a thumbs up. My mouth is already preoccupied with my favorite meal.

CHAPTER TWENTY-FIVE

JUNE

THE SIGNING HAS BEEN A *WHIRLWIND*.

Seth was true to his word. Last night he ate me out until I nearly cried from overstimulation, bundled me up in a blanket, and ate pizza with me. After that, we jumped in the shower together. Of course, that turned into him pinning me against the glass wall and fucking me so hard I screamed before we ended up in bed, in the hotel-provided fluffy robes, watching shitty movies until I fell asleep on his chest.

God, I love him so much.

He kept pin-quiet all morning, closing the electric blinds to make sure I slept in before waking me up with brunch.

And another orgasm.

Grinning, I take a long drink of the water bottle in the back room. I've already drained almost all of it. The talk was good — but the library is *busy* with the sheer amount of readers here to see me. There were a few people from the press who did early interviews with me.

It's been... nice. Slightly overwhelming, but seeing my

men in the crowd, cheering me on through every moment so far, has made it easier.

Rubbing my chest, I lean back in the chair, taking a slow breath. I get ten minutes before I need to be back out there for a final goodbye. There was a signing limit on books, but I told everyone that the pack and I brought goodie bags and they *seemed* excited.

Is it cheesy? *Maybe.* But I feel *good* for the first time in months, genuine pride in myself for reaching this point in my career where a roomful of people want to meet me, want my scribble in their book. It's all worth the anxiety and the path it took for me to get here.

My head spins a bit as I sit up. Touching my forehead, I blink slowly, glancing at the water bottle. I've not had a lot of food today, but Seth and I did eat brunch — maybe I can convince all of them to come back to the hotel with Seth and I tonight —

I look around for my phone, the room spinning as a bolt of worry pangs through me.

My phone isn't here.

Picking up the water bottle, I lift it, about to take a sip to settle my churning stomach when I notice a layer of something settled at the bottom.

My heart lurches, trying to figure out what's going on just as the door opens.

"There you are."

The man's voice sounds slurred as I slump to one side, the smell of him invading my senses — cloyingly chemical, choking me as vague memories flash through my mind — *the grocery store, the water bottles* — my eyes flutter, my heart pounding as I feel whatever was in the bottle start to drag me into unconsciousness.

"Wha —"

The stranger shushes me, unfamiliar arms wrapping around me as he picks me up. "Go to sleep, baby girl. We'll be there when you wake up."

CHAPTER TWENTY-SIX

SETH

THERE ARE so many *people* here.

It's not surprising, nowhere can keep her books on the shelves — but seeing the sheer amount of readers who want to line up and meet *my* June is staggering.

"Our event time is almost over, could one of you please go get her?" The head bookseller, Zoe, looks over at our small group — sans Theo. He's been at the snack table for ten minutes fawning over cookies decorated like June's covers.

"I'll grab her." I pull away from Bennett just as a weird flare jolts through my chest. Pausing, I exchange a look with Bennett as Arin touches his sternum.

"Maybe it's nerves" — Bennett stops himself before he moves with me toward the back hallway — "I'm coming too."

Something is undeniably *wrong* as I nudge the bond between June and I. It's not a wall — like what she does when she blocks us out when she's overwhelmed — there's an absence. Where June was, there's nothing.

Pushing through the crowd with Bennett hot on my heels,

panic sets in the second I shove the door open to the room she's been using to take a break in. It's empty, a single water bottle sitting on the table. I dart around the small space before I grab the water and unscrew the top, lifting it and sucking in a breath when I see the white powder at the bottom.

It's familiar. It's not the first time I've seen someone spike water to temporarily render a mark unconscious — flashes of memories assault me. *Sitting at bars as an unassuming beta. My cousin's voice in my ear, "Seth, just enough to knock them out, not to kill."*

"Fuck, *fuck* —" I whirl, finding Bennett in the doorway. My mind goes *feral* for a moment, blind panic hitting my bloodstream as I chuck the bottle back onto the table and dart out into the hallway, calling out, "June!"

"Seth — wait —" Bennett tries to stop me, but I throw open every fucking office door, finding them all empty, until I get to the emergency exit, where the wind ruffles my hair — *tied back with her goddamn scrunchie* — the access alleyway deserted.

"What's going on? What's happening?"

Arin's voice carries, but it's Theo's frantic shout that breaks me.

"Where is she? Where's our girl?"

Bennett's wide eyes meet mine and I just *know*. We move back down the hallway in sync.

He was with me the day I decided to leave. When I decided to prioritize *us* and the business we wanted to start together —

Shoving into the deserted office, I suck in a breath, turning to Arin sharply.

"What do you smell?"

Fuck being a beta. If I could have his nose right now, I would.

He gives me a startled look. "It smells like... chemical suppressants. Layers of them."

Theo paces. "What happened? Did someone *take* her?"

Arin shakes his head. "We need to start from the top. She *just* came back here. She got off the stage, walked back here to rest, and said she needed a couple minutes. Maybe the smell is someone else —"

"No, I don't *feel* her Arin." Theo rubs his chest, voicing everything I already know.

Under the fluorescents, Arin looks downright pallid, his voice quieter. "Charles said our security system has been alerting to nothing in the last few weeks. I called the company and they said they were sending someone out because it looked like the signal was interrupted."

Bennett goes still beside me as Theo chokes out, "And you didn't think to *tell* us that?"

Arin flounders. "I thought it was just a glitch — I don't understand — who would —"

Bennett grabs the water bottle, catching my eyes again.

I fish out my phone silently, unlocking it as I think of her running to me in that little grocery store, smelling of suppressants, rabbit-heart pounding because there was a strange man.

"We need to call the police."

I shake my head at Arin, voice low. "They won't be fast enough. I'm about to tell you and Theo something and I need you to listen." Staring at them both, I swallow my pride and guilt. "When we went back to her place, the first night we were there she said someone bumped into her at the store and he smelled like chemical perfume suppressants. There was also someone at her signing before she emerged."

Arin snarls. "Where? Can we find someone to get the footage?"

Theo cuts Arin off. "Our pack interview just aired — what about the *fucking* guy who pretended to be her brother. There was a car outside the townhouse for *weeks* when we were in London and I just thought it was someone else's — it was there even during her heat. How long has this —"

I look down at my phone, letting them both puzzle it out as Bennett grabs my elbow.

"Seth. Are you sure?"

My alpha — *our* alpha, because he's June's as much as he is mine — looks stricken as I type in a number by memory alone. I'll have to smash my phone after tonight and crush the internal chip. No one has this direct number for a reason.

"I'm not taking any chances. He's local. He'll be way fucking faster and more discreet than the cops. Someone has June." Bennett stares at me as I lift my phone to my ear, muttering, "And I'm family — I'm calling in a favor."

CHAPTER TWENTY-SEVEN

JUNE

"I TRIED so hard to get to you before your heat."

Fuck, did someone run me over with a truck?

"The designation center wouldn't let me in, my application wasn't valid."

My head is spinning as I squint up at a bright light above me.

"Luckily, I had a tracker on your car. I knew when you moved it, when you drove it from Virginia to Rochester. I had to take this opportunity when it presented itself. You were so smart to step away to the back office again."

Am I at the fucking dentist?

"You make such a pretty little omega for me, baby girl."

I don't remember making a dentist appointment. Arin would have reminded me if I had.

Memories hit me in a one-two punch — the book signing and the water bottle.

"I tried *three* times to reach you in London. First, I called your parents. It was easy when they were listed with the member registry of their club. They told me I could have you. I went to the center, but they were hesitant to let me see you because I didn't have a pack." The man comes into view, just as slimy as I remember him being in the grocery store. His hair is slicked back, eyes shifting rapidly as he rattles a medical tray next to him, adjusting the tools on it. "You're supposed to be open to pack life. So I called back and told them I was your brother, but you were already gone."

I lift my head, fighting nausea as I stare at the tray, realizing I'm *strapped* to a bed and one of the tools is a goddamn speculum.

"What —"

He shushes me, petting my hair like I'm a dog. "Don't move too much, you'll make yourself sick. I don't want you to choke on your own vomit, baby girl."

I snarl, even though I want to throw up on *him*, snapping my jaws at his hand when he gets too close to me again. "Don't *fucking* touch me."

He pulls his hand back, eyes softening, "Juniper, *baby girl.*" My blood runs cold as he gathers himself, standing a little taller. "Please stop or I'll knock you back out. The suppressants make your perfume stop." He frowns. "And I really like your smell, you smell so sweet, like spun sugar."

It's honey. I want to snarl again, but I stop myself, forcing myself to swallow fear and bile as he picks up a scalpel that shines under the harsh lighting.

"What are you doing? Why am I here?"

The man looks over at me. "Don't you remember when we met?"

My mind wracks. "The... grocery store?" What the *hell* could I have done to make one insignificant run-in with this man spiral to being strapped to a goddamn hospital bed in what looks like an abandoned apartment building? There's mold on the walls and trash along the baseboard, speaking to the level of cleanliness I have to look forward to if any of those tools get near me.

His face shutters, closing off as his eyes darken. "No, baby girl, your book signing."

Try as I might, nothing comes to mind. He grows angrier, clutching the scalpel tighter as he steps back over to the side of the bed. "For your *first book*, June. You were just a local author, signing at a card table in the front of the store on Main street."

I remember.

It was mortifying. No one knew who I was and no one came. It was me sitting at a table for *hours* while a couple booksellers took pity on me, letting me sign the store's stock. A couple people from the cafe next door walked over and made polite conversation. One man, startlingly awkward stepped up to my table, but he had shorter black hair, he didn't look this unkempt —

"I bought two copies, remember?"

He did. And when I thanked him, feeling a rush of genuine gratitude, he'd fumbled with them and said. "*You could thank me by recreating a scene or two from your book, or I could do it even better. You owe it to me. I just bought your books, you could at least be grateful.*"

I'd recoiled — and I flinch when he nears me again.

"Don't touch me."

The man frowns. "I know this may be overwhelming, but this is *fate*, June. You were such a pretty beta, but you couldn't have taken my knot back then — now you *can*. I just want to see it myself. I have to." He grabs my arm and I strain against him, shrieking as the scalpel slices across the meat of my forearm.

Blood wells from the gash, and under the light it drips down my arm, red — but with a golden sheen coating it.

The cut stings as I suck in a heaving gasp, panic lancing through me as he presses at the wound with his fingers. The man smears my blood with his thumb, holding his hand up and twisting his wrist, watching the shine under the light with wide-eyed curiosity.

"You were *made* for me. You *emerged* for me when I was at your London signing."

Adrenaline makes my heart take off. I'm going to vomit. I'm going to throw up everything in my stomach — maybe even the organ itself — because he lifts his thumb and then licks my blood from it, humming and moaning.

"I was all ready to follow you on your book tour, but then it *happened*." He turns to look at me, eyes bright with madness. "You were an *omega*, I smelled it the moment I walked inside, but that *stupid* bookseller stopped me and you ran off."

He moves around, dropping the scalpel onto the tray with the other tools. "I'm a good alpha, Juniper. I'm going to be so good to you, baby girl. No more pack. You'll be it for me, you'll have all my attention and we'll be together for life. I could *tell* you were unhappy in that interview, crying out for me, and I couldn't wait any longer."

His fingers hesitate as they brush the speculum.

"I do need to take out your birth control." The man looks up at me. "I'm glad you had it for your heat with them — I'm sorry I couldn't get you out of that townhouse, I sat there, night and day, waiting outside, but they kept leaving you with that meathead alpha. I could've taken the beta, but not him."

Theo.

The thought of one of my alphas makes me choke — tears welling in my eyes as he smoothes out my hair, cooing at me.

"It's okay, I forgive you for it. You will have my children and my children alone. We'll get rid of these bonds they've forced on you."

I freeze, a deer in headlights. *The fuck you will.*

My mind runs a mile a minute, cataloging the room, what I could do to get away from here. The traffic noise outside is minimal, and clearly no one came running when I screamed — but the bed is rusty. I might be able to break the cuffs he has me in — but I need a distraction. I need him *not* in the room with me as I try to get my half-drugged body to cooperate.

My voice is raw as I look up at him. "Please, don't do that here. Don't you have a nest for me? I'll want you" — bile burns in my throat — "as soon as it's out, I'll want you."

"I do have a nest, oh baby." He grabs my face suddenly, and I only smell cloying chemicals on his skin as he whispers, "We have to finish this before we go. If we get the implant out, we'll leave it and this city behind. Your next heat will set in and we can spend it together. I've been taking accelerants — to make my alpha stronger for you."

The *smell* makes sense now and my nausea returns with a vengeance. I'm in a *dress* — white with a wide, loose skirt — and strapped to a table. I'm painfully aware he can have it up and be between my legs in seconds. The panic makes me flinch when he touches my jaw, tilting my head back and forth, his tone tinged with a growl.

"We can break these bonds. I'll bite over them, and if that doesn't work, we'll burn them off. They'll break if we scorch your skin deep enough."

Tears overflow as I'm reduced to begging sobs. "*Please, please don't do this.*"

"Let me get you something for the pain and the anxiety." He fumbles as he steps away, like he's not entirely used to his own body. "I know you have trouble with that so hold on. I have something." He steps away from me and the gurney. My hands shake as I writhe on the bed, trying to make it rock, to fall over, for *anything* to give me a way to get out of here.

Then I feel it.

My chest sparks, like my heart is by an open flame. The adrenaline makes my focus laser in on it, the slowness in my limbs and mind fades as the anxiety overrides it — for *once* in my life, the panic response is forcing my heart to beat faster, my systems clearing away the medicine quickly as it fights *for* me. Sheer panic hits me — but it's not mine, and the man rushes out of the room as I let out a loud sob.

I turn my head back and forth, whispering, praying. The bonds are obnoxiously loud in my chest — they have to be close to me, but I don't know how to let them know that I'm *here.*

I love you.

Closing my eyes, I breathe in and out, sawing gasps as I hear footsteps.

Seth. Bennett. Theo. Arin. I love you.

The door creaks as I open my eyes, but in the other room, a *BANG!* makes both the stranger and I jump. The old door flies out of his hand as he whirls toward the noise, a bottle of something rattling in his hands.

His eyes widen, and then blood sprays out the back of his head.

It's so quick. Two more hits collide — it's like an action movie. Blood sprays. The alpha's body falls. My chest aches, hyperventilating as someone in all black rushes up to the body, checking the side of his neck.

"Dead." The voice is female. She rises, ripping off a balaclava, revealing long black hair, looking at me. "Cyrus! She's here!"

"Apartment clear!" A male voice this time — and he's *big* — he fills the room when he enters it with the woman. The smell coming off her makes me jerk and she gives him a look. "I've got her." He moves fast, holstering his gun as he approaches me to get the cuffs off. "Seth Harding sent us —"

The man smells like nothing as he touches me — no perfume, no spray — just... absent. I strain against the bed, gasping out, "Did you kill him?"

The woman — an alpha from the smell of her — glances over at the body again. "Definitely dead."

I collapse back to the gurney, breathing hard as the man unstraps my arms. Flinging up, I fall almost immediately. He catches me, the female alpha grabbing my arm, slight and lithe, but *strong*.

The man, Cyrus, frees my ankles, then he moves up. "I don't think you can walk, let me carry you. Your pack is outside with our boss." His eyes find the alpha next to me, an unspoken conversation flying between them before he picks me up.

I hiccup, my eyes finding the speculum on the floor, the

tray overturned, my blood still dripping from my arm. "He — he was going to.. The..."

The female alpha's eyes drop to where I'm looking. She follows us as Cyrus steps over the man's body, carrying me out of the apartment. The woman pauses for half a moment, eyes meeting mine as she lifts her foot and slams her heavy boot down on the dead man's groin — disfiguring him for me.

CHAPTER TWENTY-EIGHT

ARIN

ONE PHONE CALL.

That was all it took.

The man in front of me doesn't waver — an echo of Seth's features on his face. They could be twins except Seth's skin is tanned and his cousin is pale. He bears a careful, composed expression — like my love's life isn't hanging in the balance of a madman's tenuous grip on reality.

Gabriel Abramowitz's eyes track the screen in front of us. I can admit when I'm out of my element, and this is one of those times. Sheer panic rushes through my bloodstream, but the other alpha just studies the cameras.

Seth steps closer, shoulders brushing like second nature, bending to mutter something in his cousin's ear. Gabriel's eyes raise, then he nods, his voice carrying. "Vivian will enter first, Cyrus will take care of any accomplices."

What the fuck have you been hiding from us?

Bennett winds his arm around Seth and I glance at Theo, chest aching as he stares at nothing, eyes lost. I move

302

closer, hand bracing against the back of his neck, so familiar, but this time, both of us are in *pain*. "She will be okay."

"I didn't even think this was a possibility." His voice is raw, blue eyes wrecked as he looks at me. "Should we have gotten her a security team? Did we put a target on her back?" Theo searches my face for answers that I don't have.

"It isn't your fault." Gabriel steps over, pushing up his sleeves to reveal a veritable crosshatch of tattoos that rival Theo's own. I can't distinguish the art in the low light as he waves a hand at the monitors. "She was being stalked, for years, from what my people have figured out in the short amount of time we've had. He clearly believes in the old ways — one alpha, one omega — pure ownership. You can't get better than Vivian and Cyrus. They'll get her back for you."

David Masterson.

The man's face is on one of the monitors, blurry information about the psychotic alpha not registering in my brain as I stare at his photo. Greasy brown-black hair hangs around his face. He was in London — he made a commotion at June's signing, only interrupted by her oncoming heat. He had a rental car parked outside our townhouse. He lived in the same building that June did, and tagged her car with a tracker, which is how he found Seth and her at the grocery store, then later the location of our home in Rochester. He paid off an employee for access to our home security network.

He saw his chance with her signing and took it.

I feel *sick*.

Gabriel looks up at me, a few inches shorter. Prime to prime. "They're going in."

We cluster around the monitors. Both of Gabriel's

people have cameras on their suits. The female alpha — Vivian — rushes in, entering the building and the camera on the man — Cyrus — catches glimpses of her as they clear the bottom floor together. The apartment building is abandoned and wasn't hard to find. When David took June, he clearly planned to be in and out as quickly as possible.

But Seth's call was faster.

The building is *filthy* through the grainy cameras. My chest smarts and I press a hand against my heart, feeling the bond tug, awareness, sleepy and panicked — June's *awake* and I watch as Cyrus kicks a door down.

David stands by a door, clutching a bottle of pills.

Cyrus doesn't hesitate.

The monitors flare with light, gunshots firing before Vivian darts around Cyrus and bends down to check the body lying on the floor. Cyrus moves, immediately clearing the rest of the apartment and my eyes dart to Vivian's body camera as she enters a room.

June is strapped to a *gurney,* medical supplies all around her.

Theo snarls, and the noise is echoed by Bennett as Seth shoves forward, staring with his mouth partially open. "Gabriel."

Gabriel touches his earpiece, talking quickly. "Is she unharmed?"

Vivian darts to June's side, her pale face sheened with sweat. She flinches away from the female alpha and Cyrus moves quickly, working to get June free from the cuffs.

I've seen enough. Turning sharply, I leave the room, the entire building, legs eating up the distance between us and the building two blocks away. Someone shouts my name, but

I ignore them, passing a van where Gabriel has two EMTs waiting.

Then I see it.

The door to the abandoned building opens, Vivian holding it as Cyrus passes her.

And I'm *running*.

The man holding June looks up sharply as I nearly knock into him, gasping, "Juniper — *June* —" Her pretty white dress is dirty as I take her from Cyrus' arms, round face pale as I wrap my arms around her, pulling her to my chest. Tears stream down my face as I press my nose against her hair, breathing her in and chasing away the smell of the other alpha at the same time.

Seth, Bennett, and Theo's presences all join us, touching her, crying too, as she shakes. I don't let her go as we make it to the EMTs, all but snarling when they check her over. One of them touches her arm as she trembles, feeling so small to me, so human and vulnerable.

As they raise her arm, I see the gash and come undone.

Her fingers cling to me when I start to move her away — I know the other alpha is dead — but I have the sudden urge to absolutely rip his body to shreds myself.

"No," June gasps, sobbing as she clamors to hold onto me. "Don't leave me."

Theo strokes her hair, half-panicked as he looks over at me. One of the EMTs starts the process of cleaning her arm as I jerk her firmly into my lap, pressing my nose against her throat, whispering, "I'm sorry. I'm so sorry, Juniper."

She shakes harder, crying, entirely soundless. Bennett cups her face, pressing his lips against her forehead as he holds onto her.

The beta EMT looks up at our pack, eyes soft. "She

doesn't need stitches and the suppressants he spiked her with will be entirely out of her system by tomorrow. They were quick acting — meant to subdue feral omegas. I have no idea how he could have accessed ones this powerful."

June turns her head, burying herself against me as she sobs harder. My heart breaks as I shush her, letting her fall apart in my arms.

Seth and Gabriel talk rapidly, stances nearly identical, only a few steps away. The female alpha approaches them, then touches Seth's arm. He looks back at June, eyes cutting before he parts from them. When he steps over, he takes June's face into his hands, pulling her nose to nose with himself.

"You're safe now, baby. You'll always be safe. I'll never let anything else happen to you."

The omega in my arms stares up at him, her expression broken. "I want to go *home*."

Bennett makes a distressed noise in the back of his throat, and my pack looks to me. Shifting, I push June into Theo's arms, bereft to let her go as she chokes on another cry, her hands grasping at me.

"Go with Theo, love." I touch her cheeks, wiping away the dirt and tears as best as I can. "I will be right there."

Gabriel approaches us as Theo swings June into his arms, his head bending down, muttering softly to her as Gabriel slows. "I will see to getting this cleaned up and quieted. Do you need a plane to get back to your home?" His eyes briefly find June and I fight the urge to rip his head from his body for even daring to look at our omega when she's this fragile and vulnerable — but he *helped* us — so I stare at the man with hands in the pocket of every powerful person in this wretched fucking city.

"We need a car to the airport."

"Of course." Gabriel nods at a black vehicle. "Take mine." He glances to Seth. "I didn't know omegas could emerge this late."

Seth gives him an annoyed look, hands on June's back as he begins to guide Theo toward the car. "Of course you didn't know — is this the first time you've left the compound in a decade?" I'm momentarily shocked by the utter *vitriol* in his tone.

"I'm busy running the family, Seth."

Bennett and I exchange a look as Theo and Seth take June to the car. Noise rushes into my ears as she makes a pained sound, calling out for Bennett. The alpha beside me joins them, leaving me alone with Gabriel.

"I want to see the body."

He looks over at me, understanding in his cool gaze, then nods.

CHAPTER TWENTY-NINE

JUNE

THE STEAM SMEARS on the mirror as I wipe it away with the side of my hand. Bare under the lights of the bathroom, I see the silver marks on me — my neck, the bite on the side of my breast, and the glimpse of the one between my thighs.

But it's the thin, red line on my arm that makes my heart stop.

I didn't need stitches, but it's still taken almost a month for the skin to stop looking angry and inflamed. I've gotten multiple shots to ward off infection from the dirty scalpel. I can't close my eyes for more than two seconds before I remember the way the alpha touched me, my stomach churning with the smell of chemicals.

Stepping away from the mirror, I look away from my reflection — haunted eyes, pale skin.

One of Theo's sweatshirts lays on my bed, waiting for me. The sheets are pulled up, which means Bennett made the bed before he and Seth slipped out of the room. Someone has been with me almost every single second of every day since that night.

I've nearly gone to the nest a few times, but I don't want *this* to be the first memory I have of spending time there with my alphas.

Tugging Theo's clothes on, I leave my wet hair to drip as I wander downstairs with my arms around myself. Noise draws me to the kitchen, where Bennett stands behind the island, apron slung around his neck and hips, chopping vegetables. Seth leans against the fridge, smiling softly at our alpha, while Theo and Arin chat off to the side.

Bennett looks up at me first. "There she is."

Theo smiles gently. "You found the sweatshirt." He comes over, pushing my wet hair back just to kiss my forehead. "Let me braid your hair for you, June." His touch soothes the simmer of anxiety under my skin as I turn into him, nodding. Theo snaps his fingers at Seth. "Scrunchie."

Seth groans, but shakes his hair out, grabbing the tie from it and flinging it at us. A laugh catches in my throat when it hits Theo right in the face. My alpha glances down at me, arching an eyebrow. "Is that funny? Your brat of a beta hitting me in the face with a scrunchie?"

My lips twitch as he grabs me by the hips, fingers dancing along my sides. Laughing, I let out a little shriek, squirming away from him, fighting as he jerks me against his chest, kissing my jaw and muttering, "Let's go to the library."

Melting into him, I let him drag me out of the kitchen and into the library. The large room already has a fire crackling. He pulls me down onto one of the couches, bending over me. Theo's hands slide over my hips as he kisses my jaw, voice gentle. "How was your shower, baby?"

Flushing, my heart flutters as I cup his face, pulling him to me so I can kiss him gently, our noses brushing. "Good." It was nice to have a few moments to myself, but it doesn't take long for the remnants of memories to creep back in. Theo's lips touch mine before he pulls me up, readjusting us so I'm between his legs, back to his chest as his fingers card through my hair, untangling it.

"Let me take care of this." He shifts, scrunchie on his wrist as he pulls the strands back.

"Thank you." My heart tugs as I stare at the fire.

Theo kisses my shoulder from behind. "I'll always take care of you." As he starts to braid, he speaks. "I thought we could redecorate your office soon. If you're feeling up to it?"

I chew on my lower lip, nodding slightly, not wanting to disrupt his work. "Yeah, we can." Closing my eyes, I lean back into him. "I'm still tired, but it's over. I need to keep moving forward."

"You're right, it *is* over, but you're allowed to take as much time as you need." Theo pauses and his fingers hesitate. "That night... we were really lucky that Seth had someone to call. We didn't waste a second, and I'm very grateful for that."

I'm grateful too. Grateful for their urgency, their love, their part in my life, and bonds in my heart.

I don't have the full story from Seth, but what he *has* said rocked me to my core. His cousin — Gabriel — oversees an entire *criminal organization* and Seth was once *a part of it*. It's not a story my beta seemed ready to tell, and maybe it isn't entirely his to share.

Theo finishes braiding my hair and I turn, crawling into his lap to burrow into him.

The door to the library opens and I don't move as I press a kiss to Theo's throat, his hands sliding up my back, under the sweatshirt. The smell of mint surrounds us as another hand touches my head, grazing the braid. Arin takes a seat at the other end of the couch, brown eyes reflective when I pull back enough to look at him.

"I thought you two were resting before lunch."

Theo snorts, fingers exploring my skin, edging on indecent. "I'm trying to convince her to let me help her fix up that sad, empty office."

I turn my head, rolling my eyes. "The office is *fine* —"

"You need more than one old desk and that god-awful chair. Let me buy you pretty things, princess. I'll get you whatever you want. I'll even buy you a new computer if you want one —"

Arin's lips twitch as he reaches for a discarded book on the coffee table. He picks it up, then flips to the first page. His accent fills the room as he silences our argument by beginning to read aloud. I huff, but it does the job of making my eyes heavier as I curl up against Theo, using him as a giant pillow.

I DOZE IN AND OUT, only rousing when Bennett and Seth enter the room, bringing with them the smell of Bennett's risotto. He places bowls on the coffee table, giving me a sheepish look. "Sorry, darling, I didn't mean to wake you."

Rubbing my eyes with a grumble, I pull away from Theo, feeling flushed and fidgety. "It's okay, I'm hungry and I need to talk to all of you."

The room is quiet as I look at Arin. Bennett and Seth crash onto the couch across from us and I pick up a bowl of food so I have something to hold as I twist the spoon, trying to find the right words. I've had a lot of time to think since everything happened — a lot of time to ruminate and roll over the options in my mind.

Worry tinges my bonds.

"I want to get my birth control implant removed."

Arin jolts, his hand coming to rest on my knee. "June —"

"Please, let me finish." I stare at him, sucking in a breath. Despite being strapped to that *fucking* table by that alpha, it's been a long time coming. All I can think about is my life in the next year, in the next *five* years, of embracing both being an omega and my own limitations. I'm so *tired* of feeling like I should be pushing aside every single one of my personal boundaries because I want to make others more comfortable.

From agreeing to signings that I can't even comprehend attending to the interview requests that have come in, hoping they can milk my pack and I for a few minutes of air time. I don't *want* to be the face of any kind of late-emerging omega rights movement. I will do my part in the ways that I can, but not at the expense of my own peace of mind.

And I've been learning about my designation. I want to work with it, instead of constantly fighting it.

Arin nods and I cling to the bowl.

"I don't want kids." Reiterating my stance, I eye each of the men around me. "But everything that I've researched says that the hormones from the implant make heat symptoms worse. There's a lot of newer research suggesting that omega bodies function better when heat cycles are uninterrupted — I don't want a repeat of how I felt in London for my second heat."

Seth's eyes soften. "You really struggled."

"I felt *awful*. I didn't even feel like myself —"

"Remove it," Arin says, catching my eyes. "We will find other solutions for birth control."

Theo's hand brushes my back. "I've had a vasectomy for years. There are alpha doctors who will make sure it never reconnects unless it's surgically done, even during a rut."

My heart pangs as I look at Arin, Bennett, and Seth. "I just don't want to take that choice away from any of you — if you *want* —"

Bennett shakes his head, holding up a hand. "Stop." After a moment, he pinches his nose. "I have to be honest. I forgot pregnancy was a risk."

A laugh of pure surprise cracks out of me as Seth shrugs. "It's not like he was going to knock *me* up."

Theo snorts as I flounder. "So that's it?"

Arin smiles. "That's it. One IUD removal, three vasectomies. Though, I now regret not getting one years ago when Theo did."

Theo's chest puffs. "I *told* you it was worth it."

"Will you take care of me when my balls hurt, baby?" Seth grabs his own food, giving me a salacious look. "Maybe massage them?"

"No." His jaw drops as I take a bite and hum softly at the burst of flavors. Bennett really is the best cook. "But the sooner you get it, the sooner we can spend my next heat here — at *home*."

Arin stills at the other end of the couch. "I'll make the calls."

A smile tugs at my lips as I look at my pack, eyes landing on my prime. "Pencil me into your busy schedule when you're healed, alpha."

CHAPTER THIRTY

JUNE

THE DOCTOR WARNED me about this, but did I listen?

No, of course not. I thought it would take *way* more time. But it's only been three days and the chills and shakes have already begun. It was a humbling experience to have a gynecologist between my spread legs while I white-knuckle gripped Arin on one side and Seth on the other, fighting tears and a panic attack.

"I suggest you take a few weeks off, because based on the pattern of your first heat" — the doctor removed her gloves, looking up at me sympathetically — *"this removal will likely usher in your second heat early as your body adjusts to its natural hormone patterns."*

I shuffle down the hallway, blankets in my arms as I move them from the laundry room to the nest. It doesn't smell like *any* of my pack and that's unacceptable.

"Hey, darling." Bennett catches my eye as I walk through the kitchen again. "Can I help you with anything?"

"No," I answer automatically, then pause. "Actually —"

Walking over to him, I drop my forehead against his chest, wrapping my arms around him, breathing out the crawling feeling under my skin and in oranges, bright and comforting. "Hug me."

He barely manages to muffle his laugh as he wraps his arms around me and kisses the top of my head. "You're warm."

"I wonder why," I snark at him, then nudge his shirt with my face, hands creeping under it to touch his skin. *So smooth.* His body is so nice — so rude to wear clothes around me —

Bennett scratches his nails through my hair, making me preen as my brain focuses on pushing his shirt up so I can see his chest, mouth watering.

"You want to go lie down in the nest and I'll get you food?"

I scrunch my nose and look up at him. "I'm not hungry."

His lips twitch. "Tell me what you need, darling."

Whining, I push his shirt up more, the uncomfortable feeling in my body making every nerve ending feel unsettled. "I was so *stupid.*" I work to get his shirt off, rewarded by the glorious sight of it falling to the floor and him standing bare chested in the kitchen like some kind of chef-god that I get to lick whenever I want.

Bennett has the audacity to laugh at me as he cups my face. "Why were you stupid?"

"Because" — I grab him, pulling him closer as my lashes flutter, feeling his lips on my cheeks, then my jaw, moving to the bond mark as we both sigh out — "I thought I had more time before this heat." Bennett's teeth graze the mark he made in my skin and I run my hands over his chest. *Mine.*

"Come to the nest with me, alpha, you're not busy right now."

"I am yours to use." He whispers the words before he kisses me.

My mind goes hazy as we back down the hall to the nest. I tug him with me, moving him how I want, making him stay as I kiss down his chest, sinking to my knees. "What about the vasectomy?"

"All done." He pulls my sweater off, looking down with dark eyes. "Done by an alpha doctor who made sure there were no more active sperm. I can find condoms if you —"

I hum, details blurring as I push my leggings down, shedding the rest of my clothes before focusing on *him*. My alpha rises above me, standing just where I left him, bare chest highlighted by the stained glass skylight above us, clad in only a pair of sweats that are strained across the front.

I can help.

Reaching forward, I pull him out, kissing the head of his cock sweetly when it appears. My eyes shut as he groans, a hand moving to my hair, gathering it as I wrap my lips around him. The *taste* of him bursts on my tongue — rich, bright, tinged with fudge and sweetness that makes me glide my tongue all over. I suck on him before I lean back, sitting on my heels.

"You can fuck me now."

Bennett stares down at me, eyes wild. "I can?"

I nod. "I just wanted to taste first."

He utters a low curse before he tackles me to the nest mattress, kissing me heatedly as he falls between my spread thighs. "You and Seth will be the fucking death of me."

Grinning, I settle back into the pile of blankets and pillows I've been arranging for the past two days. Amongst them are Theo's sheets, Arin's dress shirts, Seth's socks, and Bennett's own pajama pants — but the smells are nothing compared to the real alpha on top of me as his hands traverse my body, fingers hooking in my underwear to rid me of them.

As his hand touches my foot, he laughs. "Do you want your fuzzy socks on or off while I fuck the life out of you, sweetheart?"

"Don't care." I breathe out the words, forcing him to kiss me again, my stomach cramping as I whine, "Just need you in me, alpha, now —"

He groans, then notches at my entrance, sinking into me without another word. I cry out, wrapping a leg around him as I grind up. The first heat made me feel like I was losing my mind — but *this* — the feelings of lust, love, want, need rise to an overwhelming clamor in my body. They tangle together, following the bond between our hearts. It's like I'm in the moment but also watching it through his shared emotions, pleasure winding as he nips at my lips, thrusting slow.

Turning my head, I feel his kisses move to my bond mark again, sucking on it as I stare at the muscles in his arm. Braced above me, they keep bulging, holding his weight as he fucks me. I moan at the sight — *hottest thing I've ever seen* — wrapping my other leg around him as I grind against his knot.

"*Fuck.*"

The softly muttered curse doesn't come from myself *or* the man on top of me, and goosebumps rise on my skin as I turn to look at the open door. Seth's eyes meet mine, then wander to Bennett's body. Theo and Arin are a half-step behind him.

Sighing, I pull Bennett closer, my voice breathy with the movement of his hips. "We started without you."

Bennett grabs a handful of my hair, jerking my head to the side so he can bite at the bond mark. "So fucking tempting." He thrusts deeper, knot teasing me as I arch into him, and I feel his grin as he murmurs, "I told you I'd make them all watch me fuck you one day." Slipping out of me, he flips me, forcing my head down to the nest as I kneel, punching his hips into mine from behind. "Let them all watch as I fill this pretty pink pussy with my cum and make you messy."

I scream as I clench around him, crying out as he sets a brutal pace. It's near punishing how fast he fucks me and my omega *loves* it. I have to chase my own orgasm, reaching under myself to play with my clit, his knot slipping in and then back out, stretching me perfectly.

Bennett groans, hand on my neck as he pushes against the bond mark, a physical representation of how much we love and *know* each other.

"Are you ready for them to watch you cover me, darling?"

His hips slam into mine and I shiver under him, screaming as slick gushes out around Bennett's knot. He pushes in all the way, holding onto me as he comes with a roar and I feel myself fluttering around him, punch-drunk as he hums and kisses across my shoulders. His fingers move between us, and then he releases his knot from me early, a mixture of us dripping down the backs of my thighs as he leans away.

"What a pretty omega; flushed, fucked, and filled."

I groan, heat flashing down my skin as I roll onto my side and look at the door, my hand wandering down my body as my two other alphas and my beta eye me. Bennett bends down, kissing my stomach, nuzzling my skin as I push the mix of our release back into myself.

Arin stares, eyes dark. "Can we help you with your heat, love?"

Bennett kisses down to my thighs, breathing out against the bond mark Arin's own teeth left before he nips at it. I whine, arching up as his hands move over me, nodding my head.

"Come in."

The ghost of Bennett's touch leaves me just as Arin makes a beeline for the center of the nest. I'm barely upright before he grabs me, meeting me for a passionate kiss as his hands glide over my sated body. *My prime.* He lifts me partially and I feel the nest dip as there's other movement.

Pulling away, I turn to see Theo already mostly naked, right beside us, cock in hand as I lean over and kiss his tip with a little hum.

He groans, pushing my hair back. "I should braid this — *fuck—*" He cuts himself off as I suck him into my mouth, swirling my tongue. The sound of a bottle cap popping open draws my eyes as Seth climbs into the nest, waving the bottle of lube at me.

"Hello, baby." He gives me a sweet kiss on my cheek, ignoring Theo's cock in my mouth. Seth winks. "I love you, be with you in a minute." Then he *tackles* Bennett.

I laugh, pulling back as my head swivels, finding Arin again. He crooks a finger at me, sitting against one of the nest walls, naked and legs wide. His hair is ruffled and I crawl over to him, climbing on top before sinking down onto him with a little sigh.

His hands move over me, one finding my hair, holding

my head as I rock up and down, but he forces me to turn. "Suck. This is punishment for starting without us."

Theo stands to the side of us, just waiting and I open my lips again, diving forward with a smile as I rock on top of Arin. It's *not* a punishment — clean rainwater coats my nostrils as I bob my head, letting one of Arin's hands guide my hips. Pulling back with a moan, I kiss down Theo's length, gasping as Arin's knot kisses my swollen clit.

"I want you all."

Theo groans, switching to holding my head, pulling me back onto him and using my mouth as Arin starts to thrust up faster. I whine, mouth full, eyes wide because each time I pull back I get glimpses of Bennett and Seth, twisting together, touching, gasping, hands fisting —

Arin slams up faster as I start to clench and my hands drop from Theo's thighs, nails digging in Arin's chest as I ride him harder, hips moving as fast as I can, chasing and writhing until he grunts under me, his knot slipping in as his cock kicks, filling me with a gasp of my name.

The omega in me *preens* as I pull off Theo, a strand of spit coming with me as I stare up at him. "How do you want me?"

He groans, then drops to his knees, kissing me heatedly as Arin takes a moment to gather himself. I feel him slide out, but then his hand cups me, pushing the mess back inside as he guides me into Theo's lap. It barely takes a moment, and no effort from either of us — because Arin grabs Theo by the cock and then shoves him inside me, landing heated kisses on my back as I cry out.

The bonds sing my chest as I reach out blindly. "I want to feel you all. *Please.*"

Someone touches my hand, then Seth is there, kissing up

my arm as he murmurs, "It's okay, we've got you, baby. We've always got you."

Theo starts to move under me as Arin rubs his hands over my back. Seth drags me into a kiss, Bennett's hand on my hair, keeping us together as he kneels behind Seth and thrusts into him. Seth grunts, then kisses me even harder as my hand falls, fisting his cock, jerking my wrist.

Theo's lips sear across my shoulder, all of us moving as Arin pushes into me from behind and I go *still*.

Mine. My pack. My loves.

It takes everything to keep upright as we all move together, lips and touches blurring. Bennett groans as I rock between Arin and Theo, my skin alight with pure pleasure.

"Come for us, June."

I shudder, unsure who said it, uncaring as I climax again. Seth twitches in my hand and I feel the spill of wet over my fingers as Theo comes underneath me. Bennett jolts with a broken groan as Arin holds me up, buried deep inside me, teeth in my shoulder.

I need more.

"I can't wait for her heats to kill me. God, what a way to go." Arin laughs at Theo's declaration, half-breathless behind me. I blindly pull Theo up into a kiss, biting at his lips, some-one's hand between my legs, rubbing and making me shiver again.

This is what safety feels like. This is love. Surrounded by all four of them, all my bonds resonating with adoration, chasing away the heat with everything in them.

How could anyone ever say this isn't what life should be?

I turn my head, finding Bennett on instinct to kiss him.

"I love you." The words escape, meant for them all, the emotion reverberating down to the marrow in my bones, to my very soul. My chest warms from four different directions as someone touches my hair. Arin pulls me into a kiss. Seth's touch lingers on my chest over my heart.

"We love you too."

"Prove it."

"With pleasure, omega."

EPILOGUES

ONE YEAR LATER

EPILOGUE

THEO

"Today was *amazing*."

June comes out of the bathroom in a cloud of humidity and concentrated smells of soap and perfume, collapsing down onto my chest on the little hotel couch. The sudden weight makes me grunt, but I smile down at her flushed cheeks, running my hands over the hotel robe she has on.

Arin steps out of the bathroom and I glance down at our omega again, wondering if the flushed tinge to her skin is *just* from the warm water.

She hums, sinking into me and kissing my chest once. "Twelve cities, twenty stops, and the European signings are *done*. Do not let me do this again. I'm exhausted."

I laugh, playing with her hair as I glance down at her.

June's eyes raise, then squint. "What's that look for?"

"I'm proud of you."

She makes a little noise, cheeks darkening as she shakes her head at me, biting her lower lip. "*Theo.*" I'll never get tired of the way she says my name — or variations of it, ranging from annoyed to embarrassment to little sighs.

The emotions hit me all at once.

It's been over a *year* since Seth left our kitchen, leaving me in front of the TV, watching a newscaster flash up an image of June's face — "*As of right now, June Wald's agent has not made a comment, but we do know the author is registered as a beta. Time will tell if the rumors are true.*"

I'd stared at the screen, barely registering Bennett as he'd rushed off behind the beta. The feeling of *rightness* had hit me from that very first second, knowing from her photo alone that I'd never be the same. Then she'd been in our townhouse mere hours later, and I was right.

There was before June — and now my future is hers. I wouldn't want it any other way.

Lifting her by the chin, I press a soft kiss to the tip of her nose. "I thank the stars every day that you love me."

Her eyes water before she's kissing me back fervently. "And I *do*, Theo. I love you so much."

We linger for a moment, breathing in each other's air before I readjust us so she's resting on my chest as I sprawl across the couch. The news plays on the TV — my mother is back in Rochester, keeping an eye on the house with Charles.

The older beta has been a stalwart companion at my mother's side for a year as she went through the messy negotiations and procedures to remove herself from my fathers' control. But her vibrancy has come back — she has a little apartment in the city, and she's been helping run a community garden that Ashley buys produce and herbs from for her restaurant.

June wiggles and I glance down at her. "What?"

"Cramp." She mutters the word, nose scrunching as she calls out, "Arin? Do we have that heating —"

"Coming." He pads out of one of the bedrooms, heating pack in hand. With a kiss to her forehead, he lays it on her stomach, eyes catching mine.

We leave for Switzerland from France tomorrow.

I never thought there'd be room for... more between Arin and I, but then he touches my arm, eyes softer. "Need anything?"

"No," I grunt, holding June against me a little tighter. For years I pushed everything down, from my designation, from my own feelings toward the prime looking at us right now — but the last year has made me realize I have a lot of extra love in my heart — love that extends to more than just the woman in my arms.

June sighs, readjusting. I rub her shoulders. "We could delay the trip."

"Absolutely the fuck not," she grumbles, rolling her eyes. "I am *not* giving up a month-long spa vacation *in the Alps* where I've been promised massages and heat sex."

I laugh loudly as Arin drops onto the other end of the couch, shaking his head with a wide smile. "Okay, okay, noted." She wiggles again and when her hips graze the front of my sweats, I grab her and grunt, "Settle, or you'll be filled and fucked in five minutes."

She flashes me a challenging look. "I'd love to see you try."

"I'll hold you down —"

"I'll bite you —"

"Both of you," Arin cuts us off, half laughing, half groaning, "stop it before I separate you two. Bennett and Seth will be back in *ten minutes* with dinner. Can't you behave that long?"

June's eyes flash to mine and I see the gears working

before the slow grin spreads across her features. My hands slide to the tie on her robe, then under it, looking up at Arin as his nostrils flare.

I unwrap her like the little gift she is.

"Chop, chop," June moans as my hand wanders between her thighs, spreading her wide. Arin's eyes focus on her and even *imaging* what he's seeing — her shiny, wet cunt — makes me impossibly hard. "I want two orgasms before they're back. I *will* be eating dinner before it goes cold."

Arin and I give her three.

EPILOGUE

ARIN

I DON'T THINK I've been to Switzerland in at least five years.

June immediately suctioned herself to my side the second our plane landed, letting me lead her around the resort as the owner gave us a tour of the new facilities. Honestly, I never considered visiting in the last few years — I helped sell the land and the untouched buildings on it — but I should have. The space is beautiful and keeps making little gasps leave my omega's lips. Her fingers tighten on my arm as we step onto the private heated pool deck, featuring a jacuzzi in one corner and a sauna in the other.

"Do you approve?"

She looks up at me, hazel eyes wide as she takes it all in, before darting to Seth's side and pointing to the view of the mountains, towering tall above us. He laughs, leaning in to mutter something in her ear before she slaps his chest.

My attention wavers, giving Stefan, the owner, a polite smile. "Thank you again for allowing my pack and I to reserve this space."

The other man smiles, half-amused as he glances at

Juniper. "Call the desk if you need anything at all. What's mine is yours, the staff know the same." He walks off, leaving us as I turn and suck in a lungful of the fresh mountain air, serenity scoring through my body.

I never would have known that a single year would change so much. From June crawling into my arms in my office to the sing of a bond in my own chest, resonating with her joy now. All the paths I took that led me to this point have been worth it — being *here* is where I feel more like myself than I ever have before.

A body moves to stand beside me and I turn my head, voice low. "Theo?"

The other alpha looks at me for a moment, blue eyes bright but almost nervous. After a moment, he touches my forearm. "Arin."

I frown. "What —"

Theo leans in, and then he's kissing me.

Years. From childhood friends to forming our pack of just the pair of us, to adding Bennett and Seth to the mix, to *now*. I was with him at his worst, when he struggled with his own designation, when we both fumbled through our twenties. He saw me through the years of endless grinding to build a client list, taking *care* of me, making sure I ate and slept.

Pulling back, I stare at him for a moment, seeing the uncertainty in his posture before I grab him by the back of the neck and drag him to me, kissing him hard with a growl. "You are one *stubborn* bastard, Theo Clarke."

He laughs against my mouth, like the *brat* he is. "I know."

I give him a disgruntled look, but it doesn't stay for very long. His cheeks are flushed, hair mussed and longer than

I've ever seen it. My heart kicks, and I kiss him again, lingering as I murmur, "I love you."

It isn't the first time we've uttered it, but it's the first time I've said it and *meant* the full definition. I love him as much as I love June.

Theo touches my jaw, strong hands on my face. "I love you. It was past time to tell you."

When we part, I glance to the side, seeing June and Seth clutching each other, eyes wide and faces split with stupid grins. Theo groans, rubbing a hand over his face. "Show's over."

June squeaks, then throws herself at the two of us, pulling Theo into one side and me into the other, peppering us both with kisses. "My alphas."

I laugh as Theo grumbles, but he's smiling the entire time until he fakes a cough, excusing himself to go into our suite.

June's gaze tilts up. "What should we do first?"

My fingers slip through her silken hair, pushing it behind her ear. "Whatever you want to do, Juniper."

She leans into me, sweet perfume invading my senses as she kisses my jaw. "I'm happy as long as I'm here with my pack, with *you*."

EPILOGUE

BENNETT

IF MY SOLE task in this life is to keep Seth and June from bouncing off the walls *and* each other, causing chaos — I'll do my due diligence happily.

June throws her head back with a loud laugh as Seth picks her up and plunges them both into the heated pool. They surface a moment later, spluttering before June splashes Seth with water. They're being a little rowdy for this to be considered a *relaxing spa vacation*, but I can't help my grin as I sit on the edge of the pool, watching them.

She's in a little brown bikini that I packed, Seth in a pair of matching shorts. Mine are purple — not a color I'd normally choose, but I think Seth slipped them into my bag. Leaning back on my arms, I watch them roughhouse, play fighting between lingering pecks.

It's been a long few years.

I remember when Arin flew us out when he was working on the sale of this place, before it was a sprawling spa. I even remember finding him and Theo together in one of the saunas — the kiss this morning was *not* a shock to anyone with eyes — but I don't think they ever would have recognized their own desire for each other had the last two years not happened.

"Bennett!" June bobs in the water. "Are you getting in?"

Seth treads next to her. "Are you going to be a stick in the mud?"

I splash them both with a hand. "The mud here does have *restorative properties.*"

Seth laughs as he mockingly covers her from the spray, spinning her away from me again as her arms come up to tangle in his hair. She kisses our beta, my heart singing with the flare of our shared bonds, both of them intertwined with my heart.

I didn't know it could ever feel like this. The moment I bit her, my DNA rewrote itself — I am theirs and they're mine. As I slip into the water, I let the heat sink into my muscles, carrying the stress away. The last few years have been tiring, between building mine and Seth's business up to where it is now to the busyness of pack life.

The two people in front of me make me want to retire early — to spend the rest of my time in our kitchen, chopping basil and making dinner. I want to be free to pull June into my arms at every opportunity, to kiss her instead of rotting away on conference calls.

Swimming up to them, I slide an arm around Seth, kissing his cheek before doing the same to June. She looks up at me, her voice soft. "You came in."

"You two were having all the fun without me." I pull away, chewing on my tongue. "I need to ask you both something."

Seth's eyes cut to me as June nods immediately, reaching out and cupping my jaw. "Anything."

"What if I decided to take a step back from working? Would that be okay?"

I'm surrounded by both of them in an instant, twin hugs encompassing me. Laughing, I hold onto them both, whispering, "I want to be at home. I want to make sure our family has dinner every night. I still want to work." I direct the words at Seth. "But I'm so tired of meetings. You were better at them than me anyway, and there's no reason for everyone on the board to default to my opinion because I'm the alpha. You're *so* brilliant." My voice softens as I touch Seth's cheek. "I'm ready to make that change if you are."

His smile breaks my heart. Our lips touch as he nods. "Absolutely. Beginning the next calendar year, you're officially on sabbatical. I think they'll survive if they finally have to listen to all my ideas."

June hums, her eyes brightening. "If you'll be home more we can take cooking classes!"

I know she gets lonely sometimes. All of us know Arin will never stop working — he enjoys it too much to truly step away — and June has the same streak in her. The idea of getting out of the house with her more, since her job is so insular, makes me smile.

"I'd love that. And if you'd still like to do some traveling before you start writing your next book, I'd be happy to go with you."

She drags us both into her arms, chattering excitedly. "Arin and Theo are going to be *so* jealous. You and I can just *leave* and go wherever we want, whenever."

Seth whines, "*I'm* jealous."

Laughing, I kiss him again, bond warm as I let him go and then turn to do the same with June. Her wet hands rise, holding my face to hers. "I'm proud of you, Bennett."

We exchange a smile as Seth wraps his arms around us. "I love you two. Look at us, we're living proof that yet another one of my schemes went off without a hitch."

June laughs, shaking her head at him and splashing him with water. "Without a hitch is a *stretch*, Seth." She dives away before he can catch her, and I plunge forward, shoving Seth out of my way to see who can get to our omega first.

I'd never admit it in fear of making his ego even larger, but Seth is right.

He deserves all the credit — our futures are this bright because of his impulsivity.

EPILOGUE

JUNE

Nᴏɴᴇ of them would tell me what we're doing tonight.

I *vaguely* know that it's a dinner, and that *maybe* Arin coordinated it, but the details have been kept from me. Which is both infuriating and charming — you'd think I'd be used to it after over a year of all four of them meddling.

My brain still can't wrap around the chain of events. I went from landing in London, anxious about my first book tour, to being certain I was going to die in an elevator with two strangers, to discovering I'm actually an *omega* and going home with said strangers?

None of it feels real.

My fingers take care in smoothing the skirt of my white dress as I stare in the mirror. There are multiple rooms in this suite — almost all of them have a view of the Swiss Alps too — but one of them is the size of a nest and I staked my claim on it, assuming that they could all find other beds. Because this one is *mine*.

This place is insane — my eyes catch on the wall of windows in the bathroom, looking out on plush, pillowy snow drifts and the mountain range. Never in a million years would I have thought I'd be here.

Stepping away from the bathroom, I pick up the thin necklace Theo got me for my birthday this year, five charms dangling off it. Two were gifted with the necklace, while Arin, Bennett, and Seth each gave me their own to add. Fastening the clip, I sweep my hair up to expose the silver mark on my throat, wishing I could flash the one on my thigh and on the side of my chest too — I like seeing them. I love what they represent.

For as horrifying as New York was — the threat was temporary, and I made it through. I always do. I'm *strong*.

It took time and a therapist — but I also have my pack. Going no contact with my parents helped, even though Dad still reaches out with small congratulations for each new milestone in my career. They're filming a movie adaption of my first book next year. My career has never been better.

My parents aren't a part of my family anymore — but that's okay. I have other people.

Grace is the *sweetest* woman alive, and having another omega in close proximity is better than I could have even imagined. She's full of tips and comments to help when I get frustrated with any of my men, but especially when Arin became a single-minded, overprotective maniac after the signing. Vera and the rest of her pack visit as much as they can with their twins, and I love the two chubby babies so much. Still, I've *never* regretted asking Arin, Bennett, and Seth to get vasectomies.

I know that babies are the end goal for most packs, but I feel like my life is only beginning. I want to reach so many new career highs — Bennett is stepping back to let Seth take the reins, Theo is investing in more charitable ventures, and

Arin will work until he drops — but I love that about all of them.

Double checking myself in a mirror, I touch the necklace's charms — a honey pot, a raindrop, a tiny chocolate bar, an orange, and a mint leaf. The gold shines under the lights, reminiscent of the blood running through my own veins.

I walk out into the living area barefoot, stopping short at the sight of tiny tea lights and candles lit all over every surface, my heart catching in my throat when I see a dinner table with a white cloth draped over it.

Arin stands at the head, a huge smile overtaking his dashing features.

"I thought I might have to come get you."

Flushing, I walk over. Theo is on Arin's right, with Bennett and Seth opposite to him, a single chair waiting for me. A smile twitches on my face as I murmur, "This is so fancy."

Theo stands and pulls me into his arms, kissing the side of my head. "It's to celebrate your tour, the end of our first full year together — really all of it."

I turn into him, beaming as I breathe in his rainwater perfume before leaning up and pecking his lips. It starts a line and I flit over to Arin next, doing the same to him, Bennett, and finally Seth before I return to my seat. "Okay, everyone's had a kiss, time to eat."

Arin laughs as Theo pulls my seat out for me, then kisses my head as I peek under the cloche, my eyes widening at the expertly dressed steak on my plate. I whip the cover off, the smell of butter and herbs permeating the air along with the sides of whipped, cheesy potatoes and roasted vegetables.

"Here" — Theo reaches over, cutting my steak for me — "let me do that."

I do, wiggling happily in my seat as he cuts it into perfect, medium-rare bite-sized pieces. Seth rolls his eyes. "Whipped."

Theo gives him a mock glare. "I'm not the one who charged into a designation center for her."

I choke as I take a sip of wine and Bennett breaks out into laughter with Arin. Covering my mouth, I thank Theo softly before I pick up my fork and stab a piece of meat, groaning the second it hits my tongue. "Oh, *Bennett.*" I take a second to chew, it practically melting in my mouth. "I think that's better than yours."

He splutters. "I'll get to this point, just you wait. I'll have plenty of time to practice."

Arin looks over at him, cutting into his own food. "Are you finally stepping back?"

Bennett nods, intertwining his hand with Seth's. "I'm ready to stay at home for a while. June wasn't complaining."

"Not at all. I'm going to drive him up the *wall.*" I have plans — multiple, actually — that involve Bennett being my new buddy for every task I don't want to do alone. He just doesn't know it yet.

Theo laughs, eating his steak as Seth digs into his salmon. When I glance at Arin's plate, I see both steak *and* salmon and I cautiously extend my fork, wiggling it at the fish.

Arin takes my fork, cutting a piece and feeding it to me. "I wasn't sure if you'd like it." His voice curls around me as I hum around the food.

"It's good." I look back at my steak, stealing my fork back. "Not as good as this, though."

Theo shakes his head. "You like it near bloody."

Flashing him my teeth, I wave a pink piece of meat at him. "Need I remind you, you do too."

His bond mark isn't the only place I have his teeth marks on my skin.

Arin rolls his eyes. "Since Bennett spoke already about his plans for the next year... I thought we'd take tonight to talk about what we'll be doing." He looks around the table, his eyes landing on each of us. "If that's alright?"

Bennett takes a long drink of his wine. "Like I said, I'm taking a sabbatical at the beginning of next year and I think with my newfound time, I'll be spending a lot of it in the kitchen — and with my omega."

My cheeks flush.

"Other than that, I'll take a few trips, maybe finally go with my dad out to the Rockies. He's wanted to hike and if he drags my mothers again, they'll never survive."

I take a drink, quickly chewing a vegetable. "I'll go with Yasmin and Kary, we can stay at one of the spas while you and your dad go look at rocks."

Bennett smiles. "That sounds wonderful."

My eyes dart to Seth. "What are you doing next year?"

"Apparently working." Seth laughs, but it's lighthearted. "I'm... excited that I'll get to head a few decisions." He looks over at Bennett, his expression softening. "I already have a few ideas, and I'm wondering if I could expand us in a few different directions. We've always talked about wine, that might be worthwhile if you're serious about cooking."

Bennett tilts his head at him, a smile on his lips. "Wine... we could expand into that."

Seth shrugs. "Just a thought." He spears a piece of asparagus. "And I spoke to Gabriel before we left France."

The name of his cousin makes us all pause. Seth meets

Arin's eyes. "Things are shifting in the family and he asked if I'd step in to oversee some of the more... legal affairs, help out the businesses. It's not like I've never been involved." His voice softens. "Mine and Bennett's liquor has been sold in his clubs for years. This would just be more of a consultant role."

Arin pauses, wine glass in hand. "We can look into that."

I glance between them, then look back at my beta. "How is Gabe?"

"Still hates that nickname."

"Well he's not here, and he let me call him that when we were in New York a couple months ago." He had us over for a very lovely dinner and didn't say a word when I called him that.

"Only you would goad a mobster."

I turn my focus to Theo as Arin motions for him to take his turn.

Theo leans back, a smile on his face. "I think Bennett has the right idea — stepping back. Not that I *do* much in the grand scheme of things." He looks at me. "But my mom's experience has left a part of me wanting to develop a fund for omegas in need — ones who want to leave their packs and get out of bad situations. I thought you might want to help me. I'm going to ask her to be the charity's director, but any options are better than the ones out there."

My heart tugs as I kiss his cheek. "That sounds amazing. We should figure out some kind of fundraising for the pack to take part in."

I've avoided the calls for interviews, but our rarity and popularity hasn't faded by much. There's not been any more omegas who have had quite the same *public* emergence since mine.

Arin smiles. "Maybe *Gabe* can help get the right people in the room."

Seth chokes on his drink. "I'll ask. Charities are actually great covers."

I shoot him a look, eyes narrowing as Arin says, "And you, Juniper?"

"Oh." I glance up at the ceiling, sucking in a breath as I grin. "Well, with this release over and done with, and this tour — I think I'd like to switch up what I've been writing. I'm thinking of maybe starting something in a different genre from contemporary, just to see. And filming should start next year for the adaption of *The Pack and I*, and..." I trail off, holding up my hand so I can tick my fingers off as I talk. "Well there's the contract I have to finish up this series, so I guess I *will* be finishing my last contemporary, and with cooking classes with Bennett and spending time with Seth" — I pause, lifting my wine — "I mean, I'm not going to turn down a trip to Italy to look at winery locations."

Arin's eyes are bright as he grins. "Oh?"

I grin at him, then look at Theo. "And I can help you with the charities. I guess I'll be spinning in circles, but I kind of like it." Gone are the days spent curled up at home — but I don't regret any of it because it has come with so much joy.

"What about you?" I look over at Arin. "What are you doing next year?"

He places his utensils on the table and wipes his hands off before taking a sip of his wine. When his eyes meet mine — an unfathomable deep brown, full of kindness and love — my heart jolts like I've been shocked.

"I've brokered a lot of good deals this year, enjoyed traveling and the time it's allowed me to spend with our pack and you." Arin swallows. "But there's one place I haven't been in a long time. India."

My mouth drops open. "India?"

He nods. "I'd love to take my parents. Theresa and I have discussed it through the years, but we've always needed a reason to go. It never felt right when the family was all being pulled in different directions, but then I mentioned it to Bennett and he suggested something."

My eyes flicker over to my other alpha, frowning.

"Then I talked to Seth and Theo. We all came to an agreement."

All our bonds are quiet, like the four of them are holding themselves back and I push away from the table in confusion. "Why am I just now hearing about this?" I try to laugh, flushing at the nerves rising in my chest. "What —"

Arin stands and I give him a wide-eyed look as he steps over to me and takes my hand, making me rise. He moves us a few paces away from the dinner table and I blink as Theo, Seth, and Bennett all watch.

When I look back at Arin, he squeezes my hand.

"There's only one event I want to attend in India, Juniper." He slowly sinks down onto one knee, reaching his free hand into his pocket with a slight fumble. Tears spring to my eyes as he pulls out a small velvet box. Arin's throat works as he stares at me. "A wedding. *Our* wedding, love."

He opens the box, a gold ring glittering under the lights. A single emerald cut diamond glimmers in the center of the band, with each side profiled by two smaller round diamonds, making a set of five. It's *beautiful*, simple — entirely *me*.

Choking on a sob, I feel tears stream down my cheeks as I start to nod before he can even get the question out. Arin laughs, but it sounds half strangled as he holds my hand tighter.

"Will you marry us, Juniper? Will you let this pack love you until we're old and gray and there's nothing left for us to do but spend the rest of our days together?"

I cover my mouth, sobbing as I cling to his shaking hand, grabbing onto him to stay upright as I gasp out, "Yes. Yes, I will."

He lets out a deliriously happy laugh, then he slides the ring onto my finger. Dragging him up to me, I kiss him, laughing and crying as he rubs my back. With one hand, I fling it out, gasping, "Where are you all? Come here."

Theo's chair smacks against the floor as he rushes over, and I turn into their collective embrace, smothered in the middle of my pack — unable to believe my life, my *luck*.

EPILOGUE

SETH

THE SWISS SIDE of the Alps look unreal from the living room windows. Arin really outdid himself.

Standing in front of the wall of glass, I wrap my arms around myself. I only untangled from the pile of bodies because I needed some water, but it included leaving Bennett's side and June's warmth. My body misses it, it's like missing limbs.

We didn't even make it to the dessert that Arin ordered. He proposed, June said yes, and then she dragged us into the suite's nest.

I smile, rubbing my hand over my bare chest as I look outside at the snow, luminescent under the moonlight.

All four of us helped pick the ring — a stone for each of us, with June's diamond in the center. It made perfect sense, and, not to pat myself on the back, it was simple. She loves quiet things, even if our lives seem to be more full of adventures than ever.

The bedroom door swings open and I glance over to see June pad out, rubbing her face. Theo's large dress shirt hangs off her body and I open one arm, pulling her into my side to cuddle.

"What are you doing awake, baby?"

She makes a little grunting noise, voice laced with sleep. "I woke up and you weren't there."

My heart tugs at the words as I push back her mussed hair. When Bennett brought up the idea of proposing, I wasn't sure if she'd panic. We've all been through *so much* since we met each other, but her the most of all. And in that time, I've always reminded myself that there is no better feeling than the one of having her in my arms. It's a rightness that I've only ever felt with Bennett.

Reaching up, I rub my throat, touching my bond marks as she stares out the window at the drifting snow. She might not have my mark on her — but she's left hers on *me*. She *chose* me.

Our family never had discussions about designation. There were no discussions to be had. Each generation has an alpha that takes over the family — on the Abramowitz side, my mother's family — and I knew from a young age that it wouldn't be me. I was never bulky, strong, or a leader others defaulted to. My mother left her Jewish family, married my Chickasaw father, and took themselves off to study animals in remote places.

Over the years I found stability from the constant movement of childhood — first it was meeting Gabriel before college, working odd jobs for the Abramowitz family — then it was meeting Bennett. The rest was history.

I couldn't help but be weary of her reaction to marriage. The heat, the circumstances in New York — she has her alphas, I'm *not* someone she should be drawn to. In the back of my mind, I've always wondered if I just shoehorned my way in, if it'll be too much one day.

June tilts her head, her smile a little more coherent. "Didn't you say there's cake?"

I laugh. "Yeah, there's cake. You want some?"

She nods her head rapidly and I tug her into the kitchen, then snag the cake from the fridge. When I open the box, she lets out an adorable squeak at the piped flowers before she grabs two plates for us, the ring on her finger flashing under the dim lights.

Holding out a knife to me, she smiles. "Do the honors?"

I take it and cut us each a slice, serving her first before I whisper, "Do you really mean it?"

She pauses, half a bite to her mouth. "Mean what?"

Swallowing, I nod at the ring. "You want to marry us — *all* of us."

June takes my plate from my hands, putting the cake to the side before she grabs my face and pulls me against her, nose to nose. "Seth, *yes*." She enunciates the word, eyes deadly serious. "I wouldn't have agreed if I didn't. I wouldn't be *here* if I wasn't completely and stupidly in love with every single one of you. From Arin's ridiculous protective behavior to Theo's stubbornness to Bennett's sweetness to *you* —"

I know I'm brash — I know I make choices without thinking first —

Her fingers smooth between my brow.

"I can't explain to you how much I love you." Her lips wobble. "I don't think the words exist, and I'm a *writer*."

A choked laugh forces itself out of my chest. "I..."

"No." June shakes her head. "No, if you don't listen to anything else I say, listen to me right here, right now. I would not be here if you hadn't decided to come find me that day. If we hadn't been pushed together time and *time* again. Do you know what that felt like when I was in the elevator with you and Bennett? I kept wondering if life was playing one big cosmic joke on me — and then again, that night I..." She pauses, licking her lips. "I couldn't comprehend that I was suddenly not who I always thought I was. It was terrifying. And all I could do is keep thinking about *you*. And then there you were" — her eyes water, shining as they look at me — "buying coffee."

Wrapping my arms around her, I pull her into a kiss that tastes like frosting. She's pliant in my arms as I hold her. She keeps talking between kisses. "Fate kept giving us chances."

"I wasn't wasting the last one." I whisper the words as I wipe an errant tear from her cheek.

June smiles, her gaze so full of love that it overflows from her emotions to mine, ringing down the bond. "You mean the world to me. I love all those stupid alphas, but I also love *you*." She jabs me in the chest with a finger. "You, who knows *no* boundaries, *you* who decided I was coming home, *you* who stuck up for me in front of your pack, *you* who saw I was about to have a heat and made it your personal mission to get me *anything* I needed, *you* who I trusted enough to *do* that when everything was loud and scary and new —"

I grunt, grabbing her hand before she can poke me again. "Don't bruise me, baby."

She rolls her eyes, but threads our fingers together. "Don't ask me stupid questions then." Her expression softens. "I love you. I have loved you from the first moment we met, and if that's crazy, then let it be." She grazes my lips with hers again, voice gentle. "Because while the world may think time and time again that omegas and alphas are always linked and destined to be together, I *know* that you and I are fated. We're meant to be here, and I'm *meant* to be yours, as much as you're mine."

Holding her tightly, I pull her against my chest, but it's not *enough* — the touching isn't close to how much I want her. Leaning down, I pick her up by the backs of her thighs and place her on the counter, making our cake plates clatter as I step between her legs and kiss her harder, pushing everything I can into it.

June's legs wrap around me as she plays with my hair. "I love you, Seth Harding."

I smile up at her. "Seth Walden."

Her mouth pops open, head tilting. "No."

Shrugging, I rub her hips idly. "I thought about it when Arin told us he wanted to propose... and if that's the pack name, then why don't we all take *your* name. We don't have to." I pause at her expression. "But I thought it might be nice to make new memories associated with your surname."

June's eyes fill with tears as she peppers my entire face with kisses. "Seth Walden." She sounds awestruck as she murmurs, "I *love* it. Theo Walden. Arin Walden. *Bennett* Walden."

Groaning, I move between her thighs. "You whispering other men's names should *not* turn me on as much as it does."

She giggles, wiggling to the edge of the counter to wrap her arms around my shoulders, looking down at me with the brightest eyes. *She's so fucking gorgeous.* Her gentle curves, her soft belly, and big smiles — it's a far cry from the woman I met in London, and I feel honored I've gotten to see her bloom.

June leans to the side, stabbing a piece of cake and holding it up to my lips. I take it and she leans into me. "I like those names the more I think about them." She hums as she takes another bite herself, sliding her legs up and down my back, her feet pushing at my sweats. "It's *very* old school." She toys with me, one hand twisting my hair. "You all take my name because I'm the omega."

"I mean, it's only fitting — you own us, even if there are no collars."

"Yet." June points her fork at me. "We have a lot of years in front of us, we could get there."

I laugh loudly, my head tipping back as I snort. "You're right, we could get there."

June beams at me. "Our *wedding*." She squeaks the word. "I'm going to plan our *wedding* next year." She offers me another bite of cake, but I ignore it to press little butterfly kisses across her exposed collarbone. The fork drops from her hand.

I'm not an alpha. I don't have a bark or a snarl. I can't purr to comfort her. But as she cards her fingers through my hair, nails scratching my scalp, I'm close to making the rattling noise of pure happiness. Biology be damned.

She smells like honey, and she's *mine*.

"Seth?"

"Hm?" I kiss her chin.

"There have to be others, right?" Her voice is soft as my hands rub over her bare thighs. At my look, she clarifies, "Other omegas like me?"

"I'm sure there are, baby." I kiss her lips, our noses touching.

June lets out a little sigh of contentment. "I hope they find this kind of happiness."

THE END

(OF JUNE'S STORY)

BONUS CONTENT

Want the 17k word bonus content for Pack Walden? (and more!)

Find me on **social media** for access!

@rlrandolph on major platforms

CONTENT WARNINGS

This book contains sensitive content.

GRAPHIC (throughout the narrative, on page, explicit):

- Ableism / Chronic Illness (omegas are predisposed to chronic conditions and the world treats them as lesser for this)
- Cursing (throughout)
- Mental Health / Mental Illness / Panic Attack / Anxiety (through narrative, a character has symptoms of derealization and dissociation which is described on page)
- Sexual content (multi-pairings including: MM, MF, MMF, MMMMF)
  - See spice list for details

MODERATE (on page, appears in a few instances):

- Alcohol (characters drink casually)
- Biphobia / Homophobia / Anti-Polyamory (from side characters / family in one instance on page)
- Blood / Medical content (scenes where blood is shed and medical instruments are used)
- Body Shaming / Emotional Abuse / Sex Shaming / Fatphobia / Eating Disorder (some self, in past, and scenes including unsupportive family. A character is told not to eat, explicitly, by a parent.)
- Religious Bigotry (of the familial variety)
- Stalking / Kidnapping (on page)
- Toxic Relationship (some readers might consider Theo and June's relationship toxic)

MINOR (in reference):

- Abandonment (mentioned in regards to family)
- Abortion / Pregnancy (mentioned in right to choose, a side character is briefly implied to be pregnant, others imply worthy omegas are fertile ones. Informed discussion of birth control options between main characters.)
- Abuse (domestic abuse of side character)
- Drug Abuse (a character is drugged)
- Death / Gun Violence / Murder (a character is shot and killed in one instance, in which the death is described briefly)
- Misogyny/Sexism (present in world and how omegas are treated)
- Nausea (brief from anxiety *only*. No pregnancy of main character.)

- Sexual Abuse / Sexual Violence / Rape (a
  character fears they will be assaulted, but
  nothing occurs on page or in narrative, though
  the antagonist sees it as their right)

SPICE LIST

This is omegaverse, welcome to knotting.

- 1: MMF — double penetration, knotting
- 2: MF, MM — rough sex, blowjob, exhibitionism/voyeurism
- 3: MF — knotting
- 4: MF
- 5: MMMMF — double penetration, sharing, knotting
- 9: MF — exhibition, voyeurism, mentions of cuckolding, female masturbation, fisting, knotting
- 10: MMF — double vaginal penetration, biting/mentions of blood
- 15: MF — knotting
- 18: MF — bratting, light primal play, spanking, toy use, knotting, biting/mentions of blood
- 21: MF — biting/mentions of blood, knotting

- 22: MMF — voyeurism, exhibitionism, spanking, double penetration, degradation/punishment, edging, light choking, knotting
- 24: MF — brief mentions of eating out
- 30: MMMMF — exhibitionism, voyeurism, sharing, double penetration, blowjob, anal, knotting

GOLDEN OMEGAVERSE GUIDE

This novel takes place in an alternate universe similar to our's. Much of the world remains the same, except every human also has a **designation**.

Designations fall into three categories: alphas, betas, and omegas. This book does **not** contain shifters and/or werewolves. See below for an overview on each designation, then a more detailed list organized by term.

DESIGNATIONS:

Alphas are humans who are generally more respected and seen as leadership types.

- Alphas can be any gender.
- They have heightened senses, and are stronger physically than other designations.
- Each alpha has a scent, that can either be alluring or off-putting to others.

- Biologically alphas are fine without having an omega, though lonely, as they often want to care for someone. (Even if they have no desire to have children)
- Biologically male alphas have a **knot**, a continuous round of muscle, at the base of their penis. Biologically female alphas have the inverse, a stronger muscle inside the vagina that can **lock** during penetrative sex. Both of these biological traits are meant to aid in breeding.
- Alphas make up 30% of the population
- Alphas bleed red, but it has a silver tinted/oil-slick sheen to it.
- Alphas make up a **large** portion of people in power in the world, as culturally it's seen that they are the "better" by default, which leads to much abuse of power in the case of alphas.

Betas are humans, as we would understand them in this world.

- They have no extra qualities.
- Betas are the majority of the population, at around 65%
- Betas in the ***goldverse*** have very faint scents when not around their scent match, though there are products that can (and do) enhance these scents to the levels of alphas or omegas. It always has a slight chemical tang, though, and is easy to spot.
- Their blood is red, and has no sheen to it.

Omegas are humans that are often associated with meek, submissive, and calm characteristics.

- Omega designations typically emerge anywhere from the ages of eighteen to twenty-five during a second puberty.
- Omegas are increasingly rare, making up **less than 5% of the total population**.
- Omegas are owned, by law, by their parents, until their ownership is "transferred" to an alpha or pack.
- Biologically female omegas are often not given the choice to prevent pregnancies, with strict rules requiring an alpha signing off on them being provided birth control.
- Biologically male omegas, while unable to get pregnant, are incredibly virile, and often their sperm results in a pregnancy. They are also refused birth control.
- Omegas have red blood, but it has a golden/oil slick sheen to it.
- Omegas are generally seen as weaker, which culturally, has meant that omegas, while being sought after, aren't really treated seriously in any capacity. They're said to be too prone to whims, and it's socially accepted that any and all omegas are too emotional for any serious or leadership positions.

LIST OF TERMS:

Bark/Commands —

- Alphas have a bark, or built-in command, where their word is obeyed. The bark has to be used with intent to make it work, and doesn't work on everyone at all times.
- Varying alphas might have a stronger bark than others, leading to a hierarchy within the designation where one alpha might be stronger than another. This is also true in pack systems, where there is a pack alpha, this alpha is often the most well-respected, and likely has the strongest bark.

Bonds —

- Bonds occur between any alphas and any designation, though most common are alphas leaving a claim bite on betas or omegas that are their life partners.
- Bonds from an alpha open up a neural pathway between the alpha and the bonded, where they can feel the other person's emotions and general state of being. It's a way for alphas to check on their bonded and care for them.
- This neural pathway isn't a way to read thoughts, but more intent and general mood. They can tell if their bonded is stressed/in heightened states of emotion. The bonds can be dimmed and dulled with various medicines.

Blood — *unique to the **goldverse***

- As previously mentioned, alphas have blood that, when viewed from an angle, will appear silver. The same can be said for omegas, who's blood will appear golden. Betas have red blood that carries no sheen.
- Though it has been attempted, there is currently no chemical way to replicate the sheen on the blood of alphas or omegas, making a blood test the one true, trustworthy way to ensure a person's designation.

Claim bites (also called ***bond marks***) —

- Alphas will get the urge to mark, or bite, their partners. These bites are binding and scar.
- Bites made by alphas appear silver in color when healed, while omega bites have a golden hue.
- Bonding bite marks heal faster than other injuries, by biological design.

Designation Centers —

- Centers exist where alphas are paired with omegas, or where an omega's guardians place them with a pack for life.
- Culturally, there are many who do not agree with packs and think every alpha should have a single omega. It often has to do with religion believing that every alpha is "owed" their own omega, and to share one is to share your right.

(Making an omega an object, rather than an actual person with wants and desires)
- In the same manner, many believe that female alphas shouldn't claim female omegas, because it, biologically, cannot result in a child. The same can be said for male alphas and male omegas, or any cross-pairing that does not want children. Breeding and population continue to be hot topics.
- Designation Centers are often government affiliated, though independently run ones do exist. Alphas can buy memberships to centers to have their pack and scents listed as an option for omegas to choose from.
- There are groups that speak out for Omegas and against designation centers, choosing to say that a person's designation should be their right to disclose, and that omegas shouldn't be the "property" of their parents until sold to an alpha (often in an exchange that contains money or other collateral).

Heat (or *heat cycle*) —

- A hormonal cycle that occurs in omegas, after their designation emerges with puberty.
- The heat cycle happens roughly every three months, or four times in a calendar year (though changes have and do occur when hormones are tampered with).
- Heats last for a week (five to seven days) and are a state of heightened sexual desire and activity,

where the omega will both want comfort and
sexual satisfaction.

- For biologically female omegas, a heat will
  coincide with ovulation week if the omega is
  currently fertile and menstruating.
- For biologically male omegas, a heat will
  occur roughly three to four times a year, and
  coincide with testosterone spikes, making the
  omega want to seek release.

Heat-sickness —

- A flu-like precursor to a first heat, that makes
  omegas weaker and often accompanied by a
  fever. Some omegas are unlucky enough to get it
  multiple times/before every heat, especially if
  they have unbalanced hormones or are stressed
  prior to a heat.
- Heat sickness is one of the major signs that
  someone is about to emerge as an omega, and is
  often tested for every few months.
  - First signs include elevated heart rate and
    body temperature.

Heat Spike —

- When an omega is approaching their upcoming
  heat, flu-like symptoms will begin to present.
  Tiny "spikes" of symptoms will mimic a heat,
  often resulting in greater arousal and other
  various symptoms associated with the omega's
  regular heat.

- ○ **Symptoms that might be present include**: dizziness, pain in the body, cramping, headaches, fevers, excessive sweating, chills or shaking/trembling, nausea or vomiting, heightened arousal, heightened emotions/mood swings (whether anger, anxiety, or other), sleepiness or insomnia, appetite changes, general fatigue

Knot —

- A ring of muscle at the base of a biological male alpha's penis. This muscle swells and enlarges during intercourse, with the intent to lock the penis in the vagina during sex, to keep semen inside and higher the chance of pregnancy.
- Knots vary in size, shape, and the time it takes for them to go down. When flaccid, the knot is still present, but not as prominent.

Lock —

- A ring of muscle inside the vagina of a biologically female alpha. This ring tightens and locks when aroused and during intercourse, keeping the penetrative object inside to higher the chance of pregnancy. Locks vary in size, shape, and rigidity.

Mannerisms —

- Alphas and omegas often display animalistic mannerisms like: barking, growling, whining, whimpering, and more.
  - **See bark** for more information on commands.

Nests/Nesting —

- A uniquely omega urge to build a small, enclosed space, full of warm and comforting objects.
- This urge is often associated with heats, though it's more of a comforting room that can be kept year-round of omegas to retreat to and enjoy. It's simply a safe place for them to be.
- Many packs will have a nest room or space for their eventual or current omegas to personalize, and it varies from omega to omega.
- Nests normally are reserved for the omega to use, with it being common to ask permission before entering an omega's nest, as they might not want things shifted, or scents to change.

Perfume (*scents* or *pheromones*) —

- Biologically all humans exist with their own natural perfume or pheromones, regardless of designation.
- Scents bloom and become more potent when experiencing heightened emotions, often arousal or fear.
- Omegas have the most powerful perfumes, while

alpha perfumes are secondary and beta perfumes are very subtle.

- The scent is unique to each and every individual. Though there are certain scents that will appeal to specific individuals, these are called **scent matches**.

Packs —

- Because the number of alphas is so high compared to the number of omegas, some alphas will "pack up" with each other, to satisfy their need to caretake and want to be surrounded by like-minded people.
  - This doesn't mean they are all romantic with each other, as the relationships might be familial or platonic as well as romantic.
- Packs will also tend to choose one alpha as their **pack alpha** or **prime** who is the decision maker and leader of the pack. They tend to be the strongest of the group, whether physically, or in the case of their bark.

Rut —

- All alphas might be subject to entering a rut, triggered by an omega in a heat cycle.
- A rut is a biological response to a heat, where the alpha goes into a similar haze of desire to mate. It doesn't occur every heat, nor with every alpha and omega pairing, and is largely up to biological chance when tending to an omega in heat.

- Alphas in a rut become *highly* territorial and single-minded. They are generally seen as more dangerous during this time because they have a lack of control over their own reactions.

Scenting —

- Scenting is objectively one of the first ways to lay claim on an omega. An alpha will rub themselves on an omega (or imbue them with their signature scent) to show to others that they belong to an alpha before a bite.
- Scenting has no permanence and products exist to suppress scents or wash them free.

Scent matches —

- Scent matches are another way to describe fated mates or soulmates.
- Scents will match, or pair well with each other, and in turn connections and attachments between individuals will form faster.
- Scent matching is used in designation centers to find potential matches faster than meetings and interviews, because if a scent of an alpha is off-putting to an omega, it is highly unlikely they will be a match romantically.

Slick —

- Slick is a natural lubricant produced by all genders of omegas that make it easier for penetration of any kind. It's produced during a heat in excess, but is naturally existing in all omegas year round.

ACKNOWLEDGMENTS

First and foremost thank you to *all* the early readers of *Gold Rush* who took a chance on my book, sight unseen. I'm floored by the response to it and don't have enough space to properly thank every last one of you. Every review, post, and share means the world to me.

Thank you to my esteemed writing team: Anne-Marie (You're the best alpha reader ever) & Kai (I still don't know what the fuck a comma does and I'm inclined not to learn because you fix them so well).

Thank you to Silvy (Sarah) for reading everything I write, regardless of how off the wall it is. Thank you to Linz (FoxOfTwilight) for drawing Juniper because you loved her so much. (!!!) More thanks to: Allegra Hall, Amalia, Ana, Ash, Chey, Emily, Jean, Julia, Katie Neel, LJ Kobzina, Michaela, Nikita Navalker, Robyn, and Sarah B.

Finally, thank you to my family for supporting me even when you don't quite understand. <3

ABOUT THE AUTHOR

R.L. Randolph is a mildly feral human woman who just wants to write about people kissing for her day job. She lives near the mountains, but, ironically, has grass and tree mold allergies so she never leaves the house.

instagram.com/rlrandolph

ALSO BY R. L. RANDOLPH

Golden Omegaverse

June's Duet

Gold Rush (#1)

Gold Mine (#2)

(***more stories in the Goldverse to come***)

Romantic Suspense

The Felling Cut

(releasing Fall 2025)